# 2039

## A Novel

To Suzanne,
Thank you for your
excellent professional service,
which have improved my condition
Best Wishes

### 2nd Edition

Martin Slapin

6/21/2018

# Martin Shapiro

# 2039

**A Novel**

**2nd Edition**

# Disclaimer

This story is a work of fiction, the invention of the author, set in the future in the year 2039. The persons and situations represented are fictional and any similarity with persons or situations past or present is purely coincidental. There are many given names and surnames in the public domain. The use of names, given names or surnames, in this story may appear to be representing people, past or present. The use of a name is not intended to foist any person living or dead on that character. No imagined connection between any character in this story to a living or dead person is intended.

Also Written by the Author

**Scroll of Naska: Sojourn in Egypt**
**Caravan to Luxor: Scroll of Naska Series**
**From Prison to Power, Joseph Reigns: Scroll of Naska Series**
**Martin Shapiro's 2039**

**Martin Shapiro**
**140 Ox Hill Road**
**Norwich, Connecticut 06360**
**MShapiro2039@aol.com**
**http://www.huffingtonpost.com/martin-shapiro/**

ISBN-10: 150870533X
ISBN-13: 9781508705338

Cataloging-in Publication Data for the book
from the Library of Congress, Control No. 2015903696
CreateSpace Independent Publishing Platform
North Charleston, South Carolina

# Introduction to 2<sup>nd</sup> Edition

Dear Reader,

The earlier version of **Martin Shapiro's 2039,** was a publication of the *galleys prior to edit*––for comment and critique. Readers were asked to comment directly to me or post on Amazon. Many such comments were received in the past year. See the reviews on **Amazon** for yourselves.

This **2nd Edition** incorporates many suggestions and reflects more current events as well. This volume was updated under the tutelage of my Content/Line Editor, Rachel Starr Thomson. She is a professional author of many fine books and supplies coaching and editing services to indie authors like me. I wish to express by profuse thanks to her. Without her knowledgeable and experienced input, this writing would not be the finished product that I intended at the outset.

If you have further comments, reply to author:

MShapiro2039@aol.com.

**Or post them on AMAZON!**
**Thank you for your interest and support.**

**Best Wishes**

# Table of Non-Familiar Acronyms

| | |
|---|---|
| AGL | Above Ground Level |
| AGV | Automatic Government Vehicle |
| AWACS | Airborne Warning and Control System |
| BUV | Big Utility Vehicle |
| CEO | Chief Executive Officer |
| CIA | Central Intelligence Agency |
| CMMATTV | Canadian Military Medium All-Terrain Tactical Vehicle |
| CNBC | Business News Cable Network |
| CSIS | Canadian Security Intelligence Service |
| DHS | Department of Homeland Security |
| EATO | European Atlantic Treaty Organization |
| EC | Eastern Connecticut |
| EMT | Emergency Medical Technician |
| ESOP | Employee Stock Ownership Plan |
| EST | Eastern Standard Time |
| ETA | Estimated Time of Arrival |
| FAV | Federal Automatic Vehicle |
| FBO | Airport Fixed Base Operator |
| FCC | Federal Communications Commission |
| FDA | Food and Drug Administration |
| FFL | French Foreign Legion |
| G, Gs | The weight of gravity |
| GD | General Dynamics |
| GI | Government Issue |
| GNP | Gross National Product |
| GPS | Global Positioning System |
| ICU | Intensive Care Unit |
| IDF | Israel Defense Force |
| LNG | Liquefied Natural Gas |

| | |
|---|---|
| LTV | Light Terrain Vehicle |
| MDH | MHD spelled wrong |
| mgk | Megakilowatts |
| MHD | Magnetohydrodynamics |
| MI5 | British Military Intelligence (Section 5) |
| MIT | Massachusetts Institute of Technology |
| MP | Military Police |
| MSH | MHD spelled wrong |
| MSNBC | Microsoft NBC Cable New Network |
| MST | Mountain Standard Time |
| MTV | Medium Terrain Vehicle |
| NATO | North Atlantic Treaty Organization |
| NGO | Non-Government Organization |
| NSA | National Security Agency |
| NYU | New York University |
| PRC | People's Republic of China |
| QC | Quebec |
| RCMP | Royal Canadian Mounted Police |
| RPI | Rensselaer Polytechnic Institute |
| SASS | South African Secret Service |
| SHS | Senior Health System |
| SNL | Saturday Night Live |
| SS | Senior Stipend |
| SSE | Super Sonic Executive |
| SSTSO | Single-Stage To Sub-Orbit |
| TASMG | Theater Aviation Sustainment Maintenance Group |
| TSA | Transportation Security Administration |
| UK | United Kingdom |
| UN | United Nations |
| US | United States |
| USPS | United States Postal Service |

# Chapter Zero
# James Bond Movie
*Ida*

"What's happening today, Ida?" Jon asked me.

"Nothing really. After the last three hectic days, we deserve quiet. Do you want to see a movie? The new James Bond film, *See Sea Saw,* is playing down the street, and the Israelis said they would protect us if we walk in daylight."

"Is that the one where the world is building colonies on the sea floor to survive the deadly air pollution and global warming? And 007 is helping the West defend their territory from the Chinese mafia?"

"Yes, yes . . . that's the one. I've heard it has wonderful underwater photography and action scenes. That's your stuff as a retired submariner."

"The rumors at the Boat say underwater enclosures are actually being tested now. Sure Ida, let's go." Jon said.

\*\*\*

It was the early Saturday show. The theatre was filled with kids, popcorn, polka-dot communicators and plenty of noise. The box office didn't want to take our American money but Jon finally laid down a fifty-dollar bill. The seller pocketed it, put in her own Canadian cash, and gave Jon two tickets and a Canadian ten dollar bill. We knew the value of our dollar was down, but two tickets to an afternoon movie for US forty bucks?? Huh?

We walked in. The noise was incredible; the screen played ads in French. The next-to-the-last row was nearly empty, just a few adults scattered across. All aisle seats were taken. We moved in, a few seat from the aisle, and sat there. As the lights dimmed, the previews began. Our row and the one behind filled up.

I looked around. We seemed to be surrounded by men—surly men.

At the end of the first preview, the man behind Jon leaned forward and whispered, "Go to the men's room *now*. I have a message from Matthew."

The man behind stood up and made his way to the aisle.

Jon looked at me. "I'll be right back."

I whispered, "Will you be safe? And coming back?"

The man next to me leaned closer and mumbled in an Israeli accent, "He'll be safe—and back."

After Jon passed me going toward the aisle, the mumbler stood up and followed. It made me feel a bit better.

In the next instant, two more men from the back row squeezed out and followed. I got panicky. I tried to watch the screen, but I was constantly turning to look over my shoulder at the head of the aisle. The third preview started and then the fourth. The dialog was in French with English subtitles, and I didn't have time to read them.

The public announcement clip started—emergency exits to the sides, turn off communicators, trash barrels at exits, and a ten-minute intermission to refill popcorn and buy more drinks and candy. That much, I could make out. The house lights went to zero; the theatre turned pitch-black as the widely advertised Bond theme music blared and the crowd roared. Moments later, the movie started. The crowd roared again.

The trademark opening action sequence began: underwater shots; men and women swimming, wearing white against a dark blue sea; with whales, sharks, barracudas, and smaller fish of many species, all heading deeper. The aroma of the seashore pumped into the theatre. The camera showed many of the predator fish feeding on the littler guys.

Divers with breathing gills in red suits were creeping up on them, exotic weapons of some sort in their hands. There was some narration, but I couldn't read the subtitles and watch the aisle at the same time. A huge enclosure—a massive, clear bubble with a city under construction on the sea floor—came into view. This was what Jon said was rumored to be secretly in testing.

I turned to see Jon returning to me, holding popcorn, drinks and a piece of paper. The man who'd been next to me was right behind him. As they pushed into the row, the last two men returned behind us. The seat behind Jon remained empty.

Jon put his face close to mine with his finger to his lips.

"Later," he said. He sat back in his seat and adjusted himself to watch the show, reading the subtitles.

"What's that paper you're holding?" I asked.

"Shhhhhh . . . *I said... later!*" He lifted the snacks. "Popcorn? Water?"

As Bond was being served to a swirling school of giant barracudas, with a close up of their sharp teeth, the screen sputtered and died—the theatre went pitch-black. The only light came from the glowing "Porte de Sortie" signs around the perimeter.

The audience groaned and shouted protests.

"What . . . what happened to the picture?"

The noise was intense. The screen quickly relit, silencing the crowd.

*Intermission Dix Minutes*
*Rafraîchissements est Maintenant Ouverte !*

"Intermission, ten minutes," the English subtitles said, with a large countdown clock amid blinking graphics of eats and treats sold you-know-where. The crowd collectively sighed. The aisles filled with kids racing to the washrooms and the refreshment counters.

3

The Israeli leaned in. "C'mon, join the crowd. We'll slip out and leave in this commotion."

We did as told, taking our coats and our things. He led us out a side exit from the lobby, hidden by the surging crowd of youthful patrons shouting their orders at the snack bar in French. The dozen servers had less than ten minutes to satisfy the horde.

Outside, Jon helped me with my coat and scarf, then buttoned his own. We put on our gloves and walked briskly toward the flat.

The Israeli followed behind. He stayed on the walk as we went down the drive to the front door. After I entered, I looked back. He was gone.

# Chapter 1
# News Flash

*Independent Thunder Cloud*
*The News the Government Doesn't Want You To Know*
**FBI Invades Private Home in Connecticut**

**Norwich, CT January 24.** With a hastily signed search warrant from the Surveillance Court in Washington, DC, the FBI Monitor Division battered down the door of a private home in a prominent neighborhood to execute their search while the residents were not at home. Neighbors watched as a government-issue black AGV pulled to the front of the house while two more agents dropped from a drone onto their tennis court. Other drones circled overhead. After finding the garage empty, the agents used a ram to smash the rear door.

The home belongs to Jonathon and Ida Kadish, long-time residents of Broadway in Norwich. Mr. Kadish is a vice president and senior engineer at the United States Submarine Industries, a division of the Defense Industries Cabinet in Groton known locally as "The Boat." The company is the former Electric Boat Division of General Dynamics, the only builder of submarines in the country. Ida Rabinow Kadish is the former owner of Now's American Home and Tire, a family business for over a hundred years.

The drone actuated multiple pressure sensors on the court that sent an alarm to the Norwich Police and the property manager, Mr. Roland Smith. The police responded with its mobile command station from their nearby headquarters. After confirming the identity of the agents and the search warrant, the police established a yellow tape perimeter around the property and managed the growing crowd who came out to see the activity.

The mayor, police commissioner and fire marshal arrived and confirmed the activity with the police chief. None would comment to the press.

The FBI would only say that the search warrant was granted after three of the five communicators in the home became inoperative. When asked for a second reason, they replied, "No comment." Normally it takes at least two reasons to seek a search warrant, and in some cases even three. The FBI would not say into which category Mr. and Mrs. Kadish fell.

Neighbors who witnessed the invasion said they saw nothing removed from the house. Agents carried in cases, presumably of equipment, stayed an hour, and are presumed to have vacuumed the premises, degaussed the atmosphere and scanned and downloaded any paper or electronic data to return to their investigators. In other cases, additional listening devises have been installed in homes.

First to arrive was Mr. Smith who was not allowed to cross the perimeter. Reporters were waiting for Mr. and Mrs. Kadish when they arrived a short time later. Mr. Kadish said the damage to the door and house was fully covered by insurance as required by law. Property insurance companies are required to pay for any damage caused by the government in the execution of their lawful duties. Regarding the reasons for the invasion or what might have been taken or installed, the Kadish's replied, "No comment."

# Chapter 2
# Getting Ready
*Ida*

"Goddamn it, Ida! Are you ready?"

*No, Jonathon, you asshole, I'm not ready!* I thought.

"Almost," I called out. "I need a few more minutes and have to pee."

"Do you have the belt on?"

I adjusted the damn thing resting on my hips.

"Yes, yes. I have it on. But it's bulky. I hope I can walk with it."

"Don't worry, we'll both be okay. A little more bulk won't be noticed under our coats. I should have listened to Truman and Eric and decided this years ago when it would've been easier. When did you tell the Snyders to be here?"

Jonathon was upstairs in our house on Broadway, where we'd lived for over thirty years. We loved our home. He'd gone up there an hour ago, and I wondered what he was doing. I wanted him down here where I could look to him for assurance.

"They'll be here by ten, just before we leave. Did you check the weather for our crossing tomorrow?" I answered.

Today we'll be driving. Tomorrow we cross into Canada.

"When is the truck going to be here?" I called.

"Ida, it's not a truck, for God's sake. I've told you a dozen times. It's an FAV! And stop worrying, the weather will be fine. Did you tell Sally to walk Pepper?"

I'd always thought we were two peas in a pod, but today I wasn't sure. Forty-seven years of marriage is supposed to do that to a couple. This was a big move that he wanted—no, needed—and I was determined to stay by his side. He knew I had anxiety before travel and the anxiety leading to this trip was worse because of its purpose. I was sure he felt it too, but he'd never admit it. He would just secretly take his comfort pill.

"Yes, yes. The Snyders know the entire routine," I answered.

I continued to mindlessly pack a basket in the kitchen like I did years ago when taking the kids to the park. The required government-issued atomic clock and monitor in the kitchen chimed the note for 9:45 and asked for confirmation. I shouted, "Confirmed!"

It recognized my voice and went back to its job. The time was shown in thousandths of a second in perfect coordination with the atomic clock in the Hall of Time in Washington. Why we had to know the time so precisely, I had no idea. Sure the media, the military, the scientists watching the heavens, maybe *they* needed that precision, but why the average family? It was said that a former administration gave the project to a company controlled by relatives as a political plum. It was perfectly plausible; all the various governments had their giveaway projects to reward major supporters, whether needed by the citizenry or not.

It was Wednesday and the start of a long holiday weekend. Monday was President's Day.

I tiptoed to look in the small mirror above the old wall phone and smoothed my hair back and down my ponytail. Jonathon hung that mirror when we moved here, positioned to suit his six-foot height. At five-eight I wasn't a midget, but I had to tiptoe to reach it.

The phone was an antique, a relic of the past, a rotary dial that should have been removed long before we bought this place. But it looked content there, like it belonged somehow. It was like the tennis court in the backyard. The novelty of it in the beginning made us go out and use it. The kids invited their friends and used it more. But after they were off to college, we removed the net and the posts and it became a drone delivery pad. Jon had multiple sensors embedded throughout the court to sound an alarm to a security service if three or more were engaged at once. When a large drone landed, the sensors in the court communicated with the monitoring service, which called the police and Rollie. Big items for some neighbors were occasionally delivered here. Ten years ago when we needed a refrigerator, the postal service delivered it by drone from Keith's Appliances, right to our back yard. That's right, the USPS—the United States Postal Service.

In the early 2020s, the postal service was given exclusive right to the lower drone airspace, everything under four hundred feet AGL— above ground level—after competing commercial drones kept crashing and falling from the sky. Police and emergency responders had to vertically ascended to above four hundred feet before traveling horizontally. Below that, it had been Domino's vs. Pizza Hut, Tim Hortons vs. Dunkin' Donuts, Taco Bell vs. Chipotle, Amazon vs. Walmart vs. Eatons. Collision avoidance radar and control systems worked well enough when only two drones were involved, but when three or four wanted to occupy the same airspace, someone on the ground was usually injured—as the pizza got cold and the ice cream melted. It didn't take long for the government to cancel that system.

Awarding the space exclusively to the postal service was the key to USPS's survival. Amazon, Walmart, Hortons, and all the others had to use them if they wanted to deliver groceries and other products by drone. Small delivery drones came frequently without notice. Rollie or Jon brought the packages in. Old-style mail was delivered to the door only two days a week.

The ponytail was my old hairdo. I expected Jon to be surprised. I sighed. *Never expected to have to be ready for this. And the weather? It's calling for blizzard conditions with temperatures near 8° F this afternoon in northern New Hampshire. What are we thinking?*

"What time is Rollie to be here?" I shouted.

Jon appeared at the top of the stairs. "You don't have to shout, Ida. Hearing is not my problem. Rollie was to pick up the vehicle at eight and be here by nine-thirty. He had to go to the government depot near Hartford. We have it for four days. I expect him any time now."

My mind was confused. Whoever thought people—we—would have to leave our homes, want to leave America? Sneaking out like thieves, filing for permission to visit family in Canada, lying about our intentions, giving the IRS collateral until our return, calling in favors, carrying hoards of cash. How could life in America have become so distasteful?

*But we are far from the first.* All of Jonathon's siblings had gotten out years ago. Two of our own children lived in foreign countries. In earlier years a person had to pay a punitive tax to the IRS to leave. The tax kept growing until now, even if you were willing to leave everything—like refugees fleeing a war zone—you needed their permission to go. *And it's not so quickly granted, especially if they think you are valuable in some way.*

We had given different cover stories to different groups. To our friends we were just going to visit our daughter Rachel and her family in Sherbrooke, as we did every few years. To Jon's employer, he was taking an extra-long weekend up north. To my colleagues and the employees at Now's, I would be staying in Canada a month or so to be with our grandchildren.

Usually we went in the spring, but here it was February, President's Day weekend—winter. We hadn't visited since 2035, four years ago. People asked, "Why February to Canada?" To most, we gave the long-weekend story. It was hard to remember who we had told what, so we tried to keep it all simple and compatible. I couldn't look anyone in the eye and tell the story. I was never comfortable being deceptive.

There would be plenty of confusion when Jon's employer and my company realized we were gone for good. But it wasn't as if we'd made an impulsive decision. After nearly ten years of preparing and stalling, the proverbial straw had finally landed on us. Jonathon had been diagnosed with a medical issue for which treatment in the government health care system was no longer available for a person of his age. Rationing health care and denying seniors certain lifesaving procedures had begun as early as the mid-2020s. Now it had caught up to us.

Over the past years, we'd sent many things in small packages to each of our three kids. We moved money and hard assets too. We transferred funds to them within the allowed limits when possible. Carried diamonds and gold in small quantities when we traveled. I sent our picture albums, certain clothing, old videos, and a few family prizes that had passed through our generations. To Eric in Israel, I sent the Chanukah menorah that my great-grandparents brought from Russia in 1905.

Sending packages was routine when there were no restrictions. But restrictions were enacted, and in each succeeding year they were tightened. By early in the '30s, undocumented and unapproved transfers out of the country by private citizens were stopped. Export licenses and inspections at government facilities were required. People who tried to send things without prior approval said the goods were confiscated and the senders called in for questioning.

My neighbor Ellen told me, "I tried to send a small Whip-Master, you know, like a blender, to my daughter in Costa Rica. It was intercepted, and I was called in to explain. Two inspectors kept me an hour, and only after I agreed to pay a fine of a hundred dollars *in cash* did they allow the package to go. The blender only cost fifty-five, but they were going to confiscate it. When I asked for a receipt, the men laughed. 'No receipts,' they said. 'You just have to trust us!' and they kept laughing. The Whip-Master did finally show up in Costa Rica."

"It's hard to believe such low level bureaucrats are getting away with that stuff," I said. "More and more, it's like we're living in a third-world country."

The bigger stuff we sold on eBay, in secondhand stores and at yard sales. Secondhand sales brought big crowds and good prices. Certain imported stuff was not available anymore, or only in short supply or at very high prices. Some quality older items were better made than their modern substitutes and were in demand. Other things we just donated to charities.

But much still remained—after all, we had to live day to day. Whatever was left, we just planned to abandon. When the homeless realized we were gone and the house empty, they might cannibalize the place and squat here. It happened in other towns where the police just watched or participated. The gas, utilities, taxes, communication services, all would continue to be paid through the Cloud. Rollie too, would be paid to check the house a few times a week. And this was Broadway, where the neighbors cared about their street. I looked around at the old familiar walls and furniture, at the too-high mirror and the kitchen I'd known for thirty years. *I hope they won't let squatting happen here.*


Sally and Sam Snyder, older members of our congregation, were coming to stay to cover our escape and care for our dog. They had come to care for Pepper many times in the past when Jon and I traveled. But now we were abandoning Pepper too. We'd told the Snyders the truth. Once we confirmed our safe entry into Canada, they would take Pepper into their home, along with anything remaining in the house that was of use or value to them. They were worried about our plans and their participation. They too might be punished if our plan became exposed. Jon had explained it all to them, maybe pressured them a bit to agree. I didn't really know the details. But I was worried about them, not wanting them to have anxiety because of our mischief.

When discussing the Snyders, Jon had snapped at me, "You worry too much!"

I didn't like that attitude when he displayed it. Often he didn't worry enough!

*We'll both miss Pepper,* I thought. She had been a puppy of our previous white Scottish terrier, Salt, a male and a stud. To leave her upset me.

Jon had said, "Forget about it. We have to keep moving forward."

Months ago, I had forced him to agree that if we couldn't find a good home for her, we would cancel our plans.

He'd said, "Sure . . . sure . . . We'll see."

Who did he think he was kidding? He wouldn't cancel the plans. I wondered if he would leave without me if I decided not to go? He knew I was only doing this for him.

The mortgage company would eventually take the house—or what might be left of it. Our reverse mortgage had pretty much used all the equity in the property. Our oldest son, Truman, my lawyer in Hawaii, had worked out a financial plan for us back in 2027. The reverse mortgage was his idea.

"Get the equity out of the property without selling it," he advised.

He told us to stop accumulating anything of value here. He had us sell our art collection and furnishings and replace them with cheap prints and posters. When visiting our daughter in Canada, we smuggled as much as we could to her. When we were able, we brought things to Eric, our youngest, in Israel. But the government began restricting travel there in the early 2020s, when US–Israel relations became strained. After the diplomatic break a few years later, travel to Israel from US soil was totally cancelled, like to Cuba in the last century. Groups still visited Israel by departing from Canadian or European airports. Israel aside, we were denied tourist permits to many other destinations because of Jon's position and security clearance. To get things and means to Eric, we asked Rachel to travel or send them to him. She cooperated. Canadians were free to travel and send packages anywhere in the world—like we used to be.

We had expected to leave long before this. Year after year, successive presidents and congresses took more and more control of everything and slowly, subtly, nationalized critical industries and curtailed the people's freedoms. The NSA, FBI, and IRS had us under constant surveillance. The Treasury Department owned all the biggest domestic and international banks, and they invaded and monitored our financial means. We no longer had to make out income tax returns. The IRS did it for everyone and just sent you a bill or a refund.

Other than sending or receiving messages through the Universal Cloud, the ordinary citizen was cut off from the outside world without some kind of prior authorization. People needed a permit to go or do almost anything. And we knew from seeing others detained that the authorities were monitoring us—through our communicators, in public and private places with programs that searched our messages, sent or spoken. Surveillance cameras photographed us wherever we drove or walked. People in crowds were identified by facial recognition. There was no escape.

Families published the names of their loved ones who had been detained. New names were added in the Cloud every day. No matter how one tried to maintain some measure of privacy, with few exceptions, everyone's means, movements and conversations could be examined.

I finished the basket and put it with my luggage near the kitchen door. Jon had brought them down earlier. *What was he doing up there anyway?* I put on a kettle to make myself tea.

The vehicle arrived at 9:48. Roland knocked and just walked in, as he usually did. Pepper yelped and ran to him, lifting her front paws to his knee so he could pet her.

"Jon," I called. "Roland is here with the truck!"

I called it that because I knew it annoyed him.

"It's not a fucking tru—" He stopped short.

"Tell Rollie to come up here for my bags and then to get yours."

Roland, our handyman and driver for decades, heard the message and took the stairs two at a time. He was up there a while and when he came down, he asked for my bags. I pointed them out. Our three-month Family Visitation Permit allowed us a second full-sized suitcase each. On a one-month Vacation Permit, a traveler was allowed only one large suitcase. We carried our national registration cards, our old-style passports, and other identification. We'd been fortunate to avoid the implanted data chip under the skin that had become standard ID for everyone born beginning in 2025. If you entered a hospital, or even if you had a medical checkup, the doctors were supposed to hook you up with a chip. We'd been able to avoid it because we were in reasonably good health—me more so than Jon—and hadn't needed a government hospital in all that time.

There it was again. Everything always came around to Jon's recent troubling diagnosis. Though we both had the required national government health insurance, we still preferred the medical care in the alternative black market that existed in the shadow of the official system. The black market, also called "concierge service," had every available technological test and device scientists and engineers had devised, even more so than the national system. But they weren't allowed to have inpatient clinics nor private hospitals. Regulators and enforcers turned a blind eye to the black market because the wealthy, the military, and most of the politicians used it, and they saw that it was protected. We had the means and it offered much better service, quality, and privacy.

Rollie had taken my suitcases but not the basket. *What was with that?*

The basket contained sandwiches, fruit, cups of coffee, cold drinks, and insulated containers of drinking water—bottles of water were no longer sold. The national water supply was now homogenized, and the FDA had discredited the sale of so-called spring water. After they sued the bottlers for false advertising, stores were forced to discontinue selling it. It was another government measure to equalize resources across the population and save the environment from the pollution of making and then disposing of packaging. It didn't matter that thousands of people were put out of work. Nobody knew or cared anymore, and there were other jobs available. People were too busy trying to live their lives and survive in the current politic. The government stopped issuing economic data, always just announcing that the country was at full this or that. "Full employment" was a term they liked. *Sure, tell that to the older people looking for work while waiting for Senior Stipend!*

The FCC had bought CNN and closed all the other 24/7 news channels. Up-to-the-minute news came exclusively from the government. And the remaining media was only allowed to broadcast optimistic fluff fed to them by designated government puppets. Some clandestine news purveyors operated in the Cloud, but it was thought that the government monitored them and watched whoever tuned in. Some people believed those sources were government plants, designed to catch viewers in a sting. Jon and I agreed it was better not to know or test the system. We stayed away from those whispered sites.

I gave the basket to Roland to put in the car.

"You don't need the drinks," he said. "The FAV has a coffeemaker, a water and drink dispenser, an ice maker and a bar, a refrigerator stocked with food, and even a small-wave oven."

"Take this and put it in the car," I said. "I'm not fooling with it anymore."

Rollie always seemed to push back at me, but never at Jon. So I was generally a little short with him, and he'd come to expect it. Rollie was somewhat of a mystery to me. There was something about him that I didn't like, maybe didn't trust. Maybe it was the way he was always scanning the house with his eyes and pointing out little defects he saw. To me he was irritating. I wondered if he was jealous in some odd way. We had always been more than fair to him over the many years he had been with us. I saw no reason for him to be hostile. But what did I know?

16

Jon would say, "You're speculating," and added, "You watch too many movies and read too many stories."

And I would reply, "You spend so much time with the numbers in your head they've warped your common sense."

Similar repartee had begun even before we were married, and we regularly revived it, masking it as a comic routine that would make us laugh though sometimes it wasn't really funny. Laughing together kept us from arguing. It was our personal version of SNL, still running with an always up-and-coming cast.

When Rollie returned, I shouted to Jon, "Rollie is ready and so am I!"

"I'll be down in a minute!" Jon shouted.

"Rollie, sit on the sofa. I'll get you some tea. Five sugars, no milk, right?"

"Right, Mrs. K, as always. Thank you."

Since he was driving us and taking us to the border tomorrow, I thought to soften my tone and be kinder to him.

"Say, what's with the tinted glasses? What's it like out there?" I asked him casually.

"Bright sunshine, temps in the 20° Fs, light wind. Wind chill feels like 18°F. Blizzard conditions possible as we head north through the afternoon."

"Really?" I said.

"You know they're never wrong anymore. I don't know why you're always asking, 'Really?'" he answered sarcastically.

"C'mon now Rollie, you know old habits die hard. Growing up in the last quarter of the twentieth century things were different, much different. Those were the good old days!"

"So you like to tell me," he said. "I grew up then too, and I don't feel that way. My father was always in and out of work when I was a kid. My mother did secret housework for others to make ends meet. My father would never have allowed it if he knew. There was always tension, words between them in front of us kids."

He sat forward a little on the couch.

"Why are you going to visit Rachel now, in February? You've never done that before."

*Oh! Need I crank out a story again?*

"It's none of your business, Roland," I said, shaking my head, my desire to lighten up toward him instantly erased. *Why is he asking? I'm know Jon told him the truth.*

We had transferred my SUV to him as a gift. But he was acting stranger than usual.

"Are you hoping I'll tell you something that you can snitch and get a reward?"

"Oh no, no, Mrs. K, nothing like that," he said defensively. "I don't know . . . You haven't been to visit in three or four years, and this is not your usual season."

I hustled into the kitchen so I wouldn't be forced to look at him and shouted over my shoulder, "My daughter and her husband are going to Panama for two weeks to soak up some sun. The kids have school, so we volunteered to go up to be with them."

"Rachel always had help and a live-in nanny. What happened to them?"

I stood in the kitchen doorway with my hands on my hips.

"Roland, why are you so nosey?" I asked. "That is none of your business either! What is making you think like this all of sudden?"

"I'm sorry for asking. Mrs. K, forget it," he answered. "You're right. It's none of my business."

"Oh no, no! Too late! You brought it up, so now out with it. I want to know what's on your mind."

Rollie hesitated for a moment, maybe thinking of what to say. He'd never been so forward with me and I'd rarely seen him looking so uncomfortable.

"You're not coming back this time, are you?" he finally blurted.

He glanced around the room. "Look at this place! The fancy pictures are gone, furniture is missing and you've neglected the property.

You haven't painted in years. You never prepared for this winter like usual. Everyone's been waiting, knowing you were going to leave. People figured you were unhappy, just like all the other people at your level!"

An edge crept into his voice.

"Who did you think you were fooling? This was expected… even sooner!"

I should have been surprised, but I wasn't. I'd always suspected that he hid the truth of his attitude toward us. *"People at our level," huh? So that's it!*

Just then Jonathan came down the stairs and into the room. "What's going on here? What's this shouting? Hey, look at your hair!" he said to me with a big smile. "You look great, years younger. Now put on a baseball cap like you used to wear. That was your look! I always liked your hair that way—shows off your face. Plenty of guys looked your way. Why'd you do that today?"

As usual, without waiting for an answer, he looked at his communicator.

"Are we ready? It's almost 9:55. When are the Snyders going to be here? Say, I'll have a cup of tea too while I check on the weather."

He unfolded and sat on a bridge chair in front of the wooden box that was being used as a coffee table.

*An hour ago you were in a hurry, and now you have time for a cup of tea.* At that moment, my aggravation with the two of them and my anxiety toward the trip got the better of me.

"Make it yourself!" I said. "I have a few more things to do."

As I left the room I noticed that Jon and Rollie were making faces at each other, signals of some sort. Jon was probably asking him what had upset me.

When I returned minutes later, both were looking at and manipulating their communicators–Jon's on his wrist, Rollie's on the underside of his cap. What were they doing now? I ignored it.

Jon was always more friendly to Rollie. I was not completely in on their relationship. Life had become so confusing—no one knew whom to trust. The federal government had become paranoid about enemies in and around us, tightening the borders at every entry point. And they transferred that paranoia to we the people. It was happening even before that Boston Marathon terrorist attack years ago. But it greatly intensified after. *What a mess.*

Jon made his tea in a mug from the boiling water faucet. He looked up and gave me a nod. I returned a manufactured smile and sat down. I took a deep breath and quieted my animosity.

"How much more time do we have?" I asked.

"Not five minutes," Jon answered. "I wish the Snyders would get here already."

He was about to say something more when he jumped from his chair. "Here they come now, right on time!"

We smiled at each other. The day was finally beginning.

Pepper greeted them as she had Rollie. I took Sally to the kitchen to go over the routine and Jon took Sam upstairs.

Five minutes later we were on our way.

# Chapter 3
# Getting Ready

*Jon*

I tossed and turned all night. Didn't get a wink. I'd been like this for weeks. I was up to pee three times. The doctor said, "Comes with your age–seventy-one—and prostate issues."

Now I had those. Ida too was restless.

We went downstairs about 6:30. She made us cups of coffee. We weren't going to sleep any more that morning, not that day—unless it was in the FAV on the drive to New Hampshire.

"How do you feel??" I asked her.

"How should I feel? This is a big day, a bold move. Maybe a danger- ous trip. I'm going because of you."

"I know, I know. I keep telling myself we have an opportunity to reinvent ourselves, start a new life, to have a new adventure. Have you thought any more about where you want to land?"

"Not Canada, too cold. And we don't want to be on top of Rachel and Jacque."

"Israel?"

"Maybe. No climate is perfect," she said.

"We can split our time between two homes. Canada and Costa Rica, or Belize, or another Central American retirement state—maybe Panama? What about Canada and Israel? Vancouver is also Canada, and not under Rachel's feet. We enjoyed Vancouver when we were there."

"Jon, didn't Vancouver try to escape from Canada? With some other provinces too? That country seems ready to break apart."

I shook my head. She worried too much.

"No, no Ida! That was some time ago already. The country has a revised Federation plan and is hanging together."

I didn't want to say more about it to Ida. But maybe you can tell I liked Canada! It was prosperous, robust, sparkling. Nearly ten million expats from the US and Europe had relocated there in the past twenty years, and their internal political restlessness seemed to be over.

Long ago Quebec thought to go for independence but lost the vote three or four…, maybe even more times. Then British Columbia, with Alberta and Saskatchewan, tried to break away together. Manitoba revolted and demanded to join them. When the votes were taken, the separation didn't pass. British Columbia was acting like a bully to the other provinces. They expected to control the new state, like London controls Britain, like Washington controls the US. The others could see this, were offended and declined. "Why trade Ottawa for Vancouver," was their slogan.

Then BC threatened to leave by itself. But Alberta and the others retaliated, threatening to bypass their ports and trade through the US or to the east. The Keystone Pipeline was in place, and BC couldn't survive without being in the trade loop. So a new deal was reached. Canada stayed together, but the provinces were given more autonomy, more control over the taxes their people paid, the services provided, and the money sent to Ottawa. The model was much like what the UK had with Scotland, Wales, and Northern Ireland—after Scotland lost the independence vote a few times too.

In earlier years, you could buy your way into Canada with a modest local investment. But the buy-in price was raised to stem the flow, especially after the US threatened to prohibit people from leaving America with their assets intact. It didn't matter that Canada had higher income tax rates. The highest rates didn't affect the investment income of the wealthiest people, retirees.

Canada had become a haven for Europeans and Americans seeking to find the freedoms they knew in the past and to escape from the confiscation of their assets. Except it wasn't as easy to get into Canada anymore. But——our family connection was our ticket in!

Why was Canada so popular? It had a solid culture of freedom and democracy from the British and French. They never had a dictator, and their army didn't have the power to stage a coup. Their political system was very safe. The country had modest federal debt, huge natural resources, a vibrant population, universal health care and retirement plans that didn't break the bank—*all possible because the US provided their defense,* leaving them with meager military costs. Their politics were now stable and their economy booming.

In recent years, migration had swelled their numbers. The immigrants created a boom in consumer spending, housing and autos, across the country and up into the Arctic. The population was reported as forty-three million in 2035, up 25 percent in only twenty years. Spending by the affluent newcomers had bailed out the credit-card debt burden of their general populace.

I'd have moved there in a heartbeat years ago if Ida had agreed. *And would now too, if she would agree!*

"Jon, Vancouver was more than twelve years ago! I know you like Canada; it's always in your options. I'd like Israel to be close to Eric, Rebecca, and their kids. But your brothers and sister in Jerusalem—I can do without––after the way they treated you."

"I know, I know, and so can I. Their lives and ours have taken a very different course. We're not in contact with them now, so we don't have to be in contact there either."

I still can't get over how miffed my brothers and sister were when I didn't go into the family business. My parents always knew I wanted to be a naval officer and encouraged me. My brothers and sister never opened their mouths back then. I had no idea they were so peeved, but their animosity had become a major problem over the years until our relationship devolved into nonexistence.

"It's hard to understand that they didn't expect you to claim your share when the company was sold," Ida said. "Did they really just expect you to walk away from all that money?"

"Who knows what they thought?"

My parents left the family company to us equally. When my dad was still alive, I helped them get their first contract for navy uniforms from a billet I served at the Pentagon. Dad was elated. That order introduced them to the military and within a decade they were a major supplier of officer's uniforms for all the services, all American-made. That was their selling point, their advantage. My father heaped much credit on me in front of my siblings—like Jacob in the Bible did to Joseph, and *his* brothers hated him too. Those times were very awkward for me. But I was too naïve to see their effect on my brothers and sister.

After my parents' death, the Defense Industries Cabinet bought the company for $80 million because all its business was from the military. My share should have been $20 million, but I agreed to accept $16 to avoid court. In one way, my siblings were smarter than me. They paid their taxes, then left the country for Israel before the most aggressive penalties and with most of their money intact. They beat the diplomatic break in 2027. That was when Truman and Eric urged us to move out too.

"Please Ida, we won't live in Jerusalem. That's easy enough. There are excellent areas in the suburbs of Tel Aviv, in Eilat or even in the developments along the Mediterranean in Gaza."

Gaza was now a part of Israel and the West Bank had become a part of the new state of Palestine, including most of the Jewish settlements there. It was said that more than two-and-a-half-million, Jews and others, many of them scientists and engineers had immigrated to Israel or Palestine from all over the world. The big push had begun in the late teens and 2020s. Many believed that these numbers were light, low. China was Israel's new big brother and they had imposed the creation of the Palestinian state, solving the long-simmering Middle East crisis with money and force.

"We haven't seen the opportunities in Gaza because we've been unable to get visitors' permits. We'll be able to travel there from Canada without a problem," I said.

Ida, disheartened, answered, "This really gives me a headache. But one thing I know: we need to have a home base to put new roots down."

This was tough for her, I knew. She was giving up a lot with no clear vision of what would take its place. She would miss our home—it was her comfort zone. She had grown accustomed to the idea that we were embarking on a new phase of life, but she was at loose ends about what she wanted.

I said, "Come finish packing, and I'll bring your suitcases downstairs. I have a bit more to do myself."

We hugged and pecked each's cheeks and climbed the stairs together to finish getting ready. When she was done, she pointed at her cases and I nodded understanding.

"I'm going to pack a snack basket in the kitchen. I need these cases to add a few things from the laundry room," she said.

"We have time, no problem. I'll bring them down in a few minutes."

Upstairs, I was puttering with my jewelry, watches, and the only gun I'd ever had. Sam Snyder had agreed to package and ship the jewelry to Truman in Hawaii. Domestic transfer, no problem! When I told Rollie our true plans, he asked if he could have my pistol, the Beretta M9A1, my service sidearm. Though I loved it and wanted to take it with me, there was no way. I'd never gotten a civilian license and to show it to the police now would guarantee confiscation. Like other officers, I stole it from the navy just before I retired. I drove it off the base after a practice session and reported it missing. The Marine guards never inspected cars coming on or leaving the base in those days. Taking the weapon was no sweat. But try to get it across the border now? Fah-ged-abou-dit! We were going to be inspected on both sides, and neither country would allow an undocumented gun to cross the border. It would be confiscated and I would be detained–for questioning–or worse. Giving it to Rollie seemed to be a good idea, so I said, "Yes."

I met Rollie, a small independent building contractor, shortly after moving to Norwich. He lived nearby. Friends referred us to him when we bought the Broadway house. He had excellent references from within our social group.

He liked that I was a navy officer and he liked talking military stuff. He had been in the service himself and knew quite a bit. Over time he became my handyman. When duty sent me to sea and Ida was alone with the kids, he was especially helpful.

Ida grew up in Norwich. I was from New York. We met in college. Life was extra-stressful for her when I went to sea. She had her family company to run––and a typical deployment was for six months. I also had two tours at the Pentagon of two years each, when I was only home for weekends. Well, most weekends anyway. When gone, I counted on Rollie to care for our property and make the decisions to keep the house and cars functioning and in good repair.

Ida never warmed up to him. She claimed she could tell that he didn't like taking orders from a woman. And at her company, Now's, an auto tire, appliances, and hard goods outlet, she was used to giving the orders! Maybe she was right . . . I wasn't around to notice. When she needed something, she left Rollie notes or notified him through the Cloud. He came by when the house was empty. He had a key. I trusted him completely and established credit for him to buy things we needed.

During one of the many periodic recessions, he took a job at Home Depot up at Lisbon Landing. I was his reference. He tried to keep up with smaller moonlight jobs, but we became his principal source of extra income every month. He was thorough with the credit line and always had the receipts for me. At times Ida suspected he charged other stuff to our account, but I never found anything amiss. Maybe her suspicions were her way to remind me that she was uneasy with him.

Like a banking relationship, never entirely satisfactory but too inconvenient to change––with no assurance of improvement, Rollie was convenient for me and it was hard to contemplate a change. His attention and workmanship were good. I didn't know where to start to find a replacement, so I never bothered. How would I train one? Maybe the next would be worse. That's what I kept telling Ida and myself. She just shook her head and had no easy solution either.

I was handling the M9 when Ida called.

"Jon, please bring down my cases."

"You don't have to shout! Hearing is not my problem," I responded.

I put the pistol on the dresser and took the bags down. Ida wasn't in sight. I left them by the kitchen door and hurried back upstairs.

Again in our bedroom, I reached for the gun. It slipped from my fingers and fell to the floor. "Goddamn it!"

Ida shouted, "What?"

"Are you ready?" I shouted back, just for something to say.

I don't recall what she answered as I hurried to get finished.

I held the Beretta close to me, wrapped it in its protective oily cloth, and forced it into its holster. I dropped it in a cloth bag from the Sun Casino and put it near the door for Rollie.

It was time to strap the money belt around my waist. It contained US $250,000 in $1000 bills. The government had revived $500 and $1000 paper bills after the hyperinflation that followed the $10 trillion "bail-in" that initially shut down the banks, destroyed the value of the dollar, and put the country in turmoil for a few weeks.

I remembered it well—like I remembered 9/11, like my parents remembered the Kennedy assassination and Armstrong landing on the moon. If it weren't for the small local banks and credit unions, there would have been absolute chaos, maybe even anarchy. As the federal government lost its footing, the states and municipalities stepped up their presence. The governors called up their guard, the cities their police. They generally held the peace. The smaller banks, not connected to the international financial mess, kept local economies functioning. Together they created a temporary local currency to keep money circulating and commerce moving.

At the end of the crisis, the Treasury acquired all the major banks by tender offer on the NYSE. Citibank, Wells Fargo, Bank of America, JP Morgan, and a dozen more, now all gone, the way of the dinosaurs. The government stepped into their place. The ultimate "too big to fail" became the US Treasury.

Bank shareholders were compensated with more printed dollars. The bloat and the float just grew and grew. But the man in the street was patient, surviving any which way until the return to a new normal, fortunately in just a few weeks. But the government grew bigger still, becoming even more pervasive in our lives.

The $1000 bills were new and stiff in ten packets of twenty-five. I pulled my shirt over the belt and tucked the tails into my slacks. Then I put a sweater over that.

"When is the truck going to be here?" Ida called.

My head shook in disbelief. If I'd told her once . . . "It's an FAV, a Federal Automatic Vehicle."

I think she kept calling it a "truck" to poke fun and provoke me. We both liked to do that to each other. If so, it was working.

I asked her about the Snyders and about Pepper. We had a few snippy exchanges.

When Rollie arrived, I was ready. I told Ida to send him upstairs to get my bags. I wanted to talk to him and give him the Beretta.

"Hey Mr. K, are you all set for this?" he asked.

"Yes, Rollie. The time's come. D-day is here."

"Are you planning to go to Israel? Your son Eric is there, right?"

"Right. At some point we'll visit and see if we want to stay."

"That could be dangerous for you, don't you think? With Israel now in the Chinese sphere and diplomatic relations suspended, maybe

Washington will want you dead and take you out with a drone or an assassin."

"C'mon, Rollie, I'm not important enough for them to spend even a dime to bother with me. I only hope they notice I'm gone."

I forced a laugh. The truth was, I really wasn't sure that Rollie was wrong. But I needed to change the subject.

"Here's my Beretta. This has been with me nearly fifty years. Never fired in combat. Hardly fired in training. Not fired since I retired from the reserves twenty years ago. Take good care of it. I always considered it a good friend."

Rollie smiled and nodded. "I'll take real good care and think of you when I practice with it. Thanks. I'll lock it in the Navigator now and pick them both up when I return."

He opened the canvas bag, looked in, and handled the cloth-covered weapon. He lifted his glasses to his forehead and did a double take looking into the bag. He turned toward me, the glasses returned to his face.

"Where are the boxes of ammo?" he asked surprised.

"There are none," I answered.

"No! None?" he stammered. "What am I going to shoot with? You know a person needs a license just to buy ammo now. I won't be able to get any!"

"There might be few or more cartridges in one of the clips, but they're more than twenty years old. I only fired at the practice range on the base. We were issued just enough ammo for our sessions. They never supplied us ammo to take home. We weren't supposed to have the pieces off the base, except aboard ship on active duty."

Rollie's face dropped. I wouldn't have believed he would be so disappointed. Frankly, I hadn't thought through the whole exercise and his surprise was funny to me.

"Please take my luggage down and lock that thing in the Navigator. Don't forget to cover the car with *your* insurance before you drive it," I said with a bit more authority.

We had transferred the title from Ida's SUV to him as a gift. Ida had agreed to that. She knew nothing about my intended disposal of the pistol.

He took my bags, and I finished boxing the jewelry.

Raised voices between Ida and Rollie reached me. I finished quickly and went down to join them.

"Hey, what's going on here, why the shouting?"

No one answered. I noticed Ida's hair and it made me smile. I told her how much I liked it, how young it made her look. To me she looked like she did back in college. I always liked her that way—in the ponytail and with a baseball cap. I guess she thought it wasn't fitting for her professional life and station in the community, because I hadn't seen that look in a long time. Whenever I suggested it, she gave me "the face." You know the face I mean? I stopped the suggestions years ago. But I wondered what had possessed her to do it today. Was it something we said at coffee? Was she turning her clock back because we were starting a new life? It was a good sign. *Maybe I should have hit my gray with one of those men's rinses?*

I sat down on a bridge chair near the sofa and saw that she and Rollie were having tea. I made myself a cup with boiling water from the automatic faucet. When I returned, Ida and I smiled at each other.

It was only another minute when the Snyders arrived. When they came through the door, I jumped for joy. Ida took Sally into the kitchen for a last-minute look around while I took Sam upstairs to give him the box to ship to Truman.

"Sam, listen," I said, "everything will be alright. Please don't worry."

Sam was shuffling from foot to foot, obviously nervous.

"As far as you know, we are going for a vacation and a visit to our daughter and grandchildren. That's what's in the official permit. You and Sally have done this for us in the past and it always worked well...

right? We always returned on time or called in to adjust plans. That's the truth, isn't it, right?"

I was snappy with him and feeling certain anxiety even as I tried to calm him down.

He nodded his head in agreement.

"If anyone asks, you'll say you were pleased when we called to report we had arrived safely. But you were shocked when we didn't return as planned and we didn't call again. You had to return to your home, so you took Pepper. You couldn't abandon her. Now that's your story . . . right?"

"I don't know, Jon . . . it's all a little scary," he said, shaking his head. "We all could go to jail if this plan of yours blows up!"

His jowls were turned down, and he had a sour look on his face. But he kept talking.

"After all, Sally and I have nothing to gain and much to lose. I'm ten years older than you, and we're surviving nicely in this system. We have some means of our own, and the government makes monthly deposits in our account, and puts food coupons into our Cloud space. Plus with the Senior Health System and Senior Center meals . . ."

It was nothing new. The same old story.

"Sam, stop, stop! You've said that many times. I know, I know!"

I just wanted to get on our way.

"Our health is good. We like the health care. Sally and I will vote for these guys for as long as we live."

"Hey, Sam, stop—stop right now!" I said tartly. "Think! You *do* have something to gain! Did you forget what you asked of me? Remember . . . US $100K, huh?"

To my greater annoyance, he just frowned more deeply.

"Yeah, that was a mistake, I'm sorry I did that now."

"But you said you needed it to help your daughter and her business. If we could give you that, you agreed to stay here and do what we needed, right?"

"Yeah, right… Okay, so here we are!"

He extended his hands, palms up, no change in his sour expression.

"Sam, thank you. Look through this box and take anything of interest to you. Ship the rest to Truman. Sally has his address. Ida and I are grateful to you and her for sticking with us. You'll see, everything will go like clockwork. C'mon now, we better get downstairs so Ida and I can leave on time. The auto Motivators, the ground controllers, will be looking for us to check in for our drive at ten o'clock."

"So where's the envelope?" he demanded. "I want to count it!"

The envelope was on the dresser. At my wit's end, I grabbed it and thrust it at him.

*What is wrong with him?*

"Here, take the envelope and open it *after* we leave! There's an extra $50K in it for you and Sally. Enjoy yourselves with a trip to Florida or something. And don't forget: give the bills to Sally to wash before you use them. New bills cause suspicion. But these are real, so nothing to worry about there."

He left the envelope on the dresser with the jewelry and we returned downstairs together.

Just minutes later, Ida and I were on our way.

The time was 10:06.

# Chapter 4

# In the FAV

*Ida*

The FAV looked like a giant licorice jellybean on tall tires. A stairway led to an entry hatch like the ones you see on private planes. Jon steadied me as I reached for the first step of the air-stair-type door with a covered chain railing to help passengers climb in. With my heavy coat and the belt around my waist, I was somewhat unbalanced. Three smaller steps and I was in.

As Jon came up the stairs, he took off a glove and tapped the side with his bare knuckles. "Ha! Graphene! Right up my alley," he chuckled. He loved advanced technology and this vehicle represented the latest.

"It's electric propelled, powered by a fuel cell," he said as he entered. "The fuel cell needs hydrogen, which is released by cracking compressed natural gas right on board. A recycling catalyst absorbs the free carbon released. As the hydrogen passes through the cell, it quietly and efficiently produces electricity without pollution. Highly efficient and the byproducts are just heat and water—totally pollution free."

I stayed quiet.

"Fuel cells are popular as auxiliary power sources on our subs. Some foreign submarines are exclusively powered this way, although their sources of hydrogen vary greatly."

"Jon, please? I've heard this lecture already. I don't care how the power is made. I only know that it's taking me away from my home for good. Please don't make my head spin on this trip."

So you get the idea. This was a very modern machine. The spacious passenger cabin was built to accommodate six people. It was luxurious, like I imagined the cabin on a private jet.

Despite my pleas, Jon was not finished. "This FAV's body has a graphene overlay on resin composite. It's stronger than steel, lightweight and bulletproof. These panels are mechanically fastened and covered with moldings. This wouldn't suffice for a submarine. Graphene used on a sub must be bonded, strong, and sealed tight—100 percent waterproof. Ida, this is the miracle material I've been adapting to submarine systems for the past twenty years."

"Jon, please stop."

I was looking forward to being with Rachel, our only daughter and her four great kids. We hadn't been to see them in three years. She and Jacque had visited us a year ago after they attended some conference in New York. We filled their car with things to get out of our house. They managed to get through Canadian customs without a problem. With Jacque speaking French in native Quebecois, "It was easy," he later told us.

Our grandkids were the greatest! Grandparents always say that. We're no different. The boy was going to be a hockey star and the girls actresses or models.

But now I wondered what there would be for me and where? I had run my father's business, Now's Home and Tire, right-sized it by closing three stores and consolidating in four locations as well as developing a significant Cloud clientele. My dad survived the big box challenge because he would only sell "Made in America" products, even when the cheapest stuff came from Japan, Korea, Taiwan, or China. "Made in America" was all over our promotions and advertising. American manufacturers of consumer goods called on us to carry their products. Loyal Americans patronized us. Even now, when almost everything is again being made in America, we retain loyal customers. Jon's family company and ours were both focused on American-made products. That was what brought us together when we first met in college.

I was used to being busy all the time. When not with the kids or work, I was director of a bank, trustee of a museum, president of my college alumni club, and a member of an active book club I'd help to start years earlier. With Jon, I participated in Jewish community activities. I was included in the wide esteem he enjoyed from that constituency. He had been president of the synagogue, the local Jewish Federation, and the Federations of Connecticut, the whole state. We were also active with civic causes. Through our work on behalf of these, we received respect at the events we attended. *Where, how, will I be able to replace those activities, those friendships and acquaintances?*

He didn't seem worried. When I brought it up to him, he would say, "I can walk into any synagogue in the world and make myself comfortable there."

And I believed him. I knew it was so! But what would I find to replace my interests and occupy my energy? And where? It seemed so easy for him, but I couldn't just sit somewhere and vegetate. Why didn't he understand and try to help me sort out some options?

Rollie, still outside, pushed a button and the air-stair door lifted up. The stairs folded in and the gull-wing door closed and sealed the compartment. He then climbed his own stairway and lifted it closed too.

Jon pointed out how the driver's station was insulated from us, separated from the back with sound-proof, one-way see-through partitions. We could see him but he could not see us. We could talk to Rollie through an intercom. His space was also generous. He could totally recline and sleep when the auto Motivators were driving. He had access to the food and drink and could connect a tube to his—you know, if he needed to…you know that too. For other services, we would have to stop.

"Is special training or a license needed to drive one of these?" I asked Jon. "Is Rollie qualified, capable?"

"Oh sure. He attended class, practiced road work, and received his license a few months ago."

Jon hadn't told me that. *No doubt Jon paid for it.*

I took off my scarf and coat and explored the many conveniences of the FAV. The leather aroma smacked of money. At our fingertips were all the things Rollie had described, plus a personal climate system and a big-screen communicator with every media option. We'd seen these up-to-date systems in stores and in the Cloud but never had our own. A tiny lavatory was behind the rearmost seats, but a person needed to be an acrobat to get there.

Jon wrote me a note and passed it over. "Welcome to the lifestyle of politicians and the 1 percent!" We had become accustomed to writing notes to each other. We felt secure that these old handwritten techniques provided just a bit of privacy from the intrusive surveillance.

In charade, I pointed to my mouth and the large communicator screen. "Boca?" I said.

Jon knew what I was asking. *Boca* was our word for busybody, gossiper. The term was inspired by people we had observed in Boca Raton, Florida, as newlyweds in 1992. When either of us said "Boca," it referred to government listeners, like virulent gossipers.

Jon openly answered, "Probably," as he nodded. "Man overboard." That was our word for watch out, or be careful.

I leaned back in my lounger, put my pillow behind my head, and closed my eyes. Yep, I had brought my favorite pillow. Just like a baby's blankie, it helped me sleep. Since we were leaving forever, I knew to take it.

I took a deep breath, murmured a little sigh, and let my mind wander . . .

Rollie had mentioned "our level." How had the US become so dramatically split between the top 10 percent and the bottom 50? How did the comfortable middle class get squeezed into only 40 percent, dominated by government workers, small business proprietors, and the professionals? Teachers, bureaucrats, technicians, monitors, police, military officers, public works laborers and the like, employees at all levels of the government—they were the real middle class. These workers, paid for by the people, had become the majority of the comfortable middle 40 percent. Good salaries, expense accounts, total safety nets, guaranteed retirement, and education for their children were theirs. Maybe we were at the bottom of the top 10 percent, but I felt we were drifting lower and lower as the federal government taxed more and more of our earnings and spied on and took a bite of our assets too. There was no firm public data for anyone to know where the edges of the brackets were. Neither the Treasury Department nor the IRS ever connected the strata to real numbers.

But money aside, it was obvious that health care for the elderly had become so burdensome that the government had begun withholding costly, lifesaving treatment to older Americans—a kind of passive euthanasia for the elderly. Retirement age had been raised to seventy-five, and aggressive health care measures began to be withheld at age seventy and over, as in Jon's recent diagnosis—unless you had a certain position. They wouldn't give a heart bypass operation to a seventy-eight-year-old retired carpenter—but they would to a congressman of similar age. That was the coup-de-gras for Jon.

Jon wanted treatment for a prostate issue and it was no longer administered in the US to men who were over seventy when diagnosed. Jon was seventy-one. The black market was not equipped for surgery or radiation therapy, so men of Jon's age had to seek it and other such procedures abroad—if they had the means and the availability to travel. We had the means but were limited as to where we could go. The government thesis was that nearly 65 percent of all men of Jon's age lived normal lives without any treatment at all, that the majority died *with* prostate cancer, not from it. That success rate was good enough for the system to discontinue the treatment for *any* man in that category, depending on status. It was totally unfair but a way to save a lot of money. We weren't willing to take the risk.

In health care, everything had changed. Everything was now done by category. No one was an individual anymore. Every person at every age was defined by one or more categories. If you had an illness—of any sort—your personal data, age, employment, family history, religion, ethnicity, color, age, symptoms, scans and lab work were sent into the Cloud, where an algorithm took over and the treatment to be given was returned. What it said was what you got. The system allowed no human intervention. The treatment was generally correct for the vast majority, but not appropriate for everyone. If you were in the minority, you probably were not going to get the best treatment for your case.

Jon calculated his own odds from what data he could find and disagreed with the system. He was livid that he was prohibited from treatment because he was over seventy and not in a privileged class. That was the final straw for him. He wanted out of America—for good! I wasn't going to let him leave by himself. I knew that if the situation were reversed, he would never let me go without him. We had promised each other *"for richer, for poorer, in sickness and in health, till"* . . . well, you know the rest. Although we weren't always on the same page with everything, those words we uttered on that wedding day so long ago, we meant. We lived by them.

We planned to spend the night at a lodge near the Canadian border in New Hampshire. Our Exit Permit directed us to cross over at Chartierville, Quebec. The permit was for a three-month stay. Rachel had rented a furnished apartment for us on a month-to-month basis. That was how we wanted it. Once there, we would apply for permanent residency. She was sure we wouldn't make Quebec our permanent home. She knew the year-round climate wouldn't suit us and that we wanted to find our own place.

I also knew that her husband, Jacque, was worried about our intrusion in his life and family. He enjoyed his distance from Jon and me. His family was a tight group of siblings and spouses, aunts, uncles, and cousins, all wrapped up in a real-estate enterprise of commercial property and retail malls. His great-grandfather, who had escaped Nazi-occupied France in 1941, started the business. Great-Grandpapa worked his way to Montreal because the language there was French.

The family council had asked Jacque to move to Sherbrooke to expand their investment territory to the east. He opened a family office and immediately made contacts with members of the Sherbrooke business community. Within a year he added some choice projects to the family portfolio, contributing to their income, growth, and success.

Though leery of our intrusion, he was willing to sign to be financially responsible for us, so it was unlikely that our residency application would be denied. Though we wouldn't need his support, it was a requirement of Canada to guarantee we would not become dependents of the state. *I'm sure he's counting on us to just sojourn there until we can clear our way elsewhere.*

I snuggled up with my pillow, closed my eyes, and hoped to sleep.

# Chapter 5
# In the FAV

*Jon*

The FAV was a cross between a large pickup truck, an old Humvee and a 2020s Cadillac Escalade. It sat high off the road on tall tires. Shiny black with dark tinted windows, it was a bigger version of the vehicles you saw on the news that preceded and followed the president's limousine. It had a double axle in the rear, one with spiked tires that could be engaged in off-road driving or inclement weather.

I marveled at all the technology that was a part of this machine, many of the same systems used on our submarines without, of course, a nuclear reactor or periscope. Ida asked me to "pipe down" as I tried to explain some of the salient features and how they related to my work.

About an hour later, I said, "Ida, it's eleven, I could use a lttle something to eat."

"Sure . . . open the basket or see what's in the fridge."

"You've been so quiet for the last twenty minutes. Where's your head?" I asked.

She kept her eyes closed, her head resting on her pillow.

"Oh…Just wandering through our situation. Thinking about how we got here and where we're going. If you'd like a turkey, Camembert, and apple on wheat, I can heat it in the wave oven. And what have you been doing in this quiet time?"

I smiled. "I too have been thinking. We're both going to be fine. We'll find ourselves––together. This is going to be a great new chapter in our lives. And what we do from now on will be together. That sandwich will be fine."

Ida left her comfortable position, unwrapped two sandwiches and put them in the oven.

"Cold drink or coffee?"

I shrugged and took the tray table out of the armrest, ready to be served.

"Listen, Jon," Ida said. "There are no stewards in this first-class cabin, so start helping yourself."

We smiled at each other and touched hands. Not a high five, just a gentle touch of affirmation. It was another little sign we did from time to time to remind one another of the more important things in life—of our commitment to each other. It was hard to talk about "love," but we both knew we loved each other. The meaning of "love" changes when you've been married almost fifty years, from your young twenties to your seventies. We hadn't talked any about it for quite a few years now.

I settled back with my sandwich, a fruit cup and a cookie. After locating a coffee pod, I starting the maker. After a few bites and a few swallows, I relaxed and slowly shook my head.

"Ida, what happened? Y2K, the new millennium—you remember that? Ushered in with great fanfare! The world didn't end like some cults predicted. The banking system, computers, and Internet didn't crash as many warned. And everyone was pretty optimistic toward the future. With the surpluses of the Clinton presidency, Bush, the son, one of the last Republican presidents, rolled back taxes for all Americans. It seemed like we were in for an era of prosperity!"

I knew the history, of course. But repeating it now and again helped make sense of it —or at least reminded us of why we were confused.

I continued, "But 9/11 shattered all that, and then he put us into two entangling wars we had no business fighting. Had they been short actions as expected, they wouldn't have mattered."

Ida sighed. "But they became huge, decade-long entanglements with changing goals that sapped our energy and treasury. The military buildup drove government spending out of control. Family lives were interrupted. Reserve service men and women were called up for duty. Our soldiers were being wounded, maimed, and killed. Many kids, family men and women from Connecticut too. Jon, I swear those countries were other Vietnams. After the initial success, *why did we have to stay so long?"*

She sat up straighter for emphasis. "What danger was there to our national security? Look how it ended, and what's there now? We didn't accomplish a single thing trying to bring that region into modern thought."

Ida and I were equally exasperated with that episode in our history.

"The notion of our security at risk was a falsehood perpetrated by Washington for only God knows what reason," I answered. "Then it was continued by his successor, Obama, because of political bickering.

"But we can't forget that I prospered at the Boat because of the military spending. Our shipyards were very busy. The damn twenty-four-hour news media just never stopped. CNN, Fox, MSNBC, radio talk jockeys. Pictures in vivid color and harsh talk—the media kept it all in our face. The treasury bled and the government just borrowed dollar after dollar. We were already at war when the last of the tax cut proposals were implemented. The Republicans could have cancelled that final cut to help pay for the wars! That would have helped the government finances. And then why did Obama extend them when they were supposed to expire?"

"Please Jon, can we talk of something else?"

I'm sorry. I'll quiet down."

I shut up, but my mind wouldn't.

That wasn't the only hemorrhage. The government social safety net had become bloated. Costs rose faster than inflation as new, expensive technology and medicines promised longer lifespans, with cures or remission for many of the ills of old age. Average lifespans had already been extended from sixty to eighty years and then to one hundred years for women, with men not far behind. The largest growing segment of the population became the hundreds and over. With longevity like that, the government could never afford its promises to the people! So they began rationing treatment to the over-seventy and retired, withholding critical care to seniors who had become dependents of the state. They tried to ease the load by phasing out Social Security and Medicare and instituting Senior Stipend and the Senior Health System in their place, deferring the starting time until age seventy-five, the new official retirement age.

I don't have to tell you that the public became incensed! Politicians were voted out. There were times it seemed riots would erupt. Heavy-handed police and state military were dispatched to keep the peace. But the new terminology and extended age remained. Those were major turning points that eventually led to our economic rebirth, with the *Re-Erected Economic Model* that began falling into place in the twenties.

"Ida you remember Barack Obama's campaign promises. He was elected to get us out of the wars, extend health insurance to all Americans and reverse the tax cuts enacted by Bush. He was planning to adjust them down on lower and middle-income earners while putting a bigger bite on the wealthy as an offset. I was encouraged by his platform. He was *my* candidate. We were long overdue to return our troops home, and it was sad that we had millions of people, children, without access to dependable health care. Those things needed to be fixed. I had mixed feeling about the taxes, but I was willing to pay our share and give back the cuts we'd gotten."

"He's still alive now, isn't he?" Ida asked.

"Who?"

"Obama."

"Yes, he is," I answered. "Still talks to the press occasionally, and golfs on Martha's Vineyard in August and Hawaii at Christmas, so I've read."

"He was my choice too," Ida said. "But he was so slow to withdraw our forces from those wars, and his initial health plan had so many flaws and lacked wide support. It wasn't thoroughly thought-out. That's what led to the Tea Party and the succeeding years where the opposition took control of Congress and were able to create gridlock in the capital. Then he bent to bipartisan pressure to extend the Bush tax cuts, continuing the huge budget deficits, trying to have guns for two wars and butter at home. That's not what he promised."

Ida leaned back and took a sip of water.

"What about the initial debacle in implementing the health plan and the criticism he received from the media and the opposition?" I asked. "It was really unfair, but he made the mistake of promising too much too soon. Any program so transformative to society needed time to work through the unexpected details and unintended consequences."

I stopped long enough to finish the sandwich and take a swallow of the coffee and a bite of the fruit.

The Affordable Care Act had finally settled in after the government bought the private and public health insurance underwriters to make a single-payer system in the fifth year or so. The participating insurance companies were too disparate with their products, too greedy for profit and too arrogant in hiding behind the government's shield. The system now worked reasonably well, but the cost was heavy. And the rationing to some of the elderly was almost criminal, though most of the time it was practical and logical. Troubling now was that the life-and-death decisions that used to be made by the family, by the patient's loved ones, were now made by the bureaucracy. A family no longer had to decide whether or not to pull the plug, because the government had already done it for them. No comatose patient lay in a gurney for a week, or even a few days in an ICU, at a cost of $25,000 or more, a day. The government just wouldn't pay for it.

"Oooh . . . what's the use? We've talked about this time after time, and the conversation never changes," I said. I finished my coffee and looked for a glass of water.

"Thank God you're done," Ida said quietly with a sigh.

We generally agreed on the issues, but I could be absolutely obsessive about certain history, and at times I felt personally responsible—as if I could or should have tried to do something about it.

"Why must you become so emotional about the miscues of both sides?" Ida asked. "That was a long time ago, and we couldn't do anything to change it then or now."

She reached over and squeezed the back of my hand as I first shook my head and then nodded. I lifted her hand, leaned down and kissed it, and then gently returned it to the armrest. I knew I had faults—a certain ego, and I could be obsessive-compulsive at times—but deep inside I liked to think I had a sensitive core and was a sympathetic soul. I knew Ida's touch was sincere, like when we held hands under the wedding canopy.

At that moment the intercom clicked and Rollie announced, "Our first rest stop is ahead. It's a Massachusetts tourist stopover with information for the traveler, toilet facilities, and vending machines. I am taking control from the Motivators and will drive us in there."

The time was near 11:20.

# Chapter 6
# First Rest Stop
*Ida*

The weather was still sunny and clear, with conditions similar to Norwich. As we pulled into the rest stop, I noticed people looking our way and children pulling on their parents' clothing, pointing to the FAV. People always fantasized about who or what was in them. Inside, I wondered what we were doing here. I was slightly embarrassed to be an object of curiosity.

"How much time do we have here?" I asked Rollie.

"Twenty minutes or so. We're a few minutes ahead of schedule," he said. "I'm ready for a bite to eat too, if it's okay with you."

"Sure. You're welcome to sit back here if you like."

"Fine, Mrs. K, but after I visit the plumbing," he said.

I was okay, so I stayed put. Jon had deployed the stair door and rushed out. Rollie followed in a run too.

I watched out the window as Jon browsed the pavilion, looking through the vending machines, probably for candy. Rollie jogged back to the FAV a few minutes later. Children and adults watched him. I presumed he attracted the interest because of his uniform. Oh, I call it a uniform, but it was just his selection of apparel for the day. He wore smartly pressed black slacks and a black turtleneck sweater with leather patches on the elbows and one on the right shoulder. He was clean-shaven, had fashionable tinted glasses and wore a black beret on his thick, salt-and-pepper hair. To me, his outfit looked like it was from a military second-hand shop. He looked like Special Forces or a Secret Service agent.

Rollie closed the driver door and joined me in the passenger compartment, trying to shake off the chill. Jon had not yet returned. Rollie unfastened a heavy curtain that he pulled across the open door. The chill in the cabin subsided somewhat.

I motioned him to the rear-facing seat opposite me. His tall, lanky frame sank into the leather, and his legs stretched into the long space between the seats. I offered him a sandwich from my basket. He looked at it and looked away. He opened a package of bologna from the refrigerator, took two slices of white bread and added a slice of cheese, some mayonnaise, mustard, catsup, and relish. He popped it in the wave oven. He put in a fresh pod and brewed a cup of coffee from the maker in the door. I gave him an apple and a few small cookies.

Jon returned and took his seat. He hit a button and the stairway retracted as the gull-wing door closed.

"Rollie says we're making good time," I said. "We gained ten minutes against the plan even with our slightly late start. But we're going to be hitting nasty weather later in upstate New Hampshire."

"Yeah, but we'll be good," Rollie said. "Your appointment at the border isn't until the morning." He sat back and bit into his lunch.

After an awkward silence, Jon asked Rollie, "How old are you now? Sixty-four or five, is it?"

I thought Jon hoped to break the tension with a bit of small talk.

"Sixty-seven," Rollie answered, "turned sixty-seven in November. Should have been my retirement age but it's not." He shook his head.

"I should be eligible for Medicare now too," he continued, "but I'm not. You know my health isn't perfect. I have diabetes—a family heirloom—and my back never fully recovered from the skiing accident twenty years ago. If I had Social Security, Medicare, and a few more odd jobs like I do for you, the wife and me could be comfortable. But I still have eight more years to work and wait."

"They're not called Social Security or Medicare anymore. Those titles were dropped years ago. SS is now Senior Stipend and Medicare is now SHS, the Senior Health System. You know that, we've talked about it before. What's wrong with you today?" Jon said, his head tilted slightly as he looked at Rollie. "And I have four more years to reach SS too."

"But you're retired navy, and you only had to do twenty years for that. Now it takes thirty for retirement in the military." Rollie seemed irritated. "Are you going to ski on this trip?"

Maybe Rollie was trying to change the subject. But Jon didn't catch it.

"You know, Rollie," he continued, "the whole idea of a 'retirement' is a *new* thing, a twentieth-century idea. From ancient times until just one hundred years ago, the rich never worked and the others never stopped. People worked until they died or became disabled. A forty- or fifty-year-old was an old man in former times. The idea of enjoying a few years without working, a so-called 'retirement,' was invented in the 1930s with Social Security—when most people only lived into their fifties! Now, a hundred years later, we live much longer and *expect* a respectable retirement—mostly paid for by the government. But they don't have enough money to pay everyone a decent, livable stipend."

I cut in and added, "People today are working beyond sixty-seven *and* seventy-five too. The huge service industry is not as hard on the body as manual labor. Few can afford to retire at sixty-seven or even seventy-five. Most don't have enough savings to last twenty or thirty more years, and SS isn't enough to fill the gap."

Jon picked up the beat. "Maybe the government should just stop trying to kid the people about having a *retirement*—and do away with it as a short-term experiment that didn't work!" he said. "It's only been kicked around for a hundred years versus eternity. *I'd call it a failure!*"

I was so surprised at Jon's provocation to Rollie.

Rollie was visibly shaken, and I wasn't sure if Jon meant what he said or was just saying something to be outrageous. Sometimes I couldn't tell. I felt that baiting Rollie like he just did might be playing with fire.

The pensive quiet returned.

So *I* made the mistake to try some small talk too.

"How are your kids? Your son is still in the army, I remember."

Rollie answered proudly, "Oh, Mrs. K, they're not kids anymore, and yes, Lee's still in and doing very well. He plans to do his *thirty years* for full retirement. He'll only be forty-eight. You know he graduated from Norwich Tech with high honors. His program in mechanical exempted him from the draft, but he enlisted anyway to get the bonus being offered back then. They sent him for advanced training, and now he's a master sergeant on Guam, in charge of a unit that maintains the rockets that are carried on drone patrol boats, choppers, and planes. His unit disassembles, inspects, and repairs the rocket motors, then reassembles them. After five more years, a dozen companies are waiting to give him offers. He'll be just fine. Never rich but solidly in the middle class, and—"

"Middle class?" Jon interrupted—a fault many people found offensive but which I knew to anticipate. Jon was quick thinking and usually liked to control a conversation.

"Sure middle class," Jon repeated. "That's the niche of most people who work for the government, like me, too. But rocket motors in the missiles—why do they need attention? They only need to work once, and poof . . . they're gone."

"That's right, but they're *only* fired in training. None has ever been fired in the Pacific in hostility. *But when one needs to be fired in combat,* you want it to work––perfectly. The solid fuel is corrosive, as are the electronics in salt air. You should know that. There's a mandatory timetable when unused missiles need to be torn down, inspected, tested, and rebuilt. After the third recycle, those missiles become available for practice. If the military doesn't use them up, the factory will have to stop production. We need to keep producing new ones to keep the factory working even though we're not at war."

"Sure, sure—the government-owned, military industrial complex needs to be fed," Jon said.

I knew Jon was being sarcastic because he was conflicted. Despite his family wealth, he was an engineer in the military industrial complex. He too was on the sucking end of the government straw, and Rollie knew it.

Rollie continued with slight sarcasm, "Just like the submarines you build and the M1Abrams tanks made in Ohio. We have more than enough, but we have to keep building or rebuilding stuff we don't need just to keep the people and skills alive and the local communities functioning. That's part of the new economic model, right?"

Rollie knew and understood more than we gave him credit for.

Again I intervened. "Rollie, Lee's been married how many years? Several children too, I remember?"

"Oh sure, they have four kids now. Both he and my daughter have four children, and maybe looking for one more. They're taking advantage of the government incentives to increase the birthrate."

Rollie stopped as he took another bite and a swallow of coffee.

Jon said, "Four kids and wanting more? Can they afford them?"

Rollie raised his eyebrows. "That's a funny question. Surely you know, Mr. K, women—in or out of marriage—are being encouraged to have more than two kids. The government pays bonuses to the mothers for each additional child after the first two. The bonuses are higher if you're married, to a man or another woman, it don't matter. The family gets lower tax rates and guaranteed lifetime health care; the children get preferential schooling and placement. I know this doesn't mean a lot to you, but it's an important benefit for my family. It's like the government owns the kids, but you get to bring them up. This is why our country is growing again."

Jon and I shook our heads. I found it hard to believe that Jon wasn't aware of that—or maybe he was still playing games with Rollie.

Rollie paused for another bite and swallow. "Even with more liberal immigration laws, our population was still falling behind in replacing and growing our workforce. Who was going to keep the system afloat, create the goods and services, and pay the taxes to support the country and shoulder the burden of the seniors?" he asked.

"I suppose we needed more people to work and pay into the system. And you say immigration wasn't enough?" Jon asked.

"Mr. K, please! *Washington didn't want it all corrected by immigrants!* America is supposed to be a melting pot, not a patchwork of ethnics and foreign languages taking over our neighborhoods and towns! Washington wanted more population from the people already here. Black, brown, red, white—they didn't care as long as the kids were raised in our schools, the US was their country, English was their language, and they would serve in the military if they didn't go to college or learn a trade."

Rollie sounded satisfied. "I can't say it was a bad plan. Now after nearly twenty years, the plan is bearing fruit. Our domestic fertility rate is 2.35 children per women. That includes all ethnic and racial groups. The Spanish, Asians, and blacks are a big part of that number.

To perpetuate a culture, a country needs a replacement birthrate of 2.1 or greater. That's the big problem in Europe, Japan, and other places. Their indigenous rates are all less than 1.5. That's why the European nations are all headed for Muslim majorities. Belgium is already there, but a third of them are not yet old enough to vote. Our birthrate was below 2.1 for decades at the end of the twentieth and the start of this century, but we're better now."

Jon and I were surprised. We had never thought about it, but if all Rollie said was true, we were impressed.

"You had three children . . . why didn't you have more?" he asked us accusingly.

"That's more than 2.1, so we did our share. You had two kids. Why didn't *you* have more?" I replied.

"Two was all we could afford in those days."

"So there's your answer," Jonathon said, nodding his head, no doubt hoping to shut him down.

Jon and I locked eyes and gave each other a nod. *We had done our share.*

***

Rollie finished his lunch, wiped his mouth with a napkin, and cleaned his hands with a moist sanitizer.

"So why are you getting out now?" he asked. "You're in the 1 percent!"

I was shocked! *Why is he trying to provoke us?* I thought. Was he picking up where he left off at the house? I looked at Jon and wondered, waited for his response.

"Please, Rollie, you don't know where we are," Jon said, his tone rebuking his friend. "No one knows. Even we don't know! People like to guess about the 'other,' look at their house, their cars, clothes, spending. But people have different priorities. You can't judge by a person's possessions or spending. That's just speculation. So stop—don't speculate about us, no matter how much you think you know. I am surprised at you!"

Jonathon was definitely caught off guard. I think he was genuinely upset.

"But you are Jews," Rollie answered . . . sort of snidely. "All the *Jews* are in the 1 percent!"

Now *that* was a surprise—a big surprise! Like a punch in the jaw! I screeched and put my hand to my mouth, trying to catch my breath. I thought Jon's eyes would jump out of his head.

"ROLLIE!" Jon exploded. "You know better than to think or say that! That's absolutely not true. Jews are in every level with everyone else. There are Jewish academics, professors, and teachers; medical workers, doctors, and nurses like your daughter; men and women in government, like your son—like me. I'm an engineer for the government. Most Jews are at the same level as your children."

Rollie looked unconvinced. "Maybe, but not at the low levels. I don't know any Jews on welfare or food coupons!"

"There are those in that category too! We know from the need to give to our community assistance programs and our Jewish Family Service. Do you think being on welfare is such an achievement that people should boast about their dependence? Jews don't think that way. For them, for us, it is nothing to be proud of!"

As he finished, Jon looked over at me and I pointed up and mouthed, "Boca?"

"Shut-up Rollie. *Now!*" Jon shouted in a whisper..., pointing up toward the ceiling.

"What? I don't care who hears us...Let whoever..."

At that instant, before Rollie could finish his words, Jon lunged and knocked Rollie's tinted glasses off his face. For the first time that day, we looked straight into Rollie's unobscured, dilated, glassy eyes.

"Jesus, Mary and Joseph!" Jon exclaimed! "You *are* on drugs —at this moment—this *very* moment! You took stuff last night or this morning! I know you have a user's license and you do recreational stuff from time to time. But why today?"

"It's none of your business, but yes, I snorted a couple of lines last night. Nothing today." Rollie answered.

"A couple of lines?" Jon shook his head. "If you did two, you did three, didn't you? After two, it is well known that users take another an hour later for a boost and then a line in the morning to fight off a hangover. Are you having a hangover, or did you do a line or more this morning to avoid one?"

Jon paused. He let his anger subside. He grew calmer.

"Why? Why would you do that knowing you had to go to Hartford early this morning and command this long drive today?" Jon said pleadingly.

"Straighten out quick and stay clean on this trip, you hear? I'm disappointed with you right now."

I could tell that Jonathon was really annoyed—maybe even having second thoughts about his relationship with Rollie. He leaned forward and thrust his finger at the cockpit.

"Isn't it time we were on our way? Move up front and get us back on the interstate."

"Then why have half the Jews moved out of the country, mostly to Israel? That's where you're going too, isn't it?" Rollie blurted.

"Get up front and get us on the road if you're not completely stoned!"

Jonathon pushed the button to open the door and deploy the stairs. A cold breeze swept in on top of the chill already in the compartment.

Rollie took more time than I thought he needed to gather himself. As I studied his movements, I saw an arrogance about him that I'd felt was always there. I think he was proud of himself for speaking his feelings, maybe after decades of repressing them. Maybe he needed the coke to muster the courage. I thought he was stalling purposely to aggravate us more.

"C'mon, Rollie, get moving," Jon said again.

After the door closed behind him, Jon leaned back in his seat, relaxed his shoulders, and took a deep breath. His face was flushed, as was usual when he was perplexed or annoyed. He fumbled for his mezuzah necklace, uncapped it, and brought out a little yellow pill with a scored line down its middle. He popped it in his mouth and took a slug of water. I was used to seeing him cut those little pills in half, but to calm down after that exchange, he apparently felt he needed it all.

"What was that all about? Can he safely drive?" I wrote.

"On the interstate, the radar, sensors, and servos steer, and the Motivators watch and set the speed. He doesn't have much to do—there's not much he can fuck up even if he's completely stoned."

"Could he be dangerous?" I wrote.

"Possibly, but I really don't think so," Jon scribbled.

"What about all that talk out in the open? We know surveillance is listening or at least recording." I wrote back.

"They can't listen to everyone at once. Maybe we'll be lucky and get across the border before the listeners catch it. We have little choice, but to keep going now!"

"What was all that talk about Jews?"

"The legalization of drugs . . ." Jon wrote.

"Not now Ida, please? We'll talk later."

# Chapter 7
# Continuing Drive
*Ida*

My eyes closed, I leaned back into the welcoming upholstery to recover. My heart raced as I reviewed the venom Rollie had spit at us. I needed one of Jon's pills but was afraid to ask. I was fearful of Rollie's resentment and wondered if he had done anything to upset our plans. If Rollie wanted to hurt us he could. He knew Jon had a classified job that would leave us vulnerable to being stopped. And Jon hadn't replied to my question about anti-Semitism.

Jon was a vice president at the United States Submarine Industries, with a Level III security clearance. That had been the submarine building division of General Dynamics until the government made a tender offer for all its stock and bought GD from the public shareholders in the mid-2020s. They bought Lockheed Martin, the military divisions of Boeing, United Technologies, and General Electric, and Raytheon, plus all other big and most small defense contractors in the same way at about the same time. They acquired hundreds of contractors in all.

It was *nationalization* by purchase. It looked very capitalistic on the surface, just like their acquisition of the health care insurers in the late teens and the big banks later. The newly created Defense Industries Cabinet offered a cash price for all the outstanding shares of a target company on the New York Stock Exchange or Nasdaq and paid what seemed to be a handsome premium to the shareholders. The government just had to print the money.

The explanation to the public was that all Americans, not just the privileged class, should own these defense-focused companies. The program was a component of the Re-Erected Economic Model. Some Washington whiz kids took credit for the concept, which began to gain ground in the late teens. Among the stated objectives was to rationalize executive pay and benefits, curtail unnecessary spending, and stop dividends to investors on profits made on government contracts. Some of the savings were passed to the working men and women to put them solidly in the middle class. And any so-called "profit"—you know, excess of the contact allotment over the cost—was returned to the Treasury, a sort of dividend to all the American taxpayers.

The Defense Industries Cabinet bought Jon's family company for the same reason. They were a manufacturer of military uniforms. Each deal had something of value for every stakeholder and the public was promised that defense purchases would become less costly to society by streamlining these companies as siblings of the military. Military officers were installed to run the companies, eliminating the lavish executive contracts, lifestyles, expense accounts, and golden handcuffs, along with all the peripherals and the outrageous pension plans. Taking over the defense industry opened slots for senior officers to continue their careers beyond the mandatory active duty retirement age. With these industrial possibilities, professional military service became more attractive to top, ambitious students. The military academies were swamped with applicants and expanded to accommodate larger classes."

The corporate airplanes of the purchased companies were organized into a government airline with many regularly scheduled routes, including two daily round trips from Groton to Washington DC, locally known as the "Congressman Shuttle." Government personnel flew for free, but the public could buy tickets on a space-available basis.

Jon was in favor of these government acquisitions. At the time he said, "It eliminated certain pressure to fulfill unrealistic quarterly goals set by bean counters. The pressure was still there, but it was military-type pressure, not Wall Street pressure."

I had asked him, "If this opportunity was available when you were still active duty, would you have stayed in?"

After hemming and hawing, he'd answered, "No. I thought about staying in then and you remember we talked about it too. The top of the military pyramid is very tiny, and there's a lot of pushing and shoving by the up-and-comers to make the cut, to stay in the game. I never liked that political type of competition, and I wasn't good at it. If promoted to captain, there was that next assignment—school in Monterey, California, followed by four years in Washington. Ida, we talked long and hard at the time about whether I should continue in the active navy. You were definitely not ready for me to take those next assignments, so I yielded to your common sense. I'm not unhappy with how my career, parenting, and civic interests have unfolded since then."

That was when I answered, "Oh . . . how about your 'husband' interests, duties?" We laughed and hugged, and he said, "Am I neglecting those too?"

It was all in good fun, and he certainly didn't neglect me that night!

*But I wonder now, how critical he is to the Boat or the navy?*
Since he had taken all five milligrams of that yellow tranquilizer, there was no point in asking him then.

After ten minutes I opened my eyes and looked at the time—12:20. The afternoon continued to be bright but cold. Outside, exhaust vapors came from the cars that still burned gasoline, diesel, or LNG. Early fuel-cell cars from the twenties spewed water vapor. The total electrics had no exhaust. Cars with the auto-drive system were everywhere. You always saw more of them on the highway. We were on I-495 in Massachusetts, and I saw an exit sign to Andover and Dracut. I knew we were close to the I-93 intersection to New Hampshire. I figured there were about five more hours to go.

Moments later the communicator screen made a long beep that startled us both. We came to attention. The screen announced in writing and voice:

"Message for Ida Kadish."

After a startled look into each other's eyes, Jon pushed the "accept" icon on the console touchscreen. The face of Gil Ottenheimer, "Otch" as he was called, the CEO of Now's, filled the screen.

"Mrs. K," he said, "I'm sorry to bother you, but you just had a surprise visitor I thought you should know about. She announced herself as Evelyn Stanson and showed me credentials as an area monitor FBI division, from their Hartford office. I scanned her chip to verify her identity. But I couldn't get a full display. Our desk scanner is only allowed to view the first layer files. Scanners at the checkouts read the second and third layers too—more personal stuff, name, address, credit rating, bank account balance–but she didn't buy anything.

"She claimed to have an appointment with you, here at noon. She seemed pretty upset that you weren't here and asked where you might be. I told her you were traveling today on a visitation permit to visit your daughter in Canada. She asked if your husband was with you and I said I didn't know."

He paused. "Since I didn't know her purpose, I decided to keep quiet."

"Otch, That's fine. What did she do then? I want to know every detail."

I kept my voice calm, but inside I was getting panicky. What did the FBI want with me? Had we been turned in to the monitors after only a couple of hours on the road? Was it Rollie? *Once we cross that border tomorrow, we'll be out and safe*—I hoped.

Jon nodded a big "Yes" at me, meaning to go for more details.

Otch continued, "She looked around for a few minutes and asked about the business, our locations, our Cloud address and stuff like that. She asked to see your office, so I showed it to her. I'm sure she noticed the stains on the walls where hangings were taken down. And she looked closely at your desk, with its noticeable dust on everything. I'm sorry I didn't have that cleaned weeks ago. She swiped her finger through it on the glass top. She looked at her finger and then took a tissue from the box on your desk to wipe the dirt off. But she didn't comment. She showed me a recent picture of you from a cash machine to confirm your identity and absorbed our minidisc brochure and catalogue into her communicator. By any chance, did you have a message from the FBI that you might have missed or just not answered?"

"I don't remember now, but I'll check my log. I get so many notices from so many government and regulatory agencies—there is something coming every week."

I threw my arms up in disgust. "Otch, you know, you get them too. I don't answer for the company anymore. I rely on you to absorb them and reply to the ones that require an answer. Maybe there was a personal one in those bundles and I missed it."

Now Jon frowned at me.

"Did you ask what she wanted in particular, if you could help?"

"Yes, I did. She said it was personal."

"Okay, Otch. You did right by calling to give me a heads up. Thank you."

"Mrs. K, please let me say once again how much I and the staff appreciate what you have done for us over the past years. You've been exceedingly kind and generous, and everyone wants you to know how grateful we are. The staff . . ."

"Otch, please, please! *Man overboard,* for God's sake!" I shouted. He cut his words short.

"Don't say such things through a communicator. You get me? Huh? You can tell me when I return, understand?"

"Yes, yes, I'm sorry I spoke now. But I was afraid I might not be able to speak to you again. Have a safe trip and be happy wherever you go."

I signaled Jon to cut him off as I said, "Bye! Otch, bye!"

I couldn't hang up fast enough. For a smart businessman, he was sure dense when understanding a personal situation. Now I had that interaction to worry about too. I shook my head.

Jonathon was quietly shaking his head, no doubt subduing his steaming innards while trying to decipher the call. I recovered my messages for the past two weeks on my communicator, and sure enough: there was a message from the Bureau saying that an agent would be visiting on Wednesday, February 16, at noon. I was to respond if I would *not* be available and offer some other days and times.

*Shit! I missed it. What's going to happen now?*

I trembled at what I expected would be Jon's reaction to my goof.

I leaned over and showed him my error. He looked and nodded his understanding. Then shook his head, reached for his pad and scribbled. He flipped his pad to me and I read, "That's a bad omission. How much did you tell Otch and the others?"

*It must be taking all his energy to control himself,* I thought.

I answered out loud. "Maybe I Boca-ed to them, but I never said exactly. They did ask why I was taking the pictures and things. I said, 'Redecorating.'"

"Had you seen that message, we could have, maybe . . . adjusted our trip," Jon said quietly.

I didn't answer. Just sank back into the leather feeling very inept.

# Chapter 8
# Continuing Drive
*Jon*

The FAV slowed as we entered the interchange and circled the on-ramp for I-93 North. In minutes we would cross into Salem, New Hampshire.

The FAV moved to the outside lane and sped up. There was no speed limit for us. The Motivators could bring us to one hundred miles per hour if the road and traffic would allow. When other drivers saw an FAV in their scanners, they'd quickly move over to let us through. FAVs always had the right of way.

Thinking about Rollie's rant, I turned toward Ida.

"Not to worry—" I started.

But before I could say anything more, the communicator screen lit up again.

<blockquote>"Priority Message for J. Kadish."</blockquote>

There was a government seal in a corner of the screen.

Again I punched the "accept" icon. And again a familiar face filled the screen.

"Jon, Ida, I owe you an apology—a big apology," the caller said. "I just got off the communicator with Evelyn from the FBI. She is concerned that Ida didn't show for a scheduled interview this noon. She mentioned a few observations that had her worried. It was my fault, I'm really sorry . . . so I covered for you and bought you, uh, us . . . some time."

The caller was Admiral Keith "Mickey" Wilson, an Executive Vice President of the Boat, and my boss. He was a young, up-and-coming Annapolis/Harvard Business School guy, a key business technocrat in the Defense Industries Cabinet. I really liked him for his sharp intellect and technical knowledge, and as a promoted submariner.

"Mickey is going places!" I had said to Ida.

I guessed he was about fifty-four years old.

"Your fault?" I asked. "What do you mean? What's your fault?"

"Jon, I'm sorry we never had a chance to get together since the first of the year," Mickey started. "You've been busy, and I've been traveling almost nonstop.

"When I was doing the annual review of the staff in December, I saw you only had four or so years until retirement. So I put you in for an upgrade to Level II Security. We need to have that confirmed before your next birthday in March. Level II will give you a bigger paycheck and added benefits now, and a higher pension and benefits when you retire. The pension people retire you at your *lowest* pay grade in your previous three years. There was no time for me to waste, and I'd planned to tell you personally. I'm sorry that slipped through the cracks. This FBI agent will be reviewing your records and needs to interview Ida and you to clear you for the promotion."

I laughed incredulously. I didn't know what to say.

"Mickey, wow! Thanks! What else haven't you told me?"

"Well, the FAV you're in is a perk of Level II. Though you're not yet confirmed, you're treated as a Level II based on my submission or until you decline or are turned down. Now, as I understand this trip, you're going for the long weekend but Ida might be staying longer. I have called for your complete file and the report of the FBI investigation so far. I should have it later this afternoon. Is there anything I should know that's not in the record?"

"You know about the FBI breaking into our house last month? What was that about?"

"No, Jon. This is the first I'm hearing of it! An FBI break-in? When?"

"January 24. Showed up with an AGV and a drone. Broke down the rear door to enter. I wonder what they were looking for or took. All the people in my section know about it. Ask any one of them."

"I'll check into that. Anything else?"

I hesitated, then *lied*, "Other than that, there's nothing that's not in the record. Mickey, any chance I can stay in Canada a few days longer?"

"No, no Jon! FBI Evelyn is coming here for eleven o'clock on Tuesday to interview you. I told her I'm expecting you to be here."

Mickey paused and then continued, "Jon, everything is okay, isn't it? There are a few rumors on the shop floor that you cleaned out your desk and said a lot of good-byes to people. Anything to that?"

Mickey was on the seventh floor. I was on the fifth. It was probable that he had not been by to see my office—I only took a couple of family photos off my desk, but people who knew my office well might notice.

"You haven't had foreign travel for nearly four years. Remember Jon, under the regs, your password and security code will be suspended while you're gone. You won't have access to any messages or files here. And any attempts to gain your account will be investigated as if from hackers."

"Thanks for reminding me, but I don't plan to check in. I know the regulations. And after all, this *is* a national holiday weekend."

I ignored the former question.

"The FAV will wait at the border to return you here on Monday. Work out the time with your driver. There are more additional perks that come with Level II. You'll like them. I'll put the manual on your Cloud account, but you won't be able to access it until you return."

"But Mickey, the FAV was only approved for four days. I thought it had to be back on Saturday. I am planning to fly from Montreal on Monday." I lied.

"Jon . . . you are so naïve at times," Mickey laughed. "The government depot doesn't work the holiday weekend. There won't be anyone to receive the vehicle until Tuesday. You're automatically allowed the extra days. You come back with the vehicle. I'll have FAV Central communicate with your driver about the adjustment in plans."

We nodded, and Ida tried to force a laugh.

"Okay, that's about it. See you Tuesday morning," Mickey said.

"Right, Mickey, see you Tuesday morning."

The communicator clicked off. Ida and I were stunned. Two and a half hours away from Norwich and after ten years of preparing, our plans were already starting to unravel.

*\*\*\**

Then all of a sudden Ida leaned forward and knocked on the one-way glass partition to Rollie. "I have to pee . . . badly," she said.

Rollie clicked on the intercom and said sharply, "What?"

"I need a ladies' room quick."

"There's an executive lav behind you there," Rollie said.

"I don't want that! Please get me to a rest stop!"

"Okay. I'll ask the Motivators to take us to the nearest approved facility."

The intercom clicked off. The vehicle slowed and moved into the right-most lane. We got off at the next exit and retraced our steps back toward Salem on a state road. Rollie drove under a hotel canopy. It was only ten feet to the entrance, so Ida went without her coat. A bundled doorman helped her down the last stair, and the hotel door opened for her. A young woman with an assistant manager badge escorted her to the ladies' room.

I followed a few seconds later just to get on my feet. The hotel employees seemed giddy and no doubt wondered who we were. I greeted them and thanked them for their courtesy. The assistant manager asked if we needed anything they could provide. They were stunned by the vehicle and seemed perplexed about what to do. We declined. They escorted us back to the FAV and helped us up.

After we got settled, Rollie went into the hotel.

Ida and I felt free for the few minutes that he was gone. Despite the soundproof petitions separating us, we could still see him when he was there. His stinging diatribe was still ringing in my head.

"Feeling more private?" I whispered to Ida. "Who could have pre-dicted these complications?"

She raised her finger to her lips in the sign of quiet as she pointed to the ceiling. "Man overboard!"

I nodded agreement.

Ida wrote, "Why did you tell Mickey that you'd be there on Tuesday?"

"Ida, for crying out loud, what else could I have said at the time?"

"Okay, okay. So what do we do now?" Ida asked.

I pointed to my temple and wrote, "Use our heads."

"Are we compromised?" she wrote.

I pointed to my temple again.

After a brief pause, she said, "Rollie is taking too much time. How long has he been in there? This is an unscheduled stop. We'll fall behind."

"He took his cap with his communicator," I replied. "Maybe he had to make a call."

She scrawled, "Maybe he's turning us in right now!"

"Ida, please. You read and listen to too much fiction. Mysteries, suspense, intrigue, romance. Please don't convince yourself that there is a conspiracy of sorts here."

Rollie returned, and after adjusting himself in the cockpit, he came on the intercom and asked, "All set?"

"We've been ready for a while. Did you make your call?" Ida asked sarcastically.

"Yes, I did. I spoke with my wife and checked the weather. We'll be running into some light snow soon. I need to reengage the Motivators to get back on track."

The intercom clicked off, but this time the abrupt snap of it seemed louder—as if Rollie was turning us off too.

"Satisfied?" I wrote.

She gave me the smirk face, then leaned the other way, shook her head and closed her eyes.

# Chapter 9
# A Bit Later

*Jon*

"Quite a twist of fate!" I wrote after a little while, and nudged Ida to open her eyes. I was tempted to offer her one of my little yellow pills, but I knew she wouldn't take it and might have a few sarcastic words about them for me. So I didn't.

"Have you figured anything out?" she wrote.

"I wish I could talk with my staff at the Boat!"

I wondered what the gossip was at the office and shop—what exactly was being said and by whom?

"Mickey's call raises lots of questions," I wrote. "I took your picture and those of the kids off my desk."

"What about all the things on your walls?" she asked.

"Months earlier I took my degrees and commendations off the walls and switched them with cheap photocopies. I brought the originals home. The office doesn't look cleared out."

She nodded her understanding.

"Well, a few things are clear," I wrote again. "We didn't do a good job of covering our actions. We should have communicated better about what to say, to whom, and what to do and stuck with that."

In a low voice with my hand blocking my mouth—you know, like when a pitcher is talking to his catcher at the mound, I said, "What did you tell Otch and others at the company?"

"I never told them directly, but from my actions I'm sure they figured something was up," she answered in the same way.

Then we started talking aloud. Everything we had to say was in the public record already.

Ida said, "Once Truman set up the ESOP and I sold 80 percent of my shares in the company to the trust three year ago, they knew something was coming. Truman arranged a bank to lend $8 million to the ESOP to pay me for the stock. The Employee Stock Ownership Plan now receives dividends from the company that were previously never paid. The trust uses those dividends to repay the bank, with interest. In twelve more years the bank will be paid, and the future money can then be distributed to the plan participants, the employees."

"And you get those dividends too on your remaining shares?" I asked.

"Well, Truman gets them. I transferred those shares to him. I became purely a figurehead. You know I rarely showed up at the office and I stayed clear of the various operating committees. Otch and the other officers didn't need my shadow following them around."

"But you continued to draw salary and benefits and paid taxes, right?"

For all that was involved in that transaction, I had never taken a big interest in it. I am not a financially oriented guy. I like my engineering numbers. I was happy to let Truman work through it with his mother.

"Absolutely," Ida responded. "First we paid taxes on the proceeds. After capital gains, gift taxes and punitive penalties and then Connecticut, the remaining proceeds were just over $4 million. Most of that is now legally out of the country, along with your proceeds. My salary had to be substantially reduced, but I continue to have a more normal pay and participate in the benefits. But do you know how much we're leaving behind?"

"No, how much?"

Here, she reverted back to writing. "About US $3,500,000!" she wrote in big numbers on my pad.

*It's not as much as it used to be—years ago—but it's still good money,* I thought.

"A good portion is the 20 percent of the company I turned over to Truman, some insurance cash values, bank and investment accounts, the cars and whatever's left in the house. Truman will take possession of them. It will be a part of our legacy to him. He's reasonably pleased, although he'll have to come back to Connecticut and obtain local counsel to settle everything up."

She sat back. "From the proceeds, we made contributions to Rensselaer and Russell Sage, the Federation, and the Community Foundation, our largest beneficiaries among many others. You never knew how much we gave to support worthwhile agencies around town. I handled our tax reports, and you never even scanned them—you just signed where I pointed. That was until the IRS just sent us a notice and took our taxes from our bank account. But you know we did *much* to give back to our community."

Being sequestered in this vehicle with so much time was giving Ida and me a chance to talk about things that we never could get around to at home.

I smiled at her with satisfaction. "You're good at this stuff and like it, don't you?"

"It's what my daddy taught me," she acknowledged proudly.

***

We were again on our way north. We rejoined I-93 near Rockingham Mall. After only a few miles, there was little traffic and we were doing a hundred miles per hour. The time was about 1:10. I closed my eyes.

I had done very well in my profession, and we would have been in the middle class from my employment alone, without Ida's income or either of our capital assets. From the data I'd been able to find, our combined worth most likely put us in or near the bottom of the top 10 percent—twenty years ago. But I doubted that we're up there now.

Ida was the Chancellor of the Exchequer for our family. She knew about money and liked to manage it. She had pockets of it in many currencies in havens across the world. In Canada and Israel, it was in our kids' names. In Aruba, Cuba, Malta, Sicily, and other places, it was in shell corporations or partnership names. Truman set them up, kept track of them and had power of attorney to act on our behalf. Well . . . on *her* behalf!

Ida was also a recognizable personality in town. With a hundred employees and nearly a hundred-year history, a lot of people and their families could connect in some way to Ida or her parents. The "Now" in the company name came from their family name, Rabinow. She had shouldered the biggest embarrassment after the FBI broke into our house. She faced more questions from people as she moved around in her everyday life than I ever had to.

"I'm sorry," she said to me as we rested in the FAV seats. "Leaving my office a neglected mess was a blunder. As was not paying attention to my electronic mail."

I waved away her apology.

"The mail might have given us a heads up, but Mickey's action to recommend me for a promotion without telling me, is the real cause of this predicament. Had we known of the possible promotion, we might have given the whole plan another thought. Level II comes with enhanced benefits—look at this FAV—and I don't know the half of them. You heard Mickey; he's sending the Level II Manual to my account. But I can't access it from here. Maybe I can have the medical treatment I need under the higher clearance? Maybe we need to explore that before we close the door here?"

Ida nodded.

Shaking my head, I said, "Listen, I too was sloppy in my planning. Though I got my degrees and stuff out without suspicion, I did take your picture and the other personal stuff from my desktop just last week. Maybe Mickey or one of the others did notice, will notice—or maybe not. The originals I shipped as printed material to Rachel in the Christmas rush. The regulators loosened up with the higher workload. The package got out, and she received it. At least I knew enough not to take anything from work. That's all secret stuff owned by the government."

I shook my head, thinking over the situation.

"As for Rollie, a couple years ago he started suggesting things to do around the house. I agreed to some of the smaller items, but I was stalling on larger projects that did in fact need attention—if we were staying long term. He probably needed the work and the money, but I didn't catch on. That's what probably made him suspicious. It was a mistake that I asked him to drive on this trip. But he was the only person I knew who could become qualified with a FAV license. Helping him get it was easy. If I had known then what Mickey just told us, I would have realized we had more options—a driver from the Boat, for example."

"Okay, what's done is done," Ida answered. "We can't go back and change it. So now what are you going to do about this promotion? You seemed genuinely excited that he recommended you."

"Well, yes. Yes, I am! I always thought I deserved it. I've worked on many Level II projects over the years. Actually, people are working on projects all the time that are rated above their level of clearance. By not insisting the applicable clearance be required, the Boat is saving money, paying the engineers and technicians doing the jobs at their lower levels."

"Like they were doing to you?" Ida asked. "Why didn't you complain?"

I chuckled. *You don't complain in the government.* You get your pay even when there might not be anything to do for a week, a month or longer. I've had those periods. Waiting for the Pentagon to make up its mind or the navy to approve one modification or another. But Mickey thought enough of me to notice my age and consider the promotion as an improvement in my last few years and in my pension. Now that's a boss who's looking out for you!"

"So what now?" Ida asked, naturally confused.

"It's a new wrinkle that deserves consideration is all I'm saying."

"How are you going to see him and the FBI agent in your office on Tuesday? When you said that, I was shocked! And what do you mean,

'It deserves consideration'? What deserves consideration? Mickey calls you and gives you an attaboy, and you feel flattered? He strokes your ego and now you're reversing your plan; *'deserves consideration'* you say?"

"Ida, please! Maybe this new status will give us what we're looking for—what I need. I don't know why I said that about Tuesday. I guess I *was* flattered by his action. Now it's another issue we—I—need to resolve."

This seemed to get more complicated by the minute. Ida turned away from me and looked out the window. I leaned back and focused out my window too. We were about forty miles north of Salem, past Concord, as light snow began to fall. One second the sky was clear and the sun was shining and the next we were under the clouds. Our compartment became gloomy with the heavily tinted windows. I looked forward at Rollie. He seemed to be napping. The Motivators had reduced our speed. I wasn't a bit worried. I was familiar enough with the surveillance systems on the satellites and drones to know this weather wouldn't hamper their ability to see us.

I looked over and saw Ida napping. I fastened her seat belt and tossed a blanket over her. Neither of us had slept very much during the night. Now with all these new issues and the confinement of the driving, she deserved a nap.

Four and a half hours to go unless the weather slowed us more. Almost halfway there, past the point of no return . . . *well, maybe.*

# Chapter 10
# Four O'clock in the FAV

*Ida*

I tried to roll over and groaned as I discovered I was tied down in some way. I tried to remember where I was. I was startled to realize I'd been asleep. *What am I lying on? Where did this silk quilt come from?* These thoughts went rapid-fire through my head as I smacked my lips against the tacky, mushy morning feeling in my mouth.

I opened my eyes slowly and there was Jon sleeping on his reclining seat, a similar quilt over him. The compartment was dark, as I hadn't remembered. I raised my head, fighting against a restraint and the supine position of the seat, enough to glance the time by squinting—3:45.

The FAV was stopped, but a motor hum was constant, maybe the heater. A huge orange truck was alongside us, with an array of domed yellow lights rotating on the cab roof. I fiddled with both armrests, looking for controls like I'd find in an airliner. The back raised and the leg rest lowered in quiet cooperation as I found the right button. The driver cab was dark, and I couldn't tell if Rollie was there or not.

*What time was it when I fell asleep?* Was my exhaustion so great that I'd so quickly gotten knocked out? *Where are we?* I blinked my eyes to wake my brain. We were leaving Salem. Jon and I had words and I turned out like a light. *Is it now a couple hours later?*

I located a recessed reading light in the ceiling and clicked it on. Looking around, I found the narrow aisle to the rear lavatory. I unbuckled my seat belt and lifted and twisted myself, head ducked, to the lav. I managed to sit and do my business and then hunched over the sink, I opened a side compartment and found a low-tech toothbrush like the ones in my childhood days with individual packages of tooth cream. I made good use of them.

Maneuvering back to my seat, I found a morning blend pod of coffee, flicked it into the holder and punched the brew button. The cup holder indexed, and a clean, fresh china mug swiveled into position under the spigot. Ten seconds later, the cab was filled with the aroma of fresh coffee, and five seconds later I took my first sip. What a jolt! Beautiful! *Just like morning!*

I gave Jon's arm a little tug. It was cute how he repeated my actions in the same order as he tried to shake the sleep from his mind and body. That he was asleep didn't surprise me. After all, he did take a whole little pill. I whispered to him about the lavatory, the toothbrush and the cream packs. He had to maneuver his six-foot frame past me, bent over, stepping on my toes to get there. As he passed, he leaned down just a bit more to plant two kisses, one on my forehead and the other on my cheek. We smiled broadly at each other and I lifted my chin and blew him a kiss as he slipped behind the seat and into the lav.

On his return he asked, "Is Rollie here?"

"I can't tell," I said.

"Do you know where we are?"

"No, but it's four. Wow, look at the snow!"

It was the first time I'd focused on it—the heavy snow. It reflected orange and yellow streaks from the truck's beacons as it flew by fast, horizontal across the window. I pressed my nose to the pane and saw piles of the slushy stuff on the ground and on everything else in sight. We were in a large parking lot, in a government-reserved space near to the entrance of a highway hospitality stop.

Jon clicked the intercom. "Rollie, are you there?"

No reply.

He tried a second time.

No reply.

Jon went to his wrist communicator and punched in a digit—his Rollie button. Rollie was immediately on the huge communicator screen, much too big and bright at that moment, overpowering me.

74

"Hi! I'm inside the hospitality center," he said. "We are at the last stop on I-93 in Franconia. We'll now continue up US Route 3. You can see what the weather has become. The Motivators are sending two snow sweepers to lead us further. They should be here in a few minutes."

"About how much further to go?" Jon asked.

"Time or miles, Mr. K?"

"Both."

"About seventy-eight miles; three or so hours based on this storm. I called the lodge and told them to expect us after seven."

"But we have a dinner reservation at Chez Oretana in town," Jon said.

"The innkeepers have already cancelled that, and they'll have dinner for you at the lodge. On days like this they do dinner for the convenience of their guests. Perhaps at an extra charge?"

"No problem, Rollie," Jon said in his ordinary voice. "That's excellent!"

After all the goings-on with that guy in the morning, I wondered how Jon could be so normal with him now. *First with Mickey and now with Rollie? Guileless—it never changes.* It seemed like everything was okay again between them, but not so with me!

"If you want to come in here, there are storm boots, gloves, and coats in the back for you and Mrs. K. I'll come out to help you with them if you wish."

Jon looked at me and I shook my head. "What for?" I shrugged.

"No, Rollie. Not necessary and will only delay us moving on. Are we safe? Is this thing safe in this weather?"

"Oh, absolutely, sir! As soon as enough snow covered the road, the Motivators engaged the winter axle with the spiked tires and called that plow truck to lead us here. The snow sweepers will take us the rest of the way and be available to us tomorrow too. This is going to be a long night with this nor'easter, but we'll be fine. I'll return in five or so minutes. Bye for now."

The communicator clicked off.

"You were pretty chummy with him after all he's put us through today," I said.

"It was just the drugs talking. I've known for a while that he's a recreational user, little different than a beer or whiskey drinker. What's the use of being antagonistic? We have to be with him for another eighteen hours at least."

"Yeah, I guess you're right," I answered, reluctantly.

# Chapter 11
# Later in the FAV
*Jon*

Legalizing hallucinogenic drugs for recreational use was another controversial but successful measure in the Re-Erected Economic plan in the late twenties. After the progressive legalization of medical marijuana, with its availability, low price and easy qualification requirements, it became generally available to the public in every state for recreational use as well. From the beginning, leaving it to the states was a mistake. Each state had its own rules that created competition. A lot of people were making a lot of money, including state politicians. The right to grow, process, and dispense the stuff became a political plum, distributed in some states to family or the highest bidders. When the Congress finally cleaned up the federal laws, the FDA was given control. Then the product, potency, sources, the rules, and distribution, were normalized across all the states.

Marijuana's effect within the population was little different than that of alcohol. But you had to apply to your state for a user's license. When granted, it was added to the encoding on your chip. If you were old enough and hadn't committed any crime, buying weed at a state dispensary, having it, and using it was no longer a crime.

So if marijuana was legal, why not cocaine, crack, heroin, methamphetamines, and all the rest? Pressure to legalize all drugs grew, but this needed federal action, and the federal government insisted that it managed by Washington.

So hallucinogenics were grown and processed only by the federal government at its federal prison farms. The feds had to approve each state's distribution plan. The states were required to have their own dispensaries, *not allowed to be contracted to others,* with limited hours like motor vehicle offices. In Connecticut that meant 7:30 to 4:00 weekdays, half a day on Saturday, closed Sunday and Monday. The states were required to keep and monitor accurate sales data and usage by licensed people. The data was regularly combed to detect purchasing habits and usage, exposing possible secondary sellers. It was a hugely profitable business for government even at their low prices.

But the major benefit was the huge cost savings that ensued. The US Coast Guard and law enforcement at every level claimed the greatest savings. The judicial system saw its calendars cut dramatically, petty crime was greatly reduced, prison populations were cut in half. The illegal drug cartels and distributers lost 90 percent of their business.

Even so, the system was not without problems. Internal theft, employee embezzlement, hijacking of shipments in transit, and secondary sales to the underage and unlicensed, with price gouging and the like, were common. The problems were basically the same as with cigarettes, alcohol, and guns.

Societal enforcement became the responsibility of the family, the employer, and the place of assembly. Drug use on the job was no different from consuming alcohol on the job. Coming to work stoned was no different from coming in drunk. Legal abusers were sent to rehab instead of prison, and their licenses were withdrawn.

Between the revenue received and the costs saved, legalized drugs became a major financial benefit for the country. They made a significant impact on improving the economy and lowering the cost of government at every level.

I had long been well aware that Rollie had a recreational user license. A number of years before, when he was struggling with his contracting business, he'd had a brush with the state authorities. He was called in to explain his higher-than-usual level of purchases of one drug or another over the previous few months. His high purchases suggested to the state that he might be a reseller to unlicensed or underage users. He told me about it because he was missing time with us, and he confessed that his contracting business was failing. He swore that only he was using his purchases. Apparently he convinced the authorities and got away without an arrest or penalty.

But I never forgot the trepidation I felt that he might have to go to rehab or jail—and then I would be *forced* to find a replacement. I don't know if Ida ever knew, she never mentioned it to me. Considering the circumstances and her mistrust of him, if she knew, she would certainly have harangued me with it. And I never said anything about it to her.

*It's good that we are leaving for good, or I'd be looking for that replacement when we returned . . . Ida surely wouldn't let him in the house again after that shockingly anti-Semitic explosion of his. And I just gave him my Beretta?*

The snow sweepers arrived, and Rollie hurried out. I only recognized him by his height and beret. His parka, boots, and gloves were no doubt part of the survival gear he'd told us about. He spoke briefly with the sweeper drivers, and then all mounted their vehicles and we were off again. He announced, "ETA lodge 7:15 pm."

Ida began to violently punch buttons on the console. She started changing the channels on the communicator screen, skipping quickly through every sport imaginable, old movies, sitcoms, and then a series of pictures that initially didn't make sense.

"Go back, go back!" I called.

She scrolled back three clicks to a shot from a camera on the FAV grill. We could see the sweeper ahead and the snow falling between. The next six shots were from different cameras looking in different directions. The eighth was a dashboard shot looking at the driver, Rollie. With the ninth click, all eight shots were displayed on the multi-split screen.

"Does HE have a camera to watch us?" Ida scrawled to me.

"Man overboard!" I shouted, and we both cracked up.

When our laughter subsided, I said to her, "Did you notice the billboards on the way here before the snow blinded us? They tell another story of what has happened to our society in the last fifty years. The most modern signs—the giant, digital, color flatscreens—all advertised casinos. Casinos in Connecticut, Massachusetts, New York, Maine, Canada."

The most elaborate signs were for the Casino de Montreal on an island in the St. Lawrence. Mohegan tribal members who were friends of ours called the Montreal casino—a tourist trap. "No locals go there; that staff speaks English! Government-owned casinos with no competition don't give the patron the value they deserve," they told us.

I continued. "The older, neon-lighted reader boards hawked the lotteries—Connecticut Lotto, Mega Millions, Mass Moonlight, Multi-State Powerball, Keno. Their digital displays keep upping the first prize as more money is bet. The drawing date and time, with a countdown, are prominently displayed. 'You Can't Win If You Don't Play!' the signs warn."

The casinos and lotteries had become so pervasive that they seemed like a natural backdrop to me. We occasionally ate or saw a show at Foxwoods or the Mohegan Sun, and Ida occasionally bought a lotto ticket when the prize was huge, although we seldom checked to see if we'd won anything. But now they struck me as a window into our culture.

"I hadn't realized until now," I said, "how the overlay of gambling seems to cover everything in our society. Everything is about taking a chance—winning a big prize out of impossible odds, hoping to pull your existence out of mediocrity. The least able to lose their money forget their problems by watching overpaid entertainers for an hour or two, maybe drunk or stoned, before returning to their misery, more miserable than ever. They eat themselves into ecstasy at unlimited buffets or exotic cuisine restaurants and then scrimp or starve the rest of the month on food coupons or with little money."

Ida replied, "My father always said, 'Sports, betting, and games of chance are the pacifier of the proletariat'—that without them, there would be anarchy in this country."

"Ya know, he was right! I remember him saying that. And now it's all even more pervasive. Football pools, March Madness wagers, the lotteries and casinos. It's always lunchroom and water-cooler talk, a distraction from the truth of our regulated, routine daily lives."

Ida answered, "I thought we had turned around from that to a great degree since the new economic model was adopted. But I guess it doesn't improve everyone equally."

"That's right," I answered.

"Why is this happening? The economy is much improved now. We're at full employment. I don't understand why the government still allows this pervasive legalized gambling. They're getting plenty of tax and fee income without it."

I pointed to the ceiling and gestured with my hands. "Ida, why are you talking so openly?"

"Forget that now!" She waved me off. "Why do we care who hears us anymore? With what Rollie blurted, we can't get into worse trouble, can we?"

"Man overboard!" I mouthed.

We smiled at each other and looked at the communicator screen.

I said, "Find a game show or some other harmless nonsense to distract us from our problems, would ya?"

We both laughed.

As I leaned back I thought, *we're not so bad off after all. We have a beautiful home. We're traveling in this FAV. Here I am looking at a pending promotion, and look what we're doing—leaving just when things seem to be getting better. Some things never make sense.*

I looked at Ida in the glow of the communicator screen.

*"It's a new wrinkle that deserves consideration, huh?"* Ida snickered.

# Chapter 12
# Arriving at the Lodge
*Ida*

We arrived at the lodge just after seven with the storm beginning to taper off. An attractive middle-aged woman was there to welcome us.

"Welcome to your home away from home. I am Françi, your hostess. My husband, Frank, and our staff are at your service," she said in a French accent.

"Jon and I are happy to finally be here. Look at this weather!"

In the dark and the snow we didn't try to ogle the lodge, but I knew from the Cloud that half of it was built in the late 1800s, added to in 1970 and more recently renovated in 2030 by Françi and François.

The earliest section held a few guest rooms with uneven floors and shared toilets and baths. The middle section had another seven rooms with private accommodations, the kitchen, and the dining room. The most recent addition provided a new entryway, a formal living room, and a multi-purpose meeting room. Double outside doors interlocked the house against the winter cold and summer mosquitos. There was a generous walk-in closet by the main door for leaving bulky and often wet outerwear to hang and dry. Jon and I shed ours, as Rollie drove to the parking lot in the rear.

Françi, smiling, said, "Living here, we are used to this weather and know how to deal with it. It helps *not* to discuss it. Forget it for now; you are warm and safe here."

Rollie brought in our overnight kits and was instructed to follow a houseman to put them in our room.

After the initial pleasantries, we were ushered to a sofa by a raging fireplace in the living room to feel the warmth on our faces as glasses of warmed apple cider spiked with something, maybe vodka, were brought to us.

"Are you starving?" bubbly Françi asked, her trim body rocking in anticipation of our affirmative answer. "François has produced a winter meal suitable for royalty."

I knew she saw us arrive in the FAV with sweeper escort, and I sensed that she wondered about our connection to the government. Maybe she suddenly thought we were celebrities of sorts. I laughed at that—who, we? But it was nice to be fussed over after our long, stressful drive.

"Come, please take seats in the dining room. Other guests are having their salads, and we are expecting two more men who have reservations. We hope they arrive soon or at least call. Your driver is welcome to join the other assistants in the breakfast nook off the kitchen. But don't worry, we are all having the same meal."

I didn't care if Rollie ate or not. Another baloney sandwich from the FAV would have been okay with me. Françi bounded from the parlor to the door to the dining room, opening it and gesturing us in with a swipe of her hand.

We slid past her into the room. A long, wide table with beautiful white linen and patterned china was set for twelve. Six people were already seated and eating salad.

"May I introduce Dr. Jonathon and Ida Kadish from Norwich, Connecticut, who now join us," Françi announced.

The four gentlemen stood as all six grumbled a discordant greeting. A dark-haired man with a chef's cap and neckerchief stuck his head out the swinging kitchen door to have a look at us. François, I supposed. Our eyes met briefly and he flashed a crowning smile. I nodded to his salutation and he returned mine. He stepped out and withdrew a chair for me near to the kitchen door and next to an Asian man. Françi motioned Jon to sit directly across from me, next to an attractive blonde woman, whom I immediately judged to be in her late fifties. Françi helped Jon into his chair.

"Please, Dr. and Mrs. Kadish, enjoy your salads and the soup will be right out."

As we dug into the salad, the conversations around the table restarted with a scramble of words and voices. I picked up remarks about the weather, the travel, the destinations, the possibility of being delayed and of missing appointments. Two men were discussing the latest hockey strike or lockout, whatever they're called. They said it was now the second longest in history or something like that. On the other side of the window, the wind whistled as snow flew down across the sash.

The Asian man sitting to my left turned toward me and said in a heavy accent, "Miss Kadiss, your husband is medical doctor or scientist?"

"Oh, no. Neither," I laughed. "Our hostess made a mistake. He is not a doctor of anything. We are business people from Connecticut."

I didn't want to reveal too much without knowing who was asking.

"And what is your profession?" I asked. "What brings you here on such an inclement day?"

"Oh, I giving speech Sunday at special symposium on structural science at Dawson College of Engineering in Serbrook. I manager this year of Syntetic Materials Raboratory at Centra Maine Cowege in Auburn. Maybe your husband going to symposium too?"

I laughed. "No, no. We're going to visit our daughter and grand-children who live in Sherbrooke."

I looked across the table. The blonde lady had engaged Jon. He was spitting salad bits on her and was busily trying to wipe them off the front of her suit jacket. I shook my head and started a slow burn inside. *What's with him when he's around a woman who pays any attention to him?*

"What's your name?" I asked my neighbor.

"Ling Xi-Peng," he answered and spelled it too. "Father Taiwanese, mother American. Born in Taiwan, before it collapse into big China. I am US citizen. Parents move to California when I seventeen."

A small man in a white service jacket with a thin mustache wheeled a narrow cart out of the kitchen and collected the salad plates. He returned with empty soup bowls. With white-gloved hands, he placed one before each diner. As he opened the door to return to the kitchen, Frank wheeled another, more ornate cart into the dining room with steam rising from a yellowish-green broth in a beautiful china soup tureen with a matching ladle. Little glass cups of croutons, one for each diner, were on the cart.

"Split pea soup, vegetarian split pea," he announced. Starting with me, in white-gloved hands, he ladled out as much as each person desired and offered a cup of croutons. He moved to my left, to Mr. Ling, serving him and then each in turn. He served Françi at the head of the table and returned back down the far side, ending with Jon.

Françi lifted her spoon and said, *"Bon appetite, mesdames et messieurs!"*
And we all leaped into the steaming soup.

Small salt and pepper mills were set at everyone's place, and all became quiet as we ate, except for the occasional slurping sounds from one or another.

When most were nearly finished, Françi rang a small handbell. Frank returned to offer the guests a second helping. Not five minutes later, when the conversation returned, out came the little man to collect the empty dishes.

Dinner plates came next, followed by Frank wheeling London broil, baked salmon, and a large roast chicken. Starting with Jon this time, he carved as much or as little of each as was wanted. Family-style bowls of vegetables and potatoes were passed. After serving, Frank urged each guest to begin. *"S'il vous plait, manger mes amis. Ne laissez pas la nourriture que froid."*

"You are welcome to eat when served," Françi repeated. "No need to let your food go cold."

Everyone nodded and gurgled agreement. When the others were served, Frank carved some selections for his own plate, added vegetables, removed the gloves and sat down to his dinner at the other head of the table, nearer the kitchen door. The guests around the table greeted him with polite applause.

*"Merci beaucoup, mes amis,"* he said as he began to eat.

Xi-Peng pushed his chair back, facing me once more and said, "Pease to meet wife, Coween Finnigan."

The woman to his left leaned in, smiled, and waved. "Hi, I'm Colleen."

"Nice to meet you," I said. "My name is Ida, and my husband—that man across the table from me, who is paying all his attention to the woman across from you—is my husband, Jonathon."

She looked across and watched Jon for a few seconds. Then she asked, "Does he always act like that?"

"Oh . . . so you see it!" I said. "Will you tell him so, to back me up? I know he'll say I'm imagining it!"

I immediately liked her. I could see they were fortyish.

"I'll introduce you to him after dinner."

"How long have you two been married?" Colleen asked.

"Forty-seven years. Can you imagine? And look how he acts with a stranger! That woman must be complimenting him about something. Do you have children?" I asked her.

"Yes, two. A daughter, eighteen, and a son, fifteen."

"And you're going with your husband to the symposium, I presume."

"Oh, yes. I'm a full-time mom, and I welcome any chance to get away for a few days. My mother came to visit from Cape Cod to look after our son. Our daughter is at college."

She paused, then asked politely, "And you?"

"Oh, our kids are grown, and we are grandparents. Our daughter lives in Sherbrooke and I'm intending to visit for a while."

"How nice!" she said sparkling genuinely.

Yes, I decided, I definitely liked her.

"How long have you been married?" I asked her. "Where did you meet?"

"Let's see . . . we're married nineteen years, and we met in college."

"Jon and I met in college too. Next year will be his fiftieth reunion year. He was Class of 1990."

"Wow!" she said. "You must be older than you look."

"Thanks," I said with a chuckle. "With today's health care, seventy is the new fifty-five. We still have time to start a new life if we wish."

"Is that what you're planning?" Colleen asked.

I quieted right down. I had dropped my guard. *What exactly did I just say? Why did she ask that?* I wondered if I had become paranoid. *You set yourself up for that one, didn't you?*

"No, no. I just was saying . . . that there would still be time to do so if one wished. Seventy isn't so old after all. What colleges did you attend?"

"You won't know them. They're both out-of-the-way schools in New York State."

I said, "Try me!"

I was happy that she was willing to move to a new subject.

"Well, I was at Russell Sage, a college for women, and Xi-Peng was at Rensselaer Polytech, both in Troy, near Albany. Have you heard of them?"

I stood momentarily. "You've got to be kidding! That's uncanny! Jon and I met when we were at those very schools. He was Class of '90, I was '91."

"Ling was Class of '17 and I was '19!"

We both laughed and said at once, together, "We have to talk!"

Frank served another round of the entrée and exited to the kitchen. Françi stood and asked each guest to briefly introduce him or herself. She apologized for the two empty places at the table. "I still haven't heard from the missing guests. I hope they're safe, wherever they are."

With that, she said to the man at her right, "Okay, *Professeur,* you first."

A rugged-looking sportsman of fifty or so years, with thinning, tinted reddish hair, rose. "I'm Dr. Robert MacLeod of Toronto, a history professor at York University, and this young man opposite me is Reynold Carboni, my marital partner."

To the professor's right was Colleen. She bobbed up. "I am Colleen Finnegan, wife of this man and mother of his children!" She gestured toward Xi-Peng and quickly sat down.

Mr. Ling remained seated, nodded his satisfaction to his wife. "I am Ling Xi-Peng, born Taiwan, my mother American. I am American citizen. Manage materials laboratory at small engineering college in Maine. Making speech on Sunday at symposium at Dawson Cowege of Civil Engineering in Serbrook. Thank you." He finished with a slight bow of his head.

I decided to stand to show my full height and impose myself on that woman next to Jon.

"My name is Ida Kadish. The man sitting opposite me is *my husband.*"

I tried to bore my eyes into the blonde, but she wasn't looking toward me.

"We are headed to Sherbrooke to visit *our grown, married daughter and four grandchildren.*"

I smoothed the back of my skirt and sat down, making a face and shaking my head toward Jonathon, but I don't think he even noticed.

# Chapter 13
# At the Dinner Table

*Jon*

It was my turn. The woman next to me had me feeling anxious and I was flustered. Seated, I tried to compose myself, hands clenched together.

"My name is Jonathon Kadish—Jon will do." I said with a forced chuckle, . . . "and Ida . . ." I motioned across the table, ". . . my wife and I reside in Norwich, Connecticut—not to be confused with Norwich, Vermont."

There was a murmur of confusion, making me feel awkward and dumb.

"As Ida said, we are on to Sherbrooke to visit our family."

I finished and quickly leaned back in the chair.

Katya was next. She rose quite deliberately, adjusting her shoulders and stretching her neck, inhaling a breath to expand her chest as she smoothed her skirt in front of her flat tummy.

"I am Ambassador Katya Rocinkova from St. Petersburg. I am a commercial officer with the Russian Mission to the United Nations, and *I will* be going to the symposium which my fellow travelers will be attending." She gestured toward Xi-Peng and Colleen.

I looked across the table at them. They both seemed startled by Katya's remark. It's hard to explain, but you know the look when you see it—sort of like someone has just had a small, unexpected electric shock.

Françi jumped in. "Ambassador, the two delayed guests are also Russian."

Katya nodded. Looking disinterested, she raised her hand as if to say, "So what?"

The man to her right, very distinguished with rugged good looks, some premature gray in his ample hair and an upturned mustache stayed seated and said very quickly, "My name is Scott Matthew from Toronto, and I happen to be traveling in this neighborhood this week."

And finally the last, the thirtyish-year-old kid the professor had referred to. "I am Renny, and I'm with him," he said, pointing to Robert across the table.

The dining room was huge. The table looked able to seat sixteen if called upon. The ceiling was high, perhaps eleven feet, and a sixteen-branched brass, wood, and glass chandelier hung over the table. On the table were four lit votive candles in gleaming brass bases with glass enclosures shaped like antique lanterns, each maybe a foot tall. The place settings were impeccable. Over the years, Ida had taught me to notice such detail and to appreciate the implements and care with which a table was set. Not since a dinner in a private dining room at the Pierre Hotel in New York City had I seen such a table. That dinner was to celebrate the sale of our family company to the government. It was the last time I was with my brothers and sister in a social setting.

Françi rang the bell again. Frank and his helper came through the swinging door with cut fruit, chocolate soufflé and whipped cream. Around the table once more, dessert, coffee, and tea were served.

"An after-dinner sherry or liqueur will be served in the meeting room at your convenience," Frank announced.

As the travelers finished their dessert, they rose and excused themselves. It was just before nine o'clock.

\*\*\*

Katya had started on me as soon as I sat down. "I've been waiting for you to arrive since two," she had said quietly, quarter-turned in my direction.

I was startled. "Huh? What? That doesn't make sense."

"I know who you are and what you're intending. I want to talk to you about coming to Russia."

Wow, did that blow my mind! How could she know all that? How did she know who I was, what I did, where we were going—even our future thoughts? I was beginning to panic. I remained silent.

"You won't stay in Canada," she continued. "It is a good place, but the climate won't suit you. And Canada and America work too closely together—they will send you back if America asks. When you travel to warm places, you will be vulnerable to kidnapping, even assassination. Russia will protect you. You and your wife will be safe with us. We will fly you directly to Moscow from Montreal, as soon as Monday if you agree."

"You are out of your mind. I don't know what you're talking about. Is this some kind of joke?" I said quietly.

"Not in the least. Let me talk to you and your wife. I want to explain everything I am authorized to offer. It is a life of comfort, status, wealth, and luxury. We want you for your knowledge, your advice, your opinion on matters on which you are expert. America has not recognized your true value, or maybe they don't trust you because you are a Jew and they worry about your loyalty. We have no issues about that."

She made me think. *What am I missing?* What did I know that Russia might value so highly?

"You don't know what you're talking about!" I finally answered. "We are perfectly happy where we are, doing what we're doing. I have a few years until retirement and I'm looking forward to slowing down. Please stop your nonsense."

"What about your medical issue?" she said, dropping her voice even further.

Boy, she seemed to know a lot. Hard to believe she was guessing. How had they learned so much about me?

"It isn't like you think! Your information is wrong! Please leave me alone."

"Our information is *not* wrong. We can listen and see the same surveillance that goes to your NSA and FBI. For a hundred years you are listening to us and we are listening to you. We have the same information about ourselves and about each other."

She took a sip of water. "We have a new treatment for prostate that might interest you. I can put you in touch with our experts to listen to your options. They have already read your scans and looked at your test results. I will contact you on the local Canadian communicator in Sherbrooke on Friday to arrange an early appointment. I am here for only a few days, while the UN is in recess."

She kept talking, but that was all I heard.


I hadn't eaten much, and I began to see the daggers that Ida was sending me. I looked across to her several times, hoping to get her attention, but she seemed engrossed in conversation with the Asian and his wife. I wanted her to talk to me so I could stop the repartee with Katya, even if just to eat my dinner.

Frank was now seated to my left, so I swiveled toward him.

"François, this meal is marvelous—wonderful cuisine for a day such as this."

He nodded a voiceless "thank you" as he hurriedly ate his entrée. It was near 8:30. There was no window in the wall I faced, so I couldn't see if it was still snowing. "Is it still snowing?" I asked him.

*"Oui, oui. Il neige encore, très dur."* He pointed to the windows behind me.

I knew *"oui, oui"* was *yes, yes.* That was all I needed.

Then he leaned close to me and whispered in accented English, "Can I talk to you later? Come to the kitchen after ten o'clock. Oui?"

I looked at my communicator and nodded. "Yes."


\*\*\*

After dessert, Ida and I asked to be shown to our room. It was ample, with a queen four-poster and the aroma of sage from a basket on the dresser. It had its own small fireplace, already lit and glowing. Our overnight cases were on folding stands. *Not everything changes in twenty years,* I thought.

"Who is that hussy you were so engrossed with?" was the first thing Ida said to me.

I wasn't surprised.

"Wait till I tell you about her! It will blow your mind. It did mine."

"And you'll never believe what I learned from the Asian and his wife," she said. "They met when he was at RPI and she at Russell Sage! He was Class of '17, she '19. They asked to have a drink with us in the living room. Let's do it! What a coincidence! I want to ask who of my professors might still have been there. We can go meet them right now."

It was quite unusual that Ida didn't immediately press me further about the Russian, but she was too excited about the coincidence with the Asian and his wife. She wanted to go to them right away. We took turns washing up in the small bathroom and I changed into my "tomorrow" shirt just to feel fresher.

Katya's solicitation had me completely forgetting the issues we needed to resolve in the next twenty-four to forty-eight hours. Ida refreshed too, but we didn't talk further as we hurried to the living room.

We ran into Rollie, who was waiting in the hallway.

"Mr. K, Mrs. K, are you all right?" he asked.

"Yes, sure, why?" I replied. "Did you enjoy the dinner? Have enough to eat?"

"Plenty of food, but the company is strange. I'm one of four drivers here. We have the only FAV; the others are in civilian versions of earlier models but impressive nevertheless. One's a big, athletic Russian—with close-clipped whiskers and a pistol in a shoulder holster that he seems proud to show off. He's driving a United Nations diplomat, but wouldn't talk about him at all."

"You mean *her!*" I said.

"Oh, that's it? The diplomat's a woman! That fits with how he was behaving—projecting a sort of superior attitude, like he knew things we didn't."

"What about the other guys?" I asked.

"One's a Canadian, he didn't say from where. He didn't say much at all, only to comment on the snow. Otherwise he just ate quietly and listened. The third's an Israeli, who also looks like a bodyguard. He said he's escorting a couple but didn't say who or from where. Strange bunch. Maybe they think I'm strange too? We each have a room in the oldest section, and I'm sharing a bathroom with the Russian. It'll do for one night."

"Rollie, be careful of the Russian. Don't reveal a breath. The woman is some sort of agent, I think."

I didn't want him to know more.

Ida looked at me with a startled expression. I quickly looked back at Rollie.

"Keep your eyes and ears open. You know our room. Knock softly if you need me. What time do we need to be out in the morning?"

"The sweepers will be here at eight. It's thirty minutes to the crossing in good weather. The snow is lightening up—should stop soon. We should start out by 8:15 to get to your appointment a bit early. The morning should be clear; I don't anticipate any problems. They know how to deal with this weather up here. Breakfast is available from 6:30."

Rollie walked me a few paces away from Ida. He leaned toward me and said in a quiet voice, "Do you know anything about a communication I received from FAV Central?"

I shook my head, my stomach sinking. "No."

"They told me to wait here to return you to Norwich on Monday. They said to work out the details and time with you. They extended and upgraded my reservation here and asked if a thousand a day would cover my time—today through Tuesday. 'It will be credited to your account,' they said. I wondered if they were kidding. I asked them to repeat it!"

He smiled and nodded. "They want me to confirm the time I'm to meet you so they can alert the Motivators to clear our path on Monday."

Surprises never stopped coming!

"We'll talk about it in the morning," I said to him.

"They think you're coming back with me on Monday, right?"

"I'm waiting for you!" Ida said, annoyed.

I said to Rollie slowly and distinctly, "We'll talk about it in the morning."

Mickey had already taken action to ensure my return, I realized.

I swiveled on my heel and walked away.

# Chapter 14
# After-Dinner Drinks

*Ida*

We met Xi-Peng and Colleen in the living room. We took snifters of cognac, Courvoisier. They had Anisette. Colleen and I stood at one end of the sofa, with Jon and Xi-Peng at the other.

I started the conversation with enthusiastic chatter about Sage Hall, the house rules when I was there, the bookstore in Follet, the infirmary at Kellas Hall, and the various restaurants we had frequented on Congress and State Street near the campus. I asked if she attended the big weekends at RPI, and if Xi-Peng had been in a fraternity. Her answers were vague. She seemed to know a good bit about the school, but she seemed hesitant to share her own experiences, her personal recollections. I couldn't connect with her on any of the faculty. We were there nearly thirty years apart, so I didn't give it much thought.

But then Jon broke away from Xi-Peng and came over to me.

"This guy's a phony. I don't think he ever went to RPI—his knowledge of the school and campus are minimal. He doesn't know about the hockey program, the history of the Science Center, the old central campus, nothing! He drew a blank when I mentioned the Student Union at Fifteenth and Sage. Nobody could *visit* the campus and not know that. He's a phony!"

At that point, I began to question some of what Colleen had said and not said.

"She's not too swift on Russell Sage either," I told him.

"C'mon," Jon said as he grabbed my arm and ushered me toward them, now huddled at the other end of the sofa.

"Okay," he said to them both. "Si'down!"

Jon pulled up armchairs for us, and we sat opposite them.

"Okay," he said again, "What's this about? You never went to RPI; you've never even been to Troy, New York! What about you?" He looked at Colleen. "Are your names really Ling whatever, and Colleen? Are you really married?"

I couldn't believe that Jon had gone so far so quickly. I worried that he was going to be embarrassed because of this tantrum. He'd always had certain impulsiveness, but this was over the top. Had he totally lost it? After all, this had been a tough day of surprises. But to my shock, the couple just looked at each other, nodded, then turned toward us.

The woman answered softly, "We cannot answer you. You have no reason to know the truth." She looked around cautiously. "Lean closer and listen to me. We are with the Israeli Scientific Service and we're here to tell you that we need you, Jon, in Israel as soon as we can arrange everything to your satisfaction. Your son Eric alerted us to your plans, and we advised our Chinese friends. With our request, the Chinese have had you both under surveillance, monitoring your communications for the past six months. They and we now know your plans and considerations. We know your heart is close to us and we can offer you a package that will address all your concerns, including your health issues. You will be able to enjoy your retirement years and financial means. And of course, your security will be assured. Can we visit with you in Sherbrooke on Sunday?"

"Sunday?" I said, confused. "But *he said* . . ." I pointed to Xi-Peng, ". . . that he is giving a talk at a symposium this Sunday?"

"Ida, forget that!" Colleen whispered. "There is no talk and no symposium! That was all just a story. So was our posing as graduates of your colleges. Please, we have serious things to review with you. Can we come to your apartment in Sherbrooke on Sunday? We will have an important government figure with us to talk to you. You may even know of him."

"If there is no symposium, how, why would the Russian woman say she is going there too?" Jon asked

*"She is not going there! No one is going there!* There is no symposium going on there this weekend! *She is a Russian agent,* no doubt here to recruit you and enlist your cooperation. She said that about the symposium to warn us that we were *made*—you know, exposed. She knew or suspected who we were and that was her threat for us to keep away from you, her quarry. We worry about her. Our driver, an Israeli Special Forces agent, passed word that her driver is Dmytri, a well-known Russian assassin. I'm concerned that if you don't show cooperation with her, he is here to take you out. If you won't work for them, they might not let you work for anybody! Get it? Do you have protection here? Don't answer! We know you don't. Go with your heart and come with us. We will be sure you are free and safe."

Jon and I looked at each other in wonderment.

Colleen took a small package from her purse and pushed it toward me.

"Here, take this analog communicator. It's old technology, no longer supported here. We have activated a temporary mini-station around Sherbrooke for us to talk to you by these. They cannot be intercepted or tapped."

I pushed her hand toward Jon, to give the communicator to him.

"No!" she said. "We want *you* to be in control of this. The Russians might look for it on him, but not on you. Just open the face and it will call us. Whoever answers will know it's you and what the situation is. Don't hesitate to tell or ask them anything. That's it for now. We'll be waiting for your call to confirm Sunday, and if necessary, we can reach you by that cell too."

The couple quickly disappeared toward the bedroom wing.

I moved to the corner of the sofa. Jon remained in the chair facing me. We took each other's hands.

"What is going on here, Jon? This whole thing is nuts."

Jon explained what the Russian woman had said to him at the table, and how the Asian and his wife were startled when Katya said she was going to the symposium.

And now we knew the Israeli driver was with Ling and Colleen.

Jon was more annoyed than I expected.

"Can you imagine that Israel sends that Asian, totally unprepared, with that half-ass RPI story––and then he doesn't say a another word when I see right through him. I wonder if he really is an engineer or man of science? He didn't say a single thing to demonstrate his technical skills. Maybe he's just a Chinese spy? Least they could have done was send an Israeli!

"Oh," Jon added, "Frank asked me to stop in the kitchen after ten." We looked at the time. It was 9:35.

I looked out the window. The snow had stopped. But it was stacked on the windowsill and the yard was filled up. I could see more than a foot of the fluffy stuff on top of their rural mailbox outside the picket fence. It was beautiful to see from the house but treacherous outside.

"C'mon," Jon said. "Let's get out of here."

# Chapter 15
# Le Professeur Expounds
*Jon*

As we walked into the hallway, we heard a voice coming from the meeting room. I looked at Ida. We hunched our shoulders and turned toward the sound.

As we neared the portal, Frank called out, "Mr. and Mrs. Kadish, come sit down. Listen for a few minutes to *le professeur.*"

Sitting in an irregular circle were the professor, his mate Renny, Françi, Frank, and Scott Matthew, the guy from Toronto.

The professor looked up at us.

"Please, come in and join us. I am trying to explain how dramatically war has changed––beginning with the Korean conflict in the 1950s. Have you ever thought about it?

"Huh? Not really. What's there to think about?" I replied, shrugging. I had more important things on my mind, but maybe this would be a good distraction.

Ida and I pushed seats into the circle.

Professor MacLeod carried on as in a lecture hall.

"From ancient times until the Korean conflict, wars were mostly fought for economic reasons. Sure, history books are filled with freedom revolutions, power struggles, religious wars, accidental wars, and the like, but if you dig deeper, they were always either to capture economic assets, including people for slavery, or alternatively to overthrow an occupier so that a people could recapture themselves. Rome went to war for profit! Consciously or subconsciously, leaders calculated the cost of the war versus the spoils to be captured. If the equation was sufficiently in their favor, they sent their war machine to subdue the prize. Societies captured neighbors for the grain from their harvests, taxes

100

from their commerce, tribute from their governments, the labor of their people, the women for their men, and more soldiers for their army.

"When the cost of holding a territory became greater than the benefits, the place was abandoned. Or on occasion, subjugated people rose to overthrow their oppressor. Many times they were successful because the oppressor had become weak or didn't see a further profit in the cost to quell the rebellion. The indigenous people were usually motivated to take back their assets, control of their lives—what we might call *freedom* today."

MacLeod raised his eyebrows at us. "Do you generally agree with this thesis, Mr. Matthew, Mr. Kadish?"

Matthew answered before I could open my mouth.

"Or a rival power might think the spoils of a territory were worth the cost to supplant the existing oppressor and possess that place in their stead. Yes, I get the point you are making."

"Good!" the professor exclaimed. "So dynasties were born, flowed—many for centuries—then ebbed, only to be succeeded by an up-and-coming new dynasty that warred and plundered for the same reasons. To the victor went the spoils! Gold and power reigned!"

The professor shouted, gestured, and laughed. He was entertaining.

"So why do you say that changed with the Korean War?" Matthew asked.

"Ah-ha! Good question!" MacLeod made his exclamation point by thrusting his arm in the air. He acted surprised—but I knew immediately that the professor was using us to lead him right where he wanted to go. The others around the circle, including Ida, all seemed attentive and waiting for his reply.

"The horrific Second World War in Europe and Asia was started by aggressors who *were* fighting for resources, power, and profit—but they were doing it — while committing horrible atrocities. After they were defeated, the United Nations was brought into being and the world came together with clearer rules of war. They outlawed chemical weapons and attacks on civilians; they established standards–for the treatment of captives, the plundering of spoils, and the responsibility of parties to provide restitution for damages. With these new rules, the world began today's period of *moral* wars. The UN mounted campaigns to combat asset or power grabs by would-be oppressors, but *not* to capture the assets for themselves.

"The first such war was the Korean conflict! Get it? North Korea invaded the south for profit. The coalition of defenders, principally the United States, had no profit to gain. What did the United States and its allies gain from the Vietnam War, the Bosnia-Kosovo War? The United Nation forces were rewarded with the right to protect South Korea for seventy-five more years at the expense of the US taxpayers! There were no spoils for the victors——only more obligations!"

The professor could have been a *stage raconteur.*

"Saddam Hussein overran Kuwait for profit. An allied coalition, perhaps the largest in human history, spent billions to chase him out. Why? Kuwait was a fabricated country, carved out of what became Iraq when Britain and France sliced up the Ottoman Empire in 1922. Iraq wanted it back, like Mainland China wanted Taiwan, like Russia and Japan contested ownership of islands and Argentina and Britain fought over the Falklands. The UN evicted Iraq from Kuwait because of moral indignation! Iraq broke the rules. Countries were not supposed to do that to one another anymore. What spoils, if any, went to the victors? What restitution was Iraq forced to pay? Do you see where I'm going?"

The group nodded its understanding. The professor was visibly emotional about his subject matter.

Scott Matthew interrupted. "Now, because the world recognizes basic human rights, self-determination, and certain humanitarian rules of hot war, major nations just fight their wars differently. Nations—"

"Yes, yes!" the professor cut him off excitedly. "But wait a moment, and we'll get to that. Of course we've skipped a lot of intervening history, but most conflicts since Korea will display pretty much the same points. Through the end of the twentieth century, the wars fought were relatively small skirmishes. The major combatants were able to afford them without needing great sacrifice from their home populations. The nations defending the weak were able to provide men and guns for the fighting and still have butter on the table for the home front. While Vietnam was a challenge, it didn't unduly sap the treasury of America; it sapped the *will* of the American people! The human cost was too high. The North didn't represent *any threat* to the US homeland, after all. The South was a weak democracy at best. It was a French colony, but even the tough French Foreign Legion was forced to withdraw. To fill its military ranks, the US had to institute conscription, and that riled the public. Many conscientious objectors escaped north to Canada, just as many others have been doing since 2010—not to avoid the military, but to escape government oppression of one sort or another."

Ida sat facing the professor. I couldn't catch her eye. I was beginning to feel warm. Anxiety was coming over me and I wanted her to notice, maybe say we should leave. She didn't so I fought to ignore it.

MacLeod went on, "The conscientious objectors came to escape the political persecution and to enjoy Canadian freedom. But today, my country, Canada, has stricter rules about who can enter and how long they can stay.

"But the most glaring examples of worthless wars were in this century, the Iraq and the Afghanistan wars of the first two decades.

"The US, with only symbolic coalition partners, fought each of these wars to topple a dictator and to defeat rogue governments, but after doing so, they — didn't have a clear vision of what to do next or when or how to withdraw. After ten years, they withdrew without achieving any clear decision, win or loss, and at great cost to themselves. Not only was no profit achieved, but the US and Europe almost became bankrupt. Even after all the cost and sacrifice to the Americans, the new Iraqi regime *didn't award a single oil concession* to an American company. Later, when the West thought these wars were over, we went *another* ten years fighting one ruthless caliphate after another until China stepped in and finally seems to have subdued the region.

"These examples clearly show that wars without a profit motive are fruitless. The US spent nearly $3 trillion, plus the lives of thousands of their forces to prosecute these wars to no conclusion. Rather than profit, these so-called liberators went grossly into debt. And those countries are no more civilized today, by our Western standards, than before you intervened there!"

The professor laughed as he pointed at me.

"So, as Mr. Matthew was about to suggest, wars between the world's biggest rivals, the so-called superpowers, are now fought for and with . . . *money!*"

He jumped up as he shouted that last word.

"With oil, gas, gold, silver, uranium, potash, sugar, cocoa, wheat, corn, raw materials of all sorts, natural resources and manufactured goods, all for profit! You get what I mean? In today's world, economic supremacy beats military might. The economic winners get to buy whatever they need or want, and dictate the terms to the lesser nations unable to survive without their patronage. The biggest international players—and you know who they are—don't need to physically battle each other. They just try to dominate each other by controlling the resources needed for their populations, the technology of today and of the future, and to provide a rising standard of living for their leaders and their people. China became the number-one world economy in the early '20s, but now the United States is surging to retake the lead. India is third, the EU fourth, while Brazil, rising, is tied with staid Russia for fifth. Japan continues to drop, now sixth.

"Japan's problem is they have resisted immigration, its population has declined, its workforce is old, it has fewer women of childbearing age, and even those have a birthrate less than two. The population is not replacing itself, and its policies and demographics defy resurgence.

"Look at how the United States has turned its military might into a profit center in the past sixteen years. How it's freed itself from being an energy hostage, becoming energy independent. How, after legalizing drugs to generate revenue and cut costs and finally restructuring its debt with the bail-in, it has become like a strong, vibrant company emerging from bankruptcy, again becoming the economic leader of the world. Look how it has created incentives for citizens to have more children, learning from the decline of Japan and Europe. Does anyone think America's future is not bright?"

The professor looked around the circle. Everyone seemed engrossed. He paused and took a sip of water. François leaned toward me and whispered, "Monsieur Jon, enough of this now. Please come with me to the kitchen."

He stood, picked up his chair to move it out of the circle, excused himself and left.

Ida and I stood and thanked the professor too.

"That was most interesting and a novel way of looking at that history. But please excuse us now . . . it is late and we've had a long day."

MacLeod nodded, looking a little deflated as his audience thinned out. "Thank you for stopping by. This and much more will be in my coming book. Perhaps we can discuss it a bit more in the morning, at breakfast? I have other interesting ways to view the present and the future."

"Perhaps," I called over my shoulder, knowing it was unlikely.

Then I wondered what Frank might want. He'd been waiting for this hour since dinner.

# Chapter 16
# Meeting with François

*Jon*

Frank was waiting for us in the kitchen. We sat down in the breakfast alcove around a decorative bowl of fruit.

"Listen to me," Frank said in what seemed like less accented speech. He leaned forward and dropped his voice.

"They know what you're thinking, planning. Don't do it! Those pretending to be your friends will let you down!"

"Who knows . . . what? You're not making any sense," I said.

Ida, who had been drained, snapped alert.

"Jon, listen to me," Frank said. "You can't trust the Russians or the Chinese. Not even the Israelis. The Chinese are calling their shots."

I folded my hands and leaned forward myself.

"Why are you telling us this? Who are you? Who do *you* represent?"

In a near-whisper, he said, "Françi and I are agents of the NSA, Industrial Service Division, and Homeland Security. General George Catern, Deputy Director of the Defense Industries Cabinet, has been in personal touch with us. He told me, 'Tell him'—meaning *you!*— 'that we know everything.' Washington, and now Groton, know what you're planning. They know your history with Israel and that your son, Eric, is there. Listen, Israel is everyone's sentimental favorite and no one would stop you from helping them––if it wouldn't hurt America. But Israel is only fronting for China. The general told me to tell you and Ida, 'Don't sell out your country! The promotion that's in the works will address all your issues.' General Catern will be at your office on Tuesday to meet and debrief you together with Mickey."

He couldn't be bluffing. He'd dropped all the right names and knew the schedule. But I didn't want to hear it.

"C'mon, Ida, we're getting out of here. I don't believe a single word of this!"

"Stop! Stop, Jon. Don't go yet. I need to have an your answer."

"I don't understand this at all," Ida said. "What does Jon have that everybody is ready to fight over?"

"Good question!" I echoed. "What is it that these sides want from me?"

My head swam with confusion. But the more I thought about it, *the more I was beginning to realize that certain knowledge I thought was ordinary might be the solution to another's problem.*

"I don't know," Frank answered. "Are you working on anything top secret? Did you work on anything like that recently? Maybe you don't realize that your fifty years in our navy and on the job at the Boat have given you many pieces of our offensive and defensive weapons. You might have vital information that could help our adversaries catch up and possibly exceed our own capabilities. Why else would you be in such demand?"

Maybe he was right. When in the navy, I'd worked in every shipboard department as I punched my ticket up the chain of command. Then I skippered different models, and at the Boat, I had worked on many aspects of their engineering. But I still didn't really understand what knowledge I had that could be so powerful.

Frank continued, "America isn't perfect, but as a superpower, we are better than the rest. We know where you'll be in Sherbrooke. Your driver will be waiting here for you on Monday. You told Mickey you would be in your office at ten a.m. on Tuesday. You don't want to disappoint them."

"Is that a threat, Frank? Are you threatening me now?" I asked.

"I don't know what you're talking about." Frank shrugged, but then he met my gaze. "Take it any way you like."

I looked at Ida and she at me. I could see she was troubled. She probably saw the same in my eyes. I was stymied and didn't know what to do or say next.

Ida came to the rescue, as she usually did. "What's a federal agent doing so far from Washington anyway—and in such an isolated place?"

Ida didn't have to ask twice. Frank was more than ready to answer. He settled in his seat, relaxed, and began to talk.

"Twenty years ago in 2019, Françi and I were living near Plattsburg, New York, next to the Canadian border. I was a newly trained chef from the International Culinary Academy in Cap d'Agde on the Riviera. Françi and I met there and quickly married. I'd always enjoyed cooking and became very good at it. With family help and a bank loan, we bought a B&B on the border to Canada, on US-11 at Rouses Point.

"That was shortly after Congress passed a sweeping immigration law. Do you remember? There were twelve million undocumented foreigners living and working in the US, and more were crossing our borders all the time. The law provided a path to residency and citizenship for many of the illegals but required sealing the borders so that only properly documented foreigners would be able to enter in the future. More foreigners were to be allowed in, though, and many new categories of temporary worker permits were created. Guest workers were to be tracked and made to comply with their visas. Foreign students in the engineering and science fields were automatically to be issued green cards. But foreign students, who were required to return to their native country by their home governments, were *no longer to be granted visas to study here.*"

He emphasized that last point, leaning forward again. "No longer were we going to train foreigners in our ways and let them go home and practice them against us. That made perfectly good sense to me."

Ida and I nodded.

I remembered that law well. I agreed that we shouldn't train foreigners if we knew they were required to return to their home countries and use that knowledge against us.

Frank continued, "The trafficking on the Mexican border was the main focus, but there was plenty of action happening on this border too! The US-Canada border was the longest open bilateral border between any two countries in the world. That was before the fence was built to prevent illegal entry and exit.

"When that law was passed, there was plenty of illegal crossing of this border too, both ways—by Americans leaving and all sorts of people entering. Foreigners from anywhere in the world had easy access to Canada and then pretty easy access to cross the border into the US. Some came right through our more casually operated checkpoints. Others crossed at unguarded points in the wilderness. You might recall some publically disclosed incidents in the far west and in Maine of suspected terrorists trying to enter the US from Canada. There were many, many more cases that did not get disclosed. Also not disclosed was the vibrant local industry of guides: farmers, woodsmen, and hunters who began escorting people back and forth across the border. Those operators on the Mexican border were called *coyotajes.* We had coyotajes here too."

His eyes sparkled as he relived the memories.

"*Coyotajes?*" Ida asked. "Do you mean *coyotes,* like the wild dogs in the woods across the country?"

"Yes, Ida, that's what he means, and that is what those men are called. He can pronounce it anyway he wants," I answered.

"You can call them anything you like but they're the farmers and woodsmen that guide illegals across this border for pay."

Frank continued, "Our B&B was on land actually touching the border. We profited from the illegal traffic. We knew many of the coyotajes operating on both sides. We were sort of a stop on an underground railroad between the US and Canada. We were young, and the money and excitement were great.

"Agents from Homeland Security exposed and initially planned to prosecute us. But then they recruited us instead. We could advise them on who the coyotajes were, when they were coming, who they were bringing, and which way the traffic was going. Most of the time Homeland Security just let the traffic move. If they watched the travelers after they crossed, either in the US or in Canada, we never knew.

Occasionally a crossing had to be stopped, and they always did it in a place that would not throw suspicion on us."

Frank showed no sign of slowing down his story and my mind was beginning to drift. The flurry of solicitations by foreign agents was giving me anxiety. I wanted to get away from the kitchen and take a pill, but I kept my seat.

"At that time, Canada was tightening its immigration laws as more Americans and others sought refuge from governments, confiscations, and penalties in their native countries," said Frank. "We became a clandestine station. It was a great deal. We had the tourist business, the coyotajes business, and a salary from the government. It was a good and secure livelihood."

"But what you're describing took place in New York State. How did you get here—Pittsburg, New Hampshire?" Ida asked.

"I'm getting to it, I'm getting to it now. Be patient."

Ida could see that I was bordering on anxiety. I'm sure she wanted him to speed up the story for my sake. I sat back and took a few deep breaths.

"A few years later they asked us to move and set up here. We had proven our loyalty, and they liked that I was Quebecois and Françi was French. Much of the cross-border traffic relocated east, away from Montreal, because our authorities had become more effective there. The word got passed: Montreal to Plattsburg was a risky place to cross. The traffic moved east, here. So Homeland needed someone here. They had others such as us along that New York border."

"What is your family name?" Ida asked.

"Bernardin—we are François and Françi Bernardin. We agreed to move and set up here. Again, it was a great deal for us! We bought the property and renovated it with their money. They cut the ski trails and put in the children's playground. They advertised us as a family resort and sports recreation center with fishing, hunting, skiing, something happening in every season. They promoted us with travel agents. It was amazing. The total of the federal treasury seemed to be at our disposal! They paid for our business, invested in the improvements, paid for advertising, and gave us a stipend to run the station. We were in our thirties! Our parents wondered how we were able to afford this. We told them we won a New York lottery!"

He laughed and stood to get something to drink. "Would you like something too?"

We both accepted. He brought over glasses and a bottle of sparkling water. I was grateful—sipping it helped calm me somewhat.

"They installed a complete safety and communications bunker, and voila, we were in business! Our careers were established. We were two more people who would always be in the government's service and debt, who would always vote for the status quo."

He grinned wryly. "Business blossomed from the start. The coyotajes found us, and we knew how to handle their patronage. So now, even fifteen years later, even with the fence along the border, even with the satellite and drone surveillance, there are cracks in the network, and people are still crossing in both directions using guides. We are plugged into the scene and know the players in the trade. We keep tabs on their activity and send reports to headquarters if something is being planned."

"When did you know we were coming?" I asked, suddenly more alert to what he was saying.

"Oh, Monsieur! When you applied for your family visit permit to Sherbrooke, you were immediately directed to the New Hampshire-Chartierville crossing, and assigned here so Françi and I could monitor you. The Defense Industries Cabinet suspected you might be trying to escape and might be a target for foreign recruitment. But they didn't expect it to be this aggressive."

"Were you listening to us in the FAV driving up here?" I asked.

"Sure, sure. Listening and recording, everything!" Frank started laughing. "Quite an interesting show, oui? But it didn't matter, surveillance knew you were heading to us as planned."

Frank leaned forward again and pounded his fist on the table. "Do not bite on their bait! Yes, you are Jewish and have connections to Israel, yes? Your great-grandparents came from Kolchin, and you have a Russian heritage too, yes? But you are Americans first! Our country educated you," Frank pointed to me, "and you too Ida. You served honorably in the navy, rising in rank and responsibility. Yes, the US has gone through terrible travails in the past thirty years, but we are moving to the top of the world again and many personal freedoms will be returned to the people in the near future. We know it has been hard for Jews—and the many, many, Christians—who support Israel. Yes, there has been a backlash against Jews who are still here because of the exodus of Jews—like your siblings—to Latin America, Canada, but principally to Israel. I have been briefed that these issues will be addressed by this administration. Diplomatic contacts will be reestablished soon. Commercial relations, tourism, and travel will be normalized. Missions to the holy sites will be allowed for groups from American soil. Israeli activist organizations will be declared legal and be restarted. Contacts between the government and Israel, and the American Jewish leadership, are already in progress."

Ida and I were tired, but we listened carefully to François's every word. What he was saying now mattered.

"Don't abandon the ship now. Stay the course. You'll be rewarded, and you both will be proud of the US again. Have I said enough? Are you convinced? I would like to have your answer now, but I will need your decision in the morning before you leave."

"Why?" I asked.

"Why? You ask *why?*" Frank tilted his head and squinted his eyes. "That's a foolish question from a smart man like you! Maybe you are tired and not thinking clearly. *Why?* Because I can have you stopped from leaving the country. You can just be turned back. Or I can have you detained for questioning. Or I can let you cross the border if I know you will return. Or our own government coyotajes can come get you if necessary. Please, Jon, you know we have many options to stop you. If you decline this plea, we will find you anywhere in the world. You will not be as free as you think!"

It was hard to believe all that Frank had said, but I knew instantly that everything he said was possible. If the government had the will to stop us, they had the way and the means. No doubt about it. They had taken drastic action against individuals in the past and could do it again anytime. *Maybe Rollie knew more than me when he suggested that the US might want me killed.*

I formed my words carefully. "Can you, François, get me across the border without going through the checkpoint?"

"Which way, Monsieur?"

"Either way . . . or both?" I said. "And what about the Russian woman and the Chinese couple? How did you uncover the Chinese couple?"

"First, if I needed or wanted to, I could move you secretly across the border in either direction at any time of day in any season! Understand?"

I nodded.

"As for the Israeli representatives, they are amateurs! Israel and China were not as prepared for your move as Russia. They don't expect you to be a hard sell. They know of your efforts on behalf of the Jewish people and Israel, they know of your siblings in Jerusalem, they know of your son and grandchildren in Hertzlia and the means you have parked with him. They probably assumed you would be going there voluntarily, making *aliyah* as many have done and as you have considered at some points in the past. Oui?"

We both nodded.

"But at the last minute they must have decided to send a representative to combat the Russians and tell you personally you are wanted and welcome."

"Did you ever see that couple before?" I asked.

"No, never. But they were not hard to recognize. They came with an Israeli driver." He chuckled. "Amateurs! As soon as they arrived I knew who they represented and why. I quickly reported them to our contacts, who confirmed there was no symposium in Sherbrooke this weekend."

Frank seemed to be done, so I motioned to Ida that we should go to our room.

"How much more is it going to snow?" I asked to break the tension.

"Oh . . . it has already stopped. You'll tell me your answer in the morning, yes? I am here in the kitchen beginning from six o'clock."

"Oui," I said. "tomorrow."

I didn't have an answer at the moment.

\*\*\*

Holding hands, quietly thinking, we walked toward the guestroom wing. Ida went in, and I grabbed the empty ice bucket to get it filled down the hall. It was just eleven o'clock.

As I returned with the ice, the door to the room on the opposite side of the hallway opened, and a head swung out and faced me. It was Matthew. I was shocked.

"Mr. Kadish," he said, his voice clear and sharp, "I work for a private security firm in Canada. A trillionaire industrialist wants you to visit him in Calgary next week. He retained my services to guard you from here to Sherbrooke, during your stay in Sherbrooke and until we can safely fly you to Calgary. He only said to say that he has 'a proposition for you that you will not be able to decline.' Six of our best agents are assigned to safeguard you and your wife once you are across the border. You should not be able to detect them. We have swept the apartment your daughter has rented for you and it is clean. Our agents are there now, watching, protecting it. Once there, you will be contacted again to make the travel arrangements. A private jet will be provided for you and your wife. Please don't say anything to anyone about this. Not even to her. She will be briefed with you on the flight."

I was stunned, speechless. Before I could regain my composure, he pulled his head inside the door and shut it. I could hear the lock click into place and the safety chain slide down its slot.

# Chapter 17
# From Kitchen to Guestroom

*Ida*

As we walked from the kitchen and the startling conversation with Frank, I linked my arm around Jon's. We walked slowly, casually. When we reached our room, I waited for Jon to unlock the door. He was shuffling his hand in a pocket. I wondered where his mind was.

"Do you have the key?" I asked him.

"Oh, yes." He abruptly pulled it from his pocket.

"I'm going to get some ice," he said as he took a cut glass bucket from the dresser.

Since we left the kitchen he had seemed distant, distracted. I had the feeling he was thinking about his work and what could possibly be the cause of these unexpected suitors. *How did they know so much about us?*

He seemed gone a long time. I was just beginning to worry when I heard him fumbling with the key again. I opened the door. He replaced the bucket, put some ice in a glass and poured water from a pitcher. He took a long, slow drink.

"I'm feeling warm," he said. He raised his glass toward me. "Water?"

My questions all gushed out at once. "Jon, you look pale! What took you so long? Did you see Rollie again? What are you thinking? Why are you going back to Groton on Monday? What do you know that everyone wants a piece of you?"

"No, no, no! I didn't see Rollie again!" he said, annoyed. "And this attention is a complete surprise—especially from the Defense Industries. Can we talk about this tomorrow? I feel overwhelmed right now."

He turned away from me, sitting on the bed with his glass of water looking at the wall. I felt he didn't want to look me in the face, look me in the eye at that moment. I wondered why. What might he be with-holding now?

"Sure, I'm tired too," I answered.

I used the bathroom first—removed my makeup, washed my face, and used my cleanser. Jon followed me in. I had slipped on my night-shirt. Jon was in a robe. We hugged. As we were about to separate, he pulled me close and held me tightly for a longer moment. He told me he loved me, and I whispered the same to him.

"We'll make it through," he said. "Don't worry."

I left him there to prepare for bed. I hung my clothes in the armoire and slipped under the covers.

We were exhausted, drained from the day, and we would have an early morning and busy tomorrow. I pondered all the surprises of the day—the snow, the ride, the Chinese agents, and then that last encounter with Frank. Lying down together, we kissed each other's cheeks and rolled about trying to get comfortable in the strange bed. Then I realized my pillow hadn't been brought in from the FAV. *Damn it!* There were four pillows on the bed. I checked each one. Two were foam, the others feather. I punched one of the feather pillows in the center to carve a depression for my head. It worked, and I quickly fell asleep.

I don't remember another thing until we both woke at a few min-utes to six.

A quick look out the window displayed a shadowed winter wonder-land. Ice and snow covered everything. Evergreen branches drooped, heavy with their white burden, looking decorated for Christmas. The sun was not fully up, and long, gray shadows tilted northwest in the morning twilight. I wondered if we would make it across the border.

Jon showered first, brushed his teeth, and took his morning com-plement of prescriptions. We helped each other with our belts and then completed dressing. There was much I wanted to talk about, but the schedule was tight, and I was nervous about the possibility of surveillance.

As if reading my mind, Jon whispered, "We need to talk. So much has happened since we left Norwich and arrived here. I have more to tell you. But we need real privacy."

"My thoughts exactly," I answered.

That short exchange made me feel calm and safe and ready for breakfast.

# Chapter 18
# Breakfast

*Ida*

We arrived at the dining room a bit before six-thirty as a young woman finished setting the table. The breakfast hour was flexible; it could be taken individually from six-thirty until ten. I heard our arrival announced in the kitchen, and Franci raced out to greet us, still wiping breakfast from her lips and chin with a cloth napkin. The assistant followed, holding steaming pots of coffee.

"Oh . . . Mr. and Mrs. Kadish! Please seat yourselves wherever you wish. You're the first to arrive. Anne has fresh coffee or decaf here, which would you prefer? And can we bring you fresh-squeezed orange juice or another juice of your choice?"

It was hard to believe Franci was a secret agent. We took a quick look around, and I motioned to chairs, side by side, in front of a lavishly appointed mahogany buffet. Anne came over and poured us coffee. We both asked for orange juice. She placed the coffee pots on their station at the buffet.

Franci stood to one side as she motioned to the buffet. "There are some cold cereal selections; sliced, diced, or whole fruit; whole milk, 2%, 1%, skimmed, half & half, light cream, and heavy cream. Yogurt of many sorts, of course. Fresh croissants baked by François; other breads—banana, pumpkin, and zucchini; butter and spreads, local preserves, and honey. Refill your coffee from there too if you wish."

Hands clasped and body bobbing left and right, she continued her practiced monologue. A fine performance, I thought, but then I remembered her profession was a B&B hostess before becoming connected to the NSA.

"Frank will make you as many an *eouf* as you wish—regular or French toast with cinnamon raisin bread, thick-sliced egg bread, or

119

French bread. Pancakes or waffles with apple or blueberry compote. Hot oats, groats, grits, or bits will take about fifteen minutes longer."

She laughed at her own joke. "Now then . . . ?"

Jon and I looked at each other, hiding a smile.

"Françi, thank you," I said. "We'll start at the buffet, and please ask us again in a few minutes."

*"Comme vous le souhaitez,"* she replied and started for the kitchen.

"What was that? Jon asked, his brow wrinkled.

"As you wish," she called back to us.

We split an individual box of Special K and a banana, me with skimmed, he with 2%. Jon took a croissant, butter, and some grape jelly, and small samples of the sweet breads. When Françi returned, we gave an order for eggs. After I ordered, Jon said, "Two poached on a buttered English, sausage, and home fries, please."

Shaking her finger, she said, "Sorry, Mr. Kadish, François does not allow *English* muffins in his kitchen. Croissant or French toast perhaps?"

"Pumpernickel?" he asked.

"Oui, pumpernickel, if you wish."

"Toasted." He nodded his approval, and she again withdrew to the kitchen.

"Jon," I said, "how can you fool around this morning with so much at stake—so many decisions to make? What are you thinking? What are we going to do? Will we even be able to cross the border? Yesterday's storm must have covered the roads. Will Rachel be able to get there to pick us up? I'm a wreck, and you're joking around. After all these years together, there are times I still can't figure you out!"

"That's what keeps our relationship alive, fresh!" he said, gesturing dramatically. "The unexpected, the unknown, the unlikely response, the impulsive activity! That's the secret *glue* between us . . ."

He trailed off. Then added contemplatively, "Maybe that's what the Russians want from me? *The glue!*"

"The *glue?*" I asked.

"Yes, Ida, there is a *glue!*"

I smiled, and he laughed.

But then his forehead wrinkled. I had a feeling he'd hit on something that hadn't previously occurred to him.

Frank delivered the hot food himself. "Egg white omelet with onions, mushrooms, tomatoes, no cheese, no potatoes, no toast for the lady. Poached on toasted pumpernickel, sausage, and potatoes for the gentleman," he announced as he placed the plates before us. "More coffee? Juice? What more can I prepare for you?"

"Can you sit for a minute?" Jon asked.

"Sure." Suddenly serious, Frank pulled a chair to the head of the table next to me and poured himself coffee. "What can I do for you this morning?"

I leaned across Ida and said, "Frank, I am going to visit my daughter and grandchildren today. I'm going to establish my wife in the apartment Rachel has let for us, and I will return here on Monday to travel to the Tuesday appointment in Groton. Ida will remain in Sherbrooke with our daughter. I will return there after my meetings. Today is Thursday, so I'll have four days to visit with them. Does this meet with your approval?"

This was the first I had heard of the *exact* plan. I began to seethe and shake my head. I hated to be without Jon when we traveled! But I would be with our daughter. That would work for a while.

Frank replied, "Okay, but remember: we have the means to find you and return you here with or without your consent. Don't do anything foolish."

Jon nodded as he looked at the scowl on my face. My heart raced as I thought of being apart while he returned to face his boss. What if he didn't or couldn't return? At that moment I was disgusted with this entire adventure. We hadn't fooled anyone but ourselves.

"Let's get out of here, back to the room. You have a lot of explaining to do," I whispered to Jon with suddenly watery eyes.

Footsteps clacked, and we looked up to see the professor and Renny enter the room. MacLeod took the chair opposite Jon, Renny the one opposite me.

I pushed my chair back, stood and said, "I'm going to our room. Are you coming?"

I expected Jon to stand and join me. He didn't. The bastard just nodded his head and said, "I'd like a few more minutes with the professor. I'll join you shortly."

# Chapter 19
# Breakfast
*Jon*

As soon as Frank left the table, Ida looked at me and said, "You *are* going to Groton for that Tuesday meeting, aren't you? You're leaving me in Canada with Rachel. What if they don't let you back? What will happen to us?"

Her eyes began to water as she waited for my reply.

At the same instant, Robert MacLeod and Renny came noisily into the room, taking seats across from Ida and me. Ida turned her head and looked away from them.

The professor greeted us heartily as Anne offered coffee or decaf and Françi began her spiel, word for word as she had recited it to us.

In the next instant, the professor leaned toward me.

"Thank you for stopping by last night. I enjoyed having you listen to my analysis."

Ida stood abruptly. "I'm going to the room, are you coming?"

"I'll be there in a few minutes," I said. "Don't forget we leave at eight."

She never turned or responded. She just hurried away.

After giving his order and collecting some cereal, the professor asked, "So, Mr. Kadish, your country has emerged from oblivion and is reasserting itself in the world, but only after trampling on its citizens' rights and asserting its military power for profit. How's that for a breakfast opener?"

I knew exactly what he was saying, but I refused to admit it to him.

"What exactly do you mean?" I asked.

"Come now, you know what I'm saying. In the last almost twenty years, Washington has monetized your military complex to become the world's largest mercenary force. Every nation that wants to avoid

Chinese, Russian, or a neighbor's domination, comes to you and pays for your protection. That massive revenue is the US's largest export earner. Add that to your drug trade, your agricultural bounty, and your energy independence, and you have the reason the US has a positive trade balance and budget surplus today. It's all exploitation and muscle."

I couldn't contest anything he said.

"Your army is the largest in the world, and your industrial complex has the means to develop and produce the most advanced weapons on the planet. But to do so, your government has again instituted conscription and nationalized the defense industry under the Defense Industrial Cabinet. The US has become the same hybrid socialized society as China and Russia, only *they* began as communist and needed to institute the free market system in some areas to compete. The US started with the free market system but needed to socialize certain aspects to balance the benefits to the population as a whole. During the twentieth-century Cold War, it was free market versus communism, but each was flawed. Now each of the major competitor nations uses a blend of these systems in order to battle with each other. Do you see my point?"

For the first time, I found his tone offensive. My shoulders stiffened as I replied.

"Professor, I am retired military, and I know full well how and what happened in America. Our country kept going to the aid of small and weaker nations––who were being persecuted in one way or another by another nation––at *our* taxpayers' expense. Later, many of those we protected became productive and rich under our umbrella. After the Second World War, we saw to the rebuilding of Germany, France, England, Japan, the Philippines, and many other places and then continued to protect them from their enemies. How long could we be expected to do that out of our own pocket? The wars you cited last night—Korea, Vietnam—were a proper example. We went to war for moral reasons and came out mostly battered, defeated, and poorer.

When the opportunity came in the modern world to be compensated for the protection we provide, we were wise to grab it. Your country, Canada, is a primary example of a rich country that enjoys our protection without contributing your proper share! We protect you as the no-man's land between Russia, China, and ourselves. If we ever fight a hot war with any of those two, it will be over Canada, as we meet them coming over the North Pole. We sell you arms; provide you with military training yet your standing military is smaller than our coast guard. Canada should be contributing $50 billion a year to us for the protection we provide."

I hadn't realized how effectively I could defend the United States when confronted.

Anne came around the table to pour fresh coffee. As she walked around the table, I stood up to go, knowing Ida was waiting for me and I was already late.

# Chapter 20
# Professor Keeps At It
*Jon*

But the professor jumped right in before I could get away.

"Look at the freedoms your people have sacrificed! You have mandatory conscription for high school dropouts and graduates. We won't even let them duck into Canada this time!"

"The draft? *Why not?* It's a good thing!" I shouted back. "If a kid is going to college or has been studying a trade, he's allowed to remain in the civilian force. But if kids are not furthering their educations or learning a skill to contribute to the common good, then they work for and are trained by the government. That applies to college graduates too, and to girls as well as boys. Our youth unemployment is now nil. Tell me how that's a bad thing!"

I was way more riled by the professor's accusations than I'd expected to be.

"Instead of the painful, divisive process of *closing* military bases, *we've filled them up!* Our bases around the country are all buzzing. Many civilians work for the military too. Total unemployment is very low. The vast majority of the people—the states, their governors, their senators, and their congressmen—all love the economic activity created by the Defense Industrial Cabinet. Anyone who doesn't can leave."

Before the full irony of that statement could hit me, the professor shouted back.

"Sure, after they *file for permission,* and concede all their assets. And *if* they can find a place that will take them, stateless and penniless! During the Vietnam War, we took your draft dodgers when our borders were wide open. Until not so many years ago, other US citizens came north too. But even Canada had to tighten our immigration rules to keep you Americans from swamping us. Remember, we built that fence together!"

I couldn't find much fault with his arguments, no matter how much his tone offended me. But I was losing time and I knew that Ida was waiting for me. I tried to excuse myself again, but he kept it up.

"So Washington printed dollar after dollar to buy the defense industry and put it under military control. Maybe there are some good points to that. But by 2024, your national debt swelled to nearly $30 trillion, your credit rating of A- was in danger, and the US interest cost alone was more than $1.2 trillion a year! Foreign entities would no longer buy your bonds. China demanded Alaska from you to redeem the $8 trillion you owed them! It wasn't so far-fetched since you bought Alaska from Russia in 1867 for what, $9 million? Many around the world thought that was funny, but everyone here was biting their nails. We were concerned that China might be ready for a hot war with you, planning an invasion to capture Alaska—a good old-fashioned war for profit. A war to wrest assets from a debtor who failed to meet their promise to repay!"

"You're right, Professor, those were hairy times," I answered quietly. "Our government had to cancel some of that debt, call it in in some way, if only to reduce the annual interest expense. But you exaggerate! Our debt to China was $4.75 trillion. They *offered $8 trillion* to buy Alaska from us."

I remembered the events well. Yes, all of North America was startled—especially the residents of Alaska. The Treasury Department commissioned appraisals by Goldman, J.P. Morgan, and the rating agencies, S&P and Moody's. The appraised value came between $9 and $10 trillion. Discussions were opened with Canada, which eventually offered $4.5 trillion for a half-ownership interest. Canada was motivated to get involved partly to keep Alaska as a North American-owned territory but also for access to its coastline, fishing grounds, ports, and natural resources. An ownership-management contract was worked out between the US and Canada, and the Alaskan residents overwhelming approved the transaction in a referendum. US citizens of Alaska were granted dual citizenship. The border was opened, and so far, the deal had proved a success.

"With your payment to us for 50 percent of Alaska," I said, "China was repaid and the world was saved from a nuclear war again, at least for a while."

"Why do you say 'nuclear war'? The world expected China to invade, to land troops on the shores of Alaska."

"'Nuclear,' because our only effective response would have been to nuke Beijing to get them to withdraw. We don't have the forces or the installations in Alaska to defend an amphibious invasion or fight a ground war. That would be silly in this day and age and you know it."

I swallowed my coffee and knew I needed to finish quickly. This guy wasn't going to let me off the hook until I did.

"We knew we needed to reduce the debt. A plan was already being considered. So *our* version of a 'bail-in' was adopted in 2023 and implemented over the next three years. In exchange for abolishing the estate tax, Congress imposed what they promised would be a one-time 12½ percent asset tax on every entity in America with net assets in excess of $6 million. The tax was imposed on corporations, individuals, universities, churches, foundations, NGOs, everyone! Every entity that had assets in excess of six million had to pay 12½ percent of the excess to the US Treasury. The NGOs screamed! Subject to the tax were the Catholic Church—all the houses of worship as such; the universities—Harvard, Yale, Duke; the foundations—Getty, Rockefeller, Gates, Buffet, Musk, the Red Cross, AARP, Hadassah, Coca Cola, Apple, Microsoft, and all the rest. Foreigners and foreign corporations with major assets in America—the likes of Honda, Toyota, Mercedes, Kia, Sony, Cameco, Samsung, and Ikea—had to pay too."

MacLeod was nodding. I sped up to cut off his chance to butt in.

"The banks and insurance companies fought the hardest. Modifications to the accounting rules and their obligations to their customers had to be adapted so banks, life and casualty insurance companies, and many other corporations wouldn't immediately fail for lack of capital due to the old formulas. Cash held in offshore deposits was given a tax holiday so it could be repatriated to pay the tax. On the personal side, less than 10 percent of individuals qualified to pay, and for those who did, it was cheaper than what would have been a larger estate tax in the future. Foreign bondholders with no domestic assets weren't touched.

"With all that, the tax turned out not to be as painful to the man on the street as it sounds. The money was due in up to three install-ments. People and entities with bonds generally sent them in to pay their tax, and the government cancelled them. The money sent in by others was used to buy back an equal number of bonds, so that money was simply redistributed in the domestic market. Sure, in the end, over $10 trillion was paid to the government, and the government owed that much less. But a great deal of it was returned to circulation. Because the total only amounted to a bit more than 6 percent of the value of the country, and because participation by individuals was so small, life went on for the vast majority without much interruption."

MacLeod opened his mouth, but again I managed to ward him off.

"These moves cut the accumulated debt and annual interest expense by a bit more than half. By 2034, the US was earning nearly a trillion-dollar annual surplus. We had a manageable debt of less than $15 trillion, a GNP of nearly twice that, full employment with a grow-ing population, and an increasing quality of life for the vast majority of our people."

I stopped to breathe. The professor pounced.

"But the government is now connected to seven out of every ten dollars circulating in your economy. That is majority socialism! And you haven't had an opposition president since the first decade of this century!"

I was becoming drained from this conversation, and Ida was going to be bullshit angry with me.

"Please, Professor. That's not totally accurate. *But I shouldn't have to tell you that it matters little who is in the White House.* Even the president of the United States has little control of the massive bureaucracy that is cemented under him and the consequences his predecessors leave behind. After the electioneering and the talking is over, they all govern the same."

By the mid-2020s, the country was being run by the plurality of moderate Democrats, called Progressives, in coalition with the moderate Republicans. The minority right-wingers (the Tea Party) and the far leftists (the Democrats) had been marginalized. Either a Progressive Democrat or a moderate Republican had been in the White House ever since, with a bipartisan majority cooperating in the Congress. Together they had soundly run the country.

And I needed to get out of there.

"So what was the rationale for taxing the churches, universities, and NGOs?" MacLeod asked.

That one, at least, I could answer quickly.

"Simple—their wealth came from untaxed funds amassed through tax-exempted contributions while they enjoyed the freedom and protection of the United States. They prospered in freedom while the government amassed its unmanageable debt. Assets from persons and businesses had already been taxed, some multiple times. It was appropriate that the wealthy, tax-exempted entities also contribute to the bail-in debt reduction program to save the America in which they prospered."

Just then Anne came out and told me, "You are wanted in the kitchen by your driver."

I welcomed the interruption! The professor could have spent the whole day with me. Don't get me wrong; I liked him. He was forthright and seemed to have no personal agenda to promote. But I was worried about Ida and overdue to be with her. Those few minutes had turned into nearly half an hour.

In the kitchen, a warmly dressed Rollie said, "The Motivators want us to be ready to leave by eight. They can only dispatch one snow sweeper to us. The others are needed elsewhere. I have the FAV warming up, and the fuel cell is charging the backup batteries. The winter axle is engaged, so I'm not expecting any difficulty getting to the border station. We'll be early for your nine o'clock."

"Fine. Please see either of our hosts and settle our accounts with your line of credit. Then pick up our cases at our room. I'm going to Ida, and we'll be ready on time."

"Yes sir," Rollie answered.

When I returned to the table, the Israeli agents had arrived. They were cruising the buffet as they called out a welcome.

"What time can we visit on Sunday?" Colleen whispered to me as I passed her on my way toward the door.

"Ida will call you on your tellie Saturday night," I answered.

She nodded and took a seat.

Before I could get out, the Russian woman entered the dining room accompanied by her driver, bodyguard, assassin, and who knew—maybe paramour? I got my first good look at him. The weapon Rollie had reported was not visible. She stopped next to me, and he behind her.

"Do not attempt contact on Monday," I whispered to Katya. "I will be visiting at my daughter's home the whole day. Make contact on Saturday, and we'll arrange an appointment for mid next week."

She didn't look happy. "I can't stay the whole week. I will call tomorrow, Friday, for an appointment."

I started to reply when all hell broke loose.

# Chapter 21
# The Sheriff
*Jon*

There was loud banging at the main door before it swung open and a tall man in a fur parka, gloves, high boots, and a trooper's hat came in, half-carrying, half-dragging a smaller man, sufficiently dressed, his face caked with dried blood from his forehead to his jaw.

"Help me, please!" the trooper shouted. "Call Frank and Françi to get some blankets. This man is hurt and nearly frozen!"

Françi came running. "Oh! That's Boris Segalov from Sochi. Where is his father-in-law, Nikelovich? These are the guests we were expecting last night!"

"They were in an automobile accident," the sheriff said. "Their car ran off the road and into a tree. With the storm, there was so little traffic it wasn't reported until an hour ago. The other man, the passenger, is dead. I need to call the coroner to pick up the body. He wore no seat belt, and the passive restraints failed to deploy. Blood covers his forehead and face. This guy had his seat belt fastened; his injuries are mostly from the abrasion of the airbag. He needs to be warmed up—might have been trapped in that car for hours. Please get a hot drink ready for when he won't choke on it. Can I put him on the sofa near the fireplace?"

Ida came running to see the commotion. "What happened?"

"We are just learning ourselves," I said, shaken.

I took Ida's hand and we watched together.

Françi's hand was over her mouth, her eyes bulged in shock. Frank took control and helped the sheriff carry the unconscious man to the sofa. They loosened his outerwear, his necktie and exposed him to the radiation of the fire.

In just minutes, the man began to stir. Anne brought a steaming mug of tea with milk and sugar. Françi brought a warm, moist towel and began to carefully dab at the dried blood on his face. The sheriff examined his limbs and all seemed stable. In another minute, they had him sitting up and were carefully giving him the tea to sip. His face was scraped, the deepest abrasions on his forehead.

Françi carefully washed the area as the young man recoiled from her touch. His eyes flashed and darted around, perhaps searching for his companion. Anne brought a first-aid kit and Françi selected an antibiotic salve to smooth on the wounds. With the tea and the salve, he began to relax and breathe more normally.

Rollie appeared and showed me his communicator. It was 7:50—time to dress. He escorted us to the front closet for our coats, boots and gloves. As we walked through the house toward the kitchen entrance, Ida and I called out our good-byes––but no one seemed to notice. All the guests were in the living room watching the proceedings. I heard Katya ask in her Russian accent, "Where did the accident happen?" But I was gone before I heard a response.

The dining room and kitchen were empty as we moved toward the door to the parking area.

"Rollie, did you settle our accounts?" I asked.

"I tried, Mr. K, but was told they had been paid."

Outside, the eight-degree wind-chill beat against our exposed skin. We turned our faces aside. Blowing snow from branches and high drifts swirled through the air. The sun was beginning to shine between the puffy white cotton balls that were drifting quickly across the sky. A path had been shoveled reaching exactly to the FAV and no further. No doubt by Rollie.

He opened the FAV door, the stairs unfolded and lowered to our feet. I helped Ida to the first stair and she scurried in. I followed. A moment later the door closed, and Rollie was set. The interior was as warm as indoors. We loosened our gear. I took my seat and looked out toward the house.

## Chapter 21  The Sheriff

Standing in a shaft of sunlight just outside the kitchen door were Scott Matthew and another man—I presumed his driver. They both wore large, aviator-style mirrored glasses, but I could visualize Matthew's eyes on me. Of course he couldn't see me through the dark-tinted glass, but somehow I knew he was staring at me. It was the first time I had seen him that morning.

A chill ran down my spine as I thought of his words in the hallway. When was I going to be able to tell Ida?

# Chapter 22
# To the Border
*Ida*

Rollie checked in with the Motivators. All business, they held us at the edge of the parking lot until they had a firm satellite fix. Jon commented that their drones probably weren't up yet, maybe due to the storm. In another minute, we were moving forward at a slow speed, north on US Route 3, auto-steering engaged.

According to the maps and catalogues I had picked up at the lodge, US 3 ended at the border where QC 257, Route Saint Hyacinthe, began. Seven hundred feet separated the two country's customs offices. The US station was a class A facility with 24/7 service. But it was on a rural road and was just a low-volume substation of the one at Canaan/Beecher Falls, Vermont. A guidebook said their posted hours could not be relied upon in unusual situations. I guessed the storm might qualify as one of those. All the references in the Cloud advised checking their coordinates for instant local conditions.

"Jon, did you or Rollie check with the station on their current situation?" I asked.

"I didn't, and I don't know about Rollie. But the Motivators wouldn't be clearing us there if service weren't available," Jon answered. "Logical?"

I shrugged.

Eighteen miles and forty minutes later, we could see for ourselves. The roads were quite clear, plowed and swept to the border and across to the Canadian station. There were four cars in the US station lot, engines on, vapor streaming from their pipes. We pulled into the lot and headed for the reserved space for government vehicles, one of the first spaces near the main door next to the handicapped spot. That certainly was an advantage in this weather.

We entered the station and queued up to the service counter behind several others. There was only one officer in the room, a mature woman working the counter. We surmised from the conversation happening around us that there was some hang-up in crossing the border that morning.

A moment later, a male officer came out of an office into the public lobby, pulling his tie tight and adjusting his indoor service cap.

"Mr. and Mrs. Kadish," he said, "you're a few minutes early. Please come into my office where we can sit and I can see what I can do for you."

Jon and I smiled to each other at what first appeared to be exceptional service being provided to us. We entered the standard GI office of the late twentieth century. The officer motioned us to sit in the visitors' chairs, and he took his seat behind the desk.

"As you may have noticed," he started, "we cannot clear any travelers at the present time to enter Canada. Our Canadian counterparts have not shown up as yet, and we reach 'no reply' when we call their command office."

He looked and sounded irritated. "Their normal hours are seven a.m. to midnight. And they do this almost every snowstorm regardless of its severity. It's very annoying to us and to those who choose this station for their transit. Can I get you a coffee or anything else to drink?"

"No, thank you, Officer Simpson, we had fresh brewed in the FAV," Jon answered. Jon must have taken the man's name from the plastic badge on his shirt pocket.

Simpson perked up at the mention of the FAV.

"Those vehicles are really something, aren't they? That's the first of that model to ever visit this station! I'd like to have a look around it later, if you don't mind."

"Help us continue our trip, and anything is possible," Jon replied. "You were telling us about the problem of the Canadian station being closed?"

"Oh . . . yes. We can clear people entering the US since they are not required to report to the Canadian station coming this way. That used to be how we did it too. But not anymore. We need to be sure you have the proper exit permit and are not taking anything out of our country that is not allowed. You understand that don't you, Mr. and Mrs. Kadish?"

That last line and his tone seemed accusatory, but I might have been hypersensitive because of the guilt I was feeling about our plans and the heft of the belt I was wearing under my dress. Exit permits had been standard procedure for the last two decades, ever since the Immigration Bill was passed by Congress and signed by the president. It was just one more major infringement on our freedom instituted through that legislation. But now my thoughts sounded like Jon.

"How did you and your staff get here today, Mr. Simpson, to work your shift?" I asked to keep the dialogue casual.

"We were yesterday afternoon's crew, and we just didn't leave. The woman out front is my wife. I've been the manager of this station for more than ten years. I called off the other shifts due to the weather, and we've manned the station for the past twenty-one hours. My second-in-command will relieve us at noon."

"Staying overnight doesn't sound comfortable," Jon remarked.

"Oh, we don't mind! There was no traffic after dark yesterday, and Sophie and I have comfy sleeping quarters here. If anyone comes the doorbell sounds a loud klaxon. We love these days. The inclement weather and the contiguous shifts earn us extra pay. This is a great billet!" Simpson beamed. "This is a great career—excellent pay, great benefits, and total security. My kids are all in government service, punching their tickets up the ladder just like we did. As long as they follow the rules and don't screw up, they'll enjoy this life too when they reach our age."

*Wow,* I thought. *Does everybody work for the government around here?* I had read somewhere that government jobs accounted for two-thirds of the US economy. Two out of three jobs—two out of every three dollars in the entire economy—were somehow traceable to federal, state, or local governments. When the government started getting its revenue by taking from Peter to give to Paul in the teens and early twenties, it was contentious. But they could always count on the support of Paul, and all the Pauls voted to keep them in power, not wanting to lose their government jobs or subsidies.

Jon once told me that was what led to the Re-Erected Economic Model. The people paying taxes couldn't support the growing number of dependents in the US. Taxpayers became poorer and fewer as many left the country. But with the new plan fully implemented—with certain industries totally under government control—the US was on a positive track again. *That's what Frank was trying to tell us last evening.* Yes, many freedoms had been curtailed, and some of the paying people had slipped into Canada or elsewhere. And here we were, trying to do the same. But the new economic model was proving to be successful, so maybe we are being too hasty in this adventure after all?

"Mr. and Mrs. Kadish," Officer Simpson interrupted my reverie, "please extend your wrists so I can scan your chips."

"We don't have any," Jon and I said simultaneously.

Officer Simpson looked surprised—or maybe shocked would be more accurate. He punched a few strokes on his communicator, no doubt touching our names on his appointment list to display our trip and permit data.

"Okay, then, let's see your National Identity Cards, passports, drivers' licenses, and other photo IDs. And your government employee card, Mr. Kadish."

I went to my handbag and Jon to his envelope. We liberated our cards and put them on the officer's desk. His big hand covered my four and dragged them over a scanner. He picked up one at a time, looked at the card, looked at the screen, and then looked at me, put it down and took the next. He examined my passport last. He nodded and slid them all back toward me as he accessed Jon's in the same way.

He looked at Jon's government employment card first and then went through his cards more quickly.

Simpson raised his eyebrows. "I see you are provisional Level II Security. You *will be required* to get a chip to have that approved. There are Level II Security areas that require a chip for entry. It would be wise for you to get one too, Mrs. Kadish. They make identification much more convenient and accessible. There are places where data from the chip is the only way entry or payment is accepted. More locations, products and services are being converted to this system every day."

He sounded like a commercial. "Your visit to Sherbrooke is approved for up to ninety-one days. Let's see . . . today is February 17. Ninety-one days will be Wednesday, May 18, unless this is a leap year, which it is not!"

Simpson looked up and laughed at his little joke. We didn't. I could see Jon was getting annoyed, impatient; the Canadian station was not open, so what was all this formality about?

"Officer Simpson, if we cannot cross into Canada from here, now, why are you putting us through this examination?" Jon asked.

"Mr. Kadish, please!" Simpson answered tartly. "This is *my* station. *I* decide what's done here! You can decide what's done at *your* station."

Jon looked at me with a scowl and a raised eyebrow. This was a perfect example of government arrogance at the interface that pisses off the public. It was an ongoing complaint—teenage cops, detectives at all levels, just-out-of-college IRS agents, local inspectors, all pushing back at the people who paid their salaries. They were just low-level bureaucrats with formidable local power who got their satisfaction by pushing others who couldn't push back. *Leadership needs to institute training and disciplinary action to straighten these civil servants out,* I thought. *Their compensation and benefits ought to be enough to satisfy them without going on a power trip too!*

And to think Jon was a civil servant too! One at a much higher grade, yet Agent Simpson felt free to talk to him in that tone.

*Jon must be steaming inside. But Simpson has the power here.*

I almost laughed out loud. The Russians, the Israelis, the Chinese, and the Deputy Director of the Defense Industries Cabinet of the United States of America might all want Jon, but he was nothing to this situational bureaucrat. For some reason, it reminded me of the agents who extorted $100 from Ellen to send a gift to her daughter. *That's almost reason enough to want to get out of this country.*

Jon stood up, lifting himself to his full six-foot height. As he slowly walked a circuit around his chair, he removed his communicator from his wrist. When he faced the agent again, he laid the piece down on Simpson's desk. The communicator was a chrome rectangle about an inch wide by an inch-and-a-half tall, with a chrome link bracelet and a snap clasp. The first link in the bracelet had the submariner dolphin emblem.

"Do you recognize this, Officer Simpson?" Jon asked tersely.

"That appears to be a Level III Security communicator," Simpson said politely. His tone was slightly more friendly.

Jon turned it over to reveal an etched seal of some sort on the back of the case. I couldn't remember ever seeing or noticing it in the past. At my angle, I could only see that something was there.

"Do you recognize this badge, Officer Simpson?"

"Yes, sir," he answered crisply.

"Do I have the authority to scan your chip if I so desire?"

"Yes, sir," he answered again.

"Would you present your chip for scanning if I so ordered you?"

"Yes sir," crisply again.

"Well, I don't think that is necessary at this time, do you?"

"No, sir. Please, I'm sorry, sir. I *am* trying to help you."

Jon picked up his communicator and replaced it on his wrist. He took a step back and sat down once again.

I was dumbfounded. What was that engraving on the back? I marveled. Jon had called it a "badge." *Could he arrest a driver for speeding?* I wondered, smiling inside.

"Please continue, Officer Simpson," Jon said in a terse tone.

"Thank you, sir. Now, do you have any idea when you plan to return and through which checkpoint? It would be helpful to have that in the record."

"Well, my wife will be staying at least a month, but I intend to return sooner."

Simpson paused, looked at his terminal again, and grimaced.

"Sir . . . that's not possible under the permit you have, sir," Simpson said quietly. "Both of you are listed on this single permit, so you must cross the border together each time—going and returning. If you wanted to return independently, you should have filed for individual permits."

"Ooooh . . ." Jon moaned quietly at this latest snag.

"Is there any way we can adjust that now?" I asked.

"No, Mrs. Kadish, not here. That can't be done at any crossing station. It needs to be done at a State Department or Homeland Security office, either in your region, which is Boston, or in Washington. My supervisor is in the Canaan/Beecher Falls office, and I know he is unable to change permits. I'm sorry. Can you adjust your plans to cross and return together?"

"Can we cross together today? Here?" Jon fought to keep his tone even. "What else can you advise regarding future travel?"

As Jon and Simpson discussed a variety of possibilities—mostly the greater restraints that would come on Jon with the Level II clearance—I slumped in my chair, my head hanging, my chin to my neck, eyes closed. It was almost ten o'clock.

"Ida, are you okay?" Jon asked. "Have you communicated with Rachel this morning?"

"Oh my God." I snapped alert. "There was no answer when I tried her at 7:30, so I left a message. Since then it's totally slipped my mind—what with the breakfast interruptions and the sheriff's arrival."

I took a zipped leather case from my pocketbook, opened it, and punched a single key on my communicator. A message from Rachel appeared on the screen.

# Chapter 22 To the Border

*Sent 7:45 AM. Chartierville station closed all day today. Can you transfer to Beecher Falls Station? I can be there for 9:30.*

I quickly showed the message to Jon. He nodded his understanding.

"Officer Simpson, can we cross today via Vermont?" Jon asked.

"I'll call my boss at Beecher Falls to see what I can find out . . . maybe arrange for you."

Simpson punched a button. "I have a couple in the newest FAV here, sir, Level II Security," he said, emphasizing our obvious status. "They have an exit permit to visit a daughter and grandchildren in Sherbrooke. I'm passing the file to you."

He hit a button, the message was sent, and the call was transferred to his ear receiver. We were cut out of the call. There was silence as he listened.

"Yes, sir; Kadish, two souls. That's right, sir."

There was a long pause.

Simpson spoke again. "No vehicle entering. Daughter in Sherbrooke will collect them on the Canadian side. Yes, the FAV will take them to the Canadian station and return. You know our problem here—no Canadian office. Sure, I'll ask them. Please stand by, sir."

Simpson lifted his face toward us and said, "The station manager can take you at five this afternoon. Okay?"

Jon touched my arm. "Ida, ask Rachel if she can pick us up then."

In another few minutes the arrangement was confirmed, and we were leaving Officer Simpson's office, accompanied by the man himself.

"Can I see the FAV now?" he asked, like a little boy wanting to see our electric trains.

"Sure, sure. Walk us out and take a look inside," Jon answered.

After more than hour, Rollie looked happy to see us. He activated the stair door, and Simpson watched in awe as the steps lowered. Jon motioned him up the stairs and followed him up, me right behind them. Inside, Simpson sat looking forward for a moment, then turned to sit looking backwards. He peered all around, trying to take in every detail.

I asked him how he liked his coffee, and he didn't know how to answer.

"Vermont Blend?" I suggested, and he nodded an emphatic yes.

"Milk, cream, sugar or sweetener?" He answered with his choices. I selected the pod and the appropriate buttons on the maker in the door, punched the to-go button, and watched as the coffee, cream, and sweetener poured into a plastic mug imprinted with the FAV number and logo, along with the date and time.

I handed the steaming mug to our eager guest. "Here, Officer Simpson, your souvenir of our visit and reminder of this storm. Thank you for your help."

"Thank you too, Mrs. Kadish! I wish you an enjoyable visit with your family."

He exited, and Jon motioned to Rollie to close the door. Alone again, we sighed and shook our heads. By intercom, Rollie asked, "Where to?"

"Back to the lodge for now," Jon answered. "Please call ahead and tell them we're coming. We have a new appointment at the Beecher Falls station at five o'clock this afternoon."

It was 10:20.

We didn't talk on the drive back to the lodge. I was still smiling inside, impressed and curious about the power of that seal or whatever it was on the back of Jon's communicator.

# Chapter 23
# Return to the Lodge
*Ida*

The sunshine gleamed off the trees. Bowed evergreens sprung up as snow slid from their branches and splashed on the wet road. Experienced New Hampshire woodsmen with their huge equipment had expertly removed the snow. The pavement was wet, slick, and shining. The snow, banked on the shoulders, made the road look like a bobsled run.

As we approached the lodge, Rollie had to wait until a large, unusual truck pulled out of the driveway heading south. We were close to it, but it was hard to define against the winter backdrop.

"What was that?" I asked Jon.

"Never saw anything like it. Was it here this morning when we left?"

Rollie pulled up to the main entrance and we entered the front door as we had yesterday. By the time we stashed all our gear in the closet, François and Françi were there to greet us. It was 11:00.

"Welcome back!" Françi said cheerfully. "We are pleased to be of service to you again, so soon."

"We have a new appointment at the Beecher Falls Station at five, so we'd like to relax here and perhaps use our room again for a few hours," I said. "Will that be okay?"

"Oh, certainly, certainly Mrs. Kadish," Françi said in her lilting accent.

"My husband will pay any additional charge. Do not hesitate to present him a bill."

Françi laughed. "Do not worry about such matters, Mrs. Kadish." She dropped her voice to a whisper. "Your charges here are covered. Come into the dining room. Frank has made Belgian chocolate *a la* Bernardin. It will definitely warm you up."

"Jon, I'm going with Françi to the dining room for a bit, okay?"

144

"Sure," he answered.

Then Frank leaned toward him and said something quietly.

"I'm going to the kitchen for some hot chocolate with Frank," Jon said––and I nodded.

Françi and I sat in the dining room. Anne served us mugs of hot chocolate and a selection of cookies and baked goods. We talked briefly about the morning excitement.

"Are all your overnight guests gone now?" I asked.

"Oh, Mr. Matthew left just a few minutes ago. Only the professeur and his mate are still here. They may stay another night."

*Oh brother... I hope Jon doesn't run into him...*

I took a sip of Frank's latest masterpiece. "This hot chocolate is delicious. Is the chocolate or the liqueur from Belgium?" I asked.

"The liqueurs are Bailey's Irish and amaretto. The chocolate is from Belgium, sent by my son from Antwerp where he lives now. He sent a case of tins for Christmas that will last until May."

We chuckled, took sips and selected a sweet cake for a bite.

"How old is your son?" I asked.

"Almost twenty-nine . . . born only five months after we were married, you see."

"But your marriage has lasted. That's good!"

"Oh, yes. François and I were meant for each other. He loves to cook and I love to manage, and with our positions in government service we are financially secure. Every day is an adventure. We were meant to do this together."

I smiled. *How would it have been if Jon worked with me, being together almost every minute of the day? I don't think we would have lasted. In our own way, we both like to cook!*

"What does your son do in Belgium?"

"It's a bit of a story. Do you have a few minutes?"

"Sure, sure. What else do I have?" I shrugged my shoulders. Besides, I really did enjoy Françi's company.

145

"Rather than wait to be drafted ten years ago, Yves enlisted in the Marines, a four-year commitment. After those four years––without discussing it with his father or me, not a single peep mind you––he enlisted in *the French Foreign Legion!* Can you imagine our shock? That's a grueling service! They ask few questions of the volunteers and exact harsh discipline and loyalty."

"How long was that for?" I asked.

"That was a five-year commitment! When I asked him why the FFL, he answered, 'Mom, you are from France, we are French. So what's the difference if I am a mercenary for the United States or for France? The US military is the largest, best-equipped mercenary force in the world. But they do no fighting. It's practice, train, and wait. It was monotonous and boring. And . . . he said, 'the food is better here!'"

She shook her head.

"That is my François's son! He made the mark, passed the physical and mental tests and survived basic training. He wrote in a letter that he loved the military life there, the harsh training, the mixed martial fighting, pushing himself beyond what he believed was his limit. He loved the adventure and the danger. We have no idea where or how he came to this. He is not allowed to tell much about his life or the service. But he said their food is the best of any military in the world. When I asked him why, he said, '*That is no secret!* We are told we eat well morning, noon and night, because a Legionnaire never knows which meal will be his last!'"

"Ohhh . . . that can't be very comforting for a mother!"

"No, of course not. We know from some postmarks he was in Mali, the South Sudan, Niger, and other places. For the last year of his service, he was with a training brigade in South Africa."

"So how did that lead to Belgium today?" I asked, intrigued by the tale. "What's he doing now?"

"Oh . . . it's the same old story. He met a girl in South Africa, a Belgian and, as fate would have it, Jewish. When his enlistment was over he followed her to Antwerp. He took a job as a security guard and a currier for a Hasidic family in the diamond business. I don't know if or how the Jewish girl fits into his work, …if at all?" Françi shrugged her shoulders. "It's a good-sized, stable company, he says. They deal in raw diamonds from South Africa. That trade still deals to some degree with cash or gold. Sometimes he travels alone to deliver payments and pick up stones. Other times he accompanies the owners to protect them and handle their needs. He's been with them less than a year, but he says he likes it and they treat and pay him well. Strange people in many ways for modern times, but they can be honest and good to work for. So he tells me."

"Does he ever go to Tel Aviv?" I asked.

"He has never said, but we don't talk too often and––never about his work. He only talks on communicators in cryptic code. He won't let himself be monitored. What I know is from his visit last November for Thanksgiving. Why Tel Aviv?"

"Our son, Eric, who is older than your boy, is a partner in a diamond business in Israel. I guess they would have no reason to know one another. My son deals in cut and polished stones—he works with design houses that sell to jewelers. There are many players and steps all over the world from the mines to the finger."

We both smiled. Françi rang the table bell. Anne scurried into the room.

"Please bring us another mug of chocolate," Françi ordered.

When Anne left, I changed the subject—I felt like this woman and I had become friends, and welcomed the chance to talk to her about our situation.

"So you know all of our business and of these foreigners chasing us," I said.

"Yes, yes, it is funny, no?" Françi replied.

"No, no! It is *not* funny at all. Jon is committed to visit our daughter and her family for this weekend, but now he needs to be in his office on Tuesday morning for an interview. I planned to stay several weeks or more in Sherbrooke. The manager of the customs station told us that because we are listed on a single permit, we have to enter and leave Canada together. He's afraid that if we both return for Tuesday or don't cross into Canada at all, we might not get another exit permit of this sort again. Jon's up for a promotion, you see, and Level II Security will eliminate most of the world for us to visit. The rest will only be with guarded, supervised groups for mission-specific purposes. We'll be under guard—to protect him, to thwart any attempt by foreigners to lure Jon away or any attempt by us to run away on our own. It's so confusing! All our plans seemed to be flawed in some way. It's a real mess."

I started to shake, and a few tears came to my eyes again. I drank a few more sips of the chocolate but then asked if I could have a glass of water. A ring of the bell and the water was at the table.

I took a long drink, then asked, "May I lay down in our room for an hour or so? Maybe I need some rest."

Françi was all sympathy. "Sure, Mrs. Kadish, at once. I'll get the key and see you there. You have nothing but your handbag? Shall I get you and your husband fresh terry robes?"

I nodded a big yes. She grabbed the robes and met me in the hall to let me into the room.

"When I return, I will tell your husband that you are resting."

"Good Françi, but please don't tell him about my sudden *mal-de-mer.*"

"Of course not," she answered as she closed the door.

The room had already been prepared for the next guest. I washed and changed into the robe. I pulled back the bedclothes and was about to lie down when I thought to check my communicator. Seating myself on the edge of the bed, I saw another message from Rachel.

> *Because of the weather and by five it will be dark, Jacque has arranged a driver to pick you up. He is a young man about*

148

*thirty, not short, not tall, a Canadian mustache. He will be wearing a bright red scarf and beret. I know you will easily find each other. He will have the keys and take you directly to your apartment. He will also pick you up tomorrow at a half after noon to bring you here. I'll have your favorite lunch. Jacque will come home and we'll be together.*

I punched the feather pillow again to make a place for my head. As I twisted to lie down, I noticed the time on the nightstand clock. It was 11:35.

# Chapter 24
# Belgian Chocolate a la Bernardin

*Jon*

Frank and I went through the dining room into the kitchen. He motioned me to the dining alcove, the round table against a semicircular bench seat with chairs on the open side where he'd revealed his true identity the night before. I slid into the bench and Frank sat in the chair next to me. A tantalizing aroma of chocolate and fresh baked cookies, vanilla, cinnamon, and something else I couldn't name, filled the air.

"Frank, I smell chocolate, vanilla, cinnamon, and . . . something else. But what is it?"

"You would have made a good cook, Mr. K. It is clove. I have some ginger, anise, and clove cookies baking right now. I use ginger, anise extract, and ground cloves for a mild, spicy flavor. You might try one after they cool."

He poured us mugs of hot chocolate and arranged a small plate of baked goods. I took a sip. The flavor was a bouquet of chocolate, coffee, and liqueur. "Beautiful," I remarked.

We lifted our mugs and saluted each other.

"What happened with the injured Russian fellow?" I asked. "What a terrible thing to have occur."

Frank nodded soberly. "It was a terrible night, especially for drivers who are not familiar with our conditions. I'm sure it wasn't the only accident, though we hope the only fatality. There were surely other fender-benders. For folks around here, they just exchange information and go on their way."

"And your guest?"

"The sheriff called the volunteer ambulance to take young Segalov to the emergency center. Then he returned to the scene to deal with the dead man, Viktor Nikelovich, and to study the situation. He needs

150

to determine the probable cause. His only man on duty was standing watch at the accident site and taking photos. To estimate the time of the accident, the coroner needs the body temperature, the time that temperature was taken, and the body weight. And the sheriff needs to get the coroner to pick up the corpse. He'll need to get a judge's permission today to order an autopsy to be done this weekend. A mere formality if he can find a judge. But it's Thursday of a holiday weekend and the day after a major storm . . . so we'll see what he can do."

"Had they been guests here previously?"

"Yes. Nikelovich and his wife stayed here once when heading to Boston from Canada, four or five years ago. About a month ago, he e-mailed and sent money for his stay together with his son-in-law."

"Oh…I said and nodded.

"Françi asked the sheriff to stop back to tell us what he learns. She promised him our Belgian chocolate, so I'm sure he'll come. What time do you have to be at Beecher Falls?"

"Five o'clock. It's dark by then. What time should we leave here?"

"Four will give you plenty of time. Will your daughter pick you up?

"Yes, I'm sure. Ida is in contact with her."

After a sip of chocolate, I continued, "Did you say the injured man's name is Segalov—Boris Segalov? I met a Russian engineer named Sergei Segalov some years ago. Perhaps they're related. Or is Segalov a common name in Russia?"

"I don't know." Frank shrugged.


"What do you know about your guest Mr. Matthew?" I asked.

"If you mean aside from him being clandestine and mysterious, then the answer is little. His charges were prepaid from a foreign account. He just left in that Canadian-military style MTV in winter camouflage. Did you see it in the parking lot this morning?"

I shook my head in wonderment.

Frank continued. "Every time he entered his room, you know, he activated a microwave frequency neutralizer. It could sense our variable listening frequency and instantly adjust to generate a canceling signal. We couldn't even hear his shower running—very clever and very mysterious. The same is true about his driver. Our people are trying to do identity searches using their facial features, but so far they've come up empty. We are trying to separate samples of their DNA from the towels, pillowcases, coffee cups, and utensils that they used. I doubt we'll be successful. Samples need to be pure and uncontaminated. Why are you asking? Did he say something to you?"

"No, no. He didn't say a word to me," I lied. "I thought he was pretty smart with the professor last night. And I thought I saw him staring at me a few times too. And I didn't see that vehicle in the lot this morning. You say it was there? Has he ever been here before?"

"Yes, once about a year and a half ago. He had the same driver and a third companion, a man of his own age. The driver stayed in the old wing, like last night. Matthew demanded the best room in the house, and for the third man, he insisted on the room across the hall from him. When they returned from dinner in the village, Mr. Matthew brought in a woman with whom he spent some of the night. Her face was lowered toward the floor—I looked at the hallway surveillance video the next morning to see if she was one of our habitual ladies of the night. But this woman seemed to be a bit older than the usual ones. The angle and definition on the video was poor. I remember thinking she was no one we knew. Sometime during the night she switched to the other man's room for an hour or so. You see what I mean? Mysterious *oui?* At five in the morning, they all left. The men returned just before seven, two hours later. We were already serving breakfast, but they went directly to their rooms and didn't come for breakfast until ten. On that day they were the last to leave."

"What is that vehicle called that they're driving?" I asked.

"It's a CMMATTV—a Canadian Military Medium All-Terrain Tactical Vehicle––in winter camouflage. It's a very advanced machine for the Canadians—four axles. It was parked along the edge of the lot against the wooded area overnight. I'm not surprised you didn't see it. The square design and variable paint program make it virtually invisible against that backdrop in this weather. The Double-MATV, as it's usually called, has been in service just about three years."

Now I was fascinated. *Maybe the exterior of that vehicle had a graphene coating and various external sensors, communicating with a design algorithm that could alter the vehicle's appearance.*

Since Frank didn't seem to mind my prying, I kept asking questions.

"Did Matthew have a Double-MATV last time he was here? Did anything else unusual happen that night?"

"I don't remember what they were driving. It was May or June, the season was different. I could check the exact date if you wish."

"Not yet. No reason as of now. Did anything different or unusual happen on that night or day?"

"Oh, yes! We will never forget. At an inn by the first lake, twelve miles to the south, a guest couple, foreigners, disappeared during the night. They were never found, and it remains a mystery to this day. I remember that they were Russian, but not much more. The story never hit the mass media—CNN had long been in FCC control at that point, and the others were probably never told about it. But the *Independent New Hampshire Press* wrote it up for a few days in the local Patch, and *The Independent Thunder Cloud* ran a short story for just a day. I'll try to find them for you. I know I printed and kept them, but I'm not sure which secret hiding place I used so I would never lose them. You know how that goes!"

We laughed. Frank stood to refill our mugs, and I took another cookie. He checked the oven for the ginger-clove batch, shut it off, and removed the cookie sheet with an insulated glove and put it on top of the oven.

"If you wish, you can try one in fifteen or twenty minutes," he said.

Françi came by and told me Ida had retired to our room. She gave me a key. I thanked her. The clock read 11:36.

As Françi disappeared, I went back to the topic at hand.

"So, could Matthew and his men be Canadian military? Can civilians get Double-MATVs? Might Matthew and his men have been involved with the disappearance of those guests from the other inn? Do you have any surveillance footage to perhaps identify the third man—and footage from the parking lot to see the vehicle on that visit?"

"Mr. K, please!" Frank said with a smile. *"I am the agent here!* I'm supposed to ask the questions." He chuckled. "Your questions are coming too fast. I don't know the answers. Give me some time and let me see what I can find."

My heart was beginning to palpitate, and my mind was cycling like the flashing of a strobe through each of my issues, not in any particular order. I knew what I needed.

"I have another major issue to ask you about, but I need a bathroom at this moment."

He pointed the way to a door across the kitchen. Thank goodness. What I needed was privacy to take my trank!

In the bathroom, I fumbled for the gold mezuzah around my neck. It was tucked underneath my sweater, shirt, and undershirt. Ida bought it for me more than thirty years ago in the Arab market of Old Jerusalem. It was a gold cylinder about three to four mm in diameter, with a handwritten parchment inside, and end caps and a little window near the top to see the scroll. At the sub-base, I had the Instrument Machine Shop remove the lower cap and retool it as a screw-on closure. By folding the little parchment and rolling it as tightly as possible then pushing it to the top of the cylinder with a Q-tip, it took only half the space in the cylinder.

I unscrewed the end cap, and five little yellow pills spilled into my palm. When had I taken one from here last? *Yes, in the FAV yesterday.* It held six.

I kept one and slid the others back into the cylinder and replaced the cap. I cupped a bit of water in my hand, popped the pill and slurped the water. When I needed a *yellow*, they had to be handy.

I returned to the table and Frank offered me a fresh cookie. I broke it in half and looked at it. The color was sort of yellow with tiny brown spots, like pepper in the batter. I took a nibble.

"Nice! Refreshing," I said, tilting my head. "I expected it to be hotter, spicier, but it's not. Very good!"

"I'm happy you like it. It changes from time to time. I don't measure when I cook or bake."

"A true artist. Now, I need to discuss a new and very troubling development with you. Maybe you can suggest a solution for Ida and me."

He looked interested. "Ask, and I'll try."

"At the border this morning, we learned that Ida and I are listed on the same exit permit, so we are required to cross and return together. You know I have to be at my office on Tuesday, and Ida was planning to stay a month or more. The border agent said only Homeland Security or the State Department at their offices in Boston or Washington can change the permit. He also said that because of my promotion to Level II, this probably would be the last unescorted international travel that I will be able to get, even to visit my daughter there in Sherbrooke. Does this sound right to you?"

Frank waved a cookie in the air. "Absolutely correct! According to the law, what he told you is so. You cannot postpone Tuesday's meeting or I will have to detain you. If Ida returns with you for Tuesday, *you* will probably not be able to visit Canada again––unescorted. Ida would be allowed individual travel, or with another person––but not with you. But having an escort, a bodyguard so to speak, will only be a minor inconvenience."

*Maybe yes, or maybe no*, I thought.

"Your crossing appointment is at five o'clock tonight, oui?"

I nodded in the affirmative.

"Monsieur, join your wife to rest, and let me think about these things. I will prepare a lunch for you. At what time would it be convenient? It is near noon now, perhaps at two or two-thirty? Or later if you like?"

"Let's say two-thirty. Please send someone to knock on our door. And be sure to get me if the sheriff returns."

"Oui, oui, Monsieur."

# Chapter 25
# To the Vermont Border
*Jon*

Ida was waiting for me when I came into the room. She was ready to jump all over me––linguistically speaking.

"Jonathon Kadish! What was that magic you pulled at the border station? I never saw that . . .uh, ...thing, engraved on your communicator. I was mentally berating Simpson as an arrogant, small-minded bureaucrat when you got up, walked around your chair, and pulled that bit. That was great! But explain it to me. What is that engraving on your communicator?"

I smiled. "Maybe you forgot and fortunately he didn't examine it closely. When I retired and entered the active navy reserve, I was a standby skipper or executive officer qualified to be called up to go to sea. But I needed an emergency shore job too. So I volunteered for the military police and the National Security Force. They were co-programs of Defense and Homeland Security. On my two weeks annual duty–– remember?––I went to Quantico, Virginia for police training. I was given a colonel rating as a navy commander and a gold badge that I could wear on my uniform. When I made Level III Security, it was automatically engraved on the back of my communicator so it would be available when I was not in uniform. If Simpson had looked closely, he would have seen that it expired eleven years ago when I turned sixty!"

"Wow, Jon! Go, guy! That was quick thinking!" Ida shook her head, beaming. "Am I proud of you! Now lie down and have a rest. Who knows what we will face at the Vermont station?"

\*\*\*

It was after four, darkness had fallen. Ida and I were again in the FAV, this time on our way to Beecher Falls, Vermont. The station parking lot was busy with cars and people rushing around in the cold and the dark. Again we pulled to the front and parked in a government space. An inspector met us at the curb, greeted us by name and ushered us directly into an interview room, bypassing a walk-thru screener chamber. I sighed a breath of relief as we bypassed that test.

The station was busy, clearing people going in both directions. We were directed to a couple's interview room. Seated behind separate desks were male and female officers. Dressing booths with ringed curtains were stationed beside them. Ida was directed to sit in front of the woman and I before the man. Looking at the ringed curtains, a shudder went through me as I felt the weight of the money belt around my middle. I wondered if Ida was terrified at that moment.

The officer held out his hand and I handed him my envelope of our identification. He handed it back after a single glance at its contents. He began to punch at his touchboard as he looked at his screen. I looked toward Ida, who was talking to the woman behind the desk. They both had muted smiles on their faces.

The officer punched in data, and a paper emerged out a circular scanner/printer slot with a red, white, and blue seal and the word *APPROVED* printed diagonally across it, with the date, time and station in tiny type across the bottom.

"This is for the Canadian inspector on the other side," he said. "They still like paper. That's all there is to it for you and the Mrs. You are all set, Colonel Kadish. Your driver may proceed to take you to the Canadian station, where they are expecting you. Thank you for your patience."

He came out from behind the desk and ushered us to the door.

\*\*\*

In another five minutes, we were cleared through Canadian customs, had found the red scarf and beret, and were on our way to Sherbrooke.

It was not yet 5:15. The dramatic improvement in service certainly wasn't random, could not have been. Simpson must have reported to his superior about the badge, and this agent didn't even ask to see it. He addressed me as "colonel." It hadn't solved any of our major issues, but it certainly greased us through the border.

In the back of the car, Ida told me, "The woman agent whispered to me that we would be on our way in only a minute. She asked, 'How is it riding in the FAV?' I told her 'Great!' She gave me a big smile and a nod."

Forty-five minutes later, we were in our apartment on the second floor of a three-story vintage house. We collapsed in old easy chairs in the parlor. Our eyes met, and we each searched for the sanity of our situation in the eyes of the other.

"Now explain to me what you are doing Monday?" Ida said.

"Man overboard!" I shouted as I pointed to the ceiling.

Ida picked the hint up in an instant. "The news!" she said.

"Sure." I went to the television—yes, they were still using television sets in Quebec—and I tuned to a news broadcast in French. With the volume high, we moved to the sofa facing the screen.

"Do you really think we are being monitored here?" Ida asked.

"I'm sure of it, and I'll tell you why in a minute. Now what were you starting to say?"

"Explain to me what you're doing Monday. I listened to what Frank explained to you, but I want to hear what you heard. Maybe I didn't get it right."

"Okay, as I understand it, four Quebecois coyotes—you know, illegal border crossing guides under contract with Frank—are going to pick me up here Monday morning and escort me through the backcountry, over the border and back to the lodge. Rollie will be waiting to take me to Connecticut. The coyotes will have clothes and equipment for me and will be with me all the way, door to door."

The plan sounded a little crazy, but I didn't have any reason to think it wouldn't work.

"Rollie will take me directly to Groton, where I'll stay at the Thames Inn. When I'm settled, he'll return to Norwich and return the FAV to Hartford on Tuesday. I'll rent a car, a BUV from Enterprise, at the inn and go to the office for my appointments on Tuesday—all of them, with Mickey, the FBI lady, and General Catern, *if he really shows up.* I'll ask Mickey for a two-week leave of absence. Frank said he'd try to get it approved in advance. Then I'll drive the rental car myself back to Pittsburg to the lodge for Tuesday night. Wednesday morning I'm to be returned here by another group of coyotes on Frank's payroll."

"I wish you didn't have to go," Ida said feebly, shaking her head. "This is all so complicated."

I wasn't surprised she felt that way, but I was hoping to get some answers out of it.

"While in Groton, I'll try to find out why the Israelis and the Russians want me. Maybe Mickey knows what I have that they think is so valuable."

I still hadn't had the quiet opportunity to tell her about Scott Matthew.

"Are you sure you can do all that—so much mental and physical activity in such a short time? Do you have enough yellow pills to see you through?"

The sarcasm in Ida's voice came through despite the news blaring in the background.

"You haven't been a navy officer for three decades."

"C'mon, Ida, don't talk like that," I said quietly. "According to Frank, the toughest parts will be the cross-country treks in each direction—about twelve miles each way, roughly four hours. But each will come after a night of sleep. The coyotes will have the necessary gear for me. I'm not worried about it. I'll be fresh Monday morning, and after the first trek, I can sleep in the FAV. The long drive to Pittsburg the next afternoon might be the most difficult part. I'll be alone and more than half the drive will be after dark. But the weather looks to be passive and I'll stop frequently to rest if necessary."

Ida leaned back and felt her forehead.

"Are you all right?" I asked. "Why are you touching your forehead?"

"No reason. Just so many new obstacles, things we never considered, never even thought of considering. Boy, were we naive or what?"

It was time to tell her.

"Ida, that's only the half of it. There's another element I have to tell you about."

I related the incident with Scott Matthew outside our bedroom door at the lodge in painstaking detail. I told her about the trillionaire, the security detail, the visit to Calgary by private jet, the "offer not to be refused."

"It's this group that's definitely monitoring us here—'providing us security,' according to Matthew. If they're here, maybe the others are too."

Ida was aghast. I told her what Frank had said about Matthew's vehicle, his previous visit and the disappearance of a Russian couple.

"What did Frank say about the message from Scott and what it might be about?" she asked.

"Ida, *I never told Frank about that!* When I asked what he knew about Scott, he asked me what he had said to me—and I told him we didn't speak. *I lied.*"

She wrinkled her forehead at me. "Why didn't you tell him?"

"He knows too much already—about the Israelis, the Russians, and our personal situation. I like Frank but he's not a friend; he's a federal agent. I'm not ready to cave into their plans and just cancel ours. I'm going to let him use me to check out what he thinks he knows––and we'll check out what he doesn't know. Get it?"

"Yes, yes." she answered. "I'll play along as long as it doesn't get dangerous."

*Maybe it already is!* I thought.

"Don't worry, Ida, I'll be able to manage anything that comes along. It's nearly seven. Let's see what there is to eat in this house."

"Not so fast, Jon, one more thing. You and Frank were huddled in a corner for fifteen minutes after lunch. I had the idea you were talking about the accident and the sheriff."

"Yes, that too. Frank dug up a little more information about our earlier chat. The Russian couple he said went missing? They were Dr. and Mrs. Sergei Segalov—Boris's parents. Sergei was a top engineer for Sevmash Shipbuilders, the only producer of nuclear submarines for Russia, in the city of Severodvinsk on the White Sea. Their family didn't even know that they were abroad. There was no evidence of foul play, so it's still just an open missing persons case. Frank said he would check into its current status and try to learn more details."

"What's the connection with to Nikelovich?" Ida asked.

"A family one. Boris Segalov is married to the Nikelovich's daughter. Boris says about a month ago, his mother Ivanica, contacted Viktor, his father-in-law and asked him to meet her this weekend in Pittsburg."

"But she wasn't at the lodge?"

"No, that's part of the mystery."

"Is that it? Is there any more?" Ida asked.

"Boris's mother said she wanted to give Nikelovich money to deposit for her in Cyprus and she would tell him where and on what Sergei was working.

"Oh . . . and one more thing. I met his father, Sergei Segalov, about fifteen years ago at a nuclear symposium at the Cern Nuclear Collider in Switzerland, after NATO split up. The topic was packaged nuclear reactors for ship propulsion. Most of EATO was there, plus us from North America, Russia, India, China, and the rest of the usual suspects. Segalov was assigned to the Russian Yasen Class boats, and I was on our smaller Eel Class at the time. We did much the same kind of work. We lunched privately and had a wide ranging discussion, as best we could—me with the little Russian I know and he with his broken English. We laughed and got along well. We were colleagues in a strange way––and I liked him. I think he liked me too. But we never communicated again after that."

The sheriff hadn't returned by the time we left the lodge, but he had called Frank and said the crash was an unusual accident—one that didn't look like an accident at all.

"Frank said he would fill me in when I get there on Monday. C'mon now, let's see what there's to eat and then relax. I'm getting hungry."

We pieced together a meal with food Rachel had stocked in the refrigerator and pantry. It was a fun break, Ida and I working together in the kitchen, both cooking like in the early years of our marriage. It was not the meal at the lodge last night, but we enjoyed it nevertheless.

***

*Brrring . . . brrring . . .*

Somewhere a phone was ringing, sounding like an old telephone. Ida and I ran around the flat trying to find the source. It was 9:00 p.m. and we had been sitting in the dinette having tea and a cake. The ringing kept going. Finally Ida got to the bedroom where the sound seemed to be shouting, "Pick me up already, for God's sake!" A small package was rattling and ringing in her purse.

"Mrs. Kadish," an Israeli accented male voice said when she picked it up, "Is this you?"

We put our head's together so we both could listen.

"Yes, this is me," she answered.

"The agent who gave you this tellie instructed me to communicate with you. You are going somewhere tomorrow, yes?"

"Yes, we are to be picked up by a driver at half after noon," Ida said.

"You are being watched. Do not lead them to any place they do not know. Do you understand me?"

"How do you know we're being watched?" she asked.

"Because I am watching them watching you!"

"Are *they* the Russians?" she asked, turning momentarily to make eye contact with me.

"No. It is someone else we don't know. But the Russians are here too. We know of your daughter and her family. They have been to Israel many times to visit your son and do business. We know where they live and where they move. Maybe these others don't, and it would be better not to lead them to them. You know who 'them' is?"

"Yes, yes! But their driver is to take us to their home for lunch tomorrow," Ida said.

"Do not go there directly! You could put your children in danger. Make another plan. Go to their synagogue and meet them there. You can lose your tails by going through the synagogue. Do you know where it is?"

"The address? No. We were only there once, a few years ago on our last visit."

"We will get all the information and take you. At the end of your visit, you must leave in the same way. Do not let your children take you back to the flat or use their driver. Do nothing that can connect you to them. We are trying to learn who these strangers are. At noon, exactly noon tomorrow, call a taxi for the listeners to hear and we will call one or two also. When the taxis arrive they'll cause a distraction in front, fighting over who gets the fare. At the same time, we will pick you up in the back of your apartment building. Go down the back staircase and a truck will be waiting. We will tell your daughter of this change in plans."

I wanted to step away but Ida shook her head and I leaned back in again.

The voice continued. "Now, about meeting on Sunday, a diplomat is coming to talk to you but cannot come to your flat. Call Saturday night to get detailed instructions. Stay inside during the night. But do not worry if you want to walk during the day, we are protecting you."

The phone went quiet. I looked at Ida and she at me. We hunched our shoulders. I lowered the sound on the TV.

"I think we should leave this on all night in case we talk in our sleep."

That night Ida had her own pillow. She finally slept well.

# Chapter 26
# Russia Comes Knocking

*Jon*

Heavy footsteps tramped up the stairs, followed by rapid banging on the door.

Ida and I were at the kitchen table having our morning coffee and toast. She in her robe, I in sweats and slippers. It was Friday, 8:00 a.m. We'd been up about an hour in what we expected to be a quiet day. Ida rushed to the bedroom. From behind the cracked door, she could see and hear what was coming. I approached the door, wishing for the first time I had my Beretta in my waistband.

"Who's there?" I called out. "What do you want?"

I put my ear to the door, hoping to hear something from the other side. More rapid knocks startled me. I almost fell over.

"Who is there?" I shouted. "What do you want?"

"It is Katya, Mr. Kadish, Ambassador Katya Rocinkova. You haven't forgotten me so soon? We have come to talk to you."

Irritation rose in me. "Katya? Why have you come here? I asked you to call." I said harshly.

"Yes, and I told you I couldn't stay all week and asked you about today."

"Yes, I remember. Didn't we agree you were to *call* today to arrange an appointment?"

*"I am calling for an appointment right now!"*

Ida and I locked eyes. I tipped my head, a hand opened to question her. She frowned and nodded.

I yelled through the door, "You'll have to wait a minute!"

Ida threw on slacks, a sweater and a pair of slip-on shoes. When she came out of the bedroom, I opened the door.

166

On the top step was Katya. One step below stood another woman, and then the driver, the assassin, waited a few more steps down. They were dressed for the weather as in Moscow in winter. I took their outerwear from them and invited them into the living room. The women removed their shoe coverings. The driver wore old, leathery military-style boots and tracked water and dirt into the apartment. Ida looked at the mess, frowned and threw me a towel, nodding to the mess with her head. I wiped it up as everyone watched.

The new woman was shorter, younger, but trim and attractive in a Russian navy dress uniform with two stars on her shoulders. An admiral—and with a North Sea Submarine badge above her many ribbons. Ida motioned to the kitchen table so I stretched my arm and hand in that direction. "Please sit."

"Is this a short or long intrusion?" Ida asked after they were seated.

"As short or as long as you make it," Katya said. "I told Jon we are prepared to fly you to Moscow on Monday if you are willing."

Ida filled the vintage kettle and lit the gas. She put cups and saucers on the table, set down a tray with sugar and lemon and began warming milk.

"What exactly is it that you want?" I asked.

"Please don't begin so harshly, Captain Kadish," the admiral said.

"Commander Kadish— not captain," I replied.

Katya interrupted. "Oh . . . I *am* sorry! Please allow me to introduce Admiral Sara Abramoff, commander of our Atlantic Fleet. And this is Dmytri from our UN security detail, my staff."

Admiral Abramoff started again. "Forgive us for breaking into your day so abruptly, but we need to speak with you, and there is little time. I can understand your disenchantment with America. I made aliyah to Israel as a youth myself. Even after that insult, when I returned to Russia some years later, they gave me the opportunity to reach my full potential. I am also the submarine representative on the Naval

Science and Engineering Committee. It is a major assignment and a big responsibility. You commanded submarines. I have your complete service record. You should understand the responsibilities that have been entrusted to me."

"I am most impressed to have you visit," I said.

I meant it sincerely, even if I didn't like these Russians as a whole. I knew her name and most of her storied career record.

The kettle began whistling. Ida took it off the stove, added teabags, and let it brew on the hot surface. I looked at her, and she contracted a corner of her mouth as she shook her head at me. I knew the look, the face, and the message.

"We could be very good for each other," the admiral said.

Again Ida frowned and shook her head looking me in the eyes a slight smirk on one corner of her mouth.

"You can live at the Black Sea, where temperatures are mild all year. We have a special village in Anapa for newcomers. There are many people of note, who help us with . . . projects. English is the dominant language; the markets are full of familiar goods, foods, international stores, and chain restaurants. The cinema, theater, and opera are first class. There are many opportunities to socialize with others of your stature. You will be very well paid, and both you and Mrs. Kadish will have generous pensions for life."

"Others of our stature? What does that mean?" I asked.

Katya answered tersely, "Whatever you want it to mean. If you want to be with Americans, there are many there—the majority. English, French, Germans, Iranians, Arabs, Israelis, and many Asians are there too. Some of them are military, like you and Sara; others are university professors, journalists, filmmakers, international businessmen, and authors. Indeed, an intriguing group of interesting people. Most come to help us combat the growing Chinese influence."

I cocked my eyebrow at that.

Admiral Abramoff continued, "*You know that China intends to dominate the world!* Thirty years ago we were worried that Islam would dominate, but since China has contained the Middle East, it is China the world worries about now."

The admiral's voice was soft and calm; Katya's harsh and terse. I wondered, were they playing good cop, bad cop with us? Of course, I was familiar with the situation they spoke of. China dominated the Middle East once they became the biggest buyer of Arab oil. The United States withdrew from the region, and all capitalists had to write off their investments there. The stock market stumbled for about a year. China stabilized the oil autocracies in Saudi Arabia, Kuwait, the Emirates, and the rest. Iran was able to take care of itself. The fractious states of Iraq, Syria, Lebanon, and Afghanistan, virtually dissolved into their medieval forms of tribes, clans, and sheikdoms, each receiving financial support from the natural resources of the region according to some formula that China imposed. The fiefdoms were paid in yuan, the Chinese currency, which they used to purchase food and other supplies from China. The Chinese military provided the only intertribal transportation in order to deliver the ordered supplies. A hundred million Arabs became China's captive market.

Yemen was secured by a coalition of Arab armies led by Egypt and Saudi Arabia. The Saudis, by agreement, annexed Yemen, and paid Egypt liberally for the use of their forces to capture, occupy and pacify the country. Egyptian troops, and later Palestinian police, were hired and paid by Saudi Arabia to keep the peace there.

At the same time, Russia supported Egypt to push the Libyan radicals, diverse militias connected to Shi'a or Sunny extremists, south into the desert. Egypt administered the area, while the Russians operated the captured Libya's oil resources. The North African coast was stabilized.

With China and Russia policing the region, the civilized world marginalized the several hastily declared caliphates, which eventually petered out along with their affiliates. Each country was left to deal with its own local terrorists. Diplomatic relations, travel, and trade in and out of these places stopped. Those failed nations were dismissed as political states from the United Nations. China and Russia reaped some benefits of their resources and their need for trade. The rest of the world simply watched or ignored them.

The admiral continued, "America should be our natural ally in containing China rather than compete with us in the areas where they presently show no interest."

"That's an interesting point. Do you really think we can be natural allies with Russia after a hundred and twenty years as natural enemies?"

"That's not true, Captain Kadish."

"Commander—not captain," I said again, but she seemed to ignore me, intent on her own thoughts.

"America must stop thinking this way," she said. "Those days are long gone. Since the days of perestroika and glasnost under Gorbachev, then Yelsin, and the fall of the Soviet Union in the 1990s, we have become more capitalistic and you have become more communist. We are the same now. We both are energy self-sufficient, we cooperate in lower space, and we have free elections with a central legislative body. The members of China's Politburo, who rule their empire, are still elected by the Central Communist Party. Don't you see that we should be natural allies to prevent China from eventually taking over the world? Don't you see the ruthlessness with which they exploit the Arabs and how they are cleverly plundering Africa?"

"But your perestroika and glasnost didn't free your citizenry. Israel and the world's Jewry were charged a ransom before Russia would let those of our people who wanted to go, *go!*"

*"And were you allowed to leave America without an exit permit, Captain Kadish?*

I let that one go by.

170

"*Did you not pay your own ransom to leave?*

"In those days, our government felt we should be paid for the education, the health care of those wanting to leave, on a scale according to the level of their achievement, their age, and the value they were taking from the State. What is a young scientist worth, or an old one? How about a university professor, a pianist? Is America any different now?"

Ida had served the tea, and Dmytri sipped his through a cube of sugar held in his teeth. Sitting next to me, she kicked my foot under the table to stop staring at him.

"But Admiral Abramoff, what about your aggressive imperialism in *this* century—annexing the Crimea, fostering revolt in the Ukraine and other former Soviet states, intimidating them to remain in your sphere. Using your energy leverage to keep those countries off balance and in *your* orbit?"

She waved her hand in the air. "That was Putin. The joke in Russia then was that because his name ended ...*in,* he thought he was the new Josef Stalin! You get it? Both names are short and end ...*in?*"

Katya, the admiral and the assassin all laughed as though it was the funniest joke in the world and looked back and forth at each other. Ida and I just sat annoyed and watched.

"It is funnier in Russian, if you know our language," Katya said.

I cleared my throat, and they gave me their attention again.

"America and Russia are not friends, no matter what you say. We initiated sanctions against each other! You reduced oil and gas shipments to the Eurozone and raised the price to squeeze Europe while still maintaining your revenue. Putin thought he was so smart! When we came into that market a few years later with our liquid natural gas at a lower price, Europe began reducing their purchases from you. But Putin wouldn't relent. Your billionaire mafia, Putin's buddies and partners, had to have him retired—pushed aside to restore the economic balance. The billionaires wanted to take their business back.

"After that, we discontinued exporting any of our gas because our reserves were being consumed at too high a rate. That period is still fresh in our minds, and I don't mind telling you, we are suspicious of Russia to this day. Me included."

Katya looked incensed. "Mr. Kadish, you Americans quote history when it serves you and forget it when it doesn't! The Crimea was part of Russia for nearly ten centuries until Khrushchev gave it to the Ukraine in 1954. Khrushchev was a Ukrainian! Even as dictator of the Soviet Union, he had no right to give that vital land and our people there to the Ukraine. He wanted to change the facts on the ground—to give Ukraine a more important territory and hope to bind the peoples of Russia and the Ukraine tighter together, not just economically and politically, but in the coming generations with blood, with assimilation. Like the ancients did with conquests, like the ancient Israelites did in Jerusalem when they conquered the Jebusites. How do you think the Russians in the Crimea felt when they suddenly became Ukrainians because of Khrushchev's act? Crimea was part of Ukraine for only sixty years. In those two to three generations, Khrushchev's experiment failed. The Russians in the Crimea *wanted* to return to Mother Russia under Putin."

Katya paused, so I jumped in.

"So, since Putin's ouster about ten years later, you feel that the balance is restored?"

"The West was recruiting our allies in eastern Europe and inviting them into your circle of influence and commerce. Putin saw that as unfair competition against the Russian people and economy. Those countries relied on us for their energy and we on them for their trade. He felt he had to do what he did to protect our country. The status quo was about to be upset, and he felt the need to take action to right an old wrong by Khrushchev.

"Он дал нашему народу гордости, когда мы всего в ней нуждается."

"He gave our people pride when we needed it the most," Admiral Abramoff translated.

"Now a status quo was been returned to the world of the West and the United States, and we should cooperate to stop China from achieving its imperialistic visions," Katya answered.

I began to feel anxiety. I could feel my pulse throbbing, my neck heating up. I was certainly no expert in that region or its history. I needed to disengage, to calm down, cool off. I excused myself to the bathroom, and Ida got up to refill the teacups and pass around some cookies that were in the pantry.

# Chapter 27
# Round Two with Katya
*Jon*

I sat for a moment or two, splashed cold water on my face and wiped my neck. I took several deep breaths and let the air out slowly. I took my pill and returned to the table, committed to switching to a new subject. Everyone looked at me as I returned to my seat. I directed my attention to the admiral.

"Admiral Abramoff, let's talk about your forces in the Med. The Russian navy has the largest fleet. China's is much smaller, and America is no longer there. I suppose you think we should be there, supporting you?"

"Yes, absolutely!" she replied. "We were invited into the Mediterranean by Egypt when your government began to neglect the region––as you became energy self-sufficient. At first we only aided them with moral and political support, in the media and at the United Nations. Later, we helped with a few rubles to buy spare parts from you. When the US completely abandoned the region, China quickly filled the vacuum, including protecting Israel. They had no reason to be interested in North Africa—it has few natural resources besides 'sand.' So those countries came to us for friendship and support.

"Our fleet patrols the whole of the North African coast, with ports of call in each nation. They get security and economic activity from our sailors in their ports and our tourists on their beaches. Russian investors have built resorts throughout the area, and Russian tourists to Egypt are now a major input to their economy. It was we who persuaded Egypt to sell the northeast Sinai quadrant to build a new home for the Arabs of Gaza! China has a few small ships in the eastern Mediterranean that call and reprovision at Rafah, Haifa, and

Beirut. A few EATO ships patrol the waters of Spain, Italy, and Greece. Turkey, since the dissolution of NATO and the return of a secular military government, is on its own—they stay aloof, welcoming any and all who call at their ports. But with Chinese resource robbers now attacking Africa from the eastern, Indian Ocean, shore, the US should be teaming with us to protect the African Atlantic coast. You see, we are not asking you to do anything that should be against your principles."

Admiral Abramoff took a sip of tea, giving me an opening.

"But Russia continues to contest with us right up to the present day—vetoing resolutions in the Security Council that we support, condemning our allies when it suits you, and competing against us for military exports using bribery and tactics that are outlawed in our country."

"Yes . . . yeees," the admiral answered––stretching the word in quiet resignation. "We have many small differences in our culture and climate. We have our chicanery and corruption, as have you. We have our mafias, as do you. Your governments took over the illicit drug business, which was very smart. It solved a lot of problems and had a positive fiscal effect. It led the way for many others to follow your example. But it is not perfectly clean. It still has a level of government corruption, social and criminal problems. None of us are immune."

Ida had become frustrated. "Listen! You can argue and discuss these things forever to no conclusion, but we have a lunch appointment away from this flat. What is it that you want my husband to do for you to earn this wonderful life you so blissfully describe on the Black Sea?"

The admiral turned toward Katya and whispered something in Russian. The ambassador nodded, and the admiral continued.

"Captain Kadish," she said.

"Commander, *not captain!*" I said again.

"No, Commander! I respectfully call you *Captain*," she scolded. Commander was your rank, but *Captain* was your position—*skipper,* as you say. Those who command our submarines are Captains, and it is as a *Captain* that I address you!"

I nodded. Ida would recognize the flattery in the admiral's words, and I would hear about it later.

"I am here," she continued, "on behalf of the Naval Science and Engineering Committee to ask your help in the bonding of graphene for undersea integrity. We are designing and testing components for our next generation of boats. We recognize the many capabilities of the material, and we can make it in continuous sheets. Bonded to certain substrates, we can cold form it for a variety of small applications. We are having less success with hot forming. What is your experience?"

*Whoa, whoa!* I thought. *This is a revealing question! I need a moment to consider my answer.*

"You don't expect me to answer that now, do you? You would have to describe more fully your experience—show me your successes, your failures, allow me to see your results and speak to your engineers and technicians. How can I possibly understand the precise issues you are asking and judge whether I am qualified to answer?"

Inwardly, I was elated. *I knew it. I knew it!* I had guessed that that might be their problem when I stumbled on the word *glue* while making small talk with Ida at the lodge.

"What else? That can't be your only issue for me," I asked.

She nodded. "We are working on two other projects, both involving graphene. We are reviving our study of the MHD propulsion system for ships and submarines. In experiments, we have achieved nearly one hundred kilometers per hour using modified cycles and multi-systems in various geometric arrangements. We believe that with magnets of new alloys and certain components made of graphene, the serviceable life of a vessel will be worth the initial cost. And––the same is true in our development of a viable thorium 232 salt reactor."

There was a pause for me to absorb the *glasnost*, openness, of the senior Russian officer.

Ida stood and offered more tea.

*Oh,* I thought. *Bonding graphene, MHD propulsion, and thorium reactors!*

I was beginning to see what was taking shape.

I answered, "We never examined thorium beyond the 1960s. And now in this new century, the world has too much invested in uranium—mining, processing, fabricating, operating experience. For us it would be like reinventing the wheel. Yes, and the accidents too! We don't want to repeat those experiences with a new fuel, a new system. But China and India are working on prototypes with thorium."

"Of course they are!"

The admiral rose slightly from her chair and nearly shouted in my face.

"The world has depleted the easy sources of uranium and the price is up more than tenfold. And China and India are still the world's largest consumers of coal for energy generation. The contaminants are killing their people, and the $CO_2$ is fouling the world's atmosphere for everyone. They have not forgotten Three Mile Island, Chernobyl, Fukushima, and Koeberg—devastating accidents with uranium due to human error or an act of nature."

She sat back down, calming slightly but still passionate. "There are many advantages to thorium. First, it cannot be used to make a weapon, a bomb. It cannot melt down. It is four times more plentiful in the earth than uranium, it is cheap, and it is now discarded as an impurity in the processing of rare earths. Spent uranium fuel from power plants, which create a huge disposal problem, can be reprocessed as the triggers in a thorium reactor. Uranium fuel is spent after only 40 percent of atomic consumption, thorium after 70 percent. And it is believed that an initial thorium charge can be made to last the full life of the plant—maybe thirty years. Again, there are a few weak links that degrade too quickly, but the use of graphene appears to be the solution *if* the parts can be fabricated. There, now you have it! I have given you secret information to show you our sincerity in recruiting your services."

Indeed, she had given me more than I ever expected.

"But *why*, Admiral Abramoff, why?" I asked. "Why does *Russia* need to develop the thorium reactor? Why not leave it to China, India, the Canadians, or the Nords?"

"Commander Kadish," Admiral Abramoff, while demoting me, answered with a softer voice and a condescending tone. "*Wake up, Commander!*" She raised her voice to a shout again. "*Does a light-bulb not go off in your head? Are you so naïve as not to recognize the disaster in the making?*"

She looked at me seemingly dumbfounded. And I just shook my head in amazement. Maybe I *was* naïve. It didn't seem like a worthwhile project to me.

"*The thorium power plant will be the most progressive development of this century,*" she said with great emotion. "It will make available cheap, clean, and ample energy for any country that adopts it, and eventually every country will. But China already controls the rare earth supply and has thousands of tons of waste thorium from past decades. *And China will not sell the systems*; they will *lease* them! They will extract a fee from each of their client states on a per-kilowatt-hour basis! Country after country will be paying them royalties. They will control the hardware and the fuel—the royalty price, and the cost of energy to each of their client states. Power will be cheaper than it is today, but not cheap enough for any client to get out from under China's control. The hardware and fuel will be cheap, the royalties steep––like the blades for your newest razor. The royalties they collect will be like "tribute" that a captured, ancient nation paid to its conqueror. *This is* their master plan to control the world!"

Her strong emotion on the subject never waned. She sat back in her chair and took a few deep breaths, wiping her forehead and nose with a tissue. Her face was flushed. I could tell her pulse was racing and she was trying to quiet it down. I was too overwhelmed by her outburst to respond.

In another minute, she looked at Katya, and each nodded her satisfaction to the other.

"So, Mr. Kadish," Ambassador Katya said. "When can you visit to see some of the evidence of these projects and go to the Black Sea area where you might wish to reside?"

All around the table leaned back and breathed quietly. I was still trying to absorb all that had been spoken. It is hard to listen attentively to another when you're preparing to reply. I was glad that Ida was with me—she would tell me later what I'd missed. She never forgot a word.

As I was trying to think of what to say, Ida came to the rescue.

"Is that it?" she asked tersely, looking around the table. "Is that all?" Ida paused. The others remained silent.

"Okay," Ida continued, "you have given us much to think about and discuss. We will investigate the Black Sea area. We'll look into Anapa, and see what we can find in the Cloud about Americans and Jews who have elected to emigrate to you. That's all we can promise right now. But allow me one question, Admiral. Why did you go to Israel and then return to Russia?"

Admiral Abramoff squirmed in her chair, swiveled her head and shoulders a bit, and pulled down the tails of her jacket.

"I went as an idealistic youth to help defend Israel against the Arabs. I joined the IDF and volunteered for sea duty. Later I was accepted at the Technion, the MIT of Israel. I played a part in the strike on Iran. But when the United States broke relations with Israel and China took over, I wouldn't be an Israeli under Chinese domination. My family was never Zionist. We are Jewish from the Khazars—from the east—not Ashkenazim from the west. The Jewish Khazars helped found Kiev with the Rus, in the Eleventh Century, one of the beginnings of

Russia. My family fought and died for the czars, for Lenin, for Stalin and those who came after him. We died in the Russian army, in the pogroms of the Kossacks, and in the Nazi concentration camps. It was because of the stories of my grandfathers that I felt a need to help save Jewish people from the Arabs. But I never expected them to one day ally with the Chinese."

Sara Abramoff sighed and took another deep breath. I felt she had been honest with us—truly open.

"Thank you, Admiral," Ida said quietly. "You make a better case for your country than is presented in America. Can we reply directly to you in the future?"

Katya replied, "Communicate through me at my United Nations coordinates. I can relay you directly to Admiral Abramoff on secure frequencies. The United Nations provides totally secure lines for each member country back to their homeland. We can patch you in. Have you any other questions while we are here?"

While Ida had occupied them, I'd had a chance to regain my composure.

"How is Sergei Segalov?" I asked after a short pause.

The admiral and Katya, eyes wide, jumped in their seats.

"Why do you ask about him?" Katya answered coolly.

The yellow pill was working. I kept myself in control.

"We met in Switzerland many years ago, and I saw his name in your technical news from time to time. He was perfecting your nuclear pump-jet propulsion system for the Borei and Yasen Class boats. He discussed with me the need to have a standby propeller, at least one, in case the main system became inoperative. We discussed the added cost, weight, and balance. I told him that if his main system was reliable, he didn't need it, but if he wasn't sure, then a standby should at least be able to be recessed in the stern and only deployed when needed. To have it hanging off the stern all the time would cause detectible cavitation and defeat the silent running of the pump-jet system."

"You suggested that to him? When?" Admiral Abramoff asked.

I was curious about the excitement in her voice.

"At the Nautical Propulsion Symposium in Cern about twelve years ago, I think—or maybe longer? I read later that a standby propeller was excluded from the design."

"Yes, he came back from Cern committed to making the primary system so reliable that a screw would be unnecessary. Perhaps as a result of your challenge?"

"Maybe? I hope so. But I haven't seen anything from him in your technical press for more than a year. He was young, very bright. I liked him. He couldn't have retired. Is he okay?"

The question visibly startled the visitors and Ida kicked me under the table. We both waited anxiously for a response.

Katya answered slowly, "If it is the man I am thinking about, he has had some health issues and has been on a temporary leave of absence. I will send him a message that you inquired about him."

Ida kicked me again. No more follow-up questions. We rose, and the visitors followed. I helped the admiral into her coat as Dmytri helped the ambassador. We said quick good-byes.

"When can I hope to hear from you?" asked the admiral.

"In a week to ten days," Ida answered.

"Please, as soon as possible." The admiral had the last word.

After they departed, I had to wipe the floor again. Damn boots.

By then it was 10:30.

# Chapter 28
# Friday Lunch at Rachel's
*Ida*

"So . . . you were 'most impressed to have her visit,' eh *Capitan*?" I said after the Russians were gone.

"Please Ida, what did you expect me to say? She was fishing for a compliment."

"Okay, I'll give you that. But how about her saying, 'We could be very good for each other,' *huh*? What do you think she meant by *that*? You're much too old for her, Jonny boy!"

I never forget a word and Jon knew it. He didn't answer.

"So what do you think? Was she telling the truth?" I asked him.

"Her story hangs together, but her description of Russia's history and present are a lot different from what we teach in our schools. There are plenty of ways to research and verify her claims. What I don't doubt are the projects she described and the difficulties of fabricating graphene to make use of its advantages. You remember when we were joking at breakfast and I said "glue" might be what they're looking for? The answer is so simple. I can't even tell *you*, now that I know that they *don't* know!"

"Do you think she took part in the strike on Iran?"

"If she was in Israel at the time, I'd say yes. I would say "yes" about any Israeli there at the time. They all risked retaliation of some sort. Fortunately it didn't come."

We paused as I poured tea.

"Please, Ida, enough tea, already!"

"The Russians are not really a consideration for us, are they?" I asked.

"No, Ida, no. We just need to string them along before giving a reply. Maybe we should take that trip to the Black Sea just to see what

182

we can learn. What about that Dmytri? I didn't feel any warmth from him. He didn't say a single word either coming or going. How'd you like how he sipped his tea?"

I grimaced. "And the mess he made walking in and out. Maybe that sugar thing is a sign he's a Templar or a member of some Russian secret society with murderous inclinations."

I meant that as a joke, but neither of us laughed. Feeling pensive, I looked into Jon's eyes. He looked pensive too.

"Thanks for buying us some time . . . you were great at that!" he said. "I was so flustered by all those issues."

*Issues, and an attractive Russian in a navy suit, Jewish at that too!* I thought. But I decided to leave him alone about that.

"Now we need to learn where each of these invitations will lead," he said. "No one gets a decision until we make our own."

He looked at me again, taking in my slacks and sweater.

"Is that what you're wearing to Rachel's for lunch?"

"Oh, no! We don't have much time. We both better get ready. But you talked to Abramoff about things I don't understand."

"We have the whole day tomorrow. I can explain anything you ask then," he answered.

We dressed more appropriately and I reviewed the instructions the Israeli gave us the previous night. We called the taxi at noon. We followed all the instructions, and a truck was waiting at the back door of the house as promised. Three taxi drivers were arguing in front as the watchers watched. No one followed as we left.

\*\*\*

The synagogue was part of a gated community, with housing and apartments within monitored walls. If you observed the strictest adherence to the Jewish Sabbath, everything was available and convenient for you. This development model had been initiated at South Beach in

Miami in the 2020s. Because of its success, other developers had copied the concept for Jewish communities in major cities. We had been to this synagogue on our last trip, but the residences were just under construction then.

From the street side, the synagogue façade looked like an apartment house, several stories high with a canopied entry–extending to the curb. There were no signs or symbols to mark it as a Jewish house of worship––only the street number on the sides and end of the canopy. The double door entry had a bank of residential mailboxes as an additional distraction. The glass was clouded from the outside but transparent from the inside. Beyond the inner door was a security station as elaborate as any at an airport. This seeming deception had become the norm for building minority religious houses of assembly or worship because of the terrorism that had taken hold throughout the world.

We quickly entered the synagogue outer door and were quickly buzzed inside. We passed through security and entered the main lobby. Rachel was waiting. She saw me, jumped up and ran to me. We kissed, hugged, and twisted each other forth and back for a good viewing—so excited to finally be together. She gave her father a similar welcome.

Rachel whispered, "Come downstairs, there's a sitting parlor where we can talk. Jacque will meet us there in a few minutes."

We talked about the kids. She told us about their house inside the compound. We had never been there.

When comfortable, Rachel asked, "Why did Israelis call to tell us to meet you here and not send our driver? What's going on?"

"That's an intricate story. We're having a bit of mystery this visit." I laughed, and she raised her brows. "I'll tell you later," I whispered.

"Mom, now that you and Dad are here, you'll have Shabbat dinner with us tonight, and you can come back tomorrow for services. We can spend all of Shabbat together!"

"No, thank you, Rachel," Jon said. "We'll be happy to have dinner tonight, but not tomorrow. Shabbat services are not a part of our routine. Maybe we'll go to a movie. There's a cinema down the street from the flat."

Rachel nodded. Jacque arrived, and we hopped in his car for the short ride to their house.

\*\*\*

We were impressed by Jacque and Rachel's expansive home. Room by room they showed us around, pointing out the most up-to-date conveniences and energy efficiency. Rachel's housekeeper and cook, Mrs. Kellogg, had a dairy lunch set out with smoked salmon, white fish, and other seafood delicacies. There were assorted breads, butter and cheese spreads, sliced tomatoes and onion. Juice, water, coffee, and tea were the drinks. The fish tasted so much better in Quebec than in Norwich. Maybe because it was local, caught and prepared in the Maritimes just to the east.

We told them a bit of our adventures with the FAV, the blizzard, and the incredible scene at the lodge. But we didn't say anything about the attention Jon had received from Israel, Russia, and Matthew. Hopefully, when we knew more—a lot more over the coming days—we'd be able to share more with them.

# Chapter 29
# Jon and Jacque Chat
*Jon*

Our son-in-law was from a family of Orthodox Jews, but I would only call Jacque, "observant." He didn't wear a kepah, a head covering, at all times, and he dressed in ordinary business and casual clothes. Our daughter embraced his observance and didn't seem at all upset with conforming to his more strict adherence to the Jewish faith and rituals. She was brought up in a more modern Reform Jewish home where attendance to ritual was more casual.

It was always a bit awkward between him and me. In our circles in Norwich, Ida and I were perceived by both Jews and Gentiles as "observant,"––because of our active identification and participation in the community––but we fell way short of Jacque's standards. On their infrequent visit to us, he and Rachel always ate "vegetarian" in our home because they knew that we didn't keep kosher.

Finding topics of mutual interest to have a conversation was usually difficult, but I think he tried to accommodate me, and I certainly tried to accommodate him.

After lunch, Jacques and I sat together in their library/den.

"I didn't think there were enough observant Jews in Sherbrooke to make a residential project like this successful. Is the Jewish community growing?" I asked.

"Slowly," Jacque replied. "More Jewish families have moved to town these past few years . . . younger families from Montreal, Ottawa, and foreign countries. Mostly professionals or staff for the many universities here. We're about a hundred families now, maybe four to five hundred people. But not all the homeowners in this development are observant,

Orthodox, or even Jewish. These housing prices are a great value, and the community is the closest to the city center that has modern security."

I nodded.

Jacque picked up the lead. "Our biggest problem is educating our children. Sherbrooke has over a half million people—93 percent Catholic, 6 percent Protestant and other Christians, the Catholics from the French and the Protestants from the English. Jews, Muslims, Hindus, Buddhists, and others are the leftovers. The city stopped providing secular schools years ago because it was having too much trouble coping with the minorities. You know, just like in France and America. Religious sensitivities, dress codes, food in the cafeterias—the city secular schools couldn't keep up with all the wants and demands of the minorities. You know? So they just got out of the elementary and high school business. Now they contribute a per-student stipend to the Catholic, Protestant, and other approved schools, so long as they teach the secular subjects: the three R's, Canadian and world history, the French and English languages. The students are required to pass city tests on these subjects and the both spoken languages to graduate."

I nodded my understanding.

Jacque continued, "So we need to provide a similar Jewish school. The city Education Department is supportive. They will contribute the same per-student contribution they give to the others, provided we also adhere to their secular curriculum. Thankfully, we're already on it for the younger students. Grades one to eight opened last the fall in rented classrooms at St Andrew's Presbyterian House with the stipend from the city. We have plenty of qualified teachers. Our few high-school-aged kids are with families in Montreal to attend schools there. That will be necessary for quite a while."

"You're smart. You'll help to figure it out. And how's your business doing, your projects?" I asked.

I knew I was heading into a sensitive subject with him. He usually didn't want to talk about his career and the family business, at least not with me. But he seemed relaxed and it was worth a try. He could always blow the subject off.

"Oh, that's another story. Since arriving seven years ago I've closed on nine projects, in commercial real estate, of course. We sold two of them for a good profit last year. One of the remaining is struggling; I put most of my time into that. Last year was the first year I couldn't add a new project to our portfolio. I had several worthwhile opportunities, but others snatched them at higher prices. I have the feeling the coming years won't be as successful as the past."

His willingness to crack open his secret door surprised me.

"What do you mean?"

Jacque didn't look unhappy at the question—we were, after all on his turf, and he seemed to need an opportunity to talk to an interested, objective outsider.

"Please, sir, don't take this as arrogance––but since arriving here our family enterprise has made its mark in this city. We could see easy opportunities that the locals could not. Our big-city experience and imagination made all the difference. I produced meaningful projects and generated a certain reputation for success. But now I feel I'm being tracked. If I show an interest in a project or property, all of a sudden multiple interests are chasing it. I find myself in competition for everything, either having to pay more or take a pass."

"What does your family advise?"

"They say it was bound to happen sooner or later. Seven years with little competition is good. But these business shadows are now bidding up the prices of projects that decrease their probability of success. I don't understand them and I don't want to be in that game. I might just advise the family to withdraw from here, or maybe move on—perhaps to Quebec City. With more than double the population, there might be more opportunities there. What do you think?"

"Jacque, you know this is not my area of expertise. But your logic is clear. The United States went through many cycles when greedy private equity firms created the so-called leveraged buy-out, with other people's money or with so-called, junk bonds. After some notable early successes, more firms joined the game. It wasn't long before too much money was chasing too few deals, and those greedy investor groups began paying higher prices. When the cash flow of the victim company wasn't sufficient to service the debt and pay the promoters' fees, the projects soured.

"This I know: if you pay too much, even for a good business, it's a bad deal! Maybe you can find untapped potential in Quebec City––or in the Maritimes. Make visits there, look around. See how you could help improve the lifestyle in those places."

Jacque nodded. "I'll make some trips with the family in the spring. So, how's the flat working out?"

He changed the subject.


"It was the best we could find—clean and with decent furniture. We had cleaning crews work it over before you arrived."

"Jacque, thank you. It would be more than adequate for a few weeks if we weren't under such pressure.

"Listen Jacque—*please keep what I am about to say confidential.* Tell Rachel only as much as you think she should know. Your mother-in-law and I are under surveillance from several governments, including the US, Israel, and Russia. We are being followed wherever we go. The Israelis are advising us on precautions to take. They brought us to the synagogue today to keep your driver from coming to the apartment. They want us to settle in Israel and for me to help them with some technology."

"Great! That sounds like a wonderful plan. You'll be near Eric, and we can visit from time to time."

My first thought was that he was happy we were not going to stay around them, but then I responded instinctively.

"Not so quick . . . it's not so great, actually. The US knows what we're thinking and is watching me as a potential defector. I've been ordered to return to my office for a Tuesday interview. They've arranged coyotes to pick me up and ferry me back over the border on Monday morning so we can get around problems with our exit permit. If I actually try to leave the USA for good, they've threatened to find and return me.

"Ida shouldn't be alone at the apartment for the days I expect to be away. Can you help me out with this?"

"No problem, she'll stay here, no question."

"You'll have to relocate her clandestinely so the watchers don't learn where she is or who you are. We don't think they know where you live, and that needs to be kept a secret. Can you figure something out?"

Jacque looked surprised. "Wow, you guys are in a high stakes game of spies and agents, eh? Sure, Rachel and I will figure out a way. Now what day is this?"

"Monday. You have to pick her up midmorning. I hope to be away only two nights and get back here on Wednesday. The Israelis are planning for us to meet with one of their diplomats on Sunday morning–day after tomorrow. They've given Ida a secure old analog cell phone to communicate with them. We'll get exact instructions from them tomorrow night."

"Where do the Russians stand? What do they want from you?"

"They don't stand anywhere. I have no idea what they want, exactly." *I lied*, then continued, "If I seriously thought of going to them, I would consider myself a traitor to all I stand for. But I'd like to hear what they have to say. I'll probably meet with them later in the week. Right now I'm trying to think just what I might have that Russia wants or needs. I don't think I have anything that special that they don't already have."

Jacques sighed and shook his head.

"Anyway, you're not to drive us back to the flat. We'll take a taxi from the synagogue, the same way we arrived. Is there any way we can communicate with you and Rachel without it being intercepted?"

"Let me think . . . yes, yes! I can give you one of the kid's polka-dot family cells. They're programmed on a children's frequency and can only call Rachel or me. We're told they're not monitored."

"Good. Give one of those to Ida. She's our communicator and will need it when I'm away."

Jacque looked concerned. "Maybe you should stay here with us for the duration of your visit?"

"Perhaps . . . but not too quick. We can think about that later."

"Okay then, Mom will stay with us while you're away, and I'll come up with a more secure flat for you when you return," Jacque said.

"Thanks for your help. I'll do my best to keep you and Rachel in the loop."

Just then, Rachel put her head into the doorway, "Jacque, Dad, please prepare for dinner and come to the table!"

Ida was helping her finish setting for the Shabbat meal.

We each went to wash our hands and Jacque brought me a kepah to put on my head. I nodded my appreciation.

It was past five o'clock, dark outside, and the Sabbath had begun. The kids turned off the TV, and the preliminaries began. Rachel lit the candles, saying the blessings together with our granddaughters. Lighting the Sabbath candles is the duty of the woman of the house. Jacque performed the blessings and rituals over the wine, washing his hands, breaking and blessing the bread, the challah. Mrs. Kellogg served a beautiful traditional meal: chicken soup with carrots and noodles, roast chicken, vegetables, and potato kugel. We sat around the table and sang the Sabbath songs. Ida and I hadn't done that in a long time. It was beautiful. We were very proud of Rachel, Jacque and our grandchildren.

The children left the table and over dessert, Rachel and Jacque questioned us about our plans for the future. They frankly told us what *they thought we should do!* We listened, but there were so many new complications that they didn't know, it was almost comical to listen to them. Jacque gave Ida a polka-dot little phone and told her to just open it and Rachel or he would answer. Mrs. Kellogg packed some leftovers and gave the bag to me. They called us a taxi, we all bundled up and they walked us back to the synagogue.

From inside the compound, the façade was beautifully decorated in artful, tasteful motifs.

We went through to meet the cab on the street side where we had entered.

When we arrived back at the flat, we looked around but couldn't tell if there were any watchers waiting for us. Of course, we weren't supposed to see them even in daylight. Perhaps we had surprised them by returning in a taxi while seeming never to have left. From then on, we would presume they had the knowledge of the rear door.

We wouldn't use that ruse again.

# Chapter 30
# Saturday to 007
*Ida*

It was Saturday, and we were up at seven. We had a morning bite at the table like yesterday. At eight, I looked at the door, but all was quiet. I had put on my slacks and blouse and fixed my ponytail just in case of another surprise. We chatted about the kids and their house, recounting all the pleasure of the previous afternoon and dinner.

I asked Jon about MSH, or MSG or, you know, whatever they were— rare earths and thorium reactors.

"Technical terms about technical stuff. Do you really want know about them?" he asked. "You've never been very interested before."

I could tell he was a little annoyed with me asking. But too bad, I wanted to know.

"I was totally lost listening to you and the Russian admiral. Just tell me some basics so I have an idea if they come up again. The admiral mentioned China and rare earths. Start with rare earths. What are they?"

"Okay, here goes. Rare earths are a segment of atomically similar elements, some of which have uniquely special properties that are very useful, even vital to some of our high-tech equipment. As their name implies, they are usually found together in minute quantities in the ground, in some cases as a byproduct of iron mining. They are difficult and expensive to mine and refine for practical use. They are usually enmeshed with thorium, which becomes an impure waste product to those extracting rare earths. Please don't ask me to name them . . . it's been decades since I had to memorize them in chemistry class. If you want, I can look them up and forward them to you."

"No, no need to bother. But what are they good for? Where are they used?"

"They are alloyed in minute quantities with some of our normal base materials, such as copper, titanium, silver, gold, carbon, silicon, aluminum. They enhance the conductivity of those materials, along with other powerful properties—heat transfer characteristics, frequency sensitivity, and other things. Their use in magnets allows greater fidelity and miniaturization of electronic devices. They extend the power and capacity of lithium batteries, and as additives in glass and fibers, they enhance their properties for one reason or another. Without the rare earths, we wouldn't have the high-speed computing power in small packages that we have today—the communicators, the capacity and longevity of batteries and electric storage systems, the guidance and response systems in our surveillance equipment, the satellites of today. Rare earths are vital to our military equipment. Is that enough?"

"Enough!" I said.

"Good!" he said. "Is MHD next?"

"Yes, MHD is next."

I was tired of the whole topic already, but I'd started this, forced him into it, and I had to see it through.


"MHD is magnetohydrodynamics. Now, slowly: *magneto—hydro—dynamics.* It's a propulsion system for use in seawater that was never fully developed because of technical constraints. It's similar to the Russian pump-jet but would be more efficient. New alloys with traces of rare earths in magnets and graphene invite the possibility of revisiting MHD for future use on ships, both surface and submarines. The theory is simple, but the execution is much more complex. The idea is to make a super powerful, donut-shaped electromagnet from these new alloys and arrange them in a configuration so that when they are turned on and programmed in a specific sequence, they will charge seawater—because of its salt content—and force it to move through the donut hole. With magnets set in a series, the water would move progressively faster and faster until it comes out at the end like a jet!

Think of a jet engine, except water shoots out the back of a MHD system and propels a ship through the sea. Enough?"

"Sure, I got it. A jet engine using water, right?"

"Good! What next?"

"Thorium, I guess."

"Okay, thorium is very interesting," he said much more slowly. "Thorium 232 is an element close to uranium on the periodic table. Thorium has an atomic weight of 232, uranium is predominately U238, but there is also some naturally occurring U235. Maybe I should skip the chemistry lesson, huh?"

"Yeah, skip the chemistry."

"Thorium is radioactive, stable, and plentiful in the earth as thorium oxide, $ThO_2$—four times more plentiful than uranium. When separated from the oxygen, it's a shiny metal. Now here's the key part, *with the addition of a single neutron to its atom–say, in a reactor vessel–– making it thorium 233, it can behave like uranium, split, and release a ton of energy!* But here is the best part: it can't sustain a chain reaction, so it's useless for atomic bombs! Many countries are working to make a practical power plant using thorium as the fuel, but not us—that is, not the United States. Our Department of Energy claims it's backtracking, reinventing something we already have, but I don't know the real truth. In my opinion, developing domestic power using thorium fuel would be a big improvement over uranium. Maybe they just have their hands full with the natural gas and don't want to start over with a new nuclear fuel.

"China's in the lead, of course. Thorium has a number of excellent, passive safety and cost advantages over uranium, as you heard Admiral Abramoff recite. But because of politics in the 1950s, particularly the Cold War, it was bypassed in favor of uranium. At that time, the goal was uranium and plutonium for *bombs.* You get the idea? The story can go on and on if you want. Is that enough?"

I laughed. "Yes, enough on that too—but I'm not quite through with you yet!"

Ida said, *"Did you see their reaction* when you asked about Segalov? *I loved it!* You shocked the hell out of them! What do you think is that story?"

Jon smiled and laughed along with me.

"Wasn't that great! Okay... I think Segalov and his wife defected to Matthew and his trillionaire, and accepted his 'offer that can't be refused.'" The Russians are pissed, want him back. Maybe Mathew wants me to work with him. If we ever get to the end of this chain, I think all these little coincidences will turn out to be connected. In time we'll see."

"I'm sure you're right," I replied.

***

The day continued without incident—no one banging on the door, no new mysteries cropping up. After the last three hectic days, we deserved quiet.

"You mentioned a movie to Rachel yesterday. Shall we see the new James Bond movie, *See Sea Saw*? It's playing at 1:30 down the street."

After a short discussion of the picture, Jon said, "Sure, let's go!"

The afternoon was a fiasco with a packed theater, screaming legions of kids and mystery men sitting around us in the last two rows. Jon got called out to the men's washroom, and four guys escorted him there. He came back with popcorn and water, but we left at intermission, rushed out by an Israeli security guy. Going to the show had been a good idea, but we didn't expect to draw such a crowd! We also weren't expecting dubbed French with English subtitles. Anyway, I was thankful when we got back to the flat safely. Jon briefed me on all the intrigue that took place in and around the men's room.

"Matthew's man said, 'we'll be called on Thursday with the details.' He's arranged for us to fly to Calgary to meet the trillionaire on Friday."

I nodded. This stuff was almost getting to be old hat.

"The Israeli said not to forget to call for the instructions for tomorrow's meeting. He said, 'There have been some changes to the original plan.'"

"What did the American and the Russian say?" I asked as a joke—but Jon kept going.

"The Russian said the admiral is anxious and is waiting for my answer. The American told me I'd be picked up on Monday morning at seven. 'Be ready. It will be cold, but they'll bring all the gear you need for the trek.'"

"And what was that mysterious paper you were holding?" I asked slowly. "You didn't have to be so abrupt in the cinema!"

"This one?" He pulled it from his shirt pocket. He laughed.

"No mystery! It's the receipt from the snack bar. And I wanted to catch up with the movie . . . reading the subtitles was a pain."

I laughed too.

"Why didn't Matthew's man come back to the show?"

Jon winked. "He said he had seen it and didn't like the ending."

\*\*\*

Jon went off to the bedroom to rest, and I later joined him. By six p.m., we were up and around, preparing the leftovers for dinner. I warmed up the soup, the chicken, and the kugel. We sat down to a nice redux of the previous evening. When we were finished, with the kitchen cleaned and settled, Jon said, "Please call the Israelis for the details for tomorrow."

I made the call with their tellie and listened carefully. I took a few notes on my pad.

When the call ended, I told Jon, "The man said an Israeli driver will pick us up in front at 9:30 in a taxi. He also said 'to wear our Sunday best.' I asked him what that meant and why? You're never going to believe what he said."

"Well?" Jon asked.

"He said, 'You're going to the ten o'clock mass at the main cathedral downtown,'––and he hung up."

# Chapter 31
# Sunday Mass at the Cathedral
*Ida*

Jon was in the only suit he'd brought, slightly rumpled, with a shirt and tie. I'd pressed it as best I could with the ancient iron I found in the flat. I wore one of my better dresses. The temperature had moderated but was still below freezing. We wore our overcoats, scarves, hats, and gloves.

A taxi pulled up at 9:25. We hurried downstairs and let ourselves into the back seat. Cabbies usually get out to open the door. This one didn't—he was definitely an Israeli. Neither of us said a word, and he pulled out with a jerk.

The driver circled a few blocks to identify the cars following us. When satisfied, he turned toward town and slowly cruised the street by the Saint-Michel Basilica-Cathedral on a promontory in downtown Sherbrooke.

People and cars were all over, scurrying in every direction. The shoveled sidewalks kept the people confined, hemmed in by piles of snow on the edges. People leaving the earlier mass were headed away. People going to the ten o'clock were bumping and bruising their way to the open doors. Bundled men, women, and children, exhaling vapor, hurried everywhere. Parked cars pulled out as new cars waited for their spots.

Our driver waited behind a departing parishioner and got a choice space. The cars following scurried to find parking spaces of their own. On a signal from the driver, Jon and I got out, quickly blended in with the crowd, and pushed our way to the cathedral. We walked hurriedly through the arched center entry, our driver was close behind—doubling as a bodyguard, it seemed. Once inside, he ushered us to the office suite of an auxiliary bishop on the lower level. A robed monsignor welcomed us into a beautifully appointed conference room. Three people were already seated. They stood as we entered.

The conference table was a crafted wood antique, gleaming with a brilliant finish. Twelve high-backed upholstered chairs on casters circled the table. Eight electronic portraits adorned the walls, three on each side and one at each end. At the far end, at the head of the table, was the electronic image of the pope. A cardinal adorned the near end, and six bishops lined the sidewalls. The portraits looked exactly as if oil painted.

Jon whispered, "Those portraits are the earliest use of graphene for electronic display, when it could only be made in small panels."

The aroma of fresh coffee tickled our nostrils.

"Thank you for coming, Mr. and Mrs. Kadish," said a stylish middle-aged woman who appeared to be the senior person at the table.

"I am Galliah Golan, Israel's ambassador to Canada at our embassy in Ottawa."

Jon led, and we walked to that end of the table to shake hands.

In the next instant, Jon exclaimed, "You're here?" to the man to her right, slightly hidden by her shadow.

"I thought I'd seen the last of you!"

Ambassador Golan smiled. "I know you have already met Ling Xi-Peng, a member of our scientific community, whom we asked to join us for this meeting. He's on sabbatical this year with a university in Maine. And this gentleman—" she motioned to a fortyish, sun-tanned man with handsome features, dressed in corduroys and an open shirt, "—is Admiral Rishon H'Ivri, from our naval forces. Your driver is my security attaché, Zvi, and he will monitor the door while we are here. Please sit," she said cordially. "We have fresh coffee if you wish."

The driver stepped out the door, and the admiral poured coffee. The fixings were on a tray on the table. Jon and I each took a cup.

The ambassador began. "Mr. Kadish, you seem upset with Xi-Peng. How can we make you comfortable with him?"

"His attempt to fool us at the Lodge was amateurish. Who is he, really? A Taiwanese? An American? An Israeli? A communist? What's the real story with him?

"*You!*" Jonathon raised his voice and pointed at him. Mr. Ling glared back in Jon's face.

"I am all those—except communist!" He wagged his finger. "My country and yours, America, let my people down many times—threw us under bus."

He glanced at the ambassador, and she nodded for him to continue.

"We allies in World War II against Japanese. America supported Chiang Kai-shek and Republic of China. America facilitated Japanese surrender to us on Formosa. As Republic of China, we seated in United Nations in 1947 to represent *all* Chinese people. We permanent member of Security Council with veto power! Later, Communists win control of mainland in '49, but we continue to represent all Chinese at UN.

"Then, in 1970, your men Kissinger and Nixon negotiate rapprochement with Chairman Mao, and we kicked out of UN in 1971. People's Republic of China, known as PRC, given our place. My father just boy then. Only twenty countries and Vatican keep relations after we become Taiwan. We struggle to participate in world cultural and sporting events. To participate in Olympics, we forced to be called 'Chinese Taipei.' Big insult! America kick us under bus."

I didn't know any of that history, and I doubted Jon did either. WWII was nearly a hundred years ago, and it was all before we were born. Taiwan was in the Pacific, and we gave neither much thought.

"Later, Father . . . my father . . . marry American girl, navy nurse. I born in Taiwan 1997. We come to California 2015. Later Congress pass sweeping immigration law to help illegals become Americans.

Children of illegals, especially Latino in south and west. California given preference.

"Because of illegals, I have to wait for papers. Not right! No, not right! I have problem to go to university, to get scholarship and government loan. My father educated man, but no talk English, only get coolie work. Make mother sick. Need costly lawyer to work things out. Again under bus, you understand?"

Jon and I nodded.

All the Israelis had knowing smirks on their faces.

"So is that it?" I asked.

"No, Miss Kadiss, not over by long shot. Taiwan become very educated, industrialized, high-tech nation. But Communists not recognize as independent, still threaten and want our lands. US protect us, look out for our interests in many ways, for many years, decades. Taiwan was strong ally of US in region. Our relationship to America like Israel to America! We both have big enemy wanting our land, we both strong democracy. Taiwan and Israel both educated countries with solid economies, high-tech industries in dangerous neighborhoods. America protect *both* of us. Later recessions, market crash, money printing, trillion deficits, and multitrillion debt. Congress gridlocked, all world suffering. White House stumble on 'Reerected Economic Model.'"

His voice dripped with disdain as he said it.

"All start with South Korea . . . you remember Kim Jong Un, then boy-king of North Korea? He send two rockets into south and accurately hit two mountains, one near Pusan, other near Seoul. Very scary, so accurate! Demonstrate capability. You remember?"

Everyone nodded.

"South Korea ask US for more troops, ships, planes for protection. President ready to go but Congress say, 'NO! STOP!'

"Congress say, 'South Korea rich country. US taxpayer cannot afford defend South Korea out of American treasury. If South Korea

want US to rush protection, it must pay two billion dollars every week!'
Very unexpected,––*but South Korea agree!*"

"You remember that, don't you, Jon?" the ambassador asked.
After a pause, Jon nodded slightly.

"*That change world!*" Ling continued. "America get first paying protection client. They rush aid, *but there no war,* only new model how America help allies. Kim Jong Un back down. Since then, hundred billion of foreign exchange coming to US from South Korea every year. United States wake up to value of its protection. In few more years, Japan, Australia, India, Philippines, and most Southeast Asian countries paying for US protection."

He was clearly working up to his main point.

"Then America ask Taiwan for four billion a month. Congress say, 'Just for navy and air force, no ground troops—ever!'

"Taiwan refuse, say, 'NO! That not way to treat friend and ally. Too much money for limited protection! Cannot pay!'

"This you remember, it big news twenty years ago."

Jon said, "Yes, I remember that very well. I felt ashamed of the United States' action and sorry for the people of Taiwan. Your island nation was left completely vulnerable."

"Yes, yes . . . Mainland PRC take opportunity, become aggressive, surround islands, make blockade. Taiwan forced to negotiate. Sure. Okay for political parties on island, okay to elect leaders of island cities and towns––but Beijing send governor. Taiwan become twenty-third province of People's Republic of China, independent––but not independent, like Hong Kong. People and business now pay tax and for defense to Beijing. Taiwan disappear from list of nations, no more independent, no more democracy. No more Olympics. Under bus big time!"

He paused and took a sip of coffee. Having reached his high point, he seemed calmer now.

"So successful in Pacific, US turn to Europe and rest of world. NATO alliance shaky, break up after Russian aggression in Eastern Europe and chaos in Middle East. US want payment for beefed-up soldiers, equipment, in Europe. Germany, Italy, Poland, everywhere US has base, asked to pay total cost plus profit to US taxpayer for presence and protection. Even Canada and Mexico asked to pay. Almost trillion dollars is coming in by 2034. *United States become biggest, best, and most expensive mercenary in world!*"

Although his English was broken, his message was clear. Much like what the professor had preached on Wednesday. And we understood it.

"Mr. Ling, so what's the point? We know what happened. Why the history lesson?" Jon asked, annoyed—probably because he got the message loud and clear.

"Okay, now main point, main point! Listen up!"

Jon and I sat up in our chairs.

"Even *Israel* asked to pay! Imagine!"

"Israel respond, 'We don't ask your protection, just give some equipment, some money help to develop new technology.' US answer, 'No more money for new technology. For equipment, you pay full price now like everyone else.'"

Ling shook his head. "Imagine . . . Arab neighbors are bloody mess, brother fighting brother, cousin cousin. Cut unfaithful and foreigners' heads off. Send pictures on Cloud. Pope, Vatican cry out for Christians; West cry out for relief workers and journalists. Jews chased out long time before. World try to help but quit, cannot interfere. Israel *only* democratic country in region, loyal friend of US with big support by people of America, defend self at big cost and sacrifice, high-tech, successful economy—same like Taiwan—and US ready to throw Israel under bus too. Israel say same as Taiwan, 'Not act of friend, of ally!'"

He punched his finger in the air.

"But Israel more smart, prepared. *They have plan B!*"

"Let me take it from here, Ling," said Ambassador Golan.

There was a heavy pause in the room.

"Wait!" I said. Jon looked at me questioningly.

"Xi-Peng, how are you an Israeli too?" I asked.

He looked at the ambassador, who nodded her approval.

Smiling, he said, "That easy. Wife, Colleen Finnegan, Jewish! We make aliyah together in 2030. Meet in college in California."

"So Colleen Finnegan *is* her real name and she really is your wife? And you say she is Jewish?" I asked, my face flushed with surprise.

"Yes, yes, Miss Kadiss. Colleen mother maiden name, Kohen. Mother marry Irishman. They live Cape Cod, and we have good life in Israel now."

# Chapter 32
# Ambassador Golan

*Jon*

"Let me continue," Ambassador Golan said, taking control.

"Mr. Kadish, as an engineer and scientist, you may know that Israel has the fastest giant supercomputer in the world in a secret underground laboratory. It wasn't generally publicized, but many in the academic and technology space know of its existence."

This turn was unexpected.

"Yes, I've heard it exists, but I don't know much more."

"Two thousand people—executives, scientists, engineers, sociologists, psychiatrists, militarians, programmers, and technicians—work there and have built the most sophisticated computer model of how the world works that exists. We've mapped global warming under various assumptions about carbon emissions from coal for the next hundred years. We have shown that even if North America and Europe stopped *all* their $CO_2$ emissions, it would not be enough to offset the pollution of China, India, and Africa. To save the world, those three need to get off coal completely and replace it with a nonpolluting energy source. It is amazing how little the results change without a dramatic shift away from coal."

"That's not a surprise—I think we all intuitively know that," I said.

"Perhaps. But scientific analysis is more persuasive than intuition to world leaders. From hundreds of independent variables, we can create a model of what will happen in the world under almost any conditions imaginable."

"So what's the point you're hoping to get at?" I asked.

"Be patient and listen, Mr. Kadish. Give me a chance to make my point."

I nodded.

"Twenty years ago when it was clear that America would become energy independent, we ran multiple scenarios to assess the future of Israel under this and related conditions. You remember the mess that the Arab world was in with their sectarian wars and multiple caliphates back then? Even with China now controlling the region, there is still tension. But when your president, Obama, won reelection in 2012, our prime minister was certain that America would *never* attack Iran's nuclear capability, nor help Israel do it. Israel, yes we, concluded we had to plan to do it alone or with others."

"That help came from China and Saudi Arabia," interrupted the admiral.

Ambassador Golan paused, visibly annoyed, and glared at the admiral from the corners of her eyes. The admiral, acknowledging the rebuke, lowered his chin and eyes toward the table.

She continued, "It was also clear that when America became energy self-sufficient, its interests in the Middle East would dissolve. This became especially true when the next president ordered the shale gas shut in, so none would be allowed for export. Their vision was that America needed *all its reserves* for itself in order to have the *cheapest* energy in the world for the *longest* possible time. Cheap energy was needed to offset your disadvantages in other costs. This was a core of your then president's philosophy in order to rebuild and maintain the American empire into the foreseeable future. That action led to the two-tier oil pricing of today, with the world price at over $150 per barrel and the North American price at half of that.

"The implication was clear. When America no longer needed the friendship of the oil-rich Arabs, it wouldn't need to care about us! With energy self-sufficiency, it could abandon the whole Middle East problem to whoever would become the new leading customer for Arab oil! We believed the future leaders of the United States would welcome the relief. Was the United States navy really going to protect the Straits of Hormuz to ensure someone else's oil supply?"

Xi-Peng and the admiral laughed. Ida and I sat poker-faced.

"Arab oil was predicted to remain crucial on the world market, as it was still vital for the growing demand of energy-resource-poor countries like China, Japan, India, and Europe."

Ambassador Golan paused for a drink before continuing.

"Water for humans and agriculture is also scarce in many places. Our computer models predict that more future local wars might be fought to obtain water than any other resource, especially among the poorest and driest countries. This prediction led our government to renew our priority on water issues. We already were the leader in conservation, recycling, and fixed high-capacity, high-quality desalination plants using conventional energy. The object was to develop smaller, more portable, standardized desalination systems that could be easily transported, installed, and powered with small, assembly-line, packaged nuclear power plants. When we still had relations with the US, we bought such power sources from Babcock and Wilcox. You know them."

I nodded. She continued.

"B&W mass-produce nice, compact nuclear power stations that can run for twenty years without refueling, modeled after your submarine reactors. At that point, units are expected to be replaced with upgraded technology rather than be refueled."

"You're talking uranium fueled nuclear power, right?" I asked.

"Yes, of course," the ambassador chirped. "We are now producing our own uranium power supplies with a nearly thirty-year life. And you know, Mr. Kadish, we are the world's leader in both technologies now."

"Perhaps in the packaged desalination process and hardware, but there are many competitors for packaged nuclear power stations from many countries," I said.

Ambassador Golan cleared her throat, ignoring my pushback.

"As Xi-Ping said, when American aid was withdrawn, we were ready with plan B. The world knows that China has been our new 'big brother' for about twelve years. What is not so well known is that Israel has enjoyed cordial relations with the People's Republic of China since just after the Six Days War in June, 1967."

I sat back surprised that she was going to take me through this. I *knew* most of the history between Israel and China.

"In the 1970s and '80s, Israel rebuilt thousands of their old T-34 Russian tanks from World War II. We gave them new turbine engines, improved armor, new turrets with a bigger gun, and environmental systems for heat in the winter and cooling in the summer. Later, we licensed China to build our Merkava tank for their military. They were pleased and we enjoyed the royalties.

"Do you know that many Chinese leaders and intellectuals are intrigued by the Jewish people? Some see the Jews and the Chinese as the only peoples to survive from antiquity to the modern day. And *we* did so without a homeland for two thousand years! They admire that. They look to learn our secret of sustainability. We exchange many scientists, engineers, doctors, and professors to work and teach in each country every year. We always live up to our word to them and they to us. Many world leaders don't trust the Chinese, but we have never had any reason to doubt them."

Now that information was an eye-opener for me.

"When did the Suez Canal bypass happen?" I asked.

"Oh . . . you mean the so-called 'Red-Med Railway.' Twenty-five years ago or so, we agreed to allow them to build a high-speed railway from Eilat to Ashdod for containerized cargo to bypass the Suez Canal. The concept was for security and cost savings. If you remember, Egypt was fraught with upheaval and political uncertainty at the time and China was worried about getting its goods to Europe. China put up most of the money, and Chinese contractors built it. It is only two hundred kilometers long."

She looked at Ling, who said, "About 125 miles."

I nodded sarcastically. I didn't need him to convert that number for me.

"Four sets of tracks now ply that route to transfer cargo containers between the Gulf of Aqaba and the Mediterranean Sea. Red Sea terminals are in our port of Eilat and in Palestine's port of Aqaba. A container ship can be off-loaded to railcars, raced overland and reloaded in Ashdod in less than forty-eight hours. It takes an average of five days to transit the canal. That's a savings of three days and many hundreds of thousands of dollars. Saving time is saving money, lots of it. And our transit fee is lower than the canal's. We would be operating at capacity if Egypt hadn't built its second canal and lowered its price. But their bottleneck is still the Great Bitter Lake, so they've never reached their announced capacity of a hundred ships a day. Traffic is now mainly divided between the Suez and our corridor."

Again Ida and I nodded.

"And, as the world knows, China also normalized the political situation, enabling the reunification of the West Bank with Jordan to create the new state of Palestine and the building of the North Sinai enclave, surrounding Rafah, for the former Gazans. The Northeast Sinai idea was originally American. Buy the land from Egypt to build a modern city, relocate the people of Gaza, and repatriate some refugees. Your son can tell you the details of these miracles. Everyone in Israel knows the stories and has an opinion. We have rebuilt Gaza for a million new residents, with waterfront homes, high-rise apartments and condos, hotels, parks, sport facilities and family centers. Disney is committed to building a world-class theme park there in the next few years. And the airport was expanded to become our second international air portal. Gaza has become, perhaps, one the finest places in the world to holiday and live."

"You kept the name 'Gaza'?" I couldn't help asking.

"*Betach!* Of course!" the ambassador answered, shrugging her shoulders and opening her hands. "Gaza is an ancient biblical, historical name. We never change such things."

Again I couldn't help myself.

"Did Russia have a hand in the Palestinian North Sinai city-state?"

"I don't know why you ask," Ambassador Golan shrugged, "but yes, Russia was helpful in advising the Egyptians. They encouraged Egypt to put aside their pride to take a very handsome deal and get out from under an unruly, noncritical, remote piece of land. Yes, unexpectedly Russia was helpful. But it took the Chinese to put up the money and dismantle the irreconcilable Hamas fanatics."

"What happened to them, the hardcore Hamas and PLO?" I finally had the opportunity and courage to ask.

"It is not for discussion here, Mr. Kadish," the ambassador said firmly. "There are many rumors in the world and not all are correct. Even many Israelis do not know the complete truth."

I dropped my head and thought the worst.

Ida opened her hand, her elbow resting on the table. The ambassador nodded to her.

"Listen, Ambassador Golan, as woman to woman, we are happy that Israel is better off now, and America is also better off in some ways. But the Jews in America, like us, are not better off. We have lost our political standing, even in domestic matters."

Ida leaned over the table and the ambassador leaned toward her too. I marveled at my wife's ability to make a human connection with every woman she met.

"The United States no longer has diplomatic relations with Israel," Ida continued. "Trade and travel are prohibited. Israel advocacy organizations are banned and any sign of allegiance to Israel on our part makes us appear disloyal to America. Our son and Jon's siblings are there. Jewish assimilation into the fabric of America has been disrupted. Moslem organizations have gained influence. Some of their organizations promote making sharia law legal in communities where the people vote in favor of it. Even Christians are worried about being marginalized in some cities around America. America is not such a good place for us anymore, and it worries me that relations with Israel are so bad."

"Yes, yes Ida, we know," the ambassador replied in a softer voice. "But Israeli-American relations are not as bad as you portray. America never applied sanctions of any sort on us, nor did they attack our international banking relations. All they did was withdraw their ambassador—the world interpreted that as a 'diplomatic break.' We withdrew our ambassador from Washington in response. There are envoys and trade officers still in the US embassy under a charge d'affaires. The Canadian ambassador is the official US representative. Some non-defense-related trade still continues. Many American companies still have facilities and investments in Israel. Our stocks still trade on the New York and Nasdaq Exchanges. We are still the third largest nation represented on the financial markets after the US and Canada. Tourism is still strong. Christian and Jewish groups visit regularly via connections from Canada, Europe, and Latin America. Chinese and Japanese tourists have increased. It's funny—they visit our industrial, technological, and agricultural sites; our seaports, energy and water facilities, rather than our religious and antiquity sites. And of course, they visit our resorts and beaches. We've had to develop or import hospitality personnel fluent in their languages.

"And Canada is facilitating talks with Washington right now. Some of them in Ottawa with me! We are showing your State Department that we are independent and not in the pocket of China. We expect a formal return to warmer relations as soon as this summer, leading to the return of ambassadors in a year. Travel and trade ties directly from US soil will be renewed. We want our American cousins to return to full participation with us and American society."

I interrupted and said, "C'mon Ida, you're talking *woman to woman* now! When are going to ask the *big* question?"

Ida looked at me and I could see the resolve come into her eyes.

"Okay, Madam Ambassador, it's time for *tuchess afen tish!*" Ida said.

"I needn't have to translate for you, but maybe for your Mr. Xi-Peng. C'mon, put your tush on the table, show us your hand! Why do you want us in Israel? What is it that you want from Jon?"

Ida did it! I knew she could and would. Just what was needed at that moment for the conversation to advance.

The ambassador smiled and deferred to Admiral H'Ivri. He nodded that he had the ball.

"You could help us in many ways, Mr. Kadish. *I needn't tell you* that America has the best submarine technology in the world. Use of sub-surface naval vessels has expanded greatly in the past decades for exploration, maintenance, and transportation. You know the Chinese have built huge undersea LNG transport submarines that can be loaded and off-loaded submerged. The build manned subs for the military and some as drones for commercial purposes.

"Iran was contained some years ago, but with every new regime they pose a continuing threat to reemerge. They are concentrating on undersea craft now too. Though Iran is principally under Russian influence, China still buys some of their oil and navigates a fine line between Iran and us.

"Our submarines are small, designed for coastal patrol and special missions. Most are single purpose. Our fleet is a state secret, but I can tell you we need to replace older vessels and add to our fleet in the next twenty years. It is well known that our main power plants are fuel cells with propulsion by Vornado sea sled, a hybrid sort of MHD, with steering by jet ports—no noisy propellers or rudders. We can be quieter than nuclear boats. Our depth capability and underwater speeds are state secrets. But I can tell you, we have established bases on the floor of the Mediterranean and in other seas for our boats to nest, observe, do testing, even refuel. Just like a manned space station around the moon, with men going in and out for various missions— we do the same undersea! Do you know that some aspects of the new

James Bond thriller, *See Sea Saw,* are taken from *our* undersea developments, just pushing them to a higher level?

"For many things, we too are adapting graphene for lightweight, high-strength, transparent, and electronic capability. We know this is your field of expertise. You might be able to advance our progress in fewer years."

Graphene again. Why was I not surprised?

"Where do you get graphene? You have no raw material in Israel to produce it. And what about nuclear power plants in your submarines? There have been rumors that you have been moving on that too."

Ida looked at me with a wry smile. She was sensing the connections coming to the Russian conversation.

"Yes, we know about the rumors," the admiral replied laconically. "We have always been working on the development of small, packaged nuclear power plants for steam generation, electricity, and to run our desalination towers. We have a few designs that could be adapted for submarines but I promise you we have not done so. The major advantages of nuclear power in a submarine do not apply to our missions. The liquid natural gas we get from our own undersea wells suits our fuel cells. Our boats can refuel right at the source while submerged. High purity graphite is available from multiple sources and we can spin or vacuum-form our own graphene."

"What about uranium for the desalination power? Where do you get that?"

"Wherever in the world it is available at a good price when we need it. The price is now so high that the cost efficiency of nuclear generation is nearly defeated. We get uranium mostly from the Cameco Corporation, the largest producer in the world. You know them well, Kadish. Your country has a contract with them to supply your submarines. Their mines and processing plants are in Saskatchewan, Kazakhstan, the US, and a few in other places. I will visit their Canadian headquarters later this week. South Africa is also a secure supplier. You know we only need finely milled, sifted ore or yellowcake and we can refine and process it ourselves. Have you any idea how many times Dimona has been rebuilt and refueled? The original core and technology from 1963 has been replaced and upgraded multiple times."

"What about the waste from the refining and refueling process?"

"There are some things I cannot talk to you about now—but remember, the initial wastes also contain many other valuable components. You know how well we recycle things." Admiral H'Ivri gave a sinister laugh.

I took a deep breath. I had taken control of the conversation. After a quick sip of coffee, I pushed further.

"There is still a lot of mystery about how Israel made the attack on Iran's nuclear facilities, crippling them even until today. Only a few key locations were hit, yet their capability was critically incapacitated. There is speculation that Israel used nuclear bombs. Is that true?"

"Another unproven rumor!" The admiral sat back as though insulted.

It was the kind of reaction I usually ascribed to one protecting a lie.

"And another matter on which I cannot comment," he continued, "except to say it was a brilliant operation. It is well known that China and Saudi Arabia helped us. And it could not have been successfully completed without our undersea capability."

With a suggestive smile on his face, he finished, "You might be able to learn more if you make aliyah."

"If I were to work for Israel, would I be aiding the Chinese in any way?"

I think the questioned stunned them. They all looked one to the other, maybe wondering what answer would please me. The admiral had the courage to offer an answer.

"No . . . no. They have strategic nuclear boats, like you Americans and the Russians. They ply the open seas and project their power in all the oceans. Their boats and tactics are patterned after the Russian model, which helped them get started, as with aircraft carriers. Germany and England built our subs in the past, but China now builds them, our basic boats. They know our designs and swimming characteristics. We build and install our own power plants and systems for control and weapons. Their naval officers consider our boats to be 'toys for children, not oceangoing, full-service machines.' We like them to think that way."

Xi-Peng interrupted. "We also working with molten salts to carry fuel pods for packaged power plants for desalination products."

"Are you using uranium like the Canadians or trying for thorium?" I asked quickly.

Xi-Peng answered again. "We working with both, and even in combination. For some problems—graphene might be answer? When successful, these power plants may be suitable for naval vessels too. I work on such problems for variety of applications . . ."

Ida and I smiled at each other as the same subjects kept getting repeated.

"Quiet!" the admiral shouted. "Why are you talking? We are not authorized to discuss those classified projects!"

*Now there's an idea, uranium supplemented with thorium! With the supply of newly mined uranium shrinking and the price up so dramatically, maybe the introduction of thorium in a power reactor might make good sense and make the power less costly.* I thought. *But the US Energy Department would probably still see it as backsliding.*

There was a pause—a long, pregnant pause. The Israelis seemed spent. Ida was quiet. I was thinking. It all sounded interesting, but without seeing an exact project, I was not sure how much I could help them. I trembled, thinking that they might be overconfident in my ability.

The ambassador took over.

"Your son told us you are leaving America. He was pretty sure you are planning to settle in Israel of your own choice. But we wanted to take this opportunity to tell you that you need not be just another person in Israel, a statistic. There are opportunities to contribute if you wish. You have the ability to impact our security and future in an important way. Naturally, you will receive all the rights of any new Jewish immigrant, but in addition, we can have you appointed to Bar Ilan University or the Technion in a position of honor and respect from which you can work to support our efforts. That is the long and short of it."

She couldn't have known she'd pushed one of my buttons.

"Not the Technion!" I barked. "I will not be associated with that institution!"

Everyone was startled by my outburst, even Ida.

"They have sold out to the Chinese. They've had an active campus in Guangdong Province with Shantou University since the early 2020s, financed by the Li Ka Shing Foundation. I remember when Li Ka Shing gave $130 million to the Technion, only half for its Haifa campus. It was the largest personal gift given to *any Israeli university* up to that time. To me, that was a form of bribery to tap into your best scientists and technical minds. Since the Technion is a partner with China, I don't want anything to do with them. That's not for me!"

"The Technion is a world-class prestigious institution—our MIT," the admiral answered, clearly surprised by my pushback.

"Why should I care? I don't give a shit about that. I won't be connected to any institution that has a direct link to China! I'm listening to you, but I'm not making any decisions about anything right now. C'mon, Ida, it's time to leave!" I bolted out of my chair. "This discussion is over!"

"One minute, just one minute," Ida said sternly, staying seated.

"Ambassador, what about Jon's illness, his medical condition? Eric must have told you about that too."

"Yes, Mrs. Kadish. Though we haven't accessed your husband's medical tests and records, we don't believe he is in imminent danger of any sort. He has had regular checkups, and this is a very recent diagnosis. PSAs and biopsies of that gland are subject to many errors. Our doctors consider positive tests inconclusive. Further study is needed.

"If the problem should prove to be real, our medical treatments are the most advanced in the world. Our noninvasive ultrasound destruction of tumors is unique in medicine. We cure people and they are back to work that afternoon or the next day. People from across the world come to Israel for these procedures. We have world-class staff and facilities to promote medical tourism. We charge huge sums to those who can afford huge fees. To those unable to pay, we treat them without charge for humanitarian reasons. The elite of every nationality and faith come to us to get treatment. The financial success from the wealthy foreigners supports the total program. Our success rate in treating prostate cancer is the best in the world. Mr. Kadish will be evaluated, and a personal regime for treatment will be designed for him if needed. Whatever we have will be available to him. He could not come to a better place for treatment."

Ida looked and smiled at me. I kept my terse composure. I was still riled by the whole meeting. Yes, Israel had always been near the top of my list—but something about all this was gnawing at my core. I didn't want to immigrate to Israel, get China in the bargain, and find out too late that it was not the place I expected, the place I used to know. I already had that disappointment in America.

The ambassador said, "Keep that small phone while you are here in Quebec. It will reach my security staff any time you call, and they will know it is from you. Contact me if I can be helpful in any way. Thank you for coming this morning."

Ambassador Golan looked down at her communicator.

"Mr. Kadish is right. The mass is almost over, so we need to leave with the crowd, as we arrived."

"Am I able to contact Admiral H'Ivri with that cell?" I asked.

The ambassador looked at the admiral.

"Why might you want to contact me?" he asked.

"You seem to have the most specific information about what I might be doing. I might have other questions."

The admiral shrugged indecisively. The ambassador gave him a slight nod, then called for Zvi, who stood guard outside the door.

"Zvi, can Mr. Kadish reach Admiral H'Ivri with the analog cell?" she asked.

"Only if the admiral is willing to give Mr. Kadish his Com-ID. Kadish would have to ask for that number when the call is answered."

The admiral took a card from his wallet, wrote on the back, and slid it across the table to me. I looked at it and nodded.

"I'm not quite done," Ida said. "What about the strangers who are monitoring us? Your man on the phone said you know about them and are trying to identify them. Have you learned who they are?"

I was proud of Ida for remembering and asking that question. In all the discussion, I'd forgotten about our more immediate concerns.

The ambassador threw the question to Zvi.

"We have been intercepting and recording their conversations and forwarding them to our cryptology people. They are using a sophisticated encryption technique and speaking in a little-known dialect from Africa, maybe South Africa. I'm sure we will break their code and be able to understand their communications. Only I cannot say when."

Zvi paused, then said, "Come, we must move quickly to leave with the parishioners from the mass."

Everyone stood and moved to shake hands. I smiled and shook Xi-Peng's hand first. I think he was surprised.

We waited upstairs for a few minutes for the church service to be over.

# Chapter 33
# The Chabad Co-op
*Ida*

As Jon and I waited for the mass to conclude, we stood against the inside wall of the cathedral, just beside the door. I looped my arm around his. The service ended, and people filed out in streams from three aisles across the vestry. The vestry filled as some waited for others. In only a minute, the crowd syndrome was in full motion.

Zvi said, "Okay, follow me!"

Jon and I walked briskly, arm in arm, following Zvi this time. He snapped the taxi unlocked and opened the passenger door on the street side for me. I sat in and slipped to the far side. Jon was half a step behind. Zvi closed the door and took the driver's seat. The engine fired, and he maneuvered back and forth a few times to push his way into the slow-moving traffic of worshippers leaving.

Once around the first corner, Jon asked, "What are we doing for lunch? We have the rest of the day, no transportation and just the food that's in the flat."

"Zvi," I called, "is there anywhere near where we can shop?"

"The inner city is very quiet on Sunday; we would have to go to the outer perimeter. What do you want?"

"Maybe a bakery for some bread, a cake, a market for cheese, fresh vegetables, fruit?"

He remained quiet for few moments, thinking perhaps. "Yes!" he finally answered. "Sherbrooke has a co-op kosher market, run by Chabad. Today will be its busiest day. Let me check the Cloud, and we will GPS our way there."

Minutes later, we drove past a modest-sized market on a block with other Jewish shops. The storefronts that were not opened were protected by metal sliding grates, and at the market there were four doorways, two to enter and two to exit. At each entry stood a provincial policeman and a burly Chabadnik, as security. The Chabadnik was to recognize the known customers and welcome them. The policeman was to check the strangers, like us.

The wide sidewalk was filled with men, women and kids, all bundled up, milling about, talking to one another. Many pulled wire market baskets. A few were packing their things in cars. The temperature seemed warmer, but the sky was overcast.

"Have you Canadian money?" Zvi asked us over his shoulder.

Jon and I looked at each other and shook our heads.

"Not much, Zvi. We have only small change. Will they take American money or credit cards?" Jon asked.

"Maybe, but you don't want the transaction to document you or your location."

He pulled over a block away and gave us a hundred dollars Canadian. "Will this be enough?"

"We'll make it enough, thank you," I said.

"How much is this..., about––in US?" Jon asked.

"About US$130," he answered. "Your dollar has recovered some since it hit its low after your bail-in, and the emergence of other world reserve currencies."

International trade was no longer quoted or settled only in American dollars. Even Canadians preferred the yuan. The Chinese currency was more stable, backed by the world's largest cache of gold. Canada had a huge trade with China, shipping natural and refined forms of energy, grains, and other goods from their west coast. Each major economy demanded its partners trade in their currency. China paid in yuan, so the seller had to buy Chinese products with yuan to balance the accounts. In the same way, Russia demanded rubles from its energy customers, and America, Brazil, South Africa, and India did the same with their own currencies. Even some second-tier countries were able to force some of their trading partners to deal in their currency for arms or certain vital commodities. Currency trading had become a popular profession, easily making profits on the arbitrage.

"Let me give you $130 US as a trade," Jon said.

"No, no . . . don't worry about it. The ambassador would not approve. I will take you to the store and see that you are allowed entry. Then I'll return to wait here for you. Okay? Let's go!"

As we walked to the store, Jon was shaking his head.

"What are you thinking now?" I asked quietly.

"About our dollar weak against the yuan. And China's accumulated mountain of gold. No wonder the price of gold is nearly fifteen thousand dollars an ounce. We could have bought some at fifteen hundred, even twenty-five hundred along the way."

"Who says we didn't?" I answered. "Remember . . . you have a son in Hawaii named Truman."

He smiled and winked at me.

The store was busy with people pushing shopping carriages and baby carriages, with hustle and bustle all around and loud talking by patrons shouting in French and English, Moslems in Arabic, Chabadniks and store personnel in Yiddish. The place was alive! The shoppers were both Chabad and Jews in secular dress, a few Moslem women in headscarves and I was sure I saw Gentiles too. I loved it! It put the first genuine smile on my face after many days—maybe weeks.

Jon and I took a basket and looked at the baked goods, the fish and dairy cases, the fresh produce. There was no salad bar as I expected to find, as in the States. Maybe there wasn't room for one, or it wasn't considered sanitary or kosher?

The meat department was on the opposite wall, as far from the dairy as was physically possible. From the signs in French and English, apparently you had to preorder certain cuts of beef, lamb, veal, and chickens forty-eight hours in advance so they could be delivered fresh from Montreal on the second day. Milk and meat products could not be checked out in the same lanes. That was a new one to me! Only one dairy and pareve checkout lane accepted cash or credit cards. The regular customers were co-op members with prepaid accounts and automatic replenishment when their balance hit a certain limit, like an E-ZPass account to pay bridge tolls in New York. *What a good way to assure customer loyalty and limit the amount of cash transacted,* I thought.

Jon and I went through the cash checkout and left with two bags of purchases. He kept the change in Canadian. Now at least we had a bit more domestic currency.

Back at our flat, I made a salad and Jon cracked eggs to make omelets. We sat down to a lunch of salad, veggie and cheese omelets, and rugelach. We each had a bottle of Pierre Spring Water—I'd been delighted to find that Canada still had bottled water!

As we lingered over lunch, I said, "I liked that woman . . . Ambassador Golan. She's smart and represents Israel well. I was impressed by much of what she explained and how she explained it."

"Like what?" Jon asked. He sounded less than impressed. I thought he was still annoyed by Xi-Peng and the whole Chinese connection.

"How the Chinese people respect and admire Israel and the Jews, how neither has broken their word to each other. How Russia played a part in contributing to the creation of the North Sinai enclave for the Palestinians and how the Israelis have rebuilt Gaza to be a grand place to live and work. You mentioned that maybe we could settle in Gaza, and now I understand what you meant. I'm willing to look."

"So the idea of settling in Israel is growing on you?"

"In some ways, yes. But today's discussion definitely showed how the world has become divided into three main power centers. The

US pretty much has the Americas, our protectorate clients in Asia—Korea, Japan, India, and Australia—plus the leanings of Europe. China has its massive land and people, the Middle East, and growing pieces of Africa."

I paused–– and Jon spoke. "You failed to mention their claims in the South China Sea. Those potential gas fields remain undeveloped because of China's claims and because the US protects those waters for the abutting nations. Indonesia and Malaysia are large independent buffer states. They cannot afford to offend China, nor do they need US protection. Singapore is independent and safe, their international status respected by everyone.

*"But I think India is the hinge on which the future of that region pivots.* John emphasized. It's a very large country with an educated, industrious people. Their population is younger and is already bigger than China's. India will have the largest formation of new households and the largest growing middle class in the future in the world. It is new households and a growing middle class that generate a consumer economy. The years that China prohibited couples from having a second child are coming back to haunt them. Though India is composed of many sects, religions, and diverse dialects, they have the largest national population that principally speaks English. They have bought military equipment from Russia, but now they are buying military technology and protection from us. We have the better, more influential position with them now."

Jon sat back. "So that leaves Russia. Where do you see them?"

"You said they're not an option for us. That we would definitely not go there. But I was impressed by their knowledge of your diagnosis."

"Yes, they deserve credit for that, and for influencing Egypt to give up that piece of the Sinai. But the Russian Federation is still aggressive toward the independent, former members of the Soviet Union, bullying them—knowing that neither EATO nor we can do anything significant to thwart their intimidation of them, without provoking greater and wide hostilities and risk nuclear war.

"But whatever we decide, I'm being swayed to have my health issues addressed in Israel. What the ambassador said is true. They're on the leading edge of applied technology and techniques in the health-care field."

Jon stopped and took his first swig from his Pierre bottle.

"Ida, I'm concerned, truly concerned. Like . . . this recruitment by Russia and Israel is a surprise, a big surprise! I suppose a compliment to my career. But listen, I know I'm a good, experienced naval engineer, *confident in my current position.* But it's hard to pinpoint what they want, expect from me. So it's also more than a little scary."

"You know, Jon," I said softly, "this decision of ours—the one that got us here—*wasn't for the purpose of getting you a new job, was it?* Twenty years ago when a person reached seventy-one, they were generally retired or semiretired. I thought we were here trying to decide where we want to spend the rest of our lives and where you're going to get medical treatment. This move was *not* about where you were going to work!"

He nodded his head. "Yes, yes, you're right! That been easy to forget–– when these countries are knocking on our door. And I'm not sure I can meet their expectations—so that doubly removes *Russia* from contention. They will want every inch of me as compensation for what they'll see as their extraordinary effort to get me. And I'm sure that the work will not be on the Black Sea in Anapa, not at all. They'll have me chasing around that country, and we won't have the life together that we've envisioned. And what would they do if I can't deliver what they expect?"

Quiet came again for a few moments.

Jon seemed stressed. I thought I'd lighten the mood.

"I liked your Q and A with the Israeli admiral. He's quite a handsome young man!"

"Sure, sure, like me thirty years ago. You always liked me in my dress uniform."

"Yes, I did. And I liked when you were promoted in those navy cultic ceremonies, when you were *piped* aboard a ship where you were taking command. Yes, I liked those events and basked in your success. The junior officers' wives treated me like a queen." I smiled, remembering.

"Today was not unlike that. The Israelis were really rushing you, wanting you to feel that you can participate at a high level with them," I continued.

Jon answered, "I could see that. But maybe they too are expecting more than I can deliver."

"Jon, Jon, *that's not you talking!*" I said, shaking my head. "The Israelis know who and what you are, and that you can help them, I'm sure."

"Yeah . . . I suppose, Ida. But if they do, I wish they would come right out and ask, like Abramoff did."

"What you said about the Technion? I didn't know all that. The Technion and China?"

"Ida, I remember all the critical dates. The Merkava tank in 2005, the Red-Med Railway in 2012, the $130 million of Chinese money for the Technion in 2013, and the Iranian raid in 2023, all prior to the US recalling its ambassador. The relationship between our nations soured with the Iran raid, especially when some tests from space indicated that maybe atomic weapons had been used. Israel denied it, and it has never been conclusively proven. But I'm more certain now that some sort of tactical nukes *were* used, based on the way Admiral H'Ivri behaved when I asked him that question. When China publically became Israel's number-one ally, that's when we officially broke relations. I can't blame the US for that, much as it's been hard on us. But I don't want to directly contribute anything to help China. What's strange is that America didn't break relations with China . . . just Israel. I always wondered why."

"Listen to me...like we just agreed, *you don't have to work for anyone,*" I replied. "You can get medical treatment in Israel, and we can have a small condo to be near Eric, Rebecca, and their kids for a part of the year, in the best season. Maybe we should become Canadians like you've been pushing. The Israelis want you, but they were not pushing as hard as the Russians. I think we could live there part-time without immigrating."

We again sat quietly. I could tell that Jon was quantifying the pros and cons in his head to help him calculate an answer. That's the way he liked to think.

"More coffee? I asked.

"Not now, thanks. I'll stick with my bottled water."

He raised the bottle to me like a toast and drank another slug of it, capped it, then rose to clear the table. I covered the leftovers, put them away and rinsed the dishes.

It was 2:30.


"We still have to contend with the mysterious Matthew, and I have my interrogation in Groton on Tuesday," Jon remarked.

My heart sank a little. "Yes, we do. But please try to keep whatever they have to say within the context of what we've just discussed."

"Sure," Jon replied, "I'll try."

# Chapter 34
# Later on Sunday
*Jon*

We moved to the sofa after lunch to watch a bit of television. Ida swept through the channels with the ancient remote. The French stations had one hockey game after another, news in French, French-dubbed movies. She stopped at CNN International, the United States propaganda channel. In a taped show, Erin Burnett, their senior anchor, was mentoring, backing up Barry Blitzer—Wolf's grandson and a neophyte—with a report on American humanitarian efforts in some islands of Indonesia.

"Look, Jon," Ida said, "the US is not totally devoid of compassion toward the emerging world."

"Please, Ida, Washington is compassionate where they hope to gain an advantage, hope to exercise some influence. You don't see any of our government organizations trying to gain influence in central Africa, do you? Why? Because Christianity has lost the battle there and *we can't compete against China or Russia!* We won't—and we shouldn't—try to play by the African dictators' rules. Our ethical and moral standards don't fit those country's leaders. Sure some American NGOs still try to help out there. But Russia and China and other nations who are willing to pay and play by the local rules get the business. You heard Admiral Abramoff admit it. They pay off the leaders and let them deal as they please with their people. That's not the way we Americans play the game."

I became quiet, thinking back over our conversation in the church.

"It troubled me that Ambassador Golan avoided saying anything about the fate of the Palestinian dissidents in the West Bank and Gaza. I wince when I think that Israel just stood aside while China played by their own brutal rules to quell extremist minority dissent—to make them disappear. I wonder what they did and how?"

Ida frowned at me.

"Jon, please. We don't know what happened to them for sure; you're speculating. Remember—you don't have to work for them, or anybody. But we want to be able to visit our son and grandchildren in Israel."

I put a pillow behind my head, leaned back and closed my eyes. Ida went to the bedroom to change out of her church dress. For the next hour, I visualized our country losing its balance at the dawn of the twenty-first century but now coming back as new, dynamic, energy self-sufficient, its manufacturing rekindled, fiscally and financially strong and maybe with freedoms about to be restored. Maybe the deficiencies of ten, twenty years ago were being corrected? Maybe Ida and I were running from ghosts of the past? *And we hadn't really given enough thought to what we were running toward.*

Ida returned and said, "Your banter with Xi-Peng and Admiral H'Ivri intrigued me. I learned a great deal about you, even without understanding all the technical points. It reminded me of all the things I liked about you when we were in college and why I wanted to marry you."

I regarded my wife for a moment. In times of crisis I could always feel her love. I wondered if she felt mine? It was there for her. We had built a beautiful life together after all these years.

"Well, we're older and wiser now, but we're both still the same people," I answered.

***

At five o'clock as darkness fell, six or more cars drove into the apartment driveway. Three or four people came out of each, bundled up for the cold. The men wore long black or fur coats and broad-brimmed black hats. The women too were in fur, and all in hats or headscarves.

In the dark they looked Hassidic. Many carried things we couldn't identify. They entered the building, rang our doorbell and trooped up the stairs to our flat. Ida and I were shocked until we saw Rachel, Jacque, and their children among them. The others were all friends from their neighborhood.

"Rachel, Jacque, kids, what a surprise!" I said, hugging each in turn. I laughed. "Look at your outfits! How will everyone fit in this flat?"

"The men put on the hats to confuse your watchers. Don't worry, Dad, we'll all make it. C'mon in, everybody!" Rachel shouted to those still on the stairs.

The women carried baskets of food, dinner for all. Rachel brought Ida a suitcase of clothing they had talked about on Friday. The crowd was Jacque's idea, to distract the attention of the watchers on any one couple. When all were defrocked and comfortable, the rabbi led the blessing to celebrate special occasions.

Everyone chanted together,

> "Blessed are you, Lord our God, King of the Universe, who has kept us in life, given us sustenance and allowed us to reach this happy occasion."

שֶׁהֶחֱיָנוּ וְקִיְּמָנוּ וְהִגִּיעָנוּ לַזְּמַן...

Everyone cheered and laughed, ate and celebrated. Even I forgot our troubles and mixed with and met all who came. I kissed the children and felt more lighthearted than I had since this ordeal began. I enjoyed myself without the need of any chemical support.

Jacque brought a tall young man to me.

"This is my friend Lyle. He'll be bringing your equipment with the coyotes in the morning. Rachel and I have arranged to bring Ida to our home undetected. Rachel will explain it to her. You'll both be fine."

That was cryptic, and I wondered what the connection was between this fellow and the coyotes and how they connected to Jacque. But there was no chance to ask for an explanation. *Did Jews do that kind of work here in Quebec?* I wondered.

I brought Lyle to meet Ida and said that we would see him again in the morning.

When it was time to leave they dressed in their outerwear, hats, and scarves, and Jacque told the drivers, "Return by different routes!"

Ida and I laughed, wondering what the watchers were thinking and would do when the crowd left the building and split up. We were drained by the full day of tension, excitement, and contemplation, ending with this celebration.

We prepared for bed, kissed good night and snuggled under the covers.

# Chapter 35
# Cross-Country with Vulf
*Jon*

Monday morning, we were up and moving at six.

"So what's the plan for today?" Ida asked. "Tell me again—when are you leaving?"

"The American at the cinema said to be ready at seven. Last night we met Lyle, you remember. He's bringing my gear."

"Seems like a nice young man," Ida responded.

I thought to mention my quandary about Lyle, a Jew, involved with the coyotes––and that Jacque seemed to know about it. But I decided not to trouble Ida with it at that moment.

"The coyotes will take me over the border and Rollie is waiting at the lodge to take me to Groton."

She eyed me critically, probably sizing up my ability to handle the long day ahead. "Maybe you should go back to bed for another half-hour."

"Maybe, but first tell me what you discussed with Rachel yesterday."

"Well, Rachel told me firmly, 'You cannot keep playing cat-and-mouse coming and going from this flat.' While you're away she wants me to stay with her. She told me, 'Take this suitcase and go by taxi to the train station. The red beret guy, in a black beret tomorrow'—meaning today, you understand?—'will find you and bring you to our house without being followed.' She said not to leave any valuables or confidential information of any sort in the flat. It will likely be searched when we're gone. She'll send her cleaning service to pick up all our things. Jacque will find us another apartment, a place with 24/7 doormen and security. They didn't realize we would arrive with so much intrigue and mystery!"

232

"Well," I chuckled, "neither did we!"

At seven, a large, white, double-cab utility truck pulled up to the apartment. Five men in white ski suits, ski boots, hoods, large sunglasses, and backpacks got out and came to the flat. After awkward greetings, a short, broad-shouldered man became their spokesman. Everyone listened to him. His name was Vulf, or at least that's what it sounded like to me.

Vulf said, "Mr. Kadish, go to the bedroom and Lyle will give you your gear. He is six feet, like you, so the gear should fit. I hope the boots fit. They are very important. After you are dressed, put the things you'll need for your travel into the backpack, and we five will leave as we came. Lyle will stay here and be picked up in an hour wearing your topcoat and hat. We believe that will be sufficient to deflect the watchers from our tail. Okay?"

Lyle and I walked toward the bedroom. He handed me two-piece thermal underwear made of white silk from his backpack.

"Put these on and use the toilet now if you need to. It's not very convenient on the trail."

I went into the bathroom and took his suggestion. He took off his one-piece ski suit and handed it in to me, and I struggled into it, with straps, snaps, zippers, and Velcro. When I came out, he was in slacks, a sweater and shoes. He rechecked the closures of the suit and adjusted a few for better comfort. I sat on the bed and he helped me with the socks and boots. "They seem to fit well; you must be a size ten too," he said.

When I returned to the others, Ida smiled and Vulf nodded. He came over and patted me down, like he was doing a pistol frisk.

"I want to check the fit. You need room to move your limbs but not more than necessary. Are the boots feeling good?"

"Yes." I nodded.

"Okay, let's go. Lyle, you'll be picked up in about an hour. Keep a lookout for the truck."

I looked at Ida, who nodded her approval, but I could see she had some trouble, maybe fear in her eyes. *About being alone with Lyle,* I thought.

Lyle must have sensed something too.

"Please don't worry, Mrs. Kadish. Jacque and Rachel are friends and he approached me to do this because of my height. Our families are close. The son of one of Jacque's employees is a taxi driver and does these missions for extra money. That's the extent of my knowledge about all this. It seems bizarre to me too."

"What are you talking about?" Ida chided us both. "If I am anxious or nervous, it's because I know that Jon will overdo it and hurt himself!"

In another minute, I was tramping down the stairs in my white ski outfit following two of the men in front with two others behind. I sat in the middle of the second seat in the double cab. It was 7:25. Vulf started it up and pulled out of the driveway with a screech. He thundered down the street, and in minutes it seemed we were in the countryside. He said we weren't being followed. We had driven for nearly forty minutes when he pulled off the road and into what seemed to be a wildlife state park. It was 8:15.

"Everyone out!" Vulf shouted. "Man the equipment!"

Each of the four went to a compartment and started removing gear. Skis and poles, snowshoes, a sled, water cans, electrolyte drinks, protein and carbohydrate bars, even white facemasks. The small stuff was put into the backpacks, and the other gear was laid out and counted. The skis and poles were stuck standing upright in the snow. We each had a pair of gloved mittens. Everything was white.

"How are you feeling Kadish? Can I call you that?" Vulf asked. "We have a good day. Temperature in the mid-twenties, light wind from the southwest—it will be mostly to our right side. Visibility is clear with only high overcast. We start on cross-country skis. Do you want to ski with us or ride in the sled? Have you skied cross-country before?"

"Oh, yes. I've skied both downhill and cross-country a few years ago. And I'm in decent shape for my age. I swim regularly and have good stamina."

I had no idea what kind of shape I was in. I hadn't skied in twenty years and I didn't swim regularly, but I was embarrassed to admit it. My military fitness and ego from thirty or forty years ago came rushing out of my mouth.

I pointed at the gear. "Why the snowshoes?" I asked.

"There are several hills where it would take too much energy to sidestep with skis. We'll switch to snowshoes for those hills. The skis and extra items will go on the sled. *Now listen to me carefully:* do as much as you're able and willing, but don't kill yourself! We won't get paid if we don't get you there alive," Vulf laughed. "Don't worry, we'll get you to the finish line even if we have to carry you!"

I nodded my understanding. The portable stuff, including the backpacks, was loaded on the sled. One of the men helped me into my skis, handed me a pair of poles, and adjusted my hood, facemask, and sunglasses for me. I grabbed the webbed mittens. I had never used them before, but I could see their utility.

"Vulf will lead, you will be number three, I will be number four behind you with the sled. André will be number five behind me as the tail to begin. I am Milt."

"How far, how long until the lodge?" I asked.

"About fourteen miles, four to five hours depending on how you do."

"Depending on how *I do*?" I repeated. "Whatcha mean?"

"How long you can propel yourself, your ability to keep the pace, how long you need for rest stops, might we have to transport you on the sled. Stuff like that. You know, you are the cargo. It's our job to deliver you. We don't have a time limit."

"It's time to go. Is everybody ready?" Vulf called out.

I was good, anxious to step off and get started and a little insulted at being told I was the "cargo." Damned if I was going to slow things down, even if I wasn't in the best of shape of my life.

Vulf consulted a GPS app in his communicator and started out. I presumed he knew where he was going. It was 8:28. The number two skier began with six feet of separation from Vulf, and I began six feet behind him. Since I couldn't look back I didn't know quite where number four, Milt, and five, André, were, but I could hear them.

Initially the terrain was level to a bit downhill, maybe across a pasture. With the snow it was impossible to tell. The poling and skiing were comfortable, and I felt good. At the end we entered a forested region with a short uphill, then level for a bit and then another short uphill. After about six of these cycles, I was becoming winded and sweaty between the silk thermal and my skin. The separation between us doubled to ten or twelve feet each. We all exhaled steam as Vulf kept a steady pace. In another five or so minutes, we reached a minor crest, and Vulf poled a ninety degree turn to a stop and waited for the rest of us to catch up.

"Okay," he said, "are we all good? Does anyone need water or anything else before we continue?" I looked at my communicator. It was 8:50. We had been moving only twenty minutes.

The next section was a modest downhill, and we moved faster and with less effort. After a short swooshing across a valley, Vulf pulled us over for a stop, a rest, some refreshment, and an opportunity to relieve ourselves. I went off to pee with two others, then took a drink of water and ate a carb bar. I looked up the next portion of our route. The hill wasn't steep, but it was wooded and steadily uphill.

Vulf called for our first change to snowshoes. The skis were loaded on the sled, and numbers two and five grabbed the sled rope in fourth position as Milt became the number two, the man I followed. Our stop had been about ten minutes long. I wondered if that was good, bad, or average. We started out again, snowshoeing sideways and pushing off with the poles, a step at a time between the naked birches and decorated evergreens, up the incline. The two above me carved flat places for me to step. Sweat was now on my face and clouds on my sunglasses. Or my eyes were blurry. For whichever reason, I lost the ability to see the time and could no longer track our progress by the clock.

Almost to the top, Vulf shouted a warning, and everyone went down into the snow. I followed their lead. A moment later a large, low drone flew in front of our position, seeming to follow the ridgeline we were approaching. After it passed, I turned and sat up in the snow and asked Milt, "Is that normal? Does that happen often?"

"We expect it a few times each crossing. But being alert and wearing these suits protects us. The insulation and foil on the inside contain our heat. It makes us sweat but virtually eliminates our heat signature to their infrared sensors. The white on everything, even our faces, blends us in with the ground. Their chance of picking us up is only about 2 percent or less. We're good now."

We got up, and the trek continued. At the top, it was back to the skis.

Some time later, at another rest stop, Vulf passed out carb and protein bars, electrolyte drinks and candy bars. I supposed we were midway. So far I had been holding my own. The downhill and level cross-country were easier, sapping little energy. It was the snowshoe treks uphill, sideways, that were the most taxing. I knew I was slowing the group down because my gap to the number two kept getting wider. But I couldn't imagine being pulled on the sled. My pride wouldn't let me quit. We were twice more overflown by a drone and repeated the drill.

It was hours later when Vulf shouted, "Okay team! This is the last uphill."

Maybe he thought that would be encouragement. But for me, it was the opposite. I dropped to my knees. It had to be way past noon, because my groin was in pain and I was squeezing to contain my bowel. I could feel myself releasing gas as it gurgled down from my abdomen. Just as Lyle had warned, these one-piece ski suits, on winter days in this terrain, were not convenient to have a movement. No one in the team had gone off to do so.

Now, with another hill in front of me, my mind was wiped. My heart was racing, eyes blurred, and groin bloated in pain. I was overcome with a wave of anxiety—a full-blown anxiety attack. I started to think, *I can't do another hill, not this one, not any other.* I had no mental or physical energy left.

My pride left somewhere behind me, I slid from my knees to lie on my side. I was afraid I might break down; I needed a Valium but could not get to my mezuzah buried under the layers of clothing. I needed to shit but didn't speak up. I took off the mittens and facemask and put my hands over my face.

Milt pointed me out to Vulf, who hovered over me moments later.

"Can you do this? Once to the top, we have a mile of downhill and flat to the lodge. Maybe another forty minutes to the end."

"I'm sorry, boss," I managed to stammer. "My legs are rubber, my arms are stiff, I can't see. I don't think I can take another step. I'm sorry."

That was all I wanted to tell him. I thought I was going to cry.

"No problem, sir. You've been great to come this far. Top ten percent! Definitely top ten. Okay, guys, get that sled ready for Mr. Kadish. Let's get him to this crest, and maybe he'll be able to ski in on his own to the finish."

The men removed the gear from the sled and put the nearly empty backpacks on their backs. I was told to sit on the cushions and lean against the upright back of the sled. I released some gas, and the pain subsided. I squeezed my butt as tight as possible. They strapped me in across the ankles, the knees, the lap and chest. The skis and remaining gear were cleanly stacked on each side of me and a few things were tossed in my lap.

Vulf and Milt took the rope of the sled as Vulf called, "Ready?"

I can't remember what was said after that, but they began the side-step trek up the hill with the sled and me in tow. My eyes closed and my body slumped, drained, in the sled.

The next thing I knew, I was sitting on the sofa before the fire in the living room of the lodge, and Anne was handing me a hot cup of tea.

"This has sugar and milk," she said.

# Chapter 36
# Gag at the Depot
*Ida*

As I watched Jon leave in his white uniform, my moment of anxiety turned to fear. He was easy to follow with my eyes; he was the tallest in the group. The five got into the truck and drove off. No other vehicle moved. I knew Jon's pride and bluster. I prayed he wouldn't try to overdo the exercise. These were occasions when he reverted to his military mentality, believing himself able to do anything, forgetting he was seventy-one.

Less than an hour later, Lyle saw the Mercedes Q class truck that was to pick him up. He dressed in Jon's topcoat, scarf, and hat and rushed down the stairs. As he opened the truck door, he waved good-bye toward the second-floor bedroom. I was peeking out the living room window. I watched as three cars pulled seemingly out of nowhere to follow the Mercedes. I smiled and thought; *at least we seem to be working with intelligent operatives.*

The TV was on as always, but I upped the volume a bit for company. I checked the time. Almost an hour to get ready. I felt creepy alone in the flat and wanted to get going. But Rachel had told me, "Don't leave before 10:30."

In the suitcase she'd brought me were a wig, big black-rimmed sunglasses, a tweed overcoat, a scarf, a hat, a black handbag, and rubber overshoes. "Call a taxi to take you to the railroad station," she'd said. "When you get there, five other women at or near your height in the exact outfit, carrying the same suitcase, will be there. You are to meet at Tim Hortons, sit at adjoining tables, and exchange seats a few at a time for five or so minutes. You are *not to talk* to each other. You will leave together at exactly 11:15 on the big clock in the Grand Hall.

Each woman knows exactly what she's to do, where to go. You, Mother, are to walk left toward the ladies' room. The black beret will intercept you. Follow him and the instructions he gives you."

That was a bit to remember, but I was good with it. My daughter clearly knew me well. I was looking forward to this personal bit of intrigue, not focused on Jon for a change.

At the right time, I dressed as planned with the money belt around my waist. I put on the wig and looked myself over in the mirror. I wondered if Jon would like me as a blonde. I chuckled at the thought. I sat down to put on the overshoes. The rubber was thin and pliable, easy to put on, and they fit snugly. I called for the taxi, which advised that it would arrive within ten minutes. I put on the overcoat, the scarf, and the hat. While looking in the mirror, I added the big sunglasses.

*Who is that looking back at me?* I wondered. I liked the idea of this escapade. I felt like an actress in a movie. My pulse was racing, my adrenaline flowing. *I liked that I had an active part in this caper for a change. Did I just think "caper"? Wow!*

I put the rest of my valuables, Jon's money belt and my jewelry, purse, and personal stuff into the suitcase and I was ready to go. A wave went through me when I realized I was carrying half a million American bucks on my person. I shook it off and went down the stairs to get into the cab as soon as it arrived. It came and we were off to the station.

I looked at my watch. It was 10:35.

The taxi dropped me at the east entrance, and I was momentarily surprised to see another woman in exactly my outfit with the matching suitcase exit the cab in front of me. Even though I knew to expect it, the sight was still a bit of a shock. Women are usually embarrassed to be seen in the same outfit. I paid the driver, who was equally surprised—he kept looking at me, looking at her and back at me again.

"Popular style at Eaton's this season," I said and quickly walked into the station.

The time was 11:00.

I looked around and asked a passerby, "Where's Tim Hortons?"

"Grand Hall central," the man said as he pointed to his left.

I turned and walked erect, briskly looking for the sign. Three of us entered almost together. I was second, and another followed me in. The customers, seated and standing, stared in our direction. A certain buzz began to rise above the previous din. Maybe they thought we were part of a flash mob, expecting us to break out in song or dance at any moment.

The six of us gathered near the doors, lingered together, and then sat at two tables. After fifteen seconds we stood, shuffled like cards, and then sat back down. Once more we stood in a group and shuffled, and when the hall clock showed 11:15, we broke from the huddle and went our instructed ways. The man in the black beret was standing by a post on the way to the ladies' room. Catching my eye, he pointed me toward a different gate and a line of waiting taxicabs. He shuffled ahead of me and opened the door of one in the middle of the line. I didn't see the switch, but as I slid into the back seat, the beret was gone. A cabbie hat with tickets in the band and a cigarette behind his ear adorned the man in the driver's seat.

From alternate entrances, the other women crossed the drop-off lane and headed for the cabs. The six taxis pulled out almost together. At the first intersection, the first turned left and the second right. At the next, the third turned right and we turned left. I was in the fourth car. That was the last I saw of the others. My driver stayed with traffic as he said, "Duck down, *Madame,* and remove the hat, glasses, and wig. Change coats and scarves with the ones back there."

In fifteen minutes, he had me at the curb of the outside entrance to the synagogue.

"Go quickly inside. Rachel is waiting for you."

I did as told, and there she was, pacing back and forth as I came through security.

"Mom! You're here. Thank God!" Rachel said as we hugged and kissed each other's cheeks. "Come quick! Let's get out of here. My car is waiting at the inside lot."

I followed Rachel to her car, and we were off to her house. She pulled into their garage, and the door opened and closed automatically. I didn't see her push any buttons. We walked from the garage directly into a mudroom with seating and places for winter coats. It was shortly after noon.

"Oh, Rachel, I had so much fun in the disguise and playing a part in the masquerade! How did you ever plan and execute that? But I left my costume in the taxi. Will I get it back? I want Jon to see me in that! I want to give him a picture of me in that getup."

Rachel laughed. "Sure, Mom, and maybe you want a picture for yourself too. I'll have the driver bring it here later. The plan was conceived and executed by my Jacque. His family's office building rents space to a modeling and talent agency that hired the women. A detective and security agency down the hall from Jacque's office made the plan and hired the taxis. Jacque called them Saturday after dark, and we all met on Sunday morning. The agencies worked all Sunday interviewing women for the five parts and drivers for the taxis. There's a women's clothing store on the street level that provided the outfits. Jacque and I went out and bought the sunglasses, overshoes, and suitcases. Did you tell Dad about the plan?"

"Oh dear, no! He had enough to worry about with his own clandestine arrangements. I'll reach him and give him the signal that I am safely here. What about our stuff at the flat?" I asked.

"I thought to leave it there for today and send in the cleaning crew tomorrow or the day after. Is something there you really need now? You didn't leave anything valuable?" Rachel asked.

"Well, I'll need a nightgown for tonight, but I brought clean underthings for another day. I left two laundry bags from the start of the trip, Jon's and mine. Oh . . . and I need my pillow! It's sitting on top of a suitcase in a pink pillowcase."

"For tonight I can give you a nightgown. Do you need your pillow tonight?"

I felt childish for mentioning the pillow. "I can live without it tonight, but I would really like it for tomorrow."

"Okay, I get the picture. I'll have all your stuff picked up this afternoon. Mrs. Kellogg can do the laundry, and we can go shopping for whatever else you need or want. We're not staying cooped up just because you're being followed."

We both laughed. I knew the situation seemed absurd to Rachel, but it was becoming real and scary to me. I was glad she and Jacque played along so well even though they didn't really understand. Rachel made a telephone call.

"Your things will be here by four this afternoon. Are you ready for lunch? Wash up, and Mrs. Kellogg will serve us."

"Great!" I said. Putting my worries out of my mind and still invigorated by my adventure, I spritely walked the hallway to their guest quarters to wash and get comfortable.

# Chapter 37
# Returned to the Lodge
*Jon*

"What time is it?" I asked.

Anne was holding the cup of tea close to my face. I could feel the steam rising in my nose. It was comforting—reviving. I took just a sip.

Françi was on one side of me, Frank on the other. He was holding an ice pack against the back of my neck. My headgear had been removed; my snowsuit was unzipped down to my waist. From my ankles to my neck, I was feeling chilled from the soaked underwear. The shivers were coming on. My groin was in pain. I was still squeezing my butt to hold together.

"How are you doing now, Mr. Kadish?" Françi asked.

"I think I'm getting better . . . feeling more solid. What happened to me?"

"No one's sure. You lost consciousness. Did you faint or fall asleep? The coyotes carried you in and put you here not ten minutes ago."

"Vulf, Milt!" I shouted, sitting up straighter and looking for them. "Where are you? Where are they?"

"They're gone," Frank said. "Vulf said to remind you, 'top ten!' He said you would know."

I shook my head and smiled. I wanted to see Vulf, Milt, to thank the guys. I was embarrassed at how I'd ended the trek.

"I need a toilet, right away," I whispered to Frank.

Frank helped me up and to the kitchen.

"Will you be okay?" he asked.

"Fine, just wait outside."

"Would you like to soak in a bath or take a shower before you leave? I have a meal prepared for you and Rollie before you depart."

"Later, later, talk to me later."

I closed the door and fought to get my arms out of the one-piece and pull it down to my knees. The soaked silk underwear was next. Finally I sat down for the pressing need, my groin and sides in pain. With my elbows on my knees, my head in my hands, eyes closed, I released my lower muscles and felt instant relief. I took a deep breath and emptied my lungs. Another major drop contracted my abdomen, and my head began to clear. I started to breathe normally. Sitting there, I took off the boots, the suit and the pantyhose. I sat another few minutes and finished my business, flushing it away at last. I steadied myself by the sink and felt for my mezuzah. When I really needed it, it was under all those layers. I took a half of yellow and hoped my anxiety would calm down.

My communicator said 1:30.

*Sure, between the exercise and the time, my physical routine was screwed up.* No wonder I'd passed out. I was just happy I hadn't unloaded in the suit.

I opened the door a crack and asked Frank for a robe, letting him know I was naked. He returned in a minute and handed it in to me. Meanwhile, I washed myself as best I could. The heavy terry-cloth robe felt good against my body. The chills were gone.

Feeling much, much better, I stepped out of the bathroom and said to Frank, "A shower and some clean stuff is all I need. What should I do with that gear? Where's Rollie? Was he in the living room with me too?"

"Yes, yes, everyone was there . . . Rollie, the sheriff, young Segalov, and new guests. Forget the ski suit; I'll take care of it."

"Did I make a fool of myself?"

"Not in any way," Frank replied, shaking his head.

"Please take me to the shower and find my backpack with my stuff in it. I'll need shampoo and towels too."

"We have a complete overnight kit with everything. We have them for guests who arrive empty-handed. Take a shave. That will refresh you too."

Frank let me into the room Ida and I had been using. For the next twenty minutes I basked in the stinging hot water beating on my head and body. The heat and getting clean felt much better, but I could feel a sensation coming in all my muscles, joints and tendons—an unpleasant one. I knew by morning that sting would turn to pain. I flexed my left foot to calm soreness in my ankle. I had engaged body parts on that trek that were dormant for decades. I knew I was going to feel it soon, and probably for days to come. I visualized my aching body tomorrow when I had to be sharp. How would I ever make the return to Sherbrooke by that overland route?

As I rested on the bed, my mind went to the Israeli meeting. I loved the Israelis as a group. They were *my* people. But I hated that they had succumbed to the Chinese and no doubt stood by as atrocities, perhaps even executions were committed to eliminate the rabid, hostile Palestinian extremists. Sure, whatever they did might have been the best for the majority—the majority Palestinians, Arabs, and Israelis alike––but it most likely violated their victim's human rights!

"But those are the tactics of our enemies!" I said out loud.

The tactics so often used *against* the Jews through history. And just like all the times in the past, the world knew about the atrocities and watched without lifting a finger. I couldn't, wouldn't work for Israel if China would benefit. My doubts were growing. *I need to have a frank talk with Eric.* I wanted to hear his point of view and see if it might sway my inclination. The entire subject was disheartening. Ida had told me her view on Israel. A week ago I would have jumped for joy to hear it, but now I needed to talk and listen to her again. We both needed to talk to Eric and Rebecca.

*And who does Matthew represent? What trillionaire has an interest in my knowledge?*

Rollie and I sat at the kitchen table as Frank served steaming beef stew over egg noodles. It was wonderful. I had a beer, Rollie a Pepsi. We both had a second helping. My body was beginning to ache. As we ate, Frank started telling me what he had learned about the accident.

"Boris Segalov is the son of Sergei and Ivanica, the missing Russian couple from a year and a half ago. Nikelovich was the boy's father-in-law. The kid claims his mother was in touch with Nikelovich and asked him to meet her here in Pittsburg this weekend. She had money to give him for safekeeping and she would tell about the exciting work Sergei is doing."

I waved my hand dismissively. "Frank, you told me all of that before I left last Thursday. What's new? How about another helping of this stroganoff?"

Frank got up to get us the second helping. When he returned, he continued, "It turns out there is a bullet hole in the windshield of the car and in the forehead of Mr. Nikelovich who was in the passenger seat. He was shot dead as the car navigated Route 3 on its way here. The coroner hasn't determined the time of death as yet. The sheriff and his deputy think they've found the place where the shooter was waiting. They've called in help to search for evidence. Preliminary information is that the bullet is a .308 or similar, uranium-tipped round. It exited the back of the head and lodged in the headrest of the seat. Such a large slug had to come from a powerful rifle at short range to pass through the windshield, the skull, and into the cushion like that. Sheriff suspects a military-style rifle."

"Are you sure about the bullet? A uranium tip is a military round used to pierce armor. Hollow-point rounds are usually used by hunters for large game or by snipers and assassins against persons. If it's a uranium tip, he should ask the FBI to analyze it. Spent uranium from power reactors are used to make them. An analysis of the uranium composition and its waste products will tell which country the material came from. They might even be able to narrow it down to a specific power plant. That analysis can be as good as a fingerprint or retinal scan to identify the source."

"Sure, thanks. The kid is distraught, inconsolable. His wife and mother-in-law are arriving here later today to claim the body. The sheriff thinks the shooter was expecting Mrs. Segalov to be in that passenger seat and worries that she might still be in the killer's sights, wherever she is. The sheriff thinks Nikelovich was in the wrong place at the wrong time, and now he's dead. And that Sergei might also be in danger. At least part of the mystery of their disappearance has been solved. For some reason they seem to have left voluntarily, since it appears they are both living and he is working somewhere successfully. The sheriff is trying to trace Mrs. Segalov. If she's in this country, she is likely nearby or trying to get here."

"That should be easy enough through the immigration service. They have accurate records of who enters and leaves the country at each portal each day."

Thoughts flashed through my head like bolts of lightning. Maybe Nikelovich *was* the target for the bullet. Maybe the shooter knew he was in the passenger seat and the kid was driving. Or maybe the sheriff was right and the shooter expected it to be Mrs. Segalov. *Someone didn't want that meeting to take place, that's for sure. Who would want that stopped and why?*

"You checked your surveillance of last Thursday for Scott Matthew's movements. Did it appear that he'd left his room?" I asked.

"If he did, it was not by the inside hallway." Frank confirmed.

"Could he have left by a window or some other way to avoid the surveillance? And did you check to see if his driver possibly went out from the old wing?"

I wanted to know all that Frank knew about that odd couple. I needed more than he had told me on Friday afternoon when Ida and I were delayed.

Frank dodged my questions.

Instead, he asked, "Have you reason to suspect them?"

That was the second time he had asked that, and that bothered me. It made me wonder if Frank knew more than he was letting on. *Maybe his hallway surveillance picked up my initial encounter with Matthew? Maybe he saw him talking to me but couldn't hear what was said?*

"Suspect them? Why not?" I answered. They were here both times a Segalov was here––or should have been! They never said why. And then you told me about the Double-MATV. And now you are describing a military rifle and uranium bullet? Maybe that adds up to something," I said, letting sarcasm tinge my statement.

"Could be," Frank answered. "I'll check the video files further and let you know."

My suspicion of Matthew and his driver was embedded in the mysterious message that he gave me in that hallway. Replacing my curiosity, I began to feel fear—fear that my association with Scott Matthew and his trillionaire might not turn out well for Ida and me. I had to decide if I was taking that flight to Calgary on Friday. More than that, I had to decide whether or not to disclose him to Mickey tomorrow.

I was glad Frank didn't mention my return in another day in front of Rollie. He already knew too much. Especially after that rancor he'd spewed on the drive up here, I didn't want him learning any more. Though he'd been nursing a hangover from being stoned before the trip, I always believed the real truth came when a person's guard was down. *Drunks don't, can't lie,* I believed, *the same with the stoned.*

"Rollie, are we ready?" I asked abruptly, upset at him after reminding myself of his words. "Did you refuel the vehicle?"

He didn't seem to notice my change of mood.

"When you arrived with the coyotes, I alerted the Motivators. I estimated then that our departure would be about three o'clock. We're on time and can get started. I can file en route for them to take control. It won't matter that we'll already be a few miles down the road. I plan to refuel where Route 3 joins I-93, at that rest stop in Franconia."

"Okay! Please go out and get everything ready. I need to talk to Frank privately for another minute."

I waited until Rollie was safely out of the room before turning to Frank again.

"Frank, we were overflown three times by drones on the way here. They missed us each time," I said excitedly.

Frank laughed hysterically. I raised an eyebrow, annoyed, while I waited for him to quiet down enough to get his words out.

"Jon, they didn't miss you! They were *tracking* you! Each of you was wearing a GPS tracker in your gear, and yours had an identifiable icon. You were being monitored the whole way. A helicopter was ready in case of a serious mishap and they had to pull you out. But thankfully you made it the hard way—that's definitely to your credit. As Vulf said, 'Top ten!'"

He kept up the mirth. I didn't join him. Finally he leaned back in his chair and folded his arms.

"How was your meeting with the Israelis?" he asked.

"Better than I expected," I lied. I wanted him to think I was leaning their way. "I liked their precision, how they executed the meeting, where it was held, who they brought there. The conversation was very frank and I was proud to think that I am, in some way, a part of their people. Ida too was impressed, but we both still have issues with their policies and their connection to China. I am approaching my retirement years. I'm not looking for any high-stress situation."

I hoped that message would get to Mickey.

"Good thinking. In the end you'll see it's not so easy to turn your back on America."

I said quick good-byes to Frank and Françi and went out by the kitchen door to the parking lot. Rollie lowered the FAV stairs and I climbed in and got comfortable. We were on our way. We would make Groton at about 10:30 p.m. I adjusted the seat to the reclining position, strapped myself in and put the blanket over me.

I didn't remember the stop for fuel. I slept deeply and woke up about five hours later, as we slowed to leave I-495 for I-290 South, near Hudson, Mass. We were less than three hours from Groton.

# Chapter 38
# Mystery in Sherbrooke
*Ida*

Rachel's lunch was great—a zesty tomato soup with beans and a grilled cheese on kimmel rye.

"You don't want potatoes, do you?" she asked.

"No, no. Not for me."

I selected tea to drink.

As we ate, Rachel told me about an apartment Jacque was considering for us to move into when Jon returned. She took a quick look around. We were finally alone, private.

"Mom, now that Dad's not here, tell me what's going on with you two. Why this mysterious coming and going? Who is watching you and why? Don't try to evade me! I want to know the truth!"

Rachel knew all the preliminaries—the medical issue with her father and all the arrangements for leaving the US that she had already helped with, including those with her brothers. I told her about the calls from Otch and Mickey, the prospect of her dad's promotion, the FBI investigation, and how everyone seemed to know everything we were doing and planning. I told her about the Russian woman agent, her driver the assassin, the Chinese-Irish Israeli couple and the meeting with the ambassador at the cathedral on Sunday. Finally I told her about the Canadian Scott Matthew and his mysterious conversation with Jon at the lodge. And, after mulling it over, I told her about our experience at the movie and the invitation to Calgary for Friday.

"Wow," she said, aghast. "So who do you think is watching you now, here in Sherbrooke—the Russians, the Israelis, that Canadian, the Americans?"

"For sure the Russians and those Canadians. I'm not sure whether the Israelis or Americans are the third. It could be either or both.

They all have reasons to want to keep us in sight and see where we go and with whom we talk. We don't believe the US or Israel intend us any harm, but we're not sure of the others. It's really scary."

"I should think so!" Rachel said. "Jacque and I are very concerned. He's been terrific coming up with ideas to help you move around. Wasn't his orchestration of today outstanding? The modeling agency told the other women it was for a gag."

"Very creative and effective. Jon and I appreciate all you've done to help."

"What would you like to do now?" Rachel asked. "It's about two. Do you want to rest? Are you up to doing some shopping? I need to go out on some errands at four. Maybe you should rest for now and come with me then?"

"Let's do that," I said.

As I rested in the guest room, I thought about the meeting with the Israelis. I liked that woman ambassador. Come to think of it, we were surrounded by women—the Russian UN ambassador, Katya, and Admiral Abramoff, and the Israeli Ambassador and Colleen. I like seeing women in important positions, like when I was CEO of Now's. Israel was a leader in women's rights. They'd had a woman prime minister as early as Golda Meir, an immigrant from Russia and Milwaukee. I had read her biography years and years ago. She was only the third woman prime minister the world had ever seen, and just the fourth prime minister of the state of Israel . . . or was it the other way around? I had become a bit more optimistic about settling down there, maybe in Gaza as Jon had suggested. But now he was perturbed toward them. He'd been terribly noncommittal when we talked about it yesterday. Then I recalled he'd also been cynical about America and its humanitarian work in Indonesia. *I swear I don't know what that man is thinking! We need to talk to Eric and Rebecca. I hope they can help us both sort this out.*

After three-thirty, the kids were home from school. Rachel and I gave them personal attention, asking about their day, listening to their stories. Rachel gave last-minute instructions to Mrs. Kellogg, who would be leaving at five. She told Hazel, the nanny, "We'll be back about five-thirty and will feed the kids at six as usual."

And we were off.

We returned just after five-thirty to find Hazel near to hysterics.

"Calm down, calm down!" Rachel told her. "What's the problem, the problem?"

The younger kids were running around their playroom, the TV blaring, and the oldest was studying in his room, gyrating his head to earphones.

"Lower that TV now!" Rachel yelled at the kids. I don't know how they could hear her, but the volume was lowered. Rachel sat Hazel down on a stool at the kitchen counter. We sat too.

"So what's the story?" Rachel asked.

Swallowing hard and taking a deep breath, Hazel stammered, "Your husband called just after five and asked if I had seen your mother—Mrs. Kadish?" She nodded toward me.

Rachel and I nodded back.

"I said, 'Yes sir,' that you both were here before leaving for errands.

"He asked, 'Are you sure?'

"I said, 'Sure? Of course I'm sure! I know your mother-in-law. The kids know their grandma. Mrs. Kellogg has already left for the day, but she saw her too.'

"He told me to look at the five o'clock news flash on the *Sherbrooke Record* Cloud site. 'Tell Rachel to call me as soon as she gets home.' Then he hung up. So I hit the *Record's* app on my communicator and the story came right up."

She did it again and showed it to us.

Mature Woman Kidnapped
Downtown from Invaded Taxi

A taxicab was rear ended and pinned to the car in front of it as men emerged from both cars and abducted the woman passenger from the taxi, according to witnesses at the scene. The bold invasion took place at the intersection of Rue Wellington Sud and Rue King Ouest after eleven-thirty this morning. The woman was taken to the lead car, which took a right on Rue King Ouest and sped away over the bridge toward the northeast. The cabbie interviewed at the scene told this reporter that he picked up the woman at the Station de Depot and was taking her to the Eglise Saint-Stanislas. He described her as in her early or mid-sixties, blonde, about five foot eight, wearing a large chapeau, sunglasses, a colorful scarf and a tweed coat. The cabbie said the woman gave her name as Ida and told him she was from America. The police refused to comment on the incident, only to say, it would be under investigation.

Rachel and I both clasped our hands to our mouths and groaned in shock and disbelief!

"Oh my God!" Rachel gasped. "That must be one of the actresses the agency hired for the part! Oh, she must be terribly frightened . . . I hope she isn't hurt!"

I couldn't catch my breath. *They took that woman thinking she was me?* My brain screamed.

"Quick Rachel, call Jacque. See what more he knows. He's probably wondering if I've been . . . ah . . . er . . . taken."

I couldn't say the word "kidnapped." I was sick to think what might happen to that poor innocent actress.

Rachel called her husband and told him, "Mom is here, at home with me. It is surely my mom and she surely has *not* been kidnapped."

Rachel clicked it onto the wall communicator so he could see and talk to both us.

Jacque related, "Henri DeBar from the talent agency called and said one of the actresses, Shelley Demers, did not get home. Her husband was getting panicky and called the agency, saying he was getting ready to call the police. Henri stalled him and asked for some time to make a few calls first. The husband agreed."

Jacque's voice became somewhat panicky.

"When the husband reports his wife missing to the Metro and tells them of her gig with the gag, the police will call Henri. When he gets called, he asked me what he should say. If he tells them that I was the client and reveals the nature of the gag, we will all be exposed to the watchers—Ida, you and me, Rachel; even the children. I don't know if that may put us in trouble. I didn't know how to answer Henri. He told me he would try to stall if the police called but would need to have his story soon."

"Oye vey," Rachel said. "What to do?"

The news from Jacque only made me feel worse. *Maybe I need to volunteer to be taken hostage to free Mrs. Demers?* But I knew I needed to keep my head and not do anything foolish that might make matters worse. I needed to be in touch with Jon, but he wasn't planning to call, and I had already sent my "I am safe" code to his communicator.

"I'm coming home," Jacque said. "Wait for me."

Jacque was home at six, and Hazel was left to feed the children by herself—which Rachel assured me was not unusual. Jacque served us a glass of wine in the living room and we talked of the day, its success and the disaster that had followed.

"I haven't heard from the agency since that initial call," he said. "I wonder what's happening. If Mr. Demers called the police to say his wife was missing, I probably would have heard from Henri by now."

"But you haven't heard from him, right?" Rachel asked.

Jacque nodded.

"Then why not call him and see if he has any more on the incident?"

Jacque grimaced. "My preference is to let it drift a little longer."

"No, Jacque, no," Rachel and I said almost in unison. "Please call now and see if he knows anything more."

Jacque picked up his communicator, consulted his directory and punched at the pad. He transferred the signal to their living room communicator. Console-to-console conversation allowed the talkers to see each other. Each party had control of the cameras on the other end: Jacque could control the cameras looking at Henri and Henri could do the same looking at us. It was always important to look your best in the house just for these unexpected occasions. Jacque motioned for Rachel and me to move out of the cameras' range.

Henri answered looking very disheveled, wearing just a sleeveless undershirt and boxer shorts. His ample salt-and-pepper hair was almost standing straight up.

"Henri, hi. Have you heard anything further from the husband or the Metro?"

Henri looked up at the screen and asked, "Jacque, that is you?"

"Yes, yes, it's me, Henri. Do you know anything new about the Demers lady?"

"No, no, no!" Henri said, rapping his knuckles three times on a tabletop with each pronouncement. "I haven't heard again from Monsieur Demers, or from the Metro Police."

He tossed his hair and rocked his head. Suddenly he realized what he was wearing.

*"Me regardez-vous? Vous envahissez ma vie privée!"* Henri shouted as he threw a towel over the camera.

We laughed.

"How about the newspaper, Henri? Maybe you should ask what they know?" Jacque asked.

Henri said, "You do it! Oui, oui, oui!" again with three staccato raps on his tabletop. "After all, they released the *Flash D'informations*—*peut-être*—they have learned more?"

Henri, quirky, quickly disconnected, probably wishing he hadn't answered at all.

After a short discussion, Jacque called the *Record's* news department and asked for the reporter who wrote the Cloud flash. Jacque again waved us away from the view of the cameras. The reporter came on the video communicator, a young, attractive woman maybe twenty years of age.

"There is nothing new to report sir," she said matter-of-factly. "The Metro Police haven't received a complaint from anybody. Someone has to report a missing person or something to allow them to open a case file. They said, 'Maybe the woman went voluntarily? Maybe the men were her relatives? If there was foul play, someone with a relationship to the victim must file a complaint.' I asked if they checked the inter-section surveillance video and they said no. They cannot even do *that* without a complaint. Can you imagine?"

"What about the report of the cabbie?" Jacque asked. "Isn't that enough to open a file?"

She shook her head. "The Metro has the cabbie's name and car license, but they haven't been able to contact him or find the car. I gave them a video of the man I interviewed, but they told me it didn't match the picture of the driver the taxi department sent to them.

"Listen," she said, lowering her voice, "the *Record* got an anony-mous call that an act of civil disobedience would occur at that cor-ner from eleven to noon on Monday. I was sent to cover it. There was no demonstration there. Then the auto pileup happened. At first I thought it was just luck that I was there to see the woman taken. But the cabbie seemed ready to give me his story—and then he stepped back into the car and drove away while we were waiting for the Metro. Now I'm thinking it was all a setup of some sort. I'm just waiting for the next shoe to fall. I don't think this story is dead, but I don't know what's coming next."

She paused and then her eyes lit up a bit as she asked, "Wait just minute, sir," she said sharply. "What is *your* interest in this case?"

Jacque immediately disconnected and then held his breath, waiting for the reporter to return his call. His coordinates would definitely be in the paper's communication log. He quietly sipped the wine as we waited. But the call didn't come. Perhaps the young reporter was working against another deadline.

After an appropriate wait, Jacque was relieved that he and the agency were not implicated as yet. But no one knew if it was going to last.

"Henri didn't say if he had tried to check on *Mr. Demers*, did he?" Jacque said. "Maybe he has been taken too? Maybe they don't have children or local relatives who will miss them right away. We'll have to tell all this to Jon as soon as possible."

Rachel and I emphatically nodded our heads.

# Chapter 39
# Tuesday at the Boat
*Jon*

By the time I got to the Boat in Groton, I was thinking I should never have returned for the interview Mickey had booked for me with the FBI. It was way too risky. The process had me illegally reentering the USA to circumvent the mistake I'd made with our exit permit. Though Frank, a federal agent, had arranged my illegal return, would Mickey or anyone there know or care?

It wasn't just the risk that had me rethinking the plan—it was also the pain. My ego had me physically overexert myself trying to be the navy ensign I was fifty years ago. My every muscle cried out for Ben-Gay or IcyHot or whatever the modern equivalent was. I'd slept most of Monday afternoon in the FAV, so I couldn't sleep much that night. I spent an hour in a tub of hot water from eleven to midnight and another hour in the hot tub at the pool from six to seven in the morning. The massaging effect of the water jets soothed but didn't cure my kinks. I was achy and cranky. And now I needed to get to the office to undergo scrutiny. What fun? In only five days of vacation, I had broken the law and totally fucked up my natural body rhythms and routine. *All for the privilege of an FBI grilling.*

Enterprise Rent-a-Car showed up at my hotel with the only car that was available, an all-electric Dachshund by Volkswagen. It was a stretched mini, plug-in electric commuter. *This will never get me back to Pittsburg.* "Take this for now and we'll exchange it later," they said at the door. *That's always a nuisance.*

Then the guard at my office lot gave me a hard time. The car was unfamiliar and didn't have an authorized Codablock sticker to be scanned, recorded, and to automatically allow me entry. "For god's sake, this is an Enterprise Rent-A-Car! My car is being serviced," I lied.

"You should have reported to the visitor's entrance and asked for a temporary parking pass. They make 'em up on the spot. Takes no more than ten minutes."

"Goddamn it, Dennis, you know me! Are you going to let me in?" I fumed at him. *Another little bureaucrat with a bit of power, hassling me over the fucking office parking lot, for god's sake!*

"Okay Mr. Kadish, just this time," he finally agreed, shaking his finger at me. "But everyone must obey the rules. If you go out for lunch or for any reason, go to the visitor's entrance and get a temporary sticker before coming here again."

"Sure, sure," I said. "You're making me late for a meeting." It was another lie, but I couldn't stand his attitude.

I sped off to my reserved spot. I absolutely should have known then what a mistake it all was—I should have turned around and left.

The front door guards were more cordial. Because they knew I didn't have a chip, I was allowed to flash my employee card with my picture to gain access to the building. The identification scanner, not integrated with Central-Data-Com, only did a face recognition test, and I passed that as I always did. I took the elevator to the fifth floor, where the Level IIIs had their offices. The sixth floor was for the Level IIs. And the seventh was for the still higher-ups—the admirals, generals, and Level I scientists, engineers, and administrators.

Off the elevator landing there were doors to three distinct wings. I approached mine, put my right thumb on the fingerprint reader and placed my right eye up to the retinal scanner. I heard a distinct click as all three hallway doors automatically bolted—locked against me. Not the welcome I had expected! A siren started screaming. The elevator immediately began to descend, trapping me on the fifth floor landing with nowhere to go. There was no stairway, no other exit from the elevator landing. Multiple surveillance cameras pivoted in my direction. *What now?*

In seconds, Marine MPs came flying through the hallway doors, a couple with weapons at ready. I was pushed to the floor, frisked for a weapon and plastic-cuffed behind my back. Wow did that hurt my already sore arms, shoulders and neck! I was so stunned I couldn't even protest. I asked what was going on, but nobody answered me.

The elevator arrived and a Marine major, the security officer on deck that day, stepped off. He was someone I didn't know. That position rotated frequently and the security officer rarely made an appearance at the guard post. We seldom knew any of them.

By this time, spectators at each hallway were crowding the doorways to take a look at the commotion.

"What's happening? Who's that guy? Are we in danger?" came from many squeaky female voices. *Yada, yada, yada,* I thought. I could hear men talking quietly among themselves.

"Okay," the major said, standing at ease, his hands clasped behind him, "How did this imposter get this far?"

Before I could protest, someone else did it for me.

"Imposter! What are you talking about?" Merle, a colleague engineer from my department, sang out. "That is Jonathon Kadish, a distinguished member of this staff for thirty years."

"Are you sure—completely sure? The print and retina scanners identify him as Jonathon Kadish, but Main Brain says he is in Canada now. He crossed into Quebec on Thursday through Beecher Falls, Vermont."

The major paused, then continued, "Is this Jonathon Kadish or not? Is he here or in Canada?"

"Merle," I called, relief flooding me at the presence of a friend, "please get Mickey right away!"

*Main Brain* was what we called Central-Data-Com, the mysterious master computer in some secret underground bunker in who-knows-where. We were always trying to find clues to its location.

The elevator closed and began to ascend. It was being called from above. In another long minute it returned to the fifth. Mickey and a general in uniform—it had to be General Catern—stepped off. The major and the Marines snapped to attention and saluted the senior officer.

He returned their salute and ordered, "As you were."

The crowd murmured their approval.

"Major, please," said the general, "release this man into my custody. Write up and file your report according to procedure, and I will file a reply. This is Jonathon Kadish, and I had him brought from Quebec to meet with me here. I'll have the record amended to explain the circumstances. Now, all of you government workers get out of here and back to work! The circus is over for today!" the general growled.

The major and two marines stepped into the elevator and descended.

The squeakees giggled as they withdrew down the hallways. The doors closed behind them. Mickey helped me off the floor. A Marine cut the cuffs and whispered, "Sorry."

I shook both my hands at the wrists, rubbed them, then clenched and unclenched my fingers to return circulation. Everything in my body hurt. Mickey called for the elevator to return. He and the general directed me onto it and we headed to the seventh floor. It was 9:30.

In Mickey's private conference room, a place I'd been many times, I sat opposite the two senior officers. I could see General Catern's name badge on his uniform.

"Have you had your morning coffee?" Mickey asked.

"You saw the only thing I've had in the office so far today," I answered.

"How do you take it?"

"Just black will do, thank you."

Mickey called the cafeteria. "Please send a pot of regular coffee, the usual accompaniments and a selection of Danish to this conference room. Apply it to my account."

"Tell me," General Catern asked, "how did your meeting with the Chinese go?"

"I had no meeting with the Chinese, sir," I said indignantly, immediately sitting up straighter.

This was my first introduction to General Catern, and my impression was that he was an arrogant, opinionated stuffed shirt—what I thought about most army guys.

"The meeting was with the Israelis, sir, *not* the Chinese. It went well, I think."

He scoffed. "The Chinese have them in their pocket. The Israelis always pushed back against us when we were their big brother, but they're not able to do that now. The Chinese don't stand for that shit."

"I didn't sense that it's like that at all, sir. The Chinese might be a different player when it comes to Israel. The Jewish people have always intrigued the Chinese. They seem to think that the Jews and the Chinese are the only peoples to survive from antiquity to modern day."

I went through the entire routine that I'd learned at that meeting, Ambassador Golan's words rolling off my tongue.

"The Chinese have enormous economic power on both the buy and sell side of every transaction and unlike us, they are not ashamed to use it. The United States has only limited power to commandeer our economic resources for state purposes because of our private enterprise, democratic system. We are always pussyfooting around trying to make everyone happy—and that seldom works. The Chinese don't pay attention to world opinion and pretty much do as they want. It's a totally different approach to world affairs. Despite all that, my impression is that Israel can hold its own. And to be direct, sir, I never understood why we ruptured relations with Israel because of China when we never touched relations with China itself?"

Mickey raised an eyebrow. "I didn't realize you have such a keen understanding of international strategic affairs and forces," he said. "Maybe we haven't accorded you the best opportunity to serve your country."

What was with me? *Yesterday I was pissed at the Israelis, and now I'm standing up for them. I guess it's just a Jewish trait—come together to defend each other when attacked by outsiders.* The general's approach had offended me. He knew I was Jewish and had a son and grandkids in Israel.

"But *this* is your country!" the general jumped in. "You were born here, served with distinction in our submarine service and might have made admiral had you not retired. America is your number-one loyalty, and you know it! We know it too. You're a friend to this country, Kadish."

The general's recognizing my citizenship and long service to America made me feel better, and my internal defenses somewhat relaxed. The coffee arrived and that made a big difference too.

"Sir, I needed to leave the navy when I did. My next assignment would have taken me away from Groton. I had already been to the War College in Newport and was to report to the Naval Postgraduate School in Monterey. From there I was headed to four years at the Pentagon. Norwich is my wife's hometown, and she was the CEO of her parents' business. She was in the process of rationalizing it then and doing a great job. It would have been the worst time for her or me to be uprooted. We still had two kids at home. I retired to keep my marriage intact and to pursue my career here at the Boat. I love the work I do here. I'm pleased with the path my life and career have taken."

The general responded, "Diplomatic relations with Israel are very complicated. We helped finance most of their technological developments, especially in the area of military matters. They agreed never to share the technology that we transferred to them, or to which we made a financial contribution––to any other nation without our

266

express approval. Our highest tech companies all had operations or subsidiaries in Israel—most still do. But our country was in dire financial straits after the Iraq and Afghanistan wars—while Israel, with our help—had become an economic and military Mighty Mouse in their region in spite of all the Arabs against them. They were actually pretty safe because of all the internal strife going on in the Arab world. Who, other than Iran, represented a real threat to them? Our country could no longer justify spending even a billion dollars a year there. Foreign aid was reserved for Third World countries and our military aid was only available for a fee and profit. Israel declined to buy our aid and we were concerned about their pledge regarding our jointly developed technology. They tried to do an AWACS deal years—yea decades ago now that we had to stop!

"Official relations were ruptured, yes. Many connections and non-military commerce still continue in a quiet way. But I am curious about your impressions. Why do you believe the Chinese do not totally control Israel's strings?"

"You know my son Eric is over there. He keeps me peppered with articles and analysis from their local sources. The news we get here is totally skewed, skewed by our government media. They keep portraying our relations with Israel as *cold*. They don't lie outwardly—they tell only half the truth and slant it for their own purposes. I'm tired of the limitations we've placed on what was a free press and the personal freedoms we've given up in the name of security."

I realized I was off on a tangent and came back to center.

"To your question, sir, the Israelis are very smart. They play China like a fiddle. They take advantage of China's manufacturing capability to build Israeli inventions, their consumer base to buy Israeli products, and their need for Israel's research and technology to give them technological leverage. Tel Aviv is recognized as second in the world in technological innovation, second only to our Silicon Valley.

"The Israelis bend China to *their* needs. Israel has good relations with more countries than we do, maintaining independent contacts and commercial dealings. They're not only China's Silicon Valley, but they've helped their agriculture bloom, teaching a whole cadre of agricultural engineers and managers in their systems. China is much improved in water desalination and efficient recycling because of Israeli technology and know-how. It's their backbone. Israel won't let China dictate what they can trade or with whom. And the partnership is positive for Israel too—it works. Look how China solved the Palestinian problem. A few million Arab refugees were a joke to the Chinese, who have to deal with many factions within a billion people all the time! China has brought relative peace to the region with their Palestinian solution. I think China and Israel are now mutually dependent. They both understand and respect each other. It's not at all a matter of puppet and master."

I couldn't believe I'd said all that. *Why did I skip the atrocities and murders that might have been committed? Like so many now and throughout history, I can admit the truth to myself but not to others.*

"Well, I hope you're right, Kadish. I hope you're right. We haven't had relations with Israel for more than ten years, and I confess they haven't seemed to skip a beat. But I can tell you the Chinese in Asia and in Africa are not the same as in your story. They are our major adversary and the reason we get so much income for our protective services. So what do the Israelis want from you? What do the Russians want?"

There were things I wanted to tell Mickey, but not the general. I knew Mickey well and could predict his reactions. But the general was a stranger, a wild card.

"That's the jackpot question, sir. In fact, General sir, Mickey—I am hoping you can tell me? I've been trying to think of what I've done that's so valuable, the projects I've worked on in the navy and here. For the life of me, I can't think of anything I've done that would warrant this kind of pursuit. The Israelis are offering me a university position and a consulting arrangement for their coastal sub program and their use of fuel cells to power their Vornado propulsion systems. But we don't use those systems in our boats, nor do the Chinese, and my knowledge of them is limited. It's hard to think of what I can specifically bring them. But if I can help them in their local strategic mission, I don't see that as detrimental to the interests of the United States. What do *you* think they want from me? What do the Russians want?"

I purposely avoided telling them about my meeting with the Russians. And I decided not to mention graphene, thorium, or MHD.

"Hard to tell," said Mickey. "You know how we manage our projects—compartmentalized. Particular teams don't get more knowledge than they need for their portion of a project. Higher-level-security people work on certain integration, but it's only at a higher level yet that even fewer people get to know the whole system. But you've been Level III for quite a while and have worked at even higher levels without the designation. Maybe the Israelis are looking for general knowledge of many things rather than a breakthrough on some top-secret something you or we may have worked on. It's hard to tell.

"But you're not going to any other side!" Mickey continued. "As the general said, you're an American first. That's right, isn't it? I should have recommended you to Level II a long time ago, but I was under pressure to keep our costs as low as possible. That was everyone's mission while our government was recovering from the financial quagmire after Afghanistan and Iraq, the recessions, and the lingering period of stagflation until into the '20s. That included pressure to *not* promote even deserving people. I'm sorry that I let your seniority and contributions slip through the cracks of that pressure."

Mickey turned to General Catern. "I told the board that they were hampering us, me and others with similar responsibilities, by not allowing us to reward performance as private industry would have prior to our takeover. I was afraid it was a mistake and might cost us someday."

"Did you really put in my promotion in December and not tell me as you explained? Or did this come about because I started thinking of leaving?"

"Please Jon, please––don't say that anywhere, especially here!" Mickey scolded. "Just saying that *you might be leaving* could put you behind bars. You're with friends here and that's not what we want for you. Be careful how you talk."

"Sorry. And that was an unfair question. I am pleased, very pleased to be recognized with this promotion. I want to leaf through the Level II Manual, especially the medical benefits section. The Israelis have offered me individual medical analysis and personal treatment. That is very attractive to me."

"You'll see the manual when you have time at your desk."

"So what about the Russians? When are you meeting with them?" the general asked.

"Not set up yet, sir," I lied. "What will they want from me, I wonder. Can you tell me that?"

"Well, you won't have to ask them. They'll tell you straightaway. We want to know why they want you too."

"Do you have any advice for me on how to deal with them, sir?"

The general sat back in his chair, exercised his neck and shoulders as he prepared to answer. He took on a professorial posture. I was waiting for his army fluff.

"Their approach will be totally different." He said. "I gather the Israelis appealed to your peoplehood instincts with their so-called homeland and their desire for your general knowledge. The Russians will tell you point blank what they want. And it will be something they know you know. Then they'll concentrate on the rewards you will be given—an apartment in the best neighborhood, a winter dacha on the Black Sea, access to imported goods, fresh food, money."

Inwardly I was impressed. He certainly had Russia's number.

Catern continued, "They won't be looking for general knowledge. They have spied on us for a century, have moles in many of our departments, capture the same data from the Cloud about our people that we do. They may even do a better job of it! Their people are not as assimilated as we are into the Cloud network. Our surveillance of them does not yield the same fruit as theirs of us... But we have our assets on their soil too, though probably not as numerous. With our satellite reconnaissance and listening capability, we get what we need.

"This I can promise you: you'll learn more about your specific value to them than you did from the Israelis. And you'll tell that to us."

"I'm not so sure," I answered. "I need to think about that. If I agree to lead them on, to get their information and return that it to you—under what umbrella will I be protected? I'll need some definitive answers from people here and in Washington."

The meeting was interrupted by a call from the entry post. The FBI agent had arrived and was waiting to be received. Her chip scan had been approved.

"Escort her to the seventh floor and my assistant will meet her," ordered Mickey.

Mickey sent his aide, a Lt. Commander, to the elevator landing. In minutes, the FBI agent was shown into the conference room.

"Gentlemen and sir," she nodded to the general, "My name is Evelyn Stanson. I am with the FBI monitoring group in Hartford. My credentials were confirmed by your security detail. I have an appointment with Mr. Kadish at eleven o'clock."

"This is Mr. Kadish," Mickey said, pointing to me as I stood. "And this is General George Catern, Deputy Director of the Defense Industry Cabinet." The general stood and nodded toward her.

"How long do you need with Mr. Kadish? We have important government business to discuss with him," General Catern asked.

I was already distracted by the presence of the FBI. The invasion of our home three weeks earlier was burning in my mind, and I was working up my anger to ask her if she had ordered it and why. I planned to chastise her for that invasion of our privacy.

But her next words knocked every other thought out of my head.

"Excuse me, sir," she answered the general, "but I have my instructions to interrogate Mr. Kadish. He has a clean record of nearly fifty years' service, but he and his wife have been acting strangely in recent times. He has a lot of explaining to do if he is to be approved by our department for your recommended promotion.

"Have you been notified by the State Department that they received a contact from a group calling themselves, 'The Free Africa and India Coalition'?"

"No ma'am," Mickey answered. "What does that have to do with us?"

"The group claims they are holding Mrs. Kadish in Sherbrooke, Quebec. She will only be released after they meet with Mr. Kadish in Canada. They were insulted when Mr. Kadish secretly left Sherbrooke to return to the United States. They claim a contact was made and he agreed to meet with their leadership."

While we listened in stunned silence, she pulled up a message on her communicator and read it out loud:

"After he rejoins his wife and listens to our proposal, the Kadishes will be free to go wherever they please. We intend no harm to either of them."

"That's the substance of the message. Now, what's this all about, Mr. Kadish? Who are they and what do they want with you? Have you had contact with them or not? What's your story?" She asked accusingly.

All eyes around the table focused on me.

But I was panicking.

*"Ida! They have Ida?* Is that so?" I managed to say.

I looked at the FBI lady in disbelief, my eyes squinting and my forehead wrinkled. "When, how did they take her? Where? She's supposed to be with my daughter from yesterday until I return there. Ida sent me our confirmation code yesterday at . . ."

I stopped to look at the log in my communicator.

". . . at 12:30 p.m. What have you been able to confirm? I need to call her and my daughter to ensure they're safe and see what they know. This is bizarre!"

My head was spinning. The name "Free Africa and India Coalition" meant nothing to me. The only reasonable connection was to Scott Matthew and his cohort. I had to make a quick decision. I hadn't planned to tell these people about the trillionaire or any of that episode.

Evelyn said, "The message came in this morning about two hours ago. Our people in Ottawa and Montreal have been notified. State gave us access to the message. Our analysts in Washington and Boston are looking into the organization. If Mr. Kadish can reach his wife or daughter and learn what they know, that might be of help."

Mickey stood and motioned for me to follow. We went to his office where he obtained a secure analog line. He asked me for Rachel's data, so I plugged my communicator into his system and uploaded it to his network. I noticed that it was 10:50. We reached Rachel and she put Ida on the phone. Wow, was I glad to talk to her!

*"You're safe!* You've been okay all the time?" I asked. "They said you were kidnapped!"

We chatted alone as Mickey went out to give me a minute of privacy and to get the general and the FBI agent. Ida quickly told me about the masquerade and the news flash. She explained what she knew and told me about the call Jacque had gotten from the talent agency and their call to the newspaper. *Strange, very strange,* I thought.

"When the others get in here, don't bring the talent agency or Matthew up, if you can help it," I told her.

"How can I avoid that?" she replied. "That's how we learned that the Demers woman is missing."

While I thought about that, she asked, "Did you call the Snyders to tell them we arrived safely?"

"No! You're bothering me about that? I thought you would pick that up," I saidannoyed that she was bringing up such a minor detail at a time like this. "I'm tied down here!"

The noise of the others arriving interrupted our discussion of domestic affairs.

"Oops, too late, the others are coming! I'll call you again later when I'm free to talk."

Mickey turned up the speaker so all could hear Ida's recitation of the events. Because we were using analog for privacy, there was no video of Ida for them to look at. I think they were annoyed at being denied her body language with her recitation. Mickey led her debriefing. Her story was recorded and immediately translated into text in the FBI space in the Cloud. Evelyn entered it into her report. The others asked question after question, but nothing new was disclosed. Ida simply answered a lot of, "I don't know, I don't remember."

In due time the interview was terminated.

The others returned to the conference room, leaving me another minute of privacy to say good-bye. We talked quickly again about the conversation with the reporter and the news piece about the abduction. It all sounded like some kind of setup to me and Ida agreed. I told her that they should all sit tight. There would be another move by the perpetrators when they were ready. We said our good-byes. Again I said, "I'll call again later when I'm free."

I returned to the conference room and before anyone could say a word, I asked, "Who are the trillionaires in the world? How many of them are there?"

I decided to take the initiative. The three at the table all had blank faces.

"Why?" they all asked.

"Why do you want to know that?" Evelyn asked.

"A mysterious Canadian named Scott Matthew, or that's what he told me, said he works for a security company and that a trillionaire would arrange a private jet to fly Ida and me to Calgary to meet with him this week. He said, 'a trillionaire wants to make you an offer that you won't be able to decline.' Matthew said his company had been engaged to protect us, Ida and me, while we were in Canada. So I know they were watching us. I sense they're connected to this. So, who could this trillionaire be and what would *he* want from me?"

Evelyn recorded all these details as I talked. She would no doubt investigate Matthew.

After a lengthy discussion, we could come up with no likely candidates for a trillionaire, and certainly none who might have any connection to Africa or India.

When nearly an hour had passed, the general piped up, "Miz Stanson, we don't have time for you to interview Mr. Kadish today. We have too many issues to discuss with him in limited time. I will speak to your director in Washington about Mr. Kadish––so an interview might not be necessary. Please wait to hear from your superiors before continuing this assignment."

Now that was a big surprise coming from the general! Maybe he was a "good guy" after all.

Evelyn said, "Except for these most recent discrepancies, Mr. Kadish's record is clean. No material found at the Kadish home by my colleagues last month would disqualify him. His approval should not be a problem if the general explains this recent behavior to the director."

Then she turned to me and smiled. "Other than the Beretta M9A1, the service sidearm you stole from the navy, nothing was amiss. And the statute of limitations has long expired on that. All you navy boys love those handguns, and by hook or by crook, you get them."

I was disarmed. I couldn't say a word of the chastisement I had planned for her.

Mickey buzzed his Lt. Commander and instructed him to escort her out.

Then, to my further surprise, Mickey and the general dismissed me.

"We have some information to look up and matters to discuss among ourselves. Look over the Level II Manual and be prepared to ask any questions you may have. Return here at 1:15," the general said.

"Aye, aye sir," I answered.

I was miffed at that order. I would have time to call Ida, which was good, but I'd wanted to be on my way back to New Hampshire as planned. My muscles were sore and now I was tired from the sleepless night. On top of all that, I was on edge because of the kidnapping of the Demers lady and the exposure of the Canadian trillionaire incident.

I had no idea, at this point, how any of this was going to turn out.

# Chapter 40
# Tuesday in Sherbrooke
*Ida*

*Where am I? Where's Jon?* I woke searching for my bearings.

It was only Tuesday, the morning after the first night I'd slept alone in years. *Oh… Jon has his FBI interview in Groton this morning.*

So much had happened, so much to digest. When my head cleared, I wandered into the kitchen thinking, *what might this new day bring?*

Rachel and Hazel were giving the kids breakfast and getting them ready for school. Jacque had already left for his office. It was 7:15.

Rachel said, "Mom, watch this!" She hit a button from a news report she had recorded earlier.

A young man came onto the screen.

> "The Metro Police have reported that a cabbie was taken to the hospital yesterday afternoon after he was found staggering aimlessly in Parc du Domaine-Howard. When revived, he described two men who subdued him with a severe blow to his head at about eleven in the morning before taking his taxi. The police are looking for the cab at this very moment. If you see an abandoned Taxi De Sherbrooke, please call Metro right away. There is speculation that this incident might be connected with the suspected kidnapping of a woman from such a taxi shortly after eleven-thirty Monday morning at the corner of Rue Wellington Sud and Rue King Ouest. Based on the injured cabbie's complaint, an investigation will be opened at Metro."

"What do you think of that?" Rachel said to me.

"Finish with the children and let me enjoy my morning coffee. This puts a whole new wrinkle on yesterday."

I sipped the hot stuff and ate some of the kids' cereal while absorbing the new news. *The man who drove Shelley Demers was a co-conspirator— had to be—in the kidnap,* I reasoned. *Maybe Shelley was in it too. But why would her husband call the agency to report her missing and not the Metro? Why didn't he call again, or go to the Metro as he had threatened?* There had to be an explanation that would fit the circumstances.

The kids were off with the nanny, so Rachel and I went into the den with our second cup.

"Let's try to figure this out," I said. "Two men hijack a taxi at eleven near Parc du Domaine-Howard and dump the cabbie out. That's one of the cars that was hired to go to the railroad station and wait in the line for the women to come out."

"Do you think he was waiting for you?" Rachel asked.

"Stop a moment, Rachel, you're jumping ahead! Did the thugs know about the gag, or were they just looking for a taxi? Did they target that cabbie *because he had been hired to do the gag?* If so, they would have known I was going to be directed to a specific car. It was very unlikely they would get me. Were they willing to take a random impersonator *just to make someone think* I had been taken, or was Demers also a conspirator? And if she was, why did they do it? What did the perps want to accomplish? Do you see where I'm going here?"

"Then why would her husband call the agency looking for her?" Rachel asked.

"I had just thought about that too," I answered. "It's strange, but it too must have an explanation."

"Yeah. And how would they know about the gag in the first place?"

"They must have a person in the talent agency, the security firm, or the dress shop. Someone from there must have tipped them off," I said.

We both sat quietly for a while.

"Okay, so now we're back to why Demers's husband called only once––four hours after the abduction and then didn't follow up either with the Metro or the agency," Rachel said.

"The abductors could have paid Shelley off, but she didn't get to her husband until after he called Henri. She reached him later, so he went quiet. Again why? Why the phony kidnap? To whom did they want to send a message?"

"What do you mean by that?" Rachel asked.

"They were trying to send *somebody* a message––that's what it had to be! Why else would they arrange to have a reporter on that corner as a witness, have the substitute cabbie give a prepared story with my first name, and then drive off before the Metro arrived?"

"Yeah . . ." Rachel said. "They called for a reporter so the newsflash would be written." Rachel paused. "Maybe Demers was the informant, paid or volunteer. She knew exactly which taxi to pick and then acted out the abduction stunt at the intersection."

That sounded likely. "It's possible that she knew the man who became the driver, or maybe they had some electronic signal for her to home in on," I said.

"That links those two, but what is her connection to the plot and where is she now? Where is her husband? The talent agency must have a portfolio on her that maybe we can access. Shall I call Jacque?"

"Maybe we can find her dossier in the Cloud? That's the best place for us to start without leaving this den. But call Jacque. He may have heard from Henri or the Metro, although I doubt it. The cabbie has no connection to the gag. There is nothing he can say to lead to us . . . I don't think?"

Rachel looked thoughtful. "That's not true, Mom. If that cabbie was hired for the gag, then he could go back to the security agency that did that hiring."

"Oh, yes! You're right! How could I forget so quickly! You better call Jacque right away and give him early warning. Hopefully we catch him before the security company or the Metro call."

Rachel left the room to call Jacque in private. This was getting good! I was thinking what to do next. After nearly fifteen minutes, Rachel had not returned. I went to the kitchen to refill my cup with fresh hot stuff. Rachel was on an analog line to Jacque. She put her finger to her lips. I poured my coffee. Mrs. Kellogg was doing the bedrooms.

After another five minutes, Rachel hung up.

"Mom, Jacque called the security company while I hung on. They had heard from the injured cabbie and told him to keep quiet about the deal, that he would get double his money. He gets a lot of work from the agency and they're sure he'll hold his tongue. He told them the muggers knew about the gag from a woman, but that was all he remembers."

I smiled big. "Good, good! So the cabbie won't lead the police to us, and the informant was a woman. Was it Demers or another of the women—or maybe a woman employed at the talent or security agencies? Or maybe the dress shop? By knowing it's a woman, the suspect list is cut in half or more now!"

Rachel smiled too and we grabbed each other's hands and shook them with joy and pride. Though it was serious, this was getting fun.


We spent the next hour finding all we could learn about Shelley Demers in the Cloud. We found her vital data and her picture, but the name Demers was just one alias among a multitude of others, together with former addresses, Cloud names, and telephone numbers. Her real name was uncertain. The data said she had never been married. We even found her criminal record. Minor stuff, basically— petty embezzlement, shoplifting, amateur counterfeiting, and identity theft. Nothing violent. Her areas of operation were listed as Quebec, the Maritimes, and Newfoundland. There was no resident address in Sherbrooke or the vicinity.

Rachel and I were like two little girls, as giddy over each new bit of data we uncovered as adolescents looking at a site on human reproduction with schematic naked men and women.

At 10:50, the local phone rang. Rachel answered.

It was Jon calling from his office in Groton.

"Mom is with me right here!" she said. "She been here since you left yesterday morning."

Rachel looked questioningly at me, hunched her shoulders and gave the phone to me.

"Hello, Jon, how's it going for you? We had a little excitement yesterday, but I'm fine," I said.

"*Ida! You're safe? You've okay?*" he asked, seemingly panicked.

"Absolutely!" I paused. "What are you so excited about?"

"The US State Department received a communication from an unknown source that you had been kidnapped and were being held until I return. Mickey, General Catern and the FBI lady will be coming on the line in a minute to hear your story."

Well, that was a new surprise! I told Jon about the newsflash, the various phone calls by Jacque, the announcement about the cabbie this morning, and the investigation Rachel and I were doing on Shelley Demers.

"Think about what you should say. Don't bring all that up with the others if you can help it—the phone calls and all that," Jon told me.

"How can I avoid it?" I replied. "It's central to the story."

Then I asked if he'd called the Snyders to tell them we arrived safely. Boy, did he blow up!

"Hell, Ida, I'm busy here! Why can't you do that?"

"What the hell should I tell them anyway?" I asked.

"Oops, too late." He replied. "Mickey, the general and the FBI lady are coming! I'll call you next chance I get."

Mickey came on the line and asked if I was okay.

"I have you on speaker; there are others in the office with us listening. A mysterious group is claiming they kidnapped you. What can you tell us?"

I gave my reply more slowly than when I'd told Jon. He was right—I needed to think through what I said.

"I'm fine, thank goodness, but there was some excitement here yesterday. I was part of a gag, childish really and another woman in a matching outfit seems to be missing—maybe kidnapped. It's all very strange and I don't know much about it."

"Run through it, will you please?" Mickey asked.

They listened as I described in detail the gag, Jacque's orchestration of it with the talent agency and the security company, then the newsflash, the calls, and the cabbie. I did not tell them Shelley Demers's name nor the information we had just uncovered on the Cloud. They each asked a lot of questions; most I couldn't or didn't want to answer. I said a lot of, "I don't know. I don't remember."

I gave them some minor details, but none of what I planned to withhold.

Mickey thanked me. "Here, you can have the last minute alone with your husband."

Thank goodness for that. "Jon, how's it going? Are they treating you well?"

He described his aching body, his sleepless night, the obstacles getting into the parking lot, and then being subdued trying to get into his office.

I didn't tell him then that I thought it was funny.

Mickey and the general were treating him with respect and trying to rally his loyalty to America. He gave me his quick analysis that the Demers woman incident sounded like a setup. Then I unwittingly made another mistake and asked, "What are you doing for lunch?"

"How the hell do I know? *I'm not in charge here, you know!* What kind of question is that now? Do you want a weather report too?"

That was the second time I could hear he was on edge. The question *was* pretty silly of me. But it was a part of our routine, late morning conversation––me at home––he at the Boat.

"Have you taken any yellow this morning?" I asked.

"No, dear," he said, calmer now. "My anxiety is begging for it, but I'm afraid it will put me to sleep. Listen, let me go. They're waiting for me. I'll call you this afternoon if I can. Love you."

"Love you too. Get back here quick and safe."

And the call ended.

# Chapter 41
# Lunch with the Guys
*Jon*

Merle was waiting for me when I got to my office.

"Hey! What was that all about? We knew you were going to Canada for the weekend. So how'd you get back with Main Brain thinking you're still there?"

"Long, dumb story," I said as I shook my head. "Ida and I are on a single exit permit, my fault. She planned to stay and I planned to return. The permit only allows us to cross the border together, so I came cross-country and didn't come through immigration or customs."

Merle and a few others who had gathered clapped and laughed. "Good job! Way to go!" Their reaction wasn't surprising. We were always looking for ways to trip up the system and get away with it. And it was funny even when we got caught—so long as there was no penalty or discipline. Men and women doing the government's work at our level were generally allowed these infractions without recourse. My original anxiety about the interview calmed down after the FBI agent was escorted out.

The guys took me down to the café for a quick lunch. The talk was light and playful, and I forgot my troubles for twenty minutes.

Once at my desk, I called the Snyders and told them all was well and that they could return home whenever they wished. Sally thanked me. I thanked her and Sam. The call was short. I called Ida again; she was waiting for me. The time was 12:45.

"Ida, I'm sorry for startling you with that earlier call, but I was startled too. Is there anything new on the kidnapping or the mugged taxi driver?"

She related in more detail the events leading up to the moment.

"And now that they have the mugged taxi driver, an investigation will begin!"

I tried to fit all these disparate pieces of information together, but a semblance of order eluded me.

Ida asked, "Are you still planning to drive to the lodge tonight and be here tomorrow? How will you do all that driving after such a grueling day? It will be mostly after dark."

"Mickey ordered me back to the conference room for 1:15. I'm not sure how long that session will last. When I have something definite, I'll let you know. Oh, and I called the Snyders, thanked them, and said they could return home."

"Good," Ida said. "I'm sorry for putting that on you earlier . . . I wasn't thinking. But thanks for doing that. Another little item to put behind us."

We professed our love and disconnected. For the balance of the time, I leafed through the Level II Manual and found a number of increased benefits, including health care related to my diagnosis. But I was stuck on the words of Ambassador Golan about the health treatment in Israel. *Another decision to be made. The path of life is always unfolding, and new decisions and directions are opening every day.* In our case, almost every hour!

I called Enterprise to see about the vehicle exchange. They said to call again when I was ready to swap.

At 1:15 Mickey, the general, and I were back in the conference room.

"We're trying to get a line on the Free Africa and India Coalition, but nothing has come up through normal channels. Organizations come and go, and others change names and focus. If these folks are for real, our people will find them," the general said.

"*Coalition* means 'more than a single entity.' Who are they? And from what or whom do they want to 'free Africa and India'?" I asked.

"All good questions, Jon," the general said. "You've got a keen mind for investigating and understanding complex situations. Since this morning, Mickey and I have been discussing you and your situation. I think we're all surprised by these foreign interests recruiting your services."

Mickey and I nodded.

The general continued, "We think for the remaining three years of your service, we should transfer you to the Intelligence Branch and have you pursue these overtures to find out what we have, or more precisely, what *you* have that they want to tap into so badly. I've tried to reach Admiral Aitcheson, the cabinet secretary, to discuss this and see if he agrees. If I don't hear from Aitcheson this afternoon, I'll surely hear from him tonight, and we can discuss it in the morning."

Mickey noisily cleared his throat. "General, sir, you haven't ascertained whether Jon would be interested in such an assignment. Don't you think we should ask him and see if he has questions?"

The general, in his early sixties, grumbled and his face turned scarlet. "Why wouldn't he want to accept such an interesting assignment to end his stellar career in public service?" Catern grunted, spitting moisture and lunch bits into the air.

"The man is a patriot! This country is the best in the world and freedoms will be returning to the people. The government is soliciting bids to return CNN to private or public ownership. As soon as that's done, the FCC is readying licenses for the networks to begin free and independent newscasts again. The Justice Department will be required to seek judicial permission, showing plausible evidence, to obtain search warrants in the future. It won't be so easy for the FBI to just break down doors and search houses, as was done to his."

He sat back, looking smug. "Exit permits, financial deposits for travel, and penalties for leaving the country will be mitigated and the income tax system overhauled. We're not the same country we were twenty, twenty-five years ago. The government finances are in good shape. We're energy independent, and our people and industries enjoy the cheapest energy in the world. Our military and our agriculture are our biggest export revenue sources. The freedoms we all have missed in our everyday lives will return quicker than the public knows."

*Why should I believe that? Maybe it's just bullshit?* Maybe——but I planned to try to check out his claims in some way later.

Mickey took over. "Jon, we searched the Cloud just as you might and learned that there are no declared trillionaires in the world. A billion is a thousand million, and a trillion is *a thousand billion*. That's one big number! On the *Forbes* list of the world's richest people, the Walton family has the greatest wealth—they're at $435 billion. There are more Americans and others around the world with enormous wealth, but the numbers drop down from there."

"Then Matthew lied!" I said, frustrated.

"Maybe, maybe not. A coalition of three, four, or more of these wealthiest people or families could be said to be a 'trillion-aire.' Maybe something like that makes up the Free Africa and India Coalition."

The general took over. "If you are approved by Aitcheson and accept the transfer, your highest priority will be to penetrate this organization and help us determine who they are, their mission, and whether they're a threat to us."

The general was moving so fast, I hadn't the time to assimilate his idea about transferring me to Intelligence. My tired mind and aching body were affecting my ability to process the fast moving conversation.

"What about the promotion to Level II, the Russians and the Israelis?" I asked.

"Level II is a requirement to be an Intelligence agent. And we are equally interested in what the Russians and Israelis want of you. You will work these targets as simultaneously as possible or in the order that is most available to you."

"Will I be free to travel abroad, to live abroad?" I asked.

"What are you thinking, Jon?" asked Mickey.

"I'm thinking of my wife and my retirement to Canada--maybe, to be near our daughter--or to Israel to be near to our son—or maybe Central America or a tropical Caribbean Island. We've talked about a lot of places. I don't want to close all those doors."

"I believe that's possible," said Mickey.

He looked at the general, who shrugged his shoulders and nodded unenthusiastically.

"But those particulars need to come from the Intelligence Branch. Once you take up intelligence work, you almost never retire. They might call you at any time and ask you to take on a particular mission," the general added.

"So what's the next step? Where do we go from here?" I asked.

General Catern answered, "Listen, Jon, we need you to do this mission. You'll be good at it. Work out the details with Mickey here and the Intelligence Branch and get on with it. I'll get you squared away with the FBI and get your promotion approved when I get back to Washington. Mickey, I'll be back to you as soon as I hear from Aitcheson. Now I have to run. I have to get to the airport to make the three o'clock shuttle to Washington. It's hard to imagine that twenty years ago—you hear-- *just twenty years ago*—I shared a Citation with only two other officers. I'd like to see those days back again!"

Mickey and I stood and shook hands with the general. I nodded. And he left.

Mickey's shoulders visibly relaxed and we both slumped back in our chairs. I closed my eyes momentarily, but Mickey saw me. He could see I was tired.

"Why not go home and rest, and we'll meet here again tomorrow morning at nine?" Mickey said. "You look like you could use some sleep, and I should hear back from Catern by then. At that point we can make some definite plans."

"Mickey, can I have a two-week leave after tomorrow? I need to return to Ida and get on with my family visit. The Russians and that

Matthew fellow will also be looking for me. It will look fishy if I hang around here too long."

"Let's see how it goes in the morning," he answered. "Say, did you use someone from here to drive the FAV to the border? And what *did* you do with your Beretta?"

"My driver was Roland Smith from Norwich. He's been my handyman for decades. I sponsored him to get a FAV license. I gave him my sidearm—he asked for it."

Mickey nodded. I saw him jot something down, and he said, "Okay, until tomorrow."

We shook hands again, and I left.

# Chapter 42
# At the Talent Agency
*Ida*

Rachel had listened to my side of the conversation, so I filled her in with what Jon had said.

"What is the Free Africa and India Coalition? Where do we go from here, Mom?"

"If Jacque doesn't mind, I would like to see the agency's dossier on Demers. Something isn't right there. What other jobs has she done for them? How long has the agency been representing her?"

After several calls, an appointment with Henri was set at 4:00. I continued looking for data on Demers under her various aliases, but there was little left to gather. The TV flickered in the entertainment center with the sound barely on. The prattling punctuated with silly laughter of the morning talk shows in French finally gave way to the midday soaps and then the two o'clock news.

An image caught my attention, and I called to Rachel, "Come quick!"

The picture was frozen on a Taxi De Sherbrooke car in the midst of a large parking lot at the Quebec City Jean Lesage International Aéroport. The car was positioned amid piles of snow and awkwardly parked vehicles. The camera narrowed on to the rear license plate.

Rachel arrived and began translating:

> "This is the license of the missing taxi that was reported hijacked from its legal driver on Monday near Parc du Domaine-Howard in Sherbrooke. The taxi was abandoned here yesterday evening according to surveillance video at the lot. There is no apparent damage to the vehicle. Metro has not determined if the perpetrators left the area by flight or other means. The person

reported kidnapped has not been found, nor has any family member come forth to verify the missing claim. Sherbrooke Metro is transferring the investigation to the stolen vehicle unit of the Motor Vehicle Registry and the Quebec Provincial Police for further inquiry."

When the report ended, Rachel said, "I wonder if we'll hear any more about this now. It sounds like Metro is washing their hands of it."

\*\*\*

At 4:00, Rachel, Jacque and I went down the hall to the Meredith Modeling Agency offices. Their quarters were neat, with floor-to-ceiling displays of some of their more noteworthy projects. They supplied many models throughout the year for vendor displays at trade shows at the Lester Centre, including the annual auto show, boat show, home renewal shows, and the like. They placed extras in movies being shot in the area, supplied men and women for commercials for local auto, furniture, and other merchants, and sent models out for fashion shows by the department stores. They had a segment for theatrical and musical entertainment for various charitable, social, and familial functions like weddings. It was an active agency with many facets, and they were quite busy when we arrived.

We were held in reception for about five minutes until Henri DeBar whizzed in and said, "Please follow me!"

Henri was tall, suave and well-dressed, with a mane of wavy salt-and-pepper hair, sixty-plus years old and dignified.

I elbowed Rachel and whispered, "He looks a lot better than in the few moments on the communicator." We both giggled.

He walked swiftly down a long corridor, we at his heels, to a neatly appointed conference room in a corner of the building. He slammed the door shut and motioned with his hand for us to sit.

"Thank you for seeing us, Mr. DeBar," I said.

Throwing his arms in the air, he shouted, "Who is Mr. DeBar?" Shaking his head, he asked, "Is Mr. DeBar here?" He exaggerated looking around, still thrusting his arms here and there. "No, no, no!" He slammed his hand against the table for each 'no,' just as he had over the communicator.

"There is no Mr. DeBar here! Mr. DeBar was my father and he is dead! I am Henri, Henri you hear—and my twin sister is Hinda. Thank you!" And he bowed at the waist.

I was aghast, immediately intimidated by his outburst and actions. Jacque took a seat at the center of the table; Rachel sat to one side of him and I to the other. Mr. DeBar stood opposite us, his back to a long wall of windows right into the corner.

He barely missed a moment before he began yelling again. "Ohhh . . . ! *C'est une telle journée!*"

"Henri, Henri!" Jacque interrupted. "English, English, *please!*"

"Oh . . . Oui, oui, . . . oui." In his usual form, he slapped the table with each *oui*. *"Je ne me souviens pas quand, de nombreux événements importants se sont réunis pour serré à cette époque de l'année."*

*"Anglais, Anglais, veuillez, Henri, parler anglais!"* Jacque stood and shouted.

Henri sat down opposite Jacque, stretched his neck and shoulders and calmed himself, as he had to translate now for me.

"Oh...! This is such a day! I can't remember when so many important events came together so tight at this time of year. Christmas is just over and we are nowhere near Easter. Hockey banquets, figure skating, ice shows, the winter equipment show. Everyone wants new commercials, the ad agencies are asking for casting calls every day, young beautiful women, old fat women, male surfers, farmers, clerks in the Walmarté and children . . . everyone wants *new* children. No reruns! *Où puis-je les trouver? Où?"*

He paused. "Now . . .? Why are we here?" he asked, his forehead wrinkled, his eyes squinting.

Henri definitely seemed on edge, but I didn't know if it was just today or every day.

Jacque answered, "We are here to learn more about this woman Shelley Demers, your actress, who we think was kidnapped during our scene on Monday at the Station de Depot."

"Oh, yes, yes, yes . . . that?" He slapped the table three times again. "I remember now. Has she been found? We need data from her to make her a paycheck."

Jacque asked, "Have you heard from her since yesterday, or from her husband?"

"Wait!" I called out. "Wait!" I repeated––suddenly more alert. "Jacque, her data in the Cloud said she is unmarried!"

I had almost forgotten about that.

*"Juste un seul instant,"* Henri said, holding up his hand to stop us. He twisted and clicked a button on a communicator behind him and shouted, *"Madeline, Madeline, venir à la salle de conférence avec un dossier de Shelley Demers."*

He turned and faced us, folding his arms across his chest. Lazily, his eyes wandered toward the ceiling. High-heeled footsteps could be heard clicking their way toward the door of the conference room.

Henry returned his attention to us and asked in a polite, moderate voice, "Would anyone like a cup of coffee, tea, espresso, tonic? Perhaps a cake or a cookie?"

His instant charm was misleading, so unlike the humor in which he had begun. Madeline, a tall, vivacious brunette, in her fifties perhaps, strode into the room. We never got to answer his invitation for refreshments.

"This is Madeline Bessette," Henri barked. "Madeline is the *directeur* of the studio and is personally responsible for all the place-ments we make in shows, on sets, in commercials. She sees it all! One person outrageously happy—she got the part—while five others cry, still waiting for their moment in the sun!"

He shaded his eyes with his hand as if blocking the summer sun.

Madeline stood nodding her head in agreement with Henri, a big smile on her face. I had the feeling this was some practiced routine they performed from time to time when the situation called for it.

"Sir, shall I call for the refreshment cart for your guests?" Madeline asked.

"Oh, no . . . no . . . no!" Three more slaps on the table. "I offered refreshments and they declined, and they won't be staying much longer in any case. Sit down, Madeline, and stop that bobbing around! Show them the Demers dossier and let's get on with this; the day is slipping away. How long has she been in our files—a year, two?"

Henri had returned to his erratic demeanor. Madeline ignored him.

I moved over a chair so Madeline could sit between Jacque and me. She adjusted the chair and leaned forward with a simple oak-tag folder in her hands. Jacque and Rachel leaned in from one side and I from the other. Henri stood quietly looking out the window toward the street, his left hand on his right elbow and his right hand on his chin. I couldn't see it, but I had the sense that he was tapping his toe.

Madeline opened the folder. It held a single sheet of paper and a thirty-or-so-year-old picture of a woman in her late twenties or early thirties in a smart outfit from the styles of those times.

"Is this it?" Jacque asked incredulously.

"This is it! This is all we've got," Madeline said.

After seeing the meager contents, Jacque, Rachel and I all leaned back in our chairs and exhaled a big breath. Jacque took the paper from the folder and I took the picture.

I studied the picture carefully—the shoes, the arrangement of the feet, the hemline, the cinch in the narrow waist, the frilly blouse, the tailored jacket, the necklace, the hairstyle, the earrings, even the chin and mouth were me, but the eyes and nose said someone else. I remembered the days of those outfits and the joy I knew back then, with our kids growing up, my pride in our success, and Jon in his dress navy uniform. We were living the American dream.

"What exactly is this paper?" Jacque asked Madeline.

"It is our short form intake report."

"Is there a long form?"

"Oh, yes, six pages that creates a complete resume of the person's education and experience."

"Where is that one?"

"Oh, *ce est une probléme.* Shelley came in during lunch hour this past Friday and Hinda didn't want to spend the time taking a full report. She was busy and the others were out to lunch. So she did the minimum and passed her over to me for an interview. I talked to the lady for about ten minutes . . ."

My mind wandered from their conversation as I stared at the picture. *I looked that good, better even. I was a knockout in those outfits.* This woman and I were together yesterday at Tim Hortons and I didn't even know it. I might have rubbed shoulders with her when we stood and shuffled. *Where is she now? What had Shelley Demers become? What about me?* I remembered all the petty crimes she committed from the data in the Cloud. *But if we were the same then, what happened to her, to me, to bring us together in this way now?*

My mind was running away from me. I focused again to listen to Madeline.

"I could see that she was down on her luck and she asked, really begged, to have some work last weekend to get a paycheck. I wanted to help her. We had an opening for Sunday, but she didn't have the outfit needed, a business suit. I took this paper and the picture and said I would call if something came along."

I had begun feeling sorry for the Shelley Demers in that picture, and now I was feeling sorry for myself too. *We don't see it from day to day, but the years do pile up, and our once flaming youth gives way to gray hair, sagging skin, wrinkled hands and faces.*

"Then *your* gig came up on Sunday for Monday morning. A fast three-and-a-half hours work in the morning, C$500 plus a complete clothing ensemble. She had the height and she seemed to fit. We put out a casting call on the Cloud for Sunday morning and had nine or so respondents for the five slots. By noon, we had booked four; turned away three; and two others turned us down when they saw the job. We could have gone with four plus your mother-in-law, but I thought of Shelley, gave her a call, described the gig and told her to be here at eight-thirty, the next morning for wardrobe. She was excited for the job and the pay. She asked if she could be paid then and there. I said I'd try."

I returned to my reverie. *Now we live too long, don't enjoy life as much as people used to, and eventually become a burden to society. In decades past, technology was massaged to keep people healthy and alive, but now some treatments are withheld, not worth the cost—the government says—to keep us breathing a few more days. Like Jon's case that brought us here.*

I took a last look at the picture and handed it behind Madeline and Jacque to Rachel.

Madeline continued with her story. "She was prompt for wardrobe and was grateful to me for giving her the call. All the women were fitted in the dress shop downstairs and their wigs were fitted and makeup was done up here. Each was given C$100 in small bills for the taxi and the suitcase to take their personal things along with them. I gave Shelley C$300 as a personal advance against the C$500 she would be paid for the day. The women were each put in a taxi and sent on their way. They loved it! There was great merriment. And then the shoe fell. The call from Shelley's husband, or whoever that was, and the rest you know. I can tell you no more."

"This address and phone number she gave?" Jacque asked, pointing to the short form.

"That's at the university. It's a pension, more like a women's shelter than a B&B. The phone number belongs to one of those temporary devices foreigners pick up at the airport when they arrive in a new territory. It no longer has service; I tried it."

"Well, well . . . " Henri slapped the table two times and paused with his hand in the air a foot over the table. We all hushed as we stared at the threatening hand, waiting for the inevitable action. "Well!" he finally shouted as he slapped the table for the third time.

"That's it! There *ain't* no more. Not our best work, I admit, but Madeline gave her heart a chance, which I don't criticize, mind you, because she is usually right!"

He nodded toward her before carrying on.

"Has any damage been done? Is anyone harmed, injured? What has this gaffe wrought?" He paused for five seconds. "Nothing serious, no harm, no foul!" Three more slaps punctuated his words. "This woman is missing, maybe, but there is no proof of any harm."

Rachel said in a louder than usual voice, "Wait! Someone *was* injured!"

"*Qui?*" asked Henri.

"The cabbie, that's who, the cabbie," Rachel answered.

Henri rubbed his chin while shaking his head. Leaning forward toward Rachel, his eyes bearing down on hers, he asked softly, "Did Shelley cause that cabbie harm?"

"No," Rachel chirped.

"Did Madeline cause that cabbie harm?" he asked again softly, tilting his head.

"No," Rachel chirped again.

"Did *I* cause that cabbie harm?" he again asked quietly, politely.

"No, no, no!" he shouted as he bore his eyes into Rachel's, answering the question himself as he again slapped the table in his usual fashion. "Now, is there anything more?" He tried to ask kindly, seemingly exasperated.

Madeline turned to me, "Would you like to see the dossiers of the four others?"

I hadn't thought of that and instinctively I said, "*Yes*" slap! "*Yes*" slap! Paused, then "*YES!*" again, slapping the table the third time. Madeline and Rachel exploded with laughter.

"No, no, Mother!" said Jacque firmly.

"*NO!*" said Henri. "That is the personal information of our personnel, which we must protect. Thank you for coming. This meeting is over."

Henri marched to the door and disappeared down the corridor. Madeline walked us to reception; we thanked her and went on our way.

I wondered if our time with Shelley Demers was over for good.

# Chapter 43
# To Sherbrooke via Ottawa
*Jon*

It was Wednesday afternoon, already dark when we took off from Ottawa International. The helicopter provided by Homeland Security was a tactical craft not equipped for pleasant passenger travel. Frank and I were harnessed into jump seats, which was a lot like wearing parachutes. The seats were side-by-side facing aft, fixed to an interior petition. A small amber light barely illuminated the space. The cabin was cold and drafty and smelled damp. We wore large Bose headsets to moderate the *thwack-thwack* of the rotor blades and to talk through the craft's intercom.

"Young Segalov, with his wife and mother-in-law, left today with the body of Nikelovich to return to Russia." Frank said. "The sheriff learned from the TSA that neither Sergei nor his wife entered the country since that time a year and a half ago—not officially, anyway. He is now trying to check with international airlines to see if she had a reservation to the States. But that is an impossible task. We don't know where she was coming from, where she was intending to land, or if she was using a domestic or foreign carrier. All we know is her name!

"The FBI has taken over the investigation and the sheriff is now in the shadows. He hopes they'll share their findings with him, especially the analysis of the bullet."

"Not a chance!" I blurted. "Once the FBI takes control, all information sharing is over. Did you check your surveillance for any movement of Matthew's man on the night of the storm?"

"You won't believe it, Jon. Remember the storm tapered off after dinner?"

"Yes, sure," I answered.

"The Israeli left first, near midnight. The Russian next, a half-hour later, then the Canadian, Matthew's man—–and then *your man, Rollie.* They *all* went out between midnight and one-thirty."

"Rollie too?"

*Where the hell was he going?* I wondered, surprised and annoyed.

"What time did Rollie get back? Did it seem like any of them might have joined up later? Where could they go? What might have been open for them at that hour after that weather?" I asked.

"Rollie was the last to leave and the first to return. He came back at two-thirty. Gone just about an hour. I haven't the slightest idea where they might have gone or if they met up out there. The Israeli returned next, then the Russian and Matthew's man last, at about five a.m."

"Rollie wasn't the shooter . . . he couldn't have been," I said to convince myself.

*Unless the rifle and bullet were in the FAV when he picked it up.* He had been military. He might still have the skills. *But Rollie had no connection to any of those people. It made no sense, no sense at all.*

"I have an idea what Rollie might have been up to! But one of the others would more likely have been the shooter. Can you send me the videos of them, all of them, leaving and returning?" I asked.

"Sure, that'll be easy when I'm back at the lodge. Now where are you going from here?"

"We're going to Sherbrooke, aren't we?"

"Yes, yes . . . sure. But what are *you* going to be doing then?"

"I'm on a two-week vacation leave to spend time with my family. What else?" I answered.

I figured that Frank rolled his eyes.

"Please, Jon, you flew to Ottawa from DC on a State Department diplomatic flight with Gwen Lathrop, assistant to the Deputy Director of Homeland Security Intelligence. My contact doesn't even report that high. What do they have you up to now?"

Frank was reaching, but my mission now was above his pay grade.

"If there is anything you need to know, your handler will tell you."

I twisted in the seat and unplugged my headset. I tried to relax and closed my eyes. Flight time was about an hour and a half.

When we landed, Frank and I heartily shook hands and wished each other well. He did not deplane, and the helicopter buttoned up and taxied for takeoff. A captain from the QC Provincial Police and a RCMP Mountie, both in civilian dress, met me at Paquin Aviation. We went into a private office where he scanned my chip to confirm my identity. Having it done for the first time for real was cool.

"Your name is Jonathon. Is that what I call you?"

"Jon is enough."

He presented his chip and I scanned it with my new Level II communicator. It revealed that he was a member of the Royal Canadian Mounted Police connected to the Canadian Security Intelligence Service.

"I go by Duevel," he said without me asking.

The scanning automatically exchanged our contact data. We shook hands and greeted each other officially.

"Come to my car," Duevel said. "I am to drive you to meet Mrs. Kadish."

En route, we chatted about my work and he voluntarily started talking about the Free Africa and India Coalition—I was surprised he brought it up—what he knew of it, he said. But it wasn't much.

Because he'd opened the door a crack, I told him about Scott Matthew, the people at the lodge, the murder in New Hampshire and my suspicion about Matthew and his man. When I mentioned the murder, he nodded ever so slightly. I got the impression I was not telling him anything new. He was quiet at first as if trying to decide what to say, how to answer.

A long minute later, he said, "I can assure you that neither Matthew nor his man committed any murder. I cannot tell you why . . . but I'm sure you will come to agree with me."

He paused then continued, "Your flight to Calgary is at eight on Friday morning. I'll pick you and your wife up at seven-thirty to take you to the airport."

"How do *you* know about the flight and the time?" I said, again surprised. "Matthew is to contact me about the details tomorrow––Thursday."

"You're being contacted now. These *are* the details. And bring along kits for a possible few nights' stay. Do you object to me being your driver?" Duevel asked.

"You know more than what you've told me, right?" I replied.

"Be patient, Jon. Things are better when you learn them on your own."

After that, Duevel clammed up until we reached the synagogue.

"Friday at 7:30 a.m., *here*," Duevel repeated as I was leaving the car.

Ida was waiting on the other side of security. We hugged for several long moments. She wiped her eyes on the lapel of my coat, and we kept our faces together, she on her toes and me leaning down a bit. It was comforting to feel her warm breath on my neck. I squeezed her tight and exhaled a sigh on her cheek.

"Thank you," she whispered. "I was so happy when you called today and told me you were flying directly here and not driving to New Hampshire. I was happy with the bits you tried to tell me in code and I can't wait to hear it all."

"C'mon," I said. "Let's get to Rachel's. I'm hungry and I'll tell you all about it."

Rachel was waiting in her car at the far curb. Bundled against the cold, I held my lapels closed at the neck with one hand, my other arm around Ida. We hustled across the street and jumped into the back seat.

"Thank God you're back!" Rachel said excitedly. "I hope you're hungry; I have dinner for you."

"Let's just get to the house. I've been cold for the last two hours and could use a bowl of soup."

Neither Rachel nor Ida commented. They both knew I liked hot soup. Sure enough, Rachel had homemade soup and a salad. I gobbled it down. It was plenty. Rachel and Jacque understood our need for privacy, so Ida and I excused ourselves, and went from the dinner table to the guest room to get comfortable and unwind. It was near 8:30.

We lay down on the bed in our bathrobes. Ida scrunched up two pillows for me so I was almost seated and she doubled up her skinny pillow and snuggled next to me.

"Mickey and General Catern were great to me yesterday morning at the Boat. They kept pitching America, and little by little I saw they were right. I didn't tell them I had already seen the Russians, but that we—you and I—knew we could never be happy there. Then Catern attacked Israel as a puppet of China, and I came to Israel's defense and spoke vigorously about their independence. But inside, I have to tell you––I was still hurting about the brutal means by which China crushes dissent. I am impressed at how much money and effort they put into forging the peace and improving the conditions of the cooperating Arabs, but I can't get over that one detail."

Ida interrupted. "We already discussed that and agreed that we might just spend some of each year at a condo in Gaza to be with Eric, Rebecca, and the kids. And you don't have to work for Israel or anyone."

"You're right. But we have to be citizens somewhere, don't we? Please, let me go on."

"Sorry, dear."

"When I left Mickey at about 1:30, I stopped back onto the fifth floor and told Merle and the guys good-bye and that I might see them in the morning. Mickey had asked me to return for nine a.m. I looked carefully again at the health benefits for Level II. I was assured that I could get an individual assessment and be able to have a procedure if I needed one. I never realized before, Ida, that the SHS is such a tiered system! As a Level III, I couldn't have treatment, but at Level II, I can. What's with that? What more do the Level I's get in health care and other perks, I wonder?"

"Hmmmm," Ida intoned as she thought of that revelation. "We always suspected that bureaucrats at different levels got different money and benefits. Look at how the Congress treats itself! Compensation, I can understand, but health care is another story," she said.

"Well, I returned to the inn and went back to the hot tub at the pool to soak. My adrenaline was low and my aching body came back into my consciousness. I'm not so young anymore, Ida."

I paused. "After an hour I went to my room to lie down and rest. It was just four o'clock, because I tuned into CNBC and the market had just closed. I fell asleep until my communicator lit up about 5:30. It was Mickey. He said, 'I'll pick you up at 7:15 a.m. at the inn. Check out and take all your things. We're flying to DC on the *Congressman*. I asked him what was up and he answered, 'I'll fill you in on the flight.'"

"That was just this morning! Wow, you must be drained," Ida sympathized. "You woke up in Groton, flew to Washington, then to Ottawa, and now to here? Do you realize that we started this adventure last Wednesday morning? This is our eighth day now, with all its twists and turns, day after day. I have some news for you too. We've learned more about Shelley Demers since you've been gone."

"Oh, I want to know about that. But believe me when I tell you, *I know* eight days have passed! I never realized our plan was so naïve, or that we would encounter so many new people and opportunities to challenge us, our intellects, and even our relationship."

"Are we headed for a *happy ending?*" Ida asked purring, her head resting on my shoulder.

"Yes, I really think so––provided we are ready to adjust to an adventurous and unpredictable future. Can I finish this with you tomorrow? I'm dog tired."

It was after 9:30.

I got up and went to the bathroom, washed up, took my regular meds and opened my mezuzah. Only one yellow came out in my palm. I couldn't remember when I'd taken the other four. I'd have to refill it. I split the pill on its crease and took half with a splash of water. I needed sleep, but the pill would have to quiet my mind first. I needed a restful night.

After I got under the covers, Ida left for the bathroom to do her routine. In the morning, I couldn't remember her coming back to bed.

# Chapter 44
# Recap of Washington DC
*Jon*

In the morning, I continued my story over coffee in the den.

"Mickey was five minutes early driving his 2030 government Tesla T. Even at nine years old, that's one sweet machine! I love being in it. The 'T' stands for 'Total' because it's fully electric and rechargeable from sunlight. The body paint contains a photovoltaic compound that transforms sunlight into electricity for storage in the lithium-lanthanum cells. The car can operate at peak performance *and* store additional energy for at least sixteen hours of night or overcast driving. There is no cord; it never has to be plugged in. Every square inch of the body surface is a solar collector."

"If it's such a great car, how come we never got one?" Ida asked.

"They were way too expensive, they never got to a popular price. Mickey's is a company car that he was lucky to get. The Defense Industry Cabinet bought a bunch that year to support Tesla's development. Only three were allocated to the Boat. Tesla hoped to lower the price and increase output by building a totally robotic factory to make a million batteries a year. But by the time the Gigafactory got operational in Nevada, strategic materials were scarce and costs had so escalated that they offset the labor efficiencies achieved by the robotic assembly. Trying to get the factory totally powered by renewable sources took them an extra few years. Even now, I've read that Tesla takes more power from the grid than they return to it. But maybe someday?"

"I've never seen a dealership anywhere. Where do you get one?"

"It's Connecticut's issue with dealerships again—that stupid law that doesn't allow a car manufacturer to sell its own cars to the public. The law is archaic, just like the one that requires local distributors for beer and alcohol. Can you imagine? Budweiser is prohibited to have its own distribution and sell directly to retailer or restaurants. It's insane. But we're not the only state without dealers. There are about twenty still not allowing Tesla to sell its own cars to people. Outrageous! You can buy the cars online, but you have to pick them up from a company store. The nearest to us I think is in Westchester, New York."

I took a sip of my coffee, still visualizing that gorgeous vehicle. I would have loved to own one, but the price wasn't the only obstacle in my mind.

"Lastly there was the image. Ida, I couldn't visualize either of us driving a Tesla T with all the raised eyebrows and having to answer the inevitable questions."

"You are *so* right about that!" Ida said with conviction. "My employees, our friends and acquaintances would have frowned at us as ostentatious, and that's not who we are or want to be."

"Once in the car I asked Mickey, "Why are we flying to DC? I hoped to drive back to New Hampshire this afternoon and return to Sherbrooke tomorrow.""

\*\*\*

"Jon, Catern called me last night," Mickey explained. "Aitcheson and some others want to meet you and listen directly to your issues. He told me, 'Fly down tomorrow on the *Congressman* and I'll square away the schedule.'"

"Is this an interview? After all my service, I'm going to Washington for an interview? And who are these 'others'?" I asked, irritated.

"I'm not sure of the names but Homeland Security will have staff there. Calm down. To some degree, I feel responsible for your quandary. I didn't act on your promotion when you deserved it, and then I neglected to tell you after I submitted it. I'll help you through this."

\*\*\*

307

Ida listened carefully as I did my best to recall everything in detail.

"The commuter aircraft varies from day to day, but yesterday it was a Canadair Challenger 615, wide-body corporate that was acquired with the purchase of Raytheon. The leather seat coverings still carried Raytheon's emblem and initials.

"There were eight or so passengers in addition to Mickey and me. The flight was smooth and uneventful. Mickey and I reviewed the previous day's meeting with the FBI lady and General Catern, and we talked more about my meeting with the Israelis. I told him the truth about the Russian visit to our flat. He was surprised that I had omitted it. I told him that I was uncomfortable coming out with it to the general. The way he attacked Israel at the start, I didn't know if I could trust him. I told Mickey I had planned to tell him after lunch, but that meeting ended more quickly than I expected."

"What did Mickey say about the Russian meeting? Did you tell him about the murder in New Hampshire and the disappearance of Sergei and Ivanica?" Ida asked.

"He laughed because the Russian meeting went just as the general warned. 'They will tell you exactly what they want to know from you— and they'll know that you know it! Then they will ply you with the perks'—just like they did! I told Mickey we might like to visit Russia but would never live there. He smiled and said 'Good.' He hadn't known about the murder in New Hampshire and was surprised that it had a connection to Segalov. He was only aware that Sergei had dropped out of Russian scientific news for the past year or more."

\*\*\*

On the plane, Mickey had said, "We've traced a thread on the Free Africa and India Coalition. We believe it involves South Africa, India, and maybe Australia. The group revolves around energy and is related to the nuclear accident at the Koeberg nuclear station last decade. At the time, South Africa's original plan for seven uranium power plants was reduced to just the two that were under construction. We thought they would move to LNG-powered generators with the fuel coming from Australia. They did, but only with *one* of the plants. But something must have gone terribly wrong, because they converted it to coal after only two years and built the others for coal as well. They should have known better."

"They *dropped* the LNG? Why? That's our fuel of preference!"

"No one really knows, Jon. There are several theories but I never heard a definitive reason. It had to have been significant—probably involving the logistics from Australia. They know that power from coal is a health hazard for their people and that $CO_2$ emissions might eventually make the surface of the planet uninhabitable for everyone. But they also have tons and tons of domestic coal, along with their other carbons and diamonds. It's not a surprise the fuel is attractive to them. Have you seen the new James Bond movie about colonizing the ocean floors?"

"Yeah, Ida and I saw some of it in Sherbrooke until an Israeli security man made us leave at the intermission."

"Well, if we don't stop contaminating our air and causing global warming, that sea-floor idea might not be so farfetched."

"But Mickey, aren't we supposed to find another planet to move to?" I said jokingly.

"Please, Jon," Mickey said seriously. "You know the species will have died off long before that will happen. Technologically sophisticated undersea colonies, to save some of the human race and propagate the species until the atmosphere is cleaned by nature over several thousand years, might be the only answer. Those covered domes will be laminated with graphene."

"Okay, enough of that science fiction. So is this group, the *Coalition*, our friend or foe?" I asked.

"We don't think they're adversarial, but we would like to know more about them—much more. I'm sure this'll come up at today's meetings," he answered.

\*\*\*

"Ida, we were picked up at Washington National by a Homeland Security car and taken to their headquarters at the St. Elizabeths Campus in the Anacostia neighborhood of southeast Washington. It's an historic hospital grounds—where the US Coast Guard and Homeland Security share headquarters. The meeting was at the office of the Director of Homeland Security, Susan Watson.

"After shedding our outerwear, we were brought to a posh conference room suite. A buffet bar was set up in the lobby for continental breakfast. General Catern was already there and greeted us affably. He motioned us to the buffet. With our selections, he led us to a small conference room, well appointed, with a big square table for maybe twelve. The general pointed me to a seat on a corner. Mickey sat next to me, and the general sat on the right angle to me. The time was just after ten. Mickey and the general talked across me about the Super Bowl, in which I had no interest. In another minute or two, five people arrived, and the general and Mickey snapped to attention. I quickly joined them.

"The three of us moved to greet the group as the general introduced us. "Secretary Aitcheson, meet Admiral Keith Mickey Wilson and Commander Jonathan Kadish, both at the Boat.'

"We shook hands and exchanged greetings.

"Aitcheson said, I am very pleased you are able to be here today, thank you. And thank you for your important service to our cabinet and our country.'

"Mickey and I nodded.

"Aitcheson turned and introduced his deputy in charge of the Intelligence Branch, Sandy Bergman. Then we were introduced to the Director of Homeland Security, Ms. Susan Watson; her deputy in charge of their Intelligence Service, Robert Mattern; and his assistant, Ms. Gwen Lathrop. Everyone had coffee and a sweet roll, and we all sat down. After a little light banter, Director Watson cleared her throat and the meeting came to order."

\*\*\*

"Thank you all for coming on short notice," she started. "We are pleased Mr. Kadish to have you here, and I want you to know that we've been briefed on your career and on your activities this past week by our agent François Bernardin and General Catern."

She nodded to the general and he nodded back.

"We hadn't realized until reviewing your service record that you were once a member of this department as a colonel in our Military Police Reserve. Your record in that position was a big boost to our enthusiasm for meeting you today. As you might expect, we are all wondering why this big interest in you by our two major adversaries and an unknown coalition of wealthy foreigners. We recognize the pressure you have been under due to the health system and other current infringements on the American people's personal liberties. We all share your concerns. But your return to report to Admiral Wilson as you promised, demonstrates your continued loyalty to this, your country. You have served honorably for so long, we don't want you to foul it up at this late stage. We have a proposition for you."

She paused and motioned with her hand, "Mr. Mattern, Bob, please?"

Mattern leaned in toward me. "Mr. Kadish, you can continue to serve our country in a new capacity. These solicitations that you've received are an excellent opportunity for you, your wife and us, to gain important information about our rivals. The Russians have been competitive with us since Stalin. Some years have been better, others worse. They will tell you what they want and offer you big rewards."

I glanced at Mickey. He smiled and nodded at me.

"You could learn a lot on a visit to Russia," he continued. "We are also preparing to reengage with Israel, and it would be interesting to have you assess that situation and give us some feedback from the navy's point of view. You said your son keeps you informed on what he hears from the Israeli press. We would welcome your analysis and an opinion as to the extent that they are under China's thumb—or not? The State Department is coming around to believe it is in our national interest to improve our relationship with Israel, and all the cabinets are ready to challenge the current Chinese monopoly on Israel's technological developments."

Bergman put out his hand, his index finger pointing at me. Mattern paused. Bergman looked at Secretary Aitcheson, as did everyone else. The secretary gave him a nod of approval. Mattern leaned back, and Bergman spoke out.

"It is not known outside a very tight circle that we, America, also participated in the Israeli attack on Iran. We helped in many ways. Earlier administrations supplied them with the design of our B61 variable-yield atom bomb, and later administrations provided fabricated guidance tails to accurately hit targets. Israel consulted with us to narrow the many possible targets down to those whose loss would cripple Iran the most. Our military leaders agreed on eight locations and supplied them with the exact GPS coordinates to hit their weakest points. We interceded with the Saudis on Israel's behalf to allow them to traverse their airspace. The air force organized a cooperative air-training mission with the Saudis and together put fifty F-16s, F22s, and F35 series aircraft in the air to camouflage the Israeli transit. Over Saudi airspace, American and Saudi tankers refueled each of the eight attack aircraft."

Then I put my finger up, and Bergman recognized me with a nod.

"Did the president order that cooperation?" I asked.

"I can only answer by saying our military assistance was there as I've described. I can't say——in fact, don't even know——who ordered the cooperation."

I nodded and continued, "Where was China in all this? Weren't they the influence in Saudi Arabia at that time?"

"Their influence was growing, but our relationship with the Saudi leadership and military was still strong, as it was with Israeli's military. You know it wasn't a very sophisticated *surprise* attack. The Chinese supplied and launched four hundred drones from aircraft carriers in the Persian Gulf to fly below the attacking Israeli F-35Es into Iranian airspace. The drones could only fly at 320 miles per hour, so the Israeli planes had to slow down to keep above their cover. The drones were knocked out of the air like flies by the Iranian missile defense batteries. But the drones successfully absorbed Iran's strongest countermeasure—not a single Iranian missile hit an Israeli plane. For the few missiles that avoided the drones, Israel's F-35Es were equipped with a powerful Israeli-invented anti-guided missile system, one that is now standard on every commercial airliner. The system detects the electronic guidance system of an attacking missile, takes over its controls, and diverts it away from the aircraft. Simple computer hacking 101! The only defense weapon to hit the attacking planes, were old-fashioned ack-ack slugs and shrapnel from anti-aircraft guns. Two Israeli planes picked up some of that in their dive to their target. It was an interesting surprise—the high-tech, sophisticated, deadly accurate missiles were neutralized with equally high-tech defenses, but the attacker was still vulnerable to the low-tech weapons of WWII."

Everyone around the table smiled and nodded.

Bergman continued. "Israel's attack and success did us a big favor. Our policies wouldn't let us participate in the Iran attack directly. Remember––then as now––we were selling our military capabilities for very big money to dependent client states, and there was no one, not Israel or anyone else, willing to pay us to do that mission. It would have harmed our relationships to use our superpower on someone— even Iran—without getting paid. That's why we had to withdraw our ambassador from Israel."

Matter-of-factly, he said, "*You know, it's business—it was just business!*"

I threw Mickey a startled look and could tell he was learning all this for the first time too. '*You know, it's business—it was just business!*'

Boy that answer and Bergman's attitude pissed me off! Aitcheson and Watson nodded their knowing heads.

"So atomic bombs *were used!* . . . and *we* supplied the design and some components to them? Why hasn't this been disclosed? Surely there were telltale signs of nuclear debris at the sites?" Mickey asked.

Bergman started to answer, but Catern motioned with his hand to be recognized.

"Mickey, Jon, we helped Israel to use the very *lowest* tonnage nuclear explosives, dialed down to the least power necessary to take out each particular target. Every target selected had fissionable material on site in one form or another. The debris from the destroyed targets to a great degree masked the debris from the bomb. In one case, we think a secondary atomic explosion occurred from a bomb or enriched uranium in storage there. For each aircraft, there was one bomb run, one bomb, and one target, simple as that.

The general relaxed back in his chair.

Bergman followed with a smirk. "We have the best surveillance satellites and drones, so when *we say the use of atomic weapons cannot be confirmed,* it doesn't matter what anyone else says! So you see, America––through many former administrations and even to that day––was very involved, and our cooperation was then––and is essential now––for the success and continued secrecy of that mission."


"But what about the escape?" I asked. "How, where, did the attack aircraft go afterward––or were they lost? Was it a known suicide mission?"

All eyes focused on the two cabinet members, Admiral Aitcheson and Susan Watson. Director Watson turned and stared at Aitcheson. Other than the greeting, he hadn't said a word.

He shifted uncomfortably in his seat. "It looks like I'm the top navy man here so if this story is to be told, I guess it is up to me. Admiral Wilson, you are Level I, and you, Commander Kadish, are Level II. What you are about to hear is *above Level I security, you understand?* You know I was a naval aviator, and you two are both dolphins. It is *only* because you are dolphins that I will disclose this to you, on condition of you keeping it absolutely secret."

Mickey and I nodded our agreement.

"Anyone below deputy director must leave the room. That seems to be only you, Ms. Lathrop. Sorry."

Gwen Lathrop stood, collected her papers, and began to move toward the entry. "When and if I'm needed, I can be reached in my office," she said.

The door closed, and Deputy Mattern actuated a frequency neutralizer to protect the room from even incidental surveillance.

"You may begin, Admiral Aitcheson," Mattern said.

Aitcheson leaned forward and folded his hands on the conference table. "As you've heard, the way in was clean, precision-planned, and under strict control. The way out was another story. At that time, the Israelis had a few test drone-equipped early F-35s, but with the weight of the nuclear weapon, they couldn't top off with full fuel. Efforts to offload other weight failed to accomplish the range needed. The situation called for manned flight, with minimal instruments, and with small and light pilots and a refueling en route. Beginning in the first decade of this century, the IDF decided to recruit small females for fighter pilot training. Every pilot who flew the Iran mission was female, under five foot three, and 110 pounds or less. They had over thirty such pilots, trained for the mission from whom to select. The program was extraordinarily successful. But I digress, sorry. As an aviator, I am so impressed by their thinking and execution that I cannot help but talk about it. What they did, *and in secrecy*, could never happen here.

"So there were three options for escape. The primary and safest option was to climb to maximum altitude and fly south over the Straits of Hormuz and the Gulf of Oman to the Arabian Sea. A hundred miles south of Oman waited two Chinese and two Israeli submarines, each carrying a squadron of eight Israeli commandos, Navy

Seal–type units. The pilots, in near-space protection suits and wearing GPS tracking beacons, activated timed charges to totally destroy their aircraft before punching out at forty thousand feet. They were able to gain that altitude only because the weight of the bomb was gone, as was the weight of the spent fuel. Tracking and retrieving them was like picking up astronauts in the earliest days of near-space flying—a piece of cake! Unknown to either the Israelis or the Chinese, we had two of our own boats there observing and prepared to go to their aid if necessary. But it was not necessary. They did a perfect job. Six of the eight pilots made it out that way.

"The second option was to go northwest to Azerbaijan and land at the airport in the Nakhchivan Autonomous Republic of Azerbaijan, three hundred miles west of Baku. One plane and pilot, with minor damage, did that. Despite continuous Russian provocations at the time, Azerbaijan had friendly relations with Israel and they have always played host to any airplanes in trouble over its airspace.

"The third option was Saudi Arabia. It was the closest. But it was the least friendly to foreign aircraft wandering into its airspace without permission, *even in this instance* where the Saudis had made a big contribution to the mission! Anyway, the F-35E with the severest damage couldn't climb to the altitude for the run to the Arabian Sea. The pilot broke radio silence and called the King Abdul Aziz Airbase, the closest to her, but she was waved off and told to go to the strictly military Al-Kharg Air Base near Riyadh.

"The pilot answered, 'Too far . . . No Joy; November Oscar; Nyet!'

"The Aziz Airbase then suggested she ditch in the gulf near their naval base and be picked up by patrol boat. And that's what she did. She guided the plane to the edge of the water, set the explosive charges and bailed out at four thousand feet. A patrol boat picked her up . . . and were they surprised to have rescued a petite girl, twenty years old, flying that thing!

"The plane pancaked on the water, cartwheeled, and sank. Ten minutes later it exploded underwater, blowing the ears off sonar listeners and sending a modest wave to all the shores. Earthquake-listening devices picked up a blip, but it was so small it was ignored as an anomaly."

Aitcheson sat back, shaking his head with a smile. "If this operation was executed yesterday, it would be hailed as a marvel of planning and execution. But remember—*this was fifteen years ago, with only the technology available at that time!* For me, it brings back many memories of extraordinary military prowess on the part of the Israeli military: the raid on Entebbe, the bombing of Iraq's Osiris reactor and the Syrian reactor, the strikes on weapons factories in the Sudan, the interdiction of Iranian weapons en route to their enemies, strategic air strikes on IS within fifty kilometers of their borders. Actions in different decades with different top brass and different operatives, but always with the same result! Israel only exists today by the ingenuity and execution of its people. We have complete satellite videos of the entire operation in our top-secret archives. That it has been kept such a closely guarded secret for so long is a testament to the loyalty of the Israelis to their cause and the desire of all the other players—China, Saudi Arabia, Kuwait, Azerbaijan, and us—to distance ourselves from cooperating in the mission. That's it! There's no more to tell."

All at the table expressed a collective sigh.

Mickey was the first to respond. "Admiral Aitcheson, thank you sir for that thorough briefing. I wish I had been one of those skippers in our standby boats. What an exciting mission! And of such significance to the world at the time."

I stayed quiet, proud of Israel, thankful for the help of China, the Saudis, and my own America. I was convinced now that staying with America was the only place for Ida and me. But then a question popped into my head.

"Admiral, sir, what class of boat did the Israelis use? That is a long run for them without nuclear power."

"Good question, Kadish—very good question and quick think-ing!" Aitcheson replied. "In the decade before the operation, Israel with China's help, built an underwater base at about three hundred feet deep on a shelf in the Gulf of Oman, covered with a graphene-laminated clear shell. Think of it as a space station, but underwater. It was a huge technical and practical achievement. A few men are sta-tioned there for about a month's duty per visit. Israeli submarines of their more modern design can pull in and dock there, up to two at a time. There, they can be refueled and resupplied. Chinese drone tanker subs resupply the base from Chinese ports for now. Both Israel and China have research ships plying their areas, looking for other sites for similar bases. Their achievement is the basis for the current 007 movie. The capabilities of that base allowed the Israelis to put two boats into the recovery operation."

Jaws dropped across the room.

"So why was it that we broke relations with Israel not long after but not with China?" I asked.

Secretary Aitcheson sat back and looked across the table for that answer.

Bergman spoke up. "Military cooperation and political discourse are miles apart, even when there are normal relations with another state. Congress cheered the success of the mission, but the White House was embarrassed at the demonstration of military power that only *we* were supposed to possess. And we didn't anticipate how fast and tight Israel and China would publically come together. The White House was pissed, and someone had to pay. There was a shakeup at the Pentagon with the Joint Chiefs of Staff. Heads quietly rolled among the air force and navy brass, with the highest officers just transferred to more lucrative positions in the Defense Industrial Cabinet. It was politics and publicity, vs. professionals."

Bergman paused and shook his head.

"Then what to do about Israel? Their early cooperation with China was public but quiet—the battle tank deals, the AWACS electronics deal *that we got cancelled,* the Suez bypass, buying the cooperation of the Technion. We would never have guessed the manpower, money, and ruthless policies China would use to push Jordan and the Palestinians together to create a new Palestinian state. King Abdullah II was paid off to abdicate and cancel the monarchy in favor of a Palestinian Republic. An even bigger surprise was that China would spend the money and manpower to buy a large northeast sector of the Sinai from Egypt to build a new home for the people of Gaza."

"Russia helped that by encouraging the Egyptians to do it," I said.

Those around the table looked quizzically at me, maybe wondering how I knew.

Bergman continued. "I speak for all the people in this room when I tell you, Jon, that we, the United States government up and down the line never expected the Israelis to tolerate Chinese suppression of the extremist Arab military militia leaders, politicians and academics. We didn't think they would allow such a purge. After that, our confidence in Israel took a real beating. Except in ancient times and a few isolated incidents in the past century, slaughter was never a policy of Jewish warriors. The Jews suffered many more times from enemies who unleashed such vengeance on *them!* No matter how our country has changed internally, the United States would never—*never*—adopt such a strategy, and we have punished many of our own individual officers and soldiers who committed atrocities under our flag. So the president ordered State to recall our ambassador, and that was that. We needed certain resources from China, and you know they were seeking Alaska from us at the time—so breaking relations with them was not a viable option at that instantaneous moment."

It was 11:00 a.m., and everyone had grown solemn after that explanation. Secretary Watson stood up. "Let's take a short break, have a

refreshment and invite Gwen to return. I think we can speak infor-
mally from this point and finish up quickly."

\*\*\*

Ida and I were quiet for a moment as I relived that part of the meeting.
The discussion of Israel and China was sobering all over again.

"I went to the men's room to splash cold water on my face. The
men were all there except Aitcheson. It started quietly, but slowly they
began to talk, socialize, and exhibit fellowship. I was a stranger on
their turf, but I observed and respected them supporting one another.
All these little nuances were helping me see and feel a sense of common purpose with this group. Ida, I liked what I saw."

\*\*\*

When we reassembled, Mattern took the floor. "Last and perhaps most
important in this discussion, something is going on in South Africa by
and between a number of former British colonies. We can brief you in
more detail on what we know and suspect, but we want you to engage
with this group, this so-called 'Free Africa and India Coalition,' and
learn of their mission and progress. We need detailed information to
judge what our relationship to them should be. We are inviting you,
Jon, to accept this assignment as a part of the Homeland Security
Intelligence Service."

Mattern leaned back and again the room went quiet. People looked
one to another for just a moment or two. It was an awkward pause. No
one seemed to know who was supposed to talk next.

Unexpectedly, Mickey piped up. "On behalf of Jon, what are you
offering?"

Catern and Aitcheson frowned at Mickey. He ignored them.

"To begin," Mattern said, "your elevation to Level II will be approved, and the FBI will waive their requirement to interview Ida."

That was a surprise and I thought a big concession to Ida and me. I knew she would appreciate it.

Mattern cleared his throat and took a slug of water. "You will be positioned at the sixty-seventh percentile of the Level II pay grade for salary and benefits, including retirement when you reach age seventy-five."

Gwen Lathrop spoke up for the first time, adding, "You will have freedom to leave the country as needed, after letting your handler—who will be me at the outset—know in advance and provide approval. You can reside in countries that we approve for parts of the year if you wish, but you will remain US citizens. You will not be trained in combat, nor will you be issued a weapon. Intellectual data gathering and reporting will be your sole job. We all think you have the knowledge, acumen, and experience to be very good at it."

"You'll not get a better offer than this from anyone," General Catern said. "And America is still the best society in the world. In due time, sooner rather than later, we will return to the principles of our founding fathers and reach new heights. C'mon, Jon. You know that this is your future."

\*\*\*

"Ida, I wanted to call you to discuss it, but there was no opportunity. All these people seem quite normal, not what outside-Washington people think of Washington people! Yah know? You get what I mean? As I saw in the men's room, they're working hard and long hours trying to do the best job they can for the majority of Americans within this system we have now."

"So what happened then—what time was that?" Ida asked.

"About 11:45. I asked a few technical questions that different people answered, that led to a sweeping discussion about the future of

America, the proposals in the current session of Congress, the vision of the president and the integrity of the economy––and the many elements of our society that have been modified in the past twenty years to renew our vitality. The conversation came back to my medical diagnosis, my options, our children and grandchildren, my service for nearly fifty years. Then it moved on to the past week, our ride in the FAV, the lodge, the dinner, the guests, the murder, and the rest. I was fully open with them, and they offered many good observations, analyses, and suggestions. I felt good with them. I felt comfortable with them as a team. Half an hour slipped away. Ms. Lathrop invited all to lunch at their executive dining room. Aitcheson and Ms. Watson excused themselves, but the rest of us followed. It was almost 12:20."

"Okay, okay already! Save the little details for later," Ida said.

"When did you decide? How did they fly you here? I'm a little scared about all this, but I'm happy you came to a decision and we're staying Americans. Glad to skip that FBI grilling too. What about our Norwich house now?"

"During lunch, my feelings about the whole thing were confirmed, and I knew saying "yes" to them was the right thing for us. I haven't thought of the Norwich house. I guess I should call Rollie tomorrow, have him check it out, shovel any snow, and make it look lived in. We'll have to get to Truman too and tell him not to act on the house as yet. We still have to sort out where we're going to live."

***

Sitting at lunch in Washington, Mickey had said, "Here, look at this." He showed me the Level II pay scale and retirement pension on his communicator screen, holding it below the tabletop.

I turned to Ms. Lathrop. "To accomplish this mission, I should operate from the Boat and continue to liaison with Mickey. His staff is the most logical to do any research that I might need."

Gwen looked quizzical for a moment but then agreed.

"Sure," she said, "You want to appear as nothing has changed in your career or assignment."

Mickey and the general both smiled and nodded their satisfaction at being kept in the loop. Ms. Lathrop excused herself, stepped away from the table and went to her communicator for several minutes outside of earshot from the table.

When she returned, she said, "It's nearly one p.m. I've ordered your chip to be implanted in an hour and a State Department diplomatic jet to take us to Ottawa, leaving from National at three. A helicopter will take us to the airport, and a helicopter will take you from Ottawa to Sherbrooke as soon as we arrive. Others on my staff are making arrangements that I will brief you about on the flight. I am going to Ottawa with you."

General Catern added, "Your upgrade to Level II is already approved and your Level II communicator will meet you at Washington National. I'm having it made in the same wrist configuration as you have now, but in brushed stainless steel. I'm even having your Homeland Security MP badge engraved on the back. That's what's taking extra time."

***

"Will you please stop calling her 'Ms. Lathrop?'" Ida snarled. "I know you're on a first name basis already. Really . . . I don't mind. I'm not jealous. But I want to get a look at her. You've never had a female boss."

Wow, that was right—I hadn't looked at it that way until Ida pointed it out! I had never worked for a female and this one was only a few years older than my own daughter. *Maybe I'll learn how Rollie feels?* I wondered.

"And *you* have always been one. Even giving orders to me!"

We both had a good laugh as we hugged and kissed. It felt so good to finally have a decision made.

"The others left after lunch and Gwen and I continued to discuss the various possibilities with my three suitors, covering almost every possible what-if. At two, we drove across the campus to the Coast Guard dispensary, where I had to sign a slew of tablets approving and waiving stuff as a medic master chief explained what was 'on' and 'not on' the chip at this time. I rejected their offer of a local anesthetic, and they shot the chip into the back of my right hand. It felt like a needle prick for a blood draw. The chief checked it out and it's working perfectly. She also gave me access to a secure Cloud site where I can learn more about the chip, its levels and functions, and personal stuff that I might want to add to it now or in the future.

"Ida, a chip has been prepared for you too, and they are trying to see where you might get it implanted before we are required to travel again. We helicoptered to Washington National, and in minutes we were in a State Department jet and departed for Ottawa."

"So here we are! What happens next?" Ida asked.

"We have tomorrow to relax and catch our breath, then Friday morning we're off to Calgary. We need to pack a few things; we might have to stay a night or two. Our Calgary contact, Duevel, will pick us up at 7:30 outside the synagogue. He's an RCMP and CSIS intelligence officer."

"*A Mountie* is taking us to the plane to meet Matthew? Doesn't that seem strange to you?"

"Ida..., this is *all* strange! We can hardly tell the good guys from the bad. And who knows what the real motivation is behind Washington recruiting us to play this part? I feel good about this, about the people I'm working for now, but who knows? Maybe they are bad guys too."

"Anything else?" she asked.

"Oh, yes . . . I almost forgot.

"My code name is Jughead, and yours is Betty."

# Chapter 45
# Friday to Calgary
*Ida*

"Good morning, Mrs. Kadish," Duevel said as we came through the outside door. He was waiting in the cold, standing under the canopied entrance to the synagogue with the car running at the curb. "Good morning, Jon," he added.

"Please, you can call me Ida. Mrs. Kadish was my mother-in-law."

He nodded and smiled. I guessed he was in his late thirties, tall and ruggedly handsome. Had he been in a Mountie suit—I mean uniform—he would have been the perfect model for their recruiting poster. He opened the back door for me and Jon sat up front. He took the single leather bag that Jon and I shared with our overnight necessities and put it in the trunk.

"Your meeting in Calgary is at 8:30 this morning and we intend to have you there on time," he said. "Be prepared—I think you are about to have the ride of your life."

"What are you talking about?" Jon asked. "Calgary is two thousand miles away, and even with the time zone change, that is in less than three hours. How can that happen?"

"It's actually only nineteen hundred miles and Jon, as an engineer, I think you'll be impressed."

There was a pause, so I jumped at the opportunity to ask a question of my own.

"Duevel, do you know a Shelley Demers?

"Oh . . .? *Oh!* That was quite a good operation! Wasn't it?" he answered with a chuckle.

"No... I don't think it was. What was so good about it?" I answered tartly.

"Well, it was Matthew's answer to your charade, wasn't it?

"The CSIS has contacts with every security firm in the country. The one in your son-in-law's building has an association with Matthew's firm in Toronto *and* the CSIS. A woman there relayed your masquerade at once. After they received the list of actresses, Matthew recognized Demers' name. He didn't know she was here in Sherbrooke. She was an easy recruit. We told her the plan and offered C$1,000 for the gig. She jumped at the chance but held out for our guarantee of the C$500 from the agency and a first-class ticket to St. Johns, her hometown. And... a ride to the airport! I tell you, we thought her demands would never stop!"

Duevel was laughing so, he was having trouble getting the words out.

"But what was the purpose to the stunt?" Jon asked annoyed. "What good did it serve?"

"The Coalition was surprised you had returned to the US, and it confused them. They weren't sure you would return here. Their project has been unable to get any traction with any of the US authorities and they wanted to make a dramatic reappearance in Washington. The cabbie cooperated too and was paid another C$1,000. But instead of a stylish outfit, he had to take a smack on the head and a walk in the park!

His laughing continued.

"The media was alerted and the charade was leaked to the Metro. Everyone became part of it!"

Duevel almost ran a traffic light, he was slapping his knee and laughing so hard.

"It was a huge success! You, Jon, the FBI, Homeland Security, the State Department, the Department of Defense Industries, all came to attention and here you are on your way to Calgary. It was a huge success, no? *YES!*" He kept laughing.

Jon and I sat quietly, unhappy at having been duped by their operation. But I was pretty proud of myself. I thought through my analysis back at Rachel's den. I was getting damn close.

"Who made the call to the agency pretending to be Shelley's husband?" I asked.

Duevel laughed more. "Some things are top secret, so I can't answer that."

*Sure you can't, but you just did.* I finally smiled.

Duevel pulled around to a remote part of the airport. The car had to pass through outer security to enter the grounds. A guard scanned Jon and Duevel's chips. It was cool watching Jon get scanned—definitely simple and quick. I wondered why we had resisted having them for so long and when I would get mine. Duevel and the guard talked quietly. I couldn't hear them but I knew it was about me—and my lack of a chip. The guard went into his station and pushed buttons on a console. After a brief delay, he lifted his head toward the car and nodded. Duevel waved. The double-fenced gates rolled aside to let us through.

We were dropped at the curb of a drab, gray, unimpressive building.

"Walk right in there. The gates will sense Jon's chip and open. People are waiting for you, and Ida—stay close to Jon and slip through with him. I'll be in after I park the car."

The building was ringed with elaborate security, and even Jon looked puzzled as he did a 360° scan of the complex, like he might with his periscope if he were submerged. Inside was another story.

We entered a well-appointed lounge with modern, space-age furnishing. Offices ringed the perimeter and satellite pictures of the heavens and earth in different light settings adorned the walls. A man and a woman in teal jumpsuits, logo on the left shoulder, name on the right, came from a rear office to greet us.

"Welcome to PlanetSpace Quebec Skydome III. I'm Paige Taylor, your pilot for today. This is André Flower, who will help you into some necessary gear, secure you in your flight lounges and brief you on what to prepare for and expect. Our shuttle today is the Canadian *Arrow XII* for a SSTSO flight to Calgary. Please let me take your bag and have it secured in the craft. Welcome again, and please follow André to your preparation suite."

*Shuttle?* I thought I'd pee in my pants! How did we get into this? I wanted to run away. After Jon gave Paige a good looking-over, he looked at me. He could see the terror in my eyes and took my hand to follow André to wherever.

"Hold steady, Ida," Jon said. "We'll each take a yellow to calm our anxiety. We'll get through this together and it will be the experience of our lives."

Duevel caught up to us.

"What is SSTSO?" Jon asked André.

"Oh . . . that's our jargon for 'Single-Stage To Sub-Orbit.' But this is no test vehicle. *Arrow XII* has made hundreds of flights over the past years, with a perfect record. You need some protective clothing, a breathing mask and a contoured lounge seat to enjoy the flight to Calgary—and trust me, *you will enjoy it!* The space plane will take off with a normal ground roll, climb to forty thousand feet, then turn nose-up and rocket to about seventy-five miles in a parabolic arc. The rocket motor will shut down just before apogee, from which you will silently glide across the country and then down again to forty thousand, where the jet will restart to take you to landing at the Calgary International Airport."

"What about G forces and weightlessness on the trip? And total time to Calgary?" Jon asked. He nudged me to pay attention and whispered, "I'll explain later. I'm getting excited about this experience! Remember the roller coaster at Paradise Park forty years ago? This could be its sequel. But we'll still take the yellows."

"Oh, Jon! Why did you mention that awful experience? I got sick on that ride and spewed my lunch all over us. Ugh . . . it had better not be that!"

André continued, "The takeoff will feel fast but not too abnormal. On the acceleration leg at the four hundred flight level, you'll experience no more than 3.05 Gs for a few seconds, that's all. The lounge and covers will absorb a good deal of it, and it shouldn't be too uncomfortable. After forty seconds, the rocket motor will shut down and the extra G forces will diminish as you glide to apogee, the top of the parabola.

"As you pass over the peak, there will be a moment of complete weightlessness as the ship transitions from uphill to downhill. On the downward leg, which will take longer as you glide west, you will not feel complete weightlessness again at any time. The plane will make maneuvers every ten seconds to break the parabolic path slightly to cancel complete weightlessness. The loss of weightlessness also happens automatically due to the friction of reentering the lower-altitude denser air. That is the longest leg of the trip and the most delightful. Look out the portholes. Look up at the sky and down at the earth. The panorama is sensational. At flight level four hundred, the plane reverts to normal jet flight for approach and landing. Total time in the air is about forty minutes. Nineteen hundred miles and you are there in less than an hour, door to door. Cool, isn't it?"

"How many people will be on the plane?" I asked.

Now Duevel answered. "The *Arrow XII* can accommodate eight, but today it will just be you two––and three other gentlemen. They arrived a short time ago from London. We don't have time for you to meet them now, but they are going to the meeting too. A secure, black Double-MATV will meet you at the PlanetSpace Alberta Skydome II—that's Calgary—and bring all five of you to the University of Calgary, downtown campus. I suggest you keep your distance from them until you are formally introduced. But if they approach you, by all means turn on the charm."

"Are we coming back here tonight, tomorrow?" I asked.

"Ida, just stay with the meetings for now," Duevel answered politely. "Proper arrangements will fall into place after the decisions of the day.

And when you do return here, I'll be waiting to take you wherever you direct."

Jon excused himself to the men's room and left me with Duevel. When he returned, he called me over and privately slipped a small yellow pill into my hand.

"Go to the ladies' room and take this. It's nothing more than a shot of whiskey," he said.

Considering the circumstances, I did as told.

André had us sit in contoured lounge seats with formable foam that compressed to our body shape. Then he inserted a metal ring around our heads and clipped a clear plastic hemisphere to it that lowered over our faces and was secured with a foam layer applied to our shoulders and around the top of our chests. He lowered the hemisphere to test the fit and made some adjustments for each of us before carefully lifting us off the lounges and spraying a fixative on them to freeze their shape.

"These lounges will be installed on the *Arrow* as your seats for this flight, and then will be kept, stored, in the event you rebook a trip with us. An enhanced oxygen breathing mix will be piped to your mask. Remember, you will feel some compression—some pressure pushing you into the lounge—even during the ground takeoff and then more, much more so during the rocket acceleration period. We have a demo video to show you next, you'll see.

"On the down and westward leg, the eighteen minutes of partial weightlessness, sort of like floating in a swimming pool is the most incredible part of the flight. Gaze at the heavens, the stars, the earth, the moon! Make use of every second. I hope you enjoy the flight."

Duevel returned us to the waiting lounge and put us in a mini-theatre to watch the video briefing on the flight. The video showed others experiencing what we would experience in just a short time.

Everything André said was reinforced. As the program was playing, three other men took seats in the theatre.

One said in a very British accent, "Oh . . . not this again? When are they going to do a new version?"

"Aye . . . quiet!" answered an Irishman. "Sit down tere, Steele, and close yure eyes. We've all seen tis many times; so what?"

When the tutorial was over, I asked Duevel, "Does this woman really know how to fly this thing?"

"Please, Ida," Jon said, his tone implying it was a stupid question.

"No, Jon," I said firmly, "I want this man to answer the question! I'm putting my life on the line here too!"

Duevel motioned us to a cluster of studio chairs in a corner of the room.

"Paige is an absolute expert in this spacecraft. She is perhaps the most experienced on the *Arrow XII.* To prepare for today, she has calculated every phase of the flight sequence and inputted the actions and coordinates needed at the points required into the primary and backup computers. *In essence, she has made this flight twice today already.* On board, she will relax in the control station and not touch a single instrument or lever unless there is some error she made in the program or an unexpected circumstance occurs—one that has never happened in fifteen years."

"What sort of unexpected circumstance?" Jon asked.

"There could be an errant decaying satellite or tiny meteor coming close to the flight path that was not previously detected. In reality, it's hard to imagine any possibility of that. The computers will totally control the complete flight from taxi down this runway to landing in Calgary. This flight is 100 percent safe *without any such flight person on board.* If we were just moving our own people, this ship would be sent as a drone, no pilot on board at all. Paige is only going because one of your three companions insists on it when he sub-orbits––and he has the authority to command almost anything!"

331

I wondered which one that might be?

By the time we were escorted to the space plane, it was after nine o'clock. André took us one by one; Jon first, then me. Another attendant escorted the three others. There were four rows of single seats on each side, each at a porthole, with a narrow aisle in the center. Jon and I were seated in the fourth row across from each other. We could have held hands if we weren't encased in our partial cocoons. The masks were equipped with an intercom so we could at least talk. André strapped us in and locked us down.

The other three men were seated in rows one and two. Row three was empty between us. I wondered if we were intentionally being kept apart. A moment later, Paige stepped on board and sat in the single lounge at the head of the aisle in front of a narrow windshield with an array of screens, switches, pulsar lights, and who-knows-what. If that was the cockpit, or whatever they called it, it was wide open and part of the cabin. I wondered where our leather bag was. André adjusted Paige's cocoon too and backed out. The stairway was withdrawn on a track, the gull-wing hatch closed, and the plane began to move, totally silent toward the taxiway. Paige hadn't moved a muscle.

"Have they started the engine yet?" I asked Jon.

"No, we must be taxiing on electric power . . . conserves fuel. The runway here is pretty short, only six thousand feet. To be off the ground in half that distance, we are going to be slammed back on these lounges by the acceleration like we saw in the video. Be prepared."

In two minutes, we were at the runway threshold. The jet engine started with a roar and the plane began to race forward, slamming us into our contoured lounges. It was only seconds before the plane leaped into the air, climbing at a steep angle and increasing speed. I felt my skin caressing my cheekbones and my lips against my teeth. In the headset and under the hemisphere it was perfectly quiet. The ride was quiet and smooth, not a notch of vibration.

# Chapter 46
# On the Flight
*Jon*

I twisted my face toward Ida and could see the pressure on her relaxing as the jet acceleration diminished and we approached the rocket ignition level. I knew abrupt acceleration was coming and that it would be much more intense. I winked at Ida, but I could see that she was still worried. She forced a smile, then returned to facing forward, her eyes closed. Out the window, I could see the stubby delta wing receding into the fuselage. I knew what was coming . . .

Our headphones lit up just as we heard in the video:

PREPARE FOR SUBORBITAL ACCELERATION . . .
FIVE . . . FOUR . . . THREE . . . TWO . . . ONE . . .

We were crushed into the lounges like a ton of dirt had dropped on our bodies. I felt my face distort, my heart race, and my chest resist expansion for breathing. My mind was panicking. Forty seconds without breath seldom suffocated a person, especially in an oxygen-enriched atmosphere. That was probably why they had picked the forty-thousand-foot altitude to move up to rocket power—the higher up it ignited, the shorter the burn to the top. I worried about Ida. She was probably thinking she was being choked to death. I managed a small inhale against the weight as the forty seconds seemed to drag on forever.

The rocket shut down and the weight relaxed as our upward thrust diminished and we coasted to the apogee, the seventy-five mile peak of the flight. At the very peak, the pressure was gone and the craft tilted horizontally for a second, leaving us weightless for that instant—just before nosing over and starting down the parabolic path to the west. The tilting lounges reoriented us to a slightly reclined position, exactly aligning our faces with the portholes.

The earth below looked like a beach ball, bright and luminous against the pitch-black void of space. Some clouds obscured parts of North America and Europe. Above, the moon looked huge and could be seen more clearly without the interference of the atmosphere. The definition of the peaks and craters was incredible. The stars were bigger and brighter for the same reason. I could see man-made satellites, reflecting the sun moving overhead. I could discern ours from other nations, because of our flag painted on their bodies. The clarity was brilliant. I looked across to Ida. She seemed composed.

"How're you doing?" I asked through the intercom.

"I thought I was going to suffocate to death before I could breathe again," she said. "Was that a ton of bricks they dropped on us?"

"Sort of," I answered, smiling. "The worse part of the flight is now over. We'll feel a bit of weightlessness gliding down and later another less intense minute of pressure when we convert back to jet power for landing. Look out the window—the sights are marvelous. Not many get to see this with their own eyes. It's like a museum display that you'll never forget. We'll be fifteen, twenty minutes in this mode and on the ground before we realize it."

Ida turned to look out the porthole.

***

On the ground, I wanted to open my hemisphere but couldn't. My arms and body were still strapped into the lounge. The space plane pulled up to the PlanetSpace Skydome at exactly 8:00 a.m. local time.

I said through the intercom, "From door to door in less than an hour! I knew this was possible and that it was being done, but I never expected to be treated to a ride."

A walkway rose up to the fuselage and the door cracked open and lifted away. Three uniformed women entered. One attended to Paige, opening her hemisphere and releasing her restraints. She hadn't moved or touched a thing during the entire flight. Another attended the three gentlemen, and the third attended us. She opened each of our masks first.

As she began releasing Ida's restraints, she said, "Welcome to the PlanetSpace Alberta Skydome II. I'll have each of you released in a minute. My name is Jackie. We ask you to perform a few mild exercises before you deplane to be sure your heart, circulation and breathing are normal."

Jackie finished releasing Ida and told her to stay in the lounge and breathe deeply. She then did and said the same to me. Paige was already off the plane, and the men in front were all standing and going through some routine, sort of dancing around. They weren't being coached. It appeared they knew what to do from experience.

Jackie helped Ida to her feet and asked if she felt dizzy.

Ida said, "Slightly."

"Okay, stand here for a moment and hold onto the lounge while I get Mr. Kadish on his feet."

Ida nodded.

In another moment, I was standing and also feeling slightly dizzy.

"This is very normal for first-time and even some repeat flyers," Jackie said. "Stand holding on and breathe. You need to purge the extra oxygen from your systems. I'll be away from you for a few seconds."

The three men were walking off and Jackie asked the other attendant to help her with us. She opened a small hatch and took out two half-liter bottles of what looked like water.

"Here," she said, "Please drink these. This is water with a few nutrients and compounds to ignite your body systems and add electrolytes quickly to your bloodstreams. Like I said, you're oversaturated with oxygen for the moment and not used to it."

Jackie stayed with Ida. The second attendant, Cindy, stood with me. We drank the water as they watched. Jackie walked Ida forward and had her flex her limbs, arms and hands, kick her legs, and rotate her feet from the ankle.

"How do you feel now?" Jackie asked.

"Better, much better. Fine, near normal."

"Okay, then, let me take your arm and walk with you off the plane, across the space bridge and into the terminal."

Cindy did all the same with me.


A buffet bar was waiting for us, and we were directed to take something with caffeine—coffee, tea, or hot chocolate—and also something with protein, an egg or some cheese; and a small portion of carbohydrates, a miniature Danish or donut. We did as directed and paced around the room steadying our rubbery legs. The three men were watching us closely, smiling as they drank and ate their selections.

A young man came and greeted us by name. He said he was a colleague of Duevel. "It will be my pleasure to attend to you while in Calgary."

He motioned me to the men's room, where he presented his chip for me to scan. His name was Rubin. He too was a RCMP on assignment with the CSIS. I nodded with satisfaction, and offered him mine.

"That's not necessary, sir," he said. "The wrong people *never* get on the *Arrow.*"

We smiled at each other and shook hands.

"Follow me, sir. I'll get you and your wife to the meeting."

"Are the others still waiting? Are we going in the Double-MATV?"

"No sir, the Double-M has already left, sir."

That was a letdown—I'd been hoping for a look inside the military vehicle, not to mention a ride.

"Please, Rubin, call me Jon. It's been a long time since I was active duty. But oh . . . the Double-M has left? Does that mean we'll be late for the meeting?"

"Oh, no, sir . . . sorry, sir . . . oops, Jon, sir. The meeting can't proceed without you."

I looked at my watch. It said 10:30—i.e. 8:30 Calgary time. We were already late.

"How far to where we're going?" I asked.

"About eleven miles, maybe twenty minutes this time of day."

"Okay, let's make tracks!" I said.

We arrived at the downtown campus of the University of Calgary in only fourteen minutes.

"Rubin, how were you able to drive so fast and why did the cars in front move over to let you by? How can you get away with that?"

"Well, sir, this *is* a recognizable RCMP vehicle and I did engage my flashing lights in the front and back. We're allowed to use them when we are escorting notables or celebrities. You won't be late at all. And as I understand these meetings, they never start on time and the guests are always kept waiting a bit. But they'll treat you well and serve you refreshments."

I twisted to look at Ida in the back seat, "Did you hear that? You're a celebrity!"

We smiled genuine smiles now that we were on the ground and feeling normal.

Rubin dropped us off at the main entrance on 8th Avenue SW and said, "Go through security and they should direct you to either the fifth or sixth floor—to the Cameco School of Energy and Environment Conference Center. I have another assignment to do, but they will buzz me when I need to be here for you. I'll meet you at the reception center on the sixth floor when you're ready to leave."

I was scanned at the door. That was all that was needed. A guard walked us to a restricted elevator and told me, "Wave your chip at the control panel and it will know where to take you, *express*."

The elevator had no buttons. I flashed the back of my right hand across its scanner, the doors closed and the number 5 started blinking on the panel. Seconds later, the door opened on the fifth floor, and there was Scott Matthew in a suit and tie waiting to greet us.

"So happy you agreed to visit," he said, smiling and nodding to us both. "The meeting is going to be slightly delayed, but come have a refreshment and meet a few of the people who will be participating."

As we followed him down a hall, I asked, "How long will this take and what happens to us afterward?"

"May I call you Jon?" he asked.

"Sure, fine."

"And I'm Scott. Okay Jon––when the meeting is over and depending on the results, we'll learn what comes next and arrange it. Don't even think about it now; we'll have it under full control at the appropriate time."

His answer satisfied me. Why should I doubt him? They'd had it all under control so far.

We reached a small café in the corner of the building with floor-to-ceiling glass looking into the city on two sides. Three men and a woman were seated at an expanded table with empty spaces for us. A uniformed gentleman stood and waited as we approached.

"Good morning, Mr. and Mrs. Kadish, I am Major General Kyle Farwell, a director of the Cameco Corporation and dean of the Cameco School of Energy and Environment. We are very pleased to have you both here today. We have important topics about energy and the environment to discuss."

I could see that he was Canadian military.

He turned toward the others, who were now all standing.

"Meet Ms. Valeria Slack, Chairman of the DeBeers Foundation of South Africa."

With his hand shielding his mouth, he half-whispered, "You know, *DeBeers*—as in diamonds! She's a great granddaughter of Sir Ernest Oppenheimer, who took control of the DeBeers mining interests in 1927, more than a hundred years ago."

Despite his theatrical attempt to hide his words, all knew what he was saying and were smiling one to the other.

Ms. Slack smiled and nodded to each of us.

The general moved on. "Did you meet Micéal Rooney? We call him Mick. He's the minister of Energy and Environment of Ireland. He came overnight on the *Arrow XII* from the UK, which stopped to pick you and Mrs. Kadish up in Sherbrooke."

"Sorry we weren't able ta meet prior to ta flight," Minister Rooney said. "I'm me country's observer in tese meetings."

"And this fine gentleman is Kerry Langley, Chairman of the Environment Protection Agency of New Zealand, another observer nation," said General Farwell.

I shook hands with each member.

They greeted Ida and me with warmth and enthusiasm and we returned the kindness. Ida was seated next to Ms. Slack and I was put on the other side of the table between the general and the Irishman. Everyone leaped into animated conversation, about the travel, the Arrows, the weather, football, hockey, and the like. A waitress came over and took orders from all. The experienced players ordered large breakfasts. Ida and I ordered more modestly. We had already had refreshments every hour.

"Do you have time for such a meal?" I asked the table.

Everyone laughed. Valeria spoke up. "The Executive Committee meets for the first hour. We are usually called at 9:30 or shortly afterward."

Rooney added, "And if we're not ready, we let 'em wait!"

Everyone laughed again.

Rooney couldn't stop talking. "Sorry we left without ye in ta Duble-M. Ta ot'er two blokes needed ta be on time. Tey are among ta key players in tis enterprise."

I was anxious to get going—into the meeting. Ida was busily engaged with Valeria and seemed interested in their conversation. I hoped they weren't talking diamonds. The men around me were asking general questions about my background, family, and interests. I didn't find it too invasive, just the ordinary chatter when meeting a new person. They talked about their interests too. When I asked about the project and why I had been invited, General Farwell said, "We are not authorized to speak on behalf of the Coalition. It would be best to wait until you are called to meet them. And please feel free to address me as Kyle."

*So here we are, and I still don't know why or for what.* Maybe Kyle noticed me shaking my head.

# Chapter 47
# Conference with the Coalition
*Jon*

At 9:40, we were all invited into the conference room.

Kyle said softly, "Follow me, and I'll get you seated."

The room was amazing, rebuilt in the past few years we were told. There was a horseshoe-shaped table for the Coalition members and a short table at the open end for Ida and me. The tabletop was without a shred of clutter, perfectly clean, but at each seat there was an individual display screen visible through the tabletop that only that person could see. Water and mints were on a shelf below the top. A mirrored sidewall I presumed concealed producers who controlled what was on each participant's screen. Remote camera pods were everywhere. When I looked down, my screen displayed a diagram of the table with the picture, name, title, and country of those at the table. I presumed Ida had the same.

The four we had entered with quickly took their seats at the horseshoe.

At the head of the table, directly facing us, sat Steele Heath, Chairman and former CEO of British Petroleum, representing Britain. Flanking him were men from India and South Africa. The Indian, Adnan Ambuti, was a billionaire in the energy business and the South African, Khgosi Motsep, was a billionaire in gold and uranium mining. Also seated were a billionaire banker from Australia, Clive Clarke, and another billionaire—retired Chairman and CEO emeritus of Cameco, Isaak Grantsson. Cameco is the giant Canadian mining company with headquarters in Saskatchewan. It's the largest publically traded uranium mining and processing company in the world. Along with the four observers we had met in the café, I guessed this group more than made a trillionaire.

# Chapter 47  Conference with the Coalition

I knew more about Grantsson than any of the others. Cameco had long-term supply contracts for uranium fuel with the US Navy. Under Isaak's leadership, the company had opened new discoveries, acquiring what seemed to be spent mines and rehabilitating them as they found new ore with new technology. The price of uranium oxide was now about US$3,600 per pound—C$3,000. I remembered days when a *high* price was US$150 and an average price was US$30–$40.

Heath had a gold ring on his left hand that he rapped on the table to call the meeting to order. The members and observers apparently had the minutes of a previous meeting on their screens, along with an agenda for this one. My screen image—and I assumed Ida's too— was then divided in half, with the table diagram on one side and the other blank. After quickly proceeding through routine matters, Heath turned his attention to us.

"Mr. and Mrs. Kadish, thank you for your attendance. I'm sorry for the way we coerced you here, but it is of vital necessity that we try to secure your participation in solving some problems related to our mission. We were told that *you, more than anyone else in the world*, might have the knowledge and know-how to break a terrible bottleneck in our progress."

I nodded at that compliment, but being *the world's expert* on something, anything, baffled me. I raised my index finger to be recognized.

"Have you something to say at this time?" Heath asked me quizzically, head tilted, squinting with a grimace.

"Not *say*, sir, *ask?* One biting question, sir: *What does your Coalition want to free Africa and India from?*"

The South African, Mr. Motsep blurted, "From energy *DEPENDENCE!* That's what!"

The Indian, Mr. Ambuti, added more politely, "And from burning coal that is sickening our people and contaminating the world's atmosphere."

Chairman Heath regained the floor.

"Mr. Kadish, the world is in a terrible state. The division of energy and energy resources has been realigned, but is unequally distributed. The United States is in the best position with centuries' worth of natural gas reserves, an embargo against exporting any of it to the rest of us, and the lowest unit price to its industry, military and population. That is a *major* reason, among others, that America's sun is rising again."

His eyes were fixed on mine, trying, I thought, to burrow into my brain.

"Mr. Kadish!" Heath continued. "The source of all national wealth is energy! From the containment of fire to the domestication of beasts of burden, the invention of the waterwheel, the steam engine, and all the rest up until modern times––whoever was first, whoever used it most widely, whoever developed it most fully, whoever found new and better energy sources––*to that nation* went national growth and improvement in the lives of their population.

Those around the table seemed to groan an affirmation.

"Not a single intellectual, academic, or prophet has ever disputed that energy is the source of all wealth! The United States and Russia are the only major countries that are energy self-sufficient, representing only 800 million people. Smaller countries with energy independence from a local resource, such as Canada and Israel, only account for another 500 million."

Leaning forward and intensifying his stare into mine––as if it was my responsibility, he shouted, "What about the other TEN BILLION PEOPLE on this planet?" He sighed, paused, and took a sip from a glass, then continued, "China has captured the energy resources of the Middle East almost exclusively, controlling those medieval fiefdoms by paying in yuan. The benefit is that the world is a little safer now that those extremists are under their control. China has nuclear power too, and their own uranium in the ground. But they are raping the undeveloped countries of Africa of their valuable energy and precious metal resources, paying the decadent leaderships and ignoring the masses.

"India today has a greater population than China, a greater demographic of young people. But they cannot fully exploit this national resource for lack of sufficient energy at an affordable price." He nodded to Ambuti.

"South Africa, with its recent nuclear incident, is in a somewhat similar position. They have wealth in gold and diamonds and even a growing rare-earths industry, but they were forced to revert to coal for their electricity—the worst of all options, primarily because of the ecological damage to the environment and the health of their people. Sure, they are a major producer of coal, along with the money they can virtually dig out of the ground. *But that won't last forever!*"

He looked at Motsep and then focused his eyes on Ms. Slack as if scolding South Africa's still-plentiful diamond and gold resources.

He opened his arms wide; encapsulating all the seated members of the Coalition and said, "Look at us! What do the members of this Coalition have in common? Our nations are all developed former members of the British Empire. We are all democracies; we are all secular societies where one's religion, ethnicity, race, gender bias, and such, are irrelevant to citizenship and the right to dignity and opportunity! And with the exception of Canada, we are all plagued at some level by deficient energy and resultant environmental issues that threaten our populations and hamper our efforts to improve the lives of our people—*and the world itself is in desperate danger!* We have to have a viable alternative for all the coal being burned around the globe. An Israeli think tank proved through computer simulation decades ago that coal is killing the planet . . . and yet we still burn coal!"

Steele Heath relaxed back in his chair seemingly drained from his monologue. His face was flushed and he started to loosen tie––but quickly realized what he was about to do, and instantly put his hands in his lap. I knew that feeling. I had wanted to do that many times over my navy and Boat career.

"Does any member or observer wish to add anything now?" he asked.

Grantsson of Cameco was the first to speak up.

"Mr. and Mrs. Kadish, the world needs a new, clean, reliable, inexpensive source of energy, and *we know what it is!* Physicists and scientists have known since the dawn of the atomic age. America did tests and research on it in the 1950s and '60s––but abandoned it. You know what I am talking about . . . don't you? Mr. Kadish!"

The room stood still. All eyes were on me, waiting for an answer.

Until this trip, my eyes had not really been open to the scope of the energy crisis facing much of the world. I calmed myself and spoke in a quiet, controlled tone.

"Gentlemen, and Ms. Slack, thank you for having us. Had I known the mission and composition of your Coalition, it would not have been so difficult to get us here. Please, you are welcome to address me as Jon, and," I nodded toward Ida, "Mrs. Kadish as Ida." Hoping to lighten the atmosphere, I added, "My parents were Mr. and Mrs. Kadish."

The assembled nodded stoically. I cleared my throat.

"Mr. Grantsson, you are no doubt referring to a Thorium 90/232 nuclear power generation system. I know the basic overarching arguments for its development and its universal adoption. And I have a basic understanding of the reasons that it has been ignored till recently—"

I was cut off before I could continue.

"It has been ignored because America is secure with LNG for generations to come and won't participate, doesn't *need to* participate, on the long, difficult and expensive road to make a thorium reactor a reality!" Ambuti said angrily.

I glanced down to remind myself of his name—Adnan Ambuti, Chairman of Reliable Reliant, Ltd, an energy giant headquartered in Mumbai.

The South African picked up the chant. "That's why our countries have joined ranks for this mission. Together we have the motivation, natural resources, and financial means to see it through to success. But we are in a race with others. China and Russia, and a Scandinavian group, the Nords, are each pushing their own thorium program."

"You forgot the Canadians with their privately financed molten salt *uranium* reactor."

Ambuti ignored my interruption. "The first entity to achieve a reliable and exportable system and demonstrate it in their own society *will own the rest of the world!* China is the most aggressive in this pursuit and is depending on its success to actually control the world. Yes, the *entire* world—us, you, Russia, even if it takes a hundred years!"

*Wow,* I thought. *That is the same story the Russian admiral told us at the flat. And maybe the Israeli reference to thorium was on behalf of China?*

"We are well advanced in developing the many elements of the process," said Clarke, the banker from Australia. "Thorium is four times more plentiful in the earth than uranium and is a waste product from the processing of other minerals, such as iron, and especially rare earths. China has a huge stockpile as the exclusive supplier of rare earths to the world for decades. They are masters at manipulating the price and supply of these elements to render other mines uneconomical to develop or operate. That *was* the case until almost two decades ago when this Coalition united––and despite the cost––invested to produce rare earths in South Africa and India. We now have a small footprint in Australia as well. How else would we be able to ensure our freedom? We have now some modest control of the rare earths needed within our own societies. Cameco has been instrumental in supplying technology and manpower outside their corporate structure."

All assembled nodded and mumbled their agreement. Grantsson and Kyle, both connected to Cameco, nodded their assent.

I listened, trying to figure out their angle. They knew I already knew most of this.

Ambuti said, "India has one of the largest deposits of thorium oxide in the world, with easy access along our eastern border against the Bay of Bengal. We have begun to extract it from beach sand and develop processes to purify and encase it in ceramic coatings that can be used in a molten salt reactor. Others are investigating more conventional thorium fuel rods to be used with plutonium triggers. But the molten system appears to be more flexible, taking advantage of thorium's natural properties for automatic control and safety."

Heath, appearing to have cooled down, leaned forward and stared at me again.

"The United States has taken no action because of your overwhelming capitalist system that rewards private and public companies for short or at best, midterm results. To undertake a development of this magnitude, *you need to invest and invest, develop and develop for maybe thirty years––before you reap the rewards of your effort! Private capital cannot abide such a long horizon!*"

I'd had enough of his chastisement and was hot to reply.

*"It is not private capital alone that drives us!"* I responded. "The government promotes a future agenda through its purchases, its grants to universities and private research laboratories, to its own research facilities, and its subsidies for technological innovators. It seeks joint ventures with private capital to accomplish future goals. But after the Manhattan Project a hundred years ago, the uranium infrastructure was already started. Thorium is radioactive but will not sustain a chain reaction. It needs triggers to make it fissile. It cannot be used for bombs."

"*Tat*, Mr. Kadish, is its main attractions ta us today!" Rooney shouted.

"*But not then!*" I shouted back.

The rhetoric was accelerating. I lifted out of my chair as I launched into a response before anyone else could get a word in.

"The Cold War was in high gear and competition with the Soviet Union required the production of uranium and plutonium to make bombs . . . 'mutual assured destruction' by both sides was the goal. Sure, ninety years later, *now,* the political situation has changed. The Soviet Union has collapsed and atomic bomb inventories on all sides have been reduced, freeing the uranium in warheads to be reprocessed for power fuel—which is now almost all used up. And still—other countries have joined the nuclear club.

*"But I'm telling you, the time to develop thorium has passed!"*

"To do so now, as you and others are trying, is to try to rewrite history. There are huge difficulties in each component of the thorium process that you don't even know about yet. You cannot tackle the disposal of the resultant wastes; you haven't made any! Most of it is just theory at this point! And what about the inevitable accidents? Practical learning exercises, for sure—but fearsome for a population. No one can predict them. We try to conceive of all the dangers in advance and take steps to prevent them. Yet some unknown or uncontrollable factors still cause them.

"Could we have prevented the Fukushima tsunami? Is Mother Nature always predictable? Should you have anticipated the Koeberg pipe shrinkage when the pipes were being cooled for a refuel? It hadn't happened the previous times, but we know that titanium has a high coefficient of expansion and contraction when heated and cooled. That would have been the fifth refueling of Koeberg after fifty-two years of operation. Shouldn't someone have thought about possible metallurgical degradation of the titanium after so many years of irradiation, heat and stress? Shouldn't there have been a debate about whether to build a completely new power plant since Koeberg I's original calculated useful life of forty years had already been exceeded?"

They were listening. I carried on.

"We retire our submarines after thirty-three years just because *we do not know* how many more *safe,* useful years are left—not only with the power plant, but with the piping, the wiring, the hull, the electronics. The lives of the crew are at stake, and they are management's responsibility!"

I took a deep breath, leaned back in my chair and reached for water, wondering to what extent I had offended them with my defense of the United States' point of view. Now my neck was hot. My heart was racing. My temples ached as they did when I became stressed. I wanted a you-know, but I couldn't get to one at that moment.

Ida looked at me with questioning eyes, probably wondering where all that stuff was stored in me. I smiled at her and at the thought. When I returned my attention to the horseshoe, the table was silent. It stayed like that for a seemingly endless minute.

Heath broke the silence. "Jon, Ida, may we please excuse you for perhaps ten minutes? I want to consult in private with the committee."

"No problem, Mr. Heath, no problem at all. I could use a washroom at this time anyway," I said.

"Steele . . . my friends and colleagues call me Steele."

I nodded understanding.

A young woman in business attire appeared behind us. I took Ida's arm as she rose from the chair and we followed the woman through another door into a very comfortable lounge.

We were recalled in less than ten minutes. The nine participants were standing at their places. As we entered, they greeted us with polite applause. They sat when we sat. Steele motioned to Ambuti by his side, giving him the floor.

"Jon, you have shown us that you *are* the person we seek, the one we need to break the logjam in our development. Your stirring outburst, demonstrating the passion of your convictions, revealed the personality and temperament we badly need at this time. We know we must first prove to you the necessity of this development––for all mankind— and demonstrate our collective commitment so you can defend and advocate for *our mission* in the same way you just did for your current beliefs. We have no doubt that when you understand our plan, see our progress, and believe in our passion to succeed, you will enthusiastically want to join us."

The others around the table all grunted and nodded their concurrence.

Steele said, "Some of us need to brief you on specific details, but not in this forum. Those attending from South Africa and India will be returning to Cape Town later this afternoon by Arrow. We invite you and Ida to join them and visit our research headquarters in Pretoria and our thorium fuel plant at Pelindaba. Then we'll helicopter you to our test reactor plant at the site of the old Colenso Power Station. We're currently building a third reactor there, based on our experience and data from the first two. Excellent staff at each of these facilities will welcome you and hold nothing in reserve. They will answer all your questions. From there if you wish, you can Arrow with Mr. Ambuti to India on Sunday, where he'll show you our thorium mining and processing there. Have you any questions?"

My head was spinning. This was not exactly the reaction I'd expected to my outburst.

"Thank you for your kind words and invitation, but Ida and I need some private time to think and talk this whole enterprise over. We also need a briefing on living places and conditions in South Africa. If I agree to join you, we will need to agree to a specific goal and an appropriate reward if I deliver it.

"Now, if I might ask, who told you that I might have the knowledge and know-how to help you? And how long do you think my services will be needed? When will we be returned to Sherbrooke where our family is waiting?"

"Sergei Segalov recommended we recruit you," Steele answered. "He felt that you could solve our bottleneck. And you might be needed for five or six months, maybe less."

The mention of Sergei's name made me smile. I turned and nodded knowingly to Ida.

"Oh . . . will I be working with him?" I asked in optimistic anticipation.

"No, Jon . . . Segalov is dead."

# Chapter 48
# Ladies' Lunch in Calgary
*Ida*

Jonathan was shocked, visibly shaken by that disclosure, as was I. When he regained his composure, we learned that Sergei and Ivanica had been murdered—"assassinated."

"They were on holiday in Madagascar two weeks ago and were shot at close range in a pub where they were supposed to meet a potential recruit," Steele told us.

Two weeks ago was only a few days before Ivanica Segalov was to meet Nikelovich in New Hampshire.

"Did they capture the killer? Do you know who is responsible?" Jon asked.

"We have our suspicions," said Steele. "MI5, SASS, and CSIS are investigating, with help from the national agencies of other Coalition members. We have tripled the security of our facilities and our people wherever they are and wherever they travel, an expense that we had hoped to avoid. Nevertheless, we are doing what is necessary."

For the next half-hour the formality of the conversion was discarded. Jon and the committee exchanged information and ideas in an open and spontaneous free-for-all. I could see that he was becoming comfortable with them and they with him. I started to worry that he was buying into their story, and I shook my head at the thought of moving to South Africa or India. So much for waiting until he'd had a chance to discuss things with me!

At 11:45, Valeria Slack got up and came over to me.

"Let these boys talk shop. Come, I'll take you to lunch with the girls and show you around a bit. The guys always eat by themselves anyway."

I got up and whispered the plan to Jon. He smiled, nodded, and returned his attention to the discussion. Walking out with Valeria, I felt poor and underdressed. An attractive woman in about her mid-fifties, she was in a smart, clinging black dress, with an open neckline, beautiful jewelry in all the right places, and three-inch spikes. Our plans hadn't suggested a need for any such outfit for me, and our suitcase limitations wouldn't have accommodated one anyway.

"You look stunning, Valeria," I said. "I hadn't planned to—"

She cut me off. "You look terrific! I wish I could wear something like that here. Please . . . this is the most uncomfortable outfit to put on for breakfast and wear through the day. I only do so because it is expected of me in public places. These jewels are all imitations, duplicates," she said with a casual backhand wave. "The real ones are home in a vault. I don't know why I even have them. I don't ever wear them––too stressful, too many guards milling around me. And please, only my grandparents called me, Valeria. I am much more comfortable with Valerie."

I had liked her immediately when we chatted earlier and out here, I liked her even more. For all her worth, she was just another down-to-earth person, ready to play her expected role when called upon.

We stopped in a ladies' room and then walked to a private dining room, chatting all the way. When we walked in, we––or she, no doubt—was applauded, with greetings coming from five women who were already seated. She walked me around the table, introducing me to each woman. But for one, all stood and greeted us. Their dress was somewhat fancier than mine, but quite a bit less than Valerie's. Three were wives of Coalition men, and one was the provost of the Cameco School. The fifth, the woman who did not stand, was a vibrant, active, retired professor from the university—eighty-five-year-old Professor B.L. Shapiro.

"Bonny Lee is a celebrated professional who always adds the historical perspective on the topic of conversation at the table," Valerie whispered to me. She leaned over and greeted the professor heartily, introduced me, and we three exchanged some quips. Valerie laughed as we continued around the circle.

"Professor Shapiro didn't stand to greet you," I whispered. "Is she infirm in some way?"

"Oh no! She's in perfect health . . . and isn't that great!" Valerie answered, still smiling.

"Isn't *what* great?" I asked.

"That she didn't stand! *She's the only woman here who gets it!* I haven't done anything, really, to achieve my position. I only pass out what was given to me. That woman is self-made: the author of acknowledged books in her subject, a winner of awards for her contributions to her field and the general knowledge of mankind. She sits so I can have the pleasure of giving *her* respect," Valerie emphasized. "It shouldn't be the other way around with any of these women, really."

We sat and joined the conversation. An appetizer of shrimp and watermelon already waited at each place. Valerie said, "Bon appetite," and everyone began. Male servers in black slacks and smart white jackets, with high collars and a sprig of a yellow flower on their left shoulder, their name embroidered on their right, collected the used dishes as a chef and attendant wheeled out a soup cart.

"Split pea with ham," he announced.

Soup plates were quickly placed before us. I noticed that Professor Shapiro waved hers off and passed the soup course. I wondered why. *Was she not hungry, or on a special eating regime? Was it the ham? Does she keep kosher?*

We didn't keep a kosher home, but we wouldn't knowingly allow pork or shellfish into our house, as our minimal observance of the dietary laws. But Jon and I both ate shellfish and bacon out. Following Professor Shapiro, I decided too wave the soup off too.

There were choices for entrée. I chose the fish—grilled Pacific Chinook freshwater salmon, caught locally. Everything was beautifully garnished, wonderfully served, and delicious. At dessert, Valerie announced, "Ida might be coming to South Africa for, perhaps, a half-year stay."

The ladies all erupted with stories of personal experiences in South Africa, suggesting cities to live in or visit, sights to see, the seasons to select. I couldn't keep track of all the competing and conflicting suggestions.

Valerie whispered to me, "I'll tell you what you need to know when this hen party is over, which will be very soon. They are waiting for me to stand and say I have an appointment to attend."

She instantly rose and announced, "Please excuse us, ladies, but Ida and I have an appointment to attend."

Her hand clasped my shoulder and motioned for me to stand as she finished, "Thank you for a delightful lunch as always."

The women all voiced their salutations, much as when we entered. Valerie took me by the arm and turned me toward the door. We left, her heels clicking the tiles, broadcasting our movement all the way.

***

Valerie led me into an executive lounge and touched a plate on the wall and the room came alive. The lights lit, the door clicked, a blank wall became a communicator screen and soft music played. It was 1:30 p.m.

"Did that door click lock us in?" I asked.

"No, no, Ida." Valerie smiled. "It locked others out and lit up a digital display that says 'Conference In Progress.' The door is perfectly open from this side. Try it if you wish?"

I felt foolish for asking the question and dropped it. Valerie motioned me to an armchair and sat in another, angled toward me. The screen began displaying pictures of magnificent landscapes in all seasons from around the world. She started touching almost invisible buttons embedded in the side table next to her chair. A map of South

Africa displayed on the screen with different places highlighted with different symbols. As she mentioned each place to me, the symbol on the map flashed. It was a very quick study for me.

"The men's lunch will go till 2 or later. The meeting will reconvene and the questions of the day will be answered. We adjourn no later than 3:30. A number of us are booked on that Arrow to Cape Town this afternoon; departure time is 4:30. The time, of course, is flexible––because it won't leave until all the passengers arrive or cancel, and that's mostly us––and maybe you and Jon too? You have been invited. I expect to take that flight. I took it here yesterday just for this meeting."

I nodded my understanding.

"Listen, Ida, I want to quickly brief you on what might happen if your husband accepts a position on the development team. They are working mostly at the Colenso Laboratory southwest of Pretoria and Johannesburg, our largest cities––with the largest Jewish populations in South Africa, by the way. Those cities are only thirty-five or so miles apart, but are more than 250 miles from Colenso, a four-and-a-half-hour drive. It's not a daily commute distance," she said shaking her head.

As she spoke, beautiful pictures of the cities were displayed on the screen with captions describing the view.

"Durban, on the bay, is only a two-hour drive, but a less desirable place to live––in my opinion. I live in Clifton in Cape Town, which is absolutely magnificent, but it's a thousand miles from Colenso."

"Valerie, what are you trying to get at with this tour? Different cities, distance to Coleco . . ."

"Colenso, the lab is in Colenso," Valerie corrected.

"Okay, Colenso then. What are you trying to say? Please stop beating around the bush and tell me what I need to know."

"Okay Ida––the bottom line is this: there is no great place to live that's really convenient to the labs. The men work there all hours of the day and night. They get an experiment started and never leave till it's done, maybe days, a week, or more. The lab has a bachelor boarding house for the men to live and eat while on duty, a separate such place for the women there. The family men try to get two or three days off between tests to visit home, which might be anywhere in the country. Surely you've had this experience with Jon in the various positions he's had in his career?"

She didn't wait for me to answer.

"Segalov pitched your husband to the Coalition. He was very enthusiastic for us to pursue Jon's participation. He said to the committee only a few months ago, 'Get Kadish, and if Kadish comes, he will be here for maybe six months. If Jonathan cannot solve this in six months, then he won't be able to do it in six years!' Segalov was sure the solution was with graphene. You know what that is. He said your husband had 'the best knowledge of the practical applications of graphene in adverse environments in the world.'"

"Well, that will be flattering to him, and yes, when he was on sea duty early in our marriage, he was gone for six or more months at a time. But then I had children to raise and my own business to attend. I had help with the kids and in the house. I didn't have time to notice he was gone. Sometimes when he returned, I even resented it! All of a sudden he would reappear, and then I had to take care of him too—— *and I'm not talking about what you're thinking!*"

We both smiled and chuckled.

"But I did that too! In South Africa I won't have children to raise or a business to run. What the hell will I do alone if he is working that schedule in a remote place?"

"Exactly! That's the point I want you to see—because I want you to be open to my next thought. I can help you get settled in any place of your choosing, large or small, in a vibrant city or on a beach. I can introduce you to the local hierarchy, the leaders of the community, the patrons of the arts, the Jewish society——if there is one. But what I want to offer you is one of the guesthouses on our estate in Clifton, the most beautiful area in Cape Town. You can stay there. I will keep you busy, and Jon can fly over when he gets a break. I have many friends, Jews among them, who I love dearly. Jewish women are among the most educated and intelligent of South Africans. I support their charities and they help mine. I've traveled to Israel with them both on business and pleasure. Israel is an important market for our diamonds, and it is a duty of mine to occasionally visit and socialize with our clients there. Actually, it is not so far away and visiting is enjoyable. Elon Musk, born in South Africa and now a dual citizen of Canada, provides a suborbital service—an XspaceX shuttle between South Africa and Israel. You could use it to visit your son and family there while Jon is slaving at the lab."

She sat back, beaming, and waited for my answer.

"That *is* surely a generous offer, Valerie. I really thank you, and I'm happy to have such an invitation to reflect on when Jon and I have the calm and privacy to discuss our views and wishes on this project. He and I are tight. At this stage in our lives, we only do what we both agree will be good for both of us."

"Ida, thank you for hearing me out. I needed you to know this is there for you if you want it. Run with me for a few months. You'll meet the most interesting people and have a great time. You won't feel completely abandoned in a strange place without a soul by your side. Think about it. I know you'll have many questions before you and Jon decide to go forward. I'll upload my private contact information to your communicator, and you can contact me whenever you wish. C'mon, now . . . the boys might be back now. If they're not, they will be any minute."

We stood simultaneously and gave each other a friendly hug. I liked this woman. She made me feel younger and more alive again.

It was 2:15.

# Chapter 49
# Men's Lunch in Calgary
*Jon*

After the women left, the discussion became more intense.

"What is it you need that you think I can contribute?" I asked.

"Segalov was leading our team on the development of a fluoride molten salt, single-liquid thorium reactor," Grantsson of Cameco answered. "In theory, it is a practical form and would be simplest in process details, smallest in size, and safest in operation. It would also require the fewest parts. It wouldn't be necessary to locate near water for cooling, because molten thorium salt can be self-cooled through the heat exchanger while operating at atmospheric pressure."

While sitting there, I searched my mind for what I knew on this specific subject. *Let's see——a molten thorium reactor can never melt down because it operates at low temperatures in relation to its melting point of 3300°C. Uranium melts at 1132°C. But as I thought at the Israeli meeting, the idea of combining thorium with uranium was beginning to feel like a winning idea, an idea worth exploring.* But I held my tongue to save my ideas, suggestions, for a more favorable time.

Grantsson continued. "The reactors could be sized physically and by output capacity to match any specific situation. A fifty mega-kilo-watt power plant would be larger than a thirty-mgk one. Power plants as small as five, eight, or ten mgk would be very practical. These could be used to power small and medium-sized communities or a specific installation, such as a university, a hospital, or a desalination plant like Israel builds. They could be factory produced and assembled in place in a very short time. Seventy percent of the initial charge of thorium can be consumed before the resultant impurities kill the batch. Uranium fuel rods must be replaced when 40 percent of the active uranium is spent. The initial charge of thorium might last up to thirty years. So it makes sense that we match all the other components with a thirty-year life. When the thorium is spent, rather than refueling, the reactor would be totally scrapped and replaced with a new, more modern one, same as you do with your submarines, and as South Africa should have done with Koeberg."

"Okay, I get it. So what's the problem for me to solve?" I asked.

Diagrams and photographs began to appear on my screen. The seating diagram was gone.

"Jon, you know that the separation wall that acts as the barrier between the hot reactor section and the Rankine cycle is usually graphite or a reinforced carbon of some sort," Grantsson said.

I nodded. A cursor showed the parts on a cutaway schematic on my screen.

"The carbon wall is an acceptable heat conductor and should be inert to the molten salt. In conventional uranium reactors, as you know, these need attention every ten or so years. The same material doesn't even last that long in the thorium cycle because the porcelain-coated thorium beads are abrading it and causing it to be corroded more quickly."

Grantsson from Cameco seemed to have the most technical, scientific understanding of the power plant being developed.

"Segalov was convinced that graphene bonded to a substrate, maybe embedded in a sandwich of materials—likely graphite—*on both faces* was the answer, as was a process for joining that material without any rupture of the graphene protective coating. He felt the electronic properties of graphene lent it the possibility of being electronically charged from an external source to combat the corrosion and even repel the beads. He tried many combinations, some showed promise and others were total failures. On the materials that showed promise, the irregularities of the graphene at the joints failed in no time. But static tests on graphene-laminated surfaces with molten salt paste—without the ceramic-coated thorium beads—showed the ability to have the life we seek."

I stayed quiet as I scrolled through a slide show of pictures, taken at the reactor site, of failed materials and parts. I recognized some problems that we, at the Boat, had solved for application in *cold* environments. But we didn't have graphene in our reactors— the material was too new and we had stabilized our configurations and materials decades earlier. We wouldn't mess with an existing system that was functioning satisfactorily. That's why developing thorium would be rewriting history for us. The applications I had worked on for our submarines didn't have to deal as much with heat, and I didn't know how they would stand up in the elevated and abrading environment from the molten salt bath and ceramic-coated beads.

*Wait,* I thought, *did they say ceramic or porcelain? Both materials were mentioned. The properties of each are different, and maybe one is preferable to the other. Maybe there are other inert protective shells that could be used to coat the thorium pods that would be better still?*

"I recognize some issues in these photos that I have seen too. But we needed a solution for cold—you need one for heat. I would have to reacquaint myself, restudy the properties of thorium, think more about your issues, and study the results of the tests you've already run––and talk to your team about their observations, especially their experiences that are not written in the reports. If I could have worked with Segalov, I'm sure we could have cracked this barrier. It takes *teams* to solve these problems. Interaction with colleagues, discussing, arguing different points of view, brainstorming over the results of a test—that's how solutions emerge for multifaceted, complex problems such as this. Who's in charge now?"

I served up those platitudes to keep my real thoughts close to my vest.

"We have appointed Sergei's assistant as the interim head of the department. Perhaps you've heard of him—Dr. Enzo Pandolfi from the Istituto Nazionale di Fisica Nucleare del Gran Sasso. He's been with us for three years and, frankly, he was disappointed when Sergei was brought in as Laboratory Director. He felt deserving of that pro-motion. But while he has the empathy, he is lacking the passion that we are looking for. Unusual for an Italian to lack passion, huh?"

Wait, *Director? What were they saying?*

"Well, *I'm* not your Director prospect—*not me!* I hope you're not thinking that?"

A few of them exchanged glances.

"You say that now, but after a few months working there, you might change your mind. After only a few months, Segalov and Pandolfi seemed to work together compatibly. But we understand your position as of now, but we can always hope. The cost if hope is nothing!" Steele said.

A round of smiles emerged at the table, even mine.

At that point Steele said, "Let's break for lunch. We probably all need a washroom, and a private dining room is set for us. The women prefer to eat by themselves."

That last comment seemed to be directed to me. I wondered how Ida was doing and when we would be back together. I wondered what sort of brainwashing they were subjecting her to.

The men all rose and I followed their lead. Adnan Ambuti and Khgosi Motsep, the Indian and South African, closed in on each side of me. Kyle read my predicament and pulled me to the side. "Here now, let me bring you up-to-date on the Canadian position in this Coalition," he said with a chuckle.

Ambuti and Motsep dropped back to wait another opportunity to corner me. They didn't have to wait long. We all stopped in the men's room, and some had to wait their turn. When the general and I got to the dining room, there were no remaining seats together. Motsep jumped up and led me to an open seat between him and Ambuti. *No,* I thought, *not long at all.*

I was surprised when all the gentlemen held hands and bowed heads as the Irishman intoned,

"Tank you, Lord, for tis day, for tese loyal colleagues in tis great endeavor for the benefit of all mankind. Speedily guide us to success for te life and prosperity of all yure eartly children. We tank you for tis food tat we are about to receive, and we pledge to you our commitment to tis great task in the name of yure son, our Savior, Jesus . . ."

He stuttered . . . hesitated . . . stopped. He took a breath, then finished,

"And we pledge our commitment to tis great task to you, Lord God, te Father of us all. Amen."

All joined in "Amen," including me.

The group laughed in good fellowship as each made a quip at Mick for modifying his invocation to accommodate the Jewish guest.

"Well," he said, in his modest Irish brogue, "I wanted our guest te be able te say 'Amen' wit us and attest te our fellowship and goals as well."

Another laugh and a light round of applause. The gentlemen all gave him a nod of admiration for his quick thinking on both accounts.

An appetizer of jumbo shrimp cocktail with a variety of sauces was already set at our places. Steele continued as the chairman of the lunch.

"Bon appetite, everyone," he said as he tapped his ring on the table.

We all began to partake of the appetizer. Young women servers in black skirts and stockings, black shoes with a slight heel, and white waiter jackets with a high neck, a small yellow corsage on their right shoulder, and their name embroidered on the left, entered and stood back until the appetizer was finished. Within seconds the dishes were swept away and replaced with soup bowls. The chef, in full regalia, and an assistant wheeled out carts and ladled steaming French onion soup to each diner. The assistant added a toasted slice of French bread and topped it with shaved mozzarella cheese. When everyone was served, Steele again announced, "Bon appetite," and everyone carefully attacked the steaming soup.

Ambuti finished half the soup and turned to me.

"Jon, we have to beat China and Russia to this. I hope you'll help?"

I heard his words but dismissed his question. My mind had reverted to Segalov, his recommendation of me, his too-recent assassination and the events and murder in New Hampshire. I needed to remember that this was dangerous business—for my own sake and for Ida's.

"Do you know who killed the Segalovs?" I asked Ambuti.

"No, not yet, but we have suspicions."

"Is Israel helping the Coalition in any way with this project?" I asked.

"We've contacted them a few times for parts and consulting. They've responded each time and we've paid their price. They have a keen interest in this development and we believe they will patronize the first entity to demonstrate a complete, reliable system, whether it's us, China, Russia, or Norway."

Motsep, the South African, stepped in. "We have a long and successful relationship with Israel in many disciplines. They need our diamonds. In payment, we accept their military hardware, knowledge, and training––which often matches or exceeds the best in the world. Most of our relationship with Israel is open and in the public domain. Other historic cooperative efforts, in sensitive spheres, are state secrets. Like the 1979 Vela double flash is still unresolved, but many believe it was a joint atomic bomb test by Israel and us. I had not yet been born at the time, so don't ask me." He raised his arms from the elbow, his hands open toward me with a big grin on his face.

He continued, "We sell some uranium yellowcake to Israel, which they are able to refine for many applications, particularly bombs and fuel rods."

"Could the Israelis have assassinated Segalov?" I asked.

"Perhaps," said Grantsson from across the table.

Everyone was now focused on our conversation.

"Perhaps . . . Maybe they want to slow us down to help China? Or protect their uranium reactor business? The Israelis have to be watched closely––now more than in the past. They are usually good partners, but they are working in so many areas with so many countries that they are always faced with multiple conflicts of interest," added Steele.

"Would they have any reason to want Sergei dead?" I asked.

"We can't be sure, but we certainly know they have the means."

"What about the Chinese? Might they have wanted Sergei dead?"

The answer was delayed as the meal cranked into high gear. The soup plates were removed and in the next instant, the chef wheeled out an elaborate serving cart with a two-foot long roasted prime rib of beef. It was huge— *A whole side of beef, beautiful!* I thought. Its essence permeated the air. Large—I mean twelve-inch—dinner plates were on a lower shelf.

The chef went to the New Zealander first and an empty plate was put before him.

"End cut, an inch and one-eighth," the chef announced.

The New Zealander nodded and said, "Thank you, correct as usual."

"He's always the first to be served!" Kyle directed toward me.

The assistant ladled the beef with au jus, and the trailing ladies supplied a fresh napkin, serving dishes of roast potatoes, green beans and a tray of condiments. As the meal was hot, the person served was allowed to dive right in, as the New Zealander did.

The chef next wheeled the cart to me, with his entourage trailing. He put one of those plates before me.

"The next slice is medium, but there is still another end cut if you wish?"

I answered, "Medium rare, please."

The chef bellowed, "Then you wait your turn like the others!"

That brought a hearty laugh around the table. He pushed the cart around to Kyle and gave him the medium piece. From there he just went one by one with medium rare around the table. When he returned to me, he said, "The normal portion is one inch, but you can have more or less."

The rib was huge. The shrimp and soup had been a lunch by itself and my mind was not focused on eating.

"A smaller slice will be fine," I said.

But he cut me an inch anyway. The sides followed and I was aghast at the amount of food prepared, served, and as I looked around the table, being eaten at this meal—this *banquet!*

When everyone was served, the staff withdrew and silence prevailed as everyone concentrated on this centerpiece of the meal. The New Zealander relaxed back first, then slowly others joined him, and in ten minutes all were finished. I was unable to finish my portion.

"What about the Chinese? Might they have wanted Sergei dead?" I asked the table again.

"Both China and Russia had multiple reason to want him dead," Steele answered. "We believe we are neck and neck with China in this development, though they are working on a two-liquid system. If they thought or knew that Segalov was moving us more quickly to a practical solution, they would want him eliminated––and they certainly have the means to do it.

"As for the Russians—well, Segalov was a highly regarded, publically known scientist from the symposiums he attended, the papers he delivered, and the news reports of his work released by the Russians.

Just his name was a threat to competitors' programs. The Russians had an added incentive because he defected from his motherland to work for a competitor. Neither of these players, China and Russia, recognizes the difference in our philosophy. They think we are just like them—mercenary in motive, striving for greed and power. Segalov came to us to benefit mankind, not just the oligarchs of Moscow, or the politburo of Beijing."

"What about anyone else? What were Segalov and his wife doing in Madagascar anyway?"

"It's a popular place for South Africans to vacation. Nice resorts, beautiful beaches, and reasonable prices. Our rand goes a lot farther there than in other places. Apparently, Mrs. Segalov was planning to visit the US in the next few days. The investigators found an airline ticket for her to Boston and a cache of money she was planning to take. It seems the Segalovs didn't want us to know about it. As Russian citizens in South Africa on a scientific visa, either or both of them could have gone to any South African international airport and leave of their own free will. We have our suspicions regarding their attempt at this deception."

My mind started to go wild. *Maybe Segalov was frustrated, unable after a year and a half to fix the problems. Maybe the Coalition was losing faith in him, paying him a big stipend for seemingly little results. Maybe Ivanica wasn't going to return and Sergei was planning to leave soon after to join her. Maybe the Coalition also had its reasons to want them dead! Who knows, maybe it went through Pandolfi?*

The entrée plates were cleared and dessert was offered. I declined. I needed my blood in my head for the next few hours, and there was already too much of it rushing to my stomach.

Steele finished his dessert, cleared his throat to get everyone's attention, and said, "This luncheon was hosted by Australia. Next it will be Canada's turn."

A round of applause greeted Mr. Clarke, who nodded and bowed his head in recognition. This trillionaire club was quite an ensemble;

I was duly entertained and impressed. *But they're not asking me to join the committee; they want me in Africa or India to do some dirty work. Don't let this day's flattery coerce you into something you might regret,* I told myself. I needed to get with Ida.

But one last thing about the Segalov assassination was still bothering me. *The evidence—what evidence was found at the scene? They haven't said a word about it. Who was the recruit Sergei was meeting? Was that person the shooter? There had to be eyewitnesses at the pub. What about the bullet, a casing, fingerprints, footprints, surveillance videos, the roster of employees and guests at the pub, the resort, and the roster of persons departing nearby airports soon after? There had to have been lots of data and evidence that could be gathered to point to the assassin.*

"What kind of evidence was gathered that might identify the killer?" I asked the table.

"We have very little intelligence regarding the investigation as yet. The Madagascar police are in charge, with MI5, SASS, and the CSIS in close cooperation," Ambuti answered.

I just nodded my head and stayed quiet. *If it was the Coalition that took them down, that team of investigators will be worthless in releasing the truth.*

Steele stood and rapped his ring on the table, his way of ending the meal and recalling the members to the meeting.

It was 2:15.

# Chapter 50
# After Lunch
*Ida*

As Valerie opened the door, we could hear the robust chatter of male voices and a herd of footsteps tromping up the hall. We stood at the doorway until the men approached. Those in the lead gave Valerie a big smile and she joined in with them. I waited for Jon and joined up with him. We slowed our pace to fall behind.

"How did it go with you," Jon asked quietly. "Did you get a good brainwashing?"

"Pretty good, really. I had a very lovely lunch with a diverse group of women. Valerie was just great, warm and attentive. I like her a lot. How did it go with you?"

"The discussion at the meeting heated up after you left, but it was just what was needed. All that preliminary cordiality was just fluff. I learned more about Sergei and Ivanica that I'll tell you later. I don't see us as any closer to a solution to the murders or what we do next.

"All the players might have wanted them dead for different reasons, and all had the opportunity and means to do it. This bunch included. Someone is lying or staying quiet about what they know. We need some time together to think this through and decide our next move."

I agreed. Jon told me to just keep walking while he chased down General Farwell. He caught up with him in the middle of the pack, walking and chatting with some fellow colleagues. Jon and Farwell slipped to the side and stood against the hallway wall. I caught up and joined them.

Jon was asking, "Kyle, what's happening now? I have a good idea of what the Coalition wants and what I may be able to provide. I need to discuss all this with Ida, especially the invitation to South Africa and India this afternoon. We have other commitments and I'm on two weeks' vacation leave from the States. Am I needed immediately in the meeting?"

"Let me speak to Steele and Isaak about the schedule. Wait right here and I'll be back to you."

The general doubled-timed it to catch up with the herd, and we could see him pull Steele and Isaak aside and talk animatedly to them. In a minute, they continued on and Farwell returned to us.

"They said to take as much time as you need, but be ready with an answer by three o'clock—that's about forty minutes from now. Why not return to the lounge where Ida was and I'll pick you up there when it's time?"

"Thanks, General," we said together.

I led Jon back to the private lounge, closed the door and touched the plate as Valerie had—and nothing happened. No lights, no click, no scenery on the wall. While we stood there for a moment in the dark, a uniformed guard appeared and opened the door. After I explained the situation, he stepped away a few paces, talked into his communicator and returned to tell us, "It's okay now. The control room has reactivated the panel and you're good until you leave."

In the room I repeated the procedure, and everything worked fine.

Jon quipped, "Elaborate security for a university."

He looked around, shaking his head skeptically.

"Is something the matter?" I asked.

"There is obviously more than university business being done on this floor."

He scoured the room and found nothing but he was sure it was bugged.

"Man overboard," he said with a wry grin. "Let's get out of here. Back to the café."

By the time we got settled, it was 2:30.

"How do you feel about taking the rocket to South Africa this afternoon?" he asked me.

"I'm up for it if you are! Valerie wants to show me around Cape Town while you tour their facilities in other places. She said taking the *Arrow* is only four hours instead of almost twenty on a standard plane. It goes over the North Pole and aims where the rotation of the earth will bring Cape Town when we are ready to land. It's still a suborbital flight, but the rocket boost takes it higher, in two separate burns so we can take a breath in between. I'll be better ready for it this time! What excitement!"

"Excitement? Yes! I suppose it is. But the trip today, this weekend?" He paused and shook his head. "I don't think it's a good idea."

His mouth scrunched up and he continued shaking his head. "No."

I was stunned.

"You acted in the meeting as if you were hot for this assignment! I can go along with it . . . it's only six months or less."

I explained all that Valerie had told me and about her offer to use her guesthouse.

"It will be the best place for me while you are working and away—— no doubt——for days at a time. What has turned you against it?" I asked.

"There's a problem here that I can't put my finger on at this very moment. Until we know who killed the Segalovs and why, we might be putting ourselves into the same danger. I understand the Coalition's technical problems and think I have an idea for a possible solution. But I think Sergei knew he was in trouble, which was why he hoped they could get me to help him out. With him gone, I don't want to step into his shoes unless we know we are protected . . . safe. I need to sort this out with Mickey and Gwen too."

I wrinkled my nose. "Who?"

"Gwen Lathrop from Homeland Security, my boss! Remember? I need them to have the CIA stick their nose into the Segalov murders, and I have to clear this with them anyway. I need their permission to explore this assignment. And isn't Rachel waiting for us to return? Don't I owe the Russians and the Israelis at least a call-and-stall?"

I confess I was a bit deflated by his demeanor.

"Jon, whatever you say. *Whatever you say!* You're surprising me. I thought you might be excited that I've been brainwashed sufficiently and am ready to join you in this adventure. Why is it that when you're hot, I'm cold, and when I warm up, *you* cool off?"

We laughed and held hands across the little table.

At 3:00, Farwell found us and asked, "Are you ready?"

Jon got up and I followed. He turned to me and said softly, "Maybe I should do this alone."

"Not on your life! I want to be there, hear what you say and face Valerie. She was so kind to me."

We followed Farwell, entered the meeting and went to our seats.

Valerie stood to greet me. I was reminded of her talk about who gives and who receives respect when being greeted at a table. I closed my eyes just momentarily as I nodded to her, returning the compliment before I took my seat. My screen had a slide show of Cape Town and several pictures of Jon and me on the *Arrow XII,* the two of us at the PlanetSpace Skydome, Valerie and me at the luncheon, pictures of her estate by the ocean, and maps of South Africa highlighting the places where Jon would be and places we could visit on his days off. It was a totally professional show. I wondered what was on his screen.

Steele rapped his ring and asked, "Jon, do you have a reply for us?"

"Yes, sir," Jon said. "Ida and I are on a two-week vacation leave to be with our daughter, son-in-law, and grandchildren in Sherbrooke. We have plans together on Monday. Your project is of interest to me because of your humanitarian goals, and if I cannot help you in six months, then I won't be able to do so in six years."

Everyone smiled and nodded. Valeria locked eyes with me, recognizing that Jon's words exactly matched Segalov's recommendation.

But Jon wasn't done.

"I would have to visit, see your facilities, talk to Pandolfi and others, and examine your results. I would like to do that sometime soon. But I would like to return to Sherbrooke today or tomorrow. We need to continue our family visit and then accept your invitation to visit South Africa and India, perhaps in a week or two. I don't want to be anyone's boss or manager. Those navy days are long over for me. I'll be thrilled if I can break your bottleneck, receive some reward and be on my way."

Jon looked at me. I took his hand and squeezed it. I know my eyes were watery, glassy. *I was so proud of him.* I wondered if he noticed my emotion. I hoped he didn't.

Steele looked around the table at every member and observer. He polled each quietly, one on one, with his eyes. After Steele confirmed with Valerie, she rose and came over to me. She leaned over and we hugged, then kissed each other on the cheek. Everyone watched, and she returned to her chair.

Steele nodded. "If and when you need or want to contact us, you can do so through Duevel or Rubin. They have direct connection to this administration and the proper members will be immediately notified. When you wish to visit our project, we'll make the arrangements for you and Ida from wherever you wish to depart. Is this satisfactory?"

"What about Matthew, sir? Where does he fit in now?" Jon asked.

"His assignment is over. He protected you and brought you here. His tactics were not really to our liking. He will no longer be part of this operation. We've conveyed our message to you and Ida, and we're satisfied with your response at this time. The Coalition will not be watching or protecting you in Canada anymore."

"Is it possible for me to be in direct contact with General Farwell here at the university too?" Jon asked.

Steele looked at the general. Kyle paused for a moment. His eyes searched the ceiling, and then he said, "If the committee approves, then I would be pleased to have him communicate with me as well."

"All those who approve, say aye!" barked Steele.

A loud chorus of "Ayes" followed in the next instant.

"Unanimous," barked Steele again. "Jon will be given communication coordinates to reach General Farwell on our secure system.

"Mr. and Mrs. Kadish, thank you for coming today. Arrangements are in process to return you to Sherbrooke this afternoon. General, please walk them upstairs to the reception center on the sixth, where Rubin will meet them. He will have all the particulars for your return to Sherbrooke."

We rose, smiled, and said good-bye.

I linked my arm around Jon's as General Farwell walked around to us and we followed him out of the conference room.

It was 3:18.

# Chapter 51
# Flight to Montreal
*Jon*

The CanJet wasn't the *Arrow*, but the next best thing. Calgary to Montreal in two-and-a-half hours. The CanJet 002 flight departed at 6:00 p.m. MST, scheduled to arrive at Trudeau International at 10:30 EST. The airplane was a twenty-one passenger Saab Ensomvarg III, SSE, meaning Super Sonic Executive. The flight attendant told me "Ensomvarg" meant "Free Spirit" in Swedish, and this airplane certainly was that.

From Calgary, the flight arced over the Arctic Circle, where it went supersonic to Mach 2.75, about eighteen hundred miles per hour. With a 160-knot tailwind, we arrived at 9:45 p.m., less than two hours and two time zones away. The cuisine, the wine, the service were beyond first class. Three attendants ministered to the cabin, each having only seven passengers to attend. The two washrooms on board were larger than the closets on the massive people movers we usually flew in. I wondered how much these tickets cost?

Ida wondered aloud, "Did others get booted to make room for us at the last minute?"

I told her, "Forget it. Let it go. If so, it wasn't our doing! The Coalition seems to have a lot of pull around here." Smiling, I added, "It might be fun to be a part of this!"

At the airport, Rubin introduced us to the CanJet flight manager. He was extremely cordial, knowing we were guests of the Coalition.

I had looked around the departure lounge and saw a familiar face. *What's she doing here?* Gwen smiled at me but didn't move from her place, maybe not wanting to be identified by our escort, who she might correctly have presumed was connected to the Coalition. With my back to Rubin and Ida, I flashed a quick smile at her, confirming the recognition.

"Duevel will meet you at the gate in Montreal and get you to Sherbrooke tonight if you wish. If you know your arrangements there, you should communicate them to him," said Rubin.

His comment initiated a flurry of activity. Ida called Rachel and told her what we knew about our possible arrival time.

"The street side of the synagogue is locked on Shabbat when the evening services are over, about nine o'clock," Rachel answered.

Ida relayed that to me. I had totally forgotten it was Friday, the start of the Sabbath at sundown. I took the communicator from Ida.

"Rachel," I said, "Is the flat still available? You know, the old flat? I still have a key, and you *did* take it for the month."

Rachel fussed a bit. "No, no, Daddy. That won't do. Your stuff is here now, as is Mom's pillow. I have to think how we can get you *here!*"

"We have overnight kits with us. We can stay at a hotel in Montreal and come to Sherbrooke tomorrow––or to a hotel in Sherbrooke tonight. Listen, I don't want to wake up in your house in the morning and feel guilty as you walk to synagogue while Mom and I lounge around. Now what's it going to be—the flat or a hotel somewhere? We believe some, if not all, of the watchers may be gone."

"All right, Daddy, I'll get my guy to check out the flat, turn up the heat, check the sheets, and be sure there is fresh milk and a few things in the fridge. Call back when you land in Montreal and I'll advise you then."

I explained it all to Ida, and she was good with it.

"Maybe we should stay a night or two in Montreal and take in some shows and restaurants?" she added.

"Well, we'll see. Let's just play it by ear," I added.

My mind drifted off . . . it had been a crazy ten days.

Ida broke the quiet and asked, "What are you planning for the next several days?"

"Well, I don't know what's to happen next." I shrugged then nodded with my head over my shoulder. "Gwen Lathrop from Homeland Security, my boss, is here. She's sitting right there, across the lounge."

Ida hadn't met her, but she scanned the people across the room and instinctively selected Gwen from the others.

"Why do you suppose she's here? You didn't tell them we were coming here, did you?"

"I didn't, that's a good point. There are things I have to ask her. I suppose she's here to get a briefing . . . or maybe she has something to tell me?"

"*Well, you're not sitting with her, you're sitting with me!* I've never been faster than the speed of sound, not even in a rocket."

I wasn't so sure about that, but I let it pass. I smiled inside. Her attitude was just what I expected.

"No problem," I laughed. "If she needs to talk to me, she'll find a way, but I'm sitting with you!"


The flight boarded. We were in seats 5A and 5B, Gwen was in 5C across the aisle. The configuration was two seats together, the aisle and then a single seat on the other side. Ida took the aisle seat. She looked Gwen up and down, and then they seemed to smile at each other. I couldn't see Ida's face, so I didn't know *which* smile she flashed. Ida, like all women, has a multitude of variations.


When the supersonic segment was over, Ida asked Gwen to change seats with her so she could chat with me for the last half-hour. She knew we had to converse *sometime,* so I guess she wanted me to get it over with. Smiling pleasantly at each other, the girls changed seats.

Gwen asked, "How did the meeting go?"

I gave her a brief summary. "They appear to be good people with a noble mission, and I wouldn't mind trying to help them if it's possible."

She answered, "We can speak more about it at another time. What are your plans from here?"

"There's a lot to catch up on. I want to reach both the Russian and Israeli admirals. Ask a few questions to demonstrate interest and give them the stall. I want to talk with François to see what has happened in the Nikelovich murder investigation. I want to study the videos of the drivers coming and going on the murder night and check on Frank's search to find surveillance video of Matthew and his men on the day the Segalovs disappeared. Maybe Ida and I should visit there again? Hey . . . and I have to contact Rollie, my handyman, and Truman, my son, to tell them we need to return to our house in a week or two. That's very important. And there's Mickey and Washington—–and you!"

"Let me tell you a few things," Gwen said. "You know the FBI has taken over the murder investigation in New Hampshire. The preliminary report on the bullet is the uranium is Russian but it came from the North Anna power plant in Virginia, now owned by Positive Power, Inc., the national electric joint venture of the Energy Department and public shareholders. That means the bullet was manufactured in the States by one of several plants that get their uranium from North Anna's spent fuel rods. All those munitions makers are in the **Defense Industries Cabinet**."

I sat up straighter—this was not what I'd expected to hear. "You mean the US government made the bullet that killed Nikelovich?"

"Yes, that's right. But the lab can't tell how old it is, and over the years we've sold or transferred millions of those bullets to many countries—the UK group, Germany, France, Israel, Egypt, Saudi Arabia, and others. They've been distributed all over the world. Some might have found their way back to Russia in secondary sales."

"Then that's not much help in identifying the murderer. With what I've been able to learn, I can't eliminate any of the players. Russia is sure a suspect, the Segalovs being Russian defectors; and that assassin Dmytri was always lurking around. I can't eliminate Matthew and the Coalition yet either. I don't like to think it of them, but maybe they were trying to stop Segalov from jumping ship. And even the Israelis are suspect, the way Ling nudged me about graphene and thorium. Maybe they *are* working for China on this project?"

I laughed, shaking my head at the number of options.

"Please Gwen, say *we* didn't do it, did we?"

"Please, Jon, no jokes. But no, America didn't do it! We have the CIA looking into the murders on Madagascar too. We agree there appears to be a link between them and the one in New Hampshire. The CIA has put two good people on the case who have experience in Africa."

"Good," I replied. "This whole situation revolves around nuclear energy, using thorium as the fuel and graphene as the structural barrier in the heat exchanger. Because the US is so secure with our natural gas reserves, we're not in the thorium hunt. But the rest of the world is loaded with intrigue over it. It's about time we get involved, pick a side, and help!"

"We agree, Jon. I hope you're pleased to know it took *your* discomfort with our current social state to make us focus on the enormous efforts taking place around the world on this issue. Some groups domestically have been advocating for us to take thorium fuel seriously, but until now they've been ignored. Secretary Watson and Secretary Aitcheson both intend to promote thorium at the next cabinet meeting as something the Department of Energy needs to make a priority. An association group, the Thorium Energy Alliance, has been lobbying for research support for decades and has realized little traction. Maybe this incident, starting with you, will light a fire under our authorities. The top leaders of *our* cabinet departments will try."

"What about my plans for what I should do now?" I asked.

"Stall the Russians and Israelis the best you can. Try to stay neutral and confirm their invitation and your intention to visit both places. Don't bother with François; he is a small cog in the gear and won't have anything to tell that you don't know. Forget the surveillance videos––I've put Frank's handler on that, and if there's anything of interest, it will come back to me. I didn't know there were any concerns about your home in Connecticut, so certainly address those as you see fit. After your two-week leave, we all expect you to return there and use your office at the Boat as your home base. You need to return to long-term normalcy as your public posture."

"Okay, but wait! How did you know we were in Calgary? We only arrived this morning. How did you get here so fast or know how and when we would be returning?"

Gwen smiled a big smile. "Jon, didn't anyone tell you that the Level II security communicator has a GPS tracking device? We follow Level IIs all over the world. When your icon on the screen went into space this morning, it set off an alarm that had a dozen people tracking you. Main Brain calculated that the *Arrow* was headed to Calgary. They readied one of our own suborbital drones and I was airmailed to Calgary from Edwards Air Force Base––without a pilot! Now that's scary! Then we saw your icon at the U of Calgary downtown campus. On a chance, I booked myself on every flight from Calgary to Montreal and Quebec City beginning at two o'clock this afternoon. I've been running from departure lounge to departure lounge since, cancelling on every flight where you didn't show up. Impressed?"

I didn't answer. Ten days ago we were running from surveillance and now I was in it—and a part of it—up to my eyeballs! What irony!

The SSE landed at Trudeau at 9:45. Ida and I said adieu to Gwen on the plane so as not to have anything to do with her inside the airport. Duevel was waiting for us at the gate. We had our leather bag with us, nothing checked.

Duevel asked, "Where from here?"

Ida was already on the communicator to Rachel. She heard the question and leaned in. "Sherbrooke, to the flat! Rachel says it's in good shape, and she even sent over my pillow!"

"You heard the lady, to the flat in Sherbrooke! And use your flashing lights to get there fast. Everything about this day has been fast, and we don't want it to stop now."

Duevel smiled and motioned for us to follow him.

It was hard to imagine that Duevel had picked us up at the synagogue at 7:30 that very morning. We had traveled two thousand miles, attended intense meetings, had a gigantic lunch, and then returned the two thousand miles to within driving distance of our starting point at 10:00 p.m. Modern technology was astounding.

I wondered what the next quarter-century would bring.

# Chapter 52
# Saturday at the Flat
*Ida*

At eight o'clock the next morning, we were back at the table having our coffee. What a whirlwind we had been on! We were waiting for another hour to pass before we started calling around to restart our lives. Jon needed to call Truman and Rollie. I wanted to call Otch and Sally Snyder. I thought of all the things we'd sold or given away, and it was crushing.

"Listen, Jughead," I told Jon, "we're going back to Norwich to an empty house. We sold or gave away all the treasures from our past adventures, the art and sculptures we collected on our trips, the furnishings we selected and loved. Now all those dinghy walls are in need of paint or new wallpaper. The idea is depressing me."

"Betty, dear, *please*, we are returning as new people! I am no longer an engineer; you are no longer a businesswoman. We are both now *spies*! We will renovate the house to accommodate our rebirth: new colors, new furniture, new art and sculptures collected on our future travels. We need new cars. We'll get a 2040 Tesla Double T, new in the coming spring. To hell with the neighbors—let 'em squawk! How many people get this chance at our age? How many get to feel rejuvenated like I do!"

His enthusiasm was infectious. "I guess you're right. You've been promoted with a raise in pay. That's not too shabby. I'll start shopping furniture at Gorin's; they're the only classy game left in town. Rob's and Top Drawer dropped out years ago. If Chris and Todd are still available, I'll get one or both to help paint. You're right. I'm beginning to get excited for this too!"

At nine, I called Otch on the company's Saturday line. He answered.

"Otch, we're returning to Norwich after this vacation. I'll come by soon to finish redecorating my office. I intend to use it on a regular basis for a new project I'm starting."

"Great, Ida! We'll be happy to see you here again. I'm sorry about that last call and the things I started to say. I hope that didn't cause you any grief?"

I laughed to myself—he had no idea the journey we'd been on since then!

"No, Otch, no problem. It fortunately fell by the wayside."

"Is there anything the company or I can do to help you with your project . . . though I don't even know what it is at the moment?" He started laughing. "I know that anything you undertake will be to benefit others and will be successful—because that's who you are and that's what you do!"

Boy, did I need that spontaneous batch of flattery at that moment from someone other than Jughead. I knew Otch was sincere and not just jerking my chain.

"Thank you for that vote of confidence. There might be a place for the company to help—to give me cover in a way. We'll see as it goes along and I'll keep you appraised. Thanks again. I'll be in in another week or so."

As we said good-bye, I was happy with myself. If Jon was going to be Jughead from his office at the Boat, I was going to be Betty from my office at Now's. I began to imagine how my position there could cover us for travel too. Jon was right: this is like getting a whole new start in life.

I had to wait to call Sally. I knew she and Sam would be in synagogue in the morning. They were regulars every week to socialize with the congregants and to have their lunch at the Kiddush.

Jon had to wait until afternoon to call Truman; it was still the middle of the night in Hawaii. But he got to Rollie.

\*\*\*

*Jon*

"Hey Mr. K, how's it going?" Rollie asked. "Am I ever going to see you again? Everything's good here. The house is safe. I have the heat set for 60°F and the systems are working fine. Randy has been snowplowing when needed and was paid by the bank. USPS drones came a few times. I locked the things in the garage with the few pieces of junk mail that still come by carrier. The place is just as you left it."

"Good, Rollie, good!" I said, upbeat. But I felt nauseous at the thought of firing and replacing him, which I knew I would have to do.

"Listen, Rollie, I have a surprise for you and all the other speculators you talk to. Mrs. K and I will be returning in a few days or another week or so. She plans to redecorate and paint or paper all the rooms." I paused and decided to lie. "There'll be plenty of work in your off-hours from the Depot. Say, any chance I can have my Beretta back? I'll be happy to pay you for it."

"Sure, sure, no, no! It's yours. And forget about money. I took the required safety course a few days ago, and I've applied for a pistol permit, so I'll get one of my own soon anyway. You should go for the firearm license too! It's not as tough as in the past. The state has loosened the restrictions, and anyone without a criminal record can apply. It's part of the national return to the freedoms we are guaranteed by the Constitution. My permit should be here by the end of next month.

"But I was forced to give up my recreational drug license," he continued. "You can't have both. One or the other, so I'm excited about going for the pistol permit. Many of my coworkers at the Depot have the license and belong to the Sprague Rod and Gun Club. I've applied to join. They also purchased some ammo for the Beretta and we've shot it at the club range. After they calibrated the sights, bingo! Shoots right on target and I'm getting the rust out from my army days. I'm pretty good already after just a few sessions. You'll have to come and do this with us. It's great fun. I love it and you will too!"

The more he talked, the worse I felt about firing him. But there just wasn't any other choice—not after his display on the road. "Great, I'd like to try that sometime. And yeah, maybe I'll apply for a pistol permit too. But the best news you just told me was that you surrendered your drug license. I couldn't believe how out of it you were on the ride to New Hampshire!"

I was pleased that I'd been able to casually slip that into the conversation. At some point I was going to need to face that up with him.

"Oh, Mr. K, I am sorry . . . *so sorry* . . . about my mouth and behavior on that trip. I was down on myself, jealous of your success, of the FAV, of your courage to get up and leave—*and I was stoned.* Everything you said was true. I did have three lines that night and more in the morning. I took a line before going to Hartford for the FAV and another before stepping into your house. I even sniffed one when we stopped at the hotel in Salem for Mrs. K, and again that night when I went out after midnight and the storm. For whatever I said, *I'm sorry . . . very sorry.* I've thought long and hard about it, and I have no animosity toward you or the missis whatsoever—or toward any Jews in general. I know and deal with many every day! They are coworkers at the Depot with me and are our customers. They were always good customers of my contracting business, and just as you said, they're every bit as American as everyone else. My tirade at you was awful, but it has washed that crap out of my system and I'm off the drugs. I hope you'll forgive me and put that terrible episode behind us."

I believed him. Honestly, it would make me happier just to forgive the whole episode.

"I want to . . . but you are going to have to convince Mrs. K! You are going to have to say what you just said to me—to her! You will have to convince her—you're not anti-Semitic!

"And while you're at it, she always felt you didn't like taking orders from women, particularly from her. You will have to show her that's not true. You better hope she gives you a chance to stay with us. She will be home more and will be orchestrating the renovation and redecorating of the house. If you want to have a part of it, you have to get along better, *much* better, with her. She's planning to line up others too. But it's up to you to adjust your attitude and tone to make her comfortable around you. She doesn't appreciate your wisecracks and sees them as sassy and insulting. That has to stop! You hear?"

"Mr. K, yes . . . yes. We're on the same page. With my friends at the Depot, I am happy there now. With this new interest in shooting, I'm a new man. My wife is happy for me and we are doing better together. Give me the chance to prove myself and I won't let you down."

"That will be all up to Mrs. Kadish," I said.

***

*Ida*

My call to Sally brought infectious laughter. She was so happy to hear that we were returning and would take Pepper back.

"We forgot how much work even a little dog is. We haven't had our own for over twenty years. Sam almost fell on the ice taking her for a walk. Then the bending to pick up the poop––and in this weather no less!"

"Why didn't he use the plastic tongs for that?" I asked.

"Oh, Ida, he didn't like the neighbors seeing him carrying it!"

We both laughed.

She thanked me profusely for helping her daughter's business and said, "We *are* going to Florida, like Mr. K suggested––to visit my sister. Thank you so much for your kindness and generosity."

I had no idea what she was talking about. Maybe in her eighties she was getting a little senile. She gave me ten days of gossip that I listened to patiently, but only because I didn't want to be rude. I had other things on my mind—our new start, our new career.

Near the end, she said, "So you're going to be home tomorrow. What time will you come for Pepper? I want to be sure to be home."

"No, Sally, not tomorrow! Maybe a week from tomorrow! I'll call and come for Pepper as soon as I'm there."

"Sure, sure, please, and thank you and good-bye."

She hung up before I could say another word. I ran to tell Jon, "We have to go sooner rather than later; Pepper is in trouble!"

Jonathan had a longer and more complicated talk with Truman. He couldn't tell him the truth of all the adventures we had experienced. He concentrated on the promotion, the pay and pension, and the enhanced benefits, especially the medical provisions. After nearly twenty minutes of back and forth over this and that, Truman finally surrendered and wished us good health and happiness. Jon got him to agree to come east for Passover, saying we would try to have everyone together in Norwich for the first Seder.

Jon said later, "Maybe we'll divert Truman to Rachel and we'll go to Israel for Passover with Eric and his family."

Jon was sure Gwen would approve of an Israeli trip if it included some meetings with the admiral and advanced his ability to assess their relationship with China. Passover was only a month and a half away, with first Seder on Friday evening, April 8.

In the late afternoon, Jon and I walked back to the cinema and bought two tickets for the 4:30 showing of *See Sea Saw* with a C$20 bill from which he received change. We walked into a half-empty theatre, bought popcorn and drinks and picked seats of our choice in the mid-house on the aisle. We stayed to the end. We were both pissed that Israel wasn't even mentioned, that the Chinese seemed to have won and that the West came in second. Still alive though badly wounded, James Bond, the invincible 007, had suffered his first defeat!

# Chapter 53
# Return to Norwich
*Jon*

On Monday, I called Admiral H'Ivri while we still had the Israeli tellie. We had a pleasant and casual chat. With my newfound knowledge of the Iranian attack and pilot retrieval, I had more respect than ever for the IDF's capabilities. I put the Chinese out of my mind.

"I'd like to visit you and see some of the projects to which I might contribute. Ida wants to visit Gaza and look at condos, maybe as a second home."

"No problem," said H'Ivri. "We'll be delighted to take you around. I'll try to spend as much time as possible with you, but I'm busy and might have to put you with others too. Maybe we can have dinner together with our wives some evening? When are you coming?"

"We are thinking Passover in April. It's the best time to see our children and grandchildren."

"That's a tough week here. Many things are closed for vacation, and the military gives many passes—furloughs, you call them. It would help if you came a few days early or stayed a few days late. But if you are here—no matter when—we will make it work."

"When we leave Quebec, how will I be able to reach you?" I asked.

"Good question. I will have to ask. I think if you call our mission at the United Nations, they can patch you to me on a secure line. I'll get back to you with an answer and a number."

Next I called Katya at the UN to get patched to Admiral Abramoff. When I identified myself to their receptionist, she said, "Oh, Ambassador Rocinkova said she was expecting you to call and that I was to put you onto *her* line. One minute please."

I waited and waited, only staying on the line because they were playing Rachmaninoff's Piano Concerto No. 2 in C minor, Op.18, one of his most popular compositions. Naturally Katya picked up when I was completely subdued by the music.

"Mr. Kadish, what can I do for you?" she asked sharply.

"Patch me into Admiral Abramoff. I understand she has been trying to reach me."

"We are *all* trying to reach you. That's why we visited Friday, more than a week ago. Have you an answer for us?"

"Not just yet. But I have a few questions for the admiral."

"The admiral *does not want questions,* she only wants answers! Are you coming for a visit or not? If so, when? I can only patch you to her if you have answers—only answers!"

"We would like to visit to see the projects and Anapa, but my schedule is in flux, you know? Uncertain. If it is only answers you want, I'll have to call back."

"When Mr. Kadish, *when?*" she barked. "Our offer is not available forever! We have problems to solve and you are not getting younger. You might die of cancer at any time––and there are others to recruit. When we recruit someone, they either work for us or for no one! Maybe you've noticed?"

Okay, now she had really pissed me off! *Not getting younger, am I? Might die of cancer at any time, huh? Threatening to take me out if I didn't heel? Did she just infer that they did in the Segalovs?*

I took a deep breath.

"I'll call back when—and if—I have *answers!*" I said tartly. And I hung up.

I was afraid that Gwen and Mattern might not like my handling of that, but I was pissed. I wasn't going to take that threat and battering from a Russian bureaucrat.

The rest of Monday and most of Tuesday we spent with Rachel and the kids, moving around, shopping, and buying them gifts. Ida shopped for some *chachkas* for some friends and her book club. We told Rachel and Jacque almost the whole truth and that life would return to normal for the family. We talked about Passover and who would go where. The details were fuzzy and we left them to be sorted out later.

I didn't want to tip off the Coalition about our plans, so I avoided Duevel. Our time and business in Canada was up, so we took a commercial airport shuttle from Sherbrooke to Montreal and flew from there to Hartford on Wednesday, arriving at 4:15 pm. I had Rollie pick us up. He came in Ida's former Lincoln Navigator. That reminded me that we needed *two* new cars, one of which would be the Tesla TT.

Ida looked at her former Navigator and gave me the *face. You can guess which face that was!*

It quickly felt like we had never left home.

# Chapter 54
# Arrived Norwich
*Jon*

Rollie picked us up at the arrivals curb of the Bradley International Airport. As he put our luggage in the trunk, I quietly told him to apologize to Ida as he had to me on the communicator. I went to the men's room to get out of their way. I stayed away a good fifteen minutes.

When I returned, Rollie gave me a little nod, but Ida was quiet and looking a little terse. Rollie opened the passenger doors. I sat in front, Ida behind me.

On the highway a few minutes later, I said to Rollie, "We need stop to pick up some milk, eggs, and a few things for tonight and tomorrow."

"Not necessary, Mr. K. My wife picked that stuff up today when she shopped at the Food Warehouse. I put a bunch of stuff in the pantry and refrigerator when I stopped at the house to reset the thermostats. She prepared simple dinners for you too; they're on your table."

"Thanks, Rollie," I said.

Ida was totally quiet on the ride to Norwich. Rollie and I were both painfully aware of it.

When we pulled into our driveway at about 6:00 p.m., she finally spoke.

"Rollie, after you take our suitcases in, would you please drive to the Snyders to pick up Pepper? I called to say that someone was coming."

"Sure, Mrs. K," he said very politely. "Should I stop at the Pet Mart to get her usual brands on the way?"

"That would be great," Ida answered in a brighter tone.

*Rollie was starting on the right foot,* I thought.

\*\*\*

It was Friday and I still hadn't reported to Groton. Rollie called at 3:30 p.m. to say he was leaving the Depot in Lisbon and was going to stop by to bring my Beretta.

"Ida and I are just sitting down for afternoon tea," I told him.

Ida took my communicator. "You're welcome to join us for tea or hot chocolate."

He said, "I'll be there by four. I'm stopping in and will decide then."

As we sat having tea and some cookies, we heard a large drone preparing to land on our court. I got up and looked out the window. The drone was big and still about thirty feet in the air. It had USPS markings, but it was bigger than their usual delivery machines and of an unfamiliar design. I could see that its pads and weight were going to trigger the security alarm. It crossed my mind that Rollie and the Norwich police would get a call from Alarm Central.

The time was just 3:50.

The drone landed. Ida and I stayed seated at the kitchen table, expecting a postman to knock.


In the next instant, the back door crashed open, and a man dressed totally in black, his skin hidden with a Darth Vader-type mask and voice resonator, came inside. He held a long-barreled pistol with a fixed silencer, drawn and ready.

"Stay where you are and put your hands flat on the table," he resonated.

We did as instructed.

"You haven't cooperated, Kadish, and I've been sent to take you or lay you down," the garbled voice said.

My pulse was racing in my temples. Heat rose in my neck and into my face. I was more frightened that I'd ever been in my life. And I was frozen from the fear, my mind a blank.

Where Ida was sitting gave her a view of the door and the side of the intruder. Suddenly she lifted out of the chair and headed toward the sink. I was shocked.

"Sit down, where do you think you're going?" the intruder barked through his mask.

Ida turned briskly and looked straight at him, taking a full view from head to foot.

"Look at that mess!" she shouted, pointing to his wet and dirty footsteps tracked into the kitchen. She grabbed a towel.

"Listen, *Dmytri*, this is the second time you've tracked mud and snow into my house with those dirty old leather combat boots. *You clean it up this time!*" And she tossed the towel at him.

Her action startled him and he arched sideways against the table, maybe trying to avoid the towel coming at him in the air. His gun hand pointed up and a round discharged into the ceiling. *Pssssst*, it sounded, the silencer suppressing the escaping gases from the explosive charge. The spent casing rolled on the floor.

As he leaned away, my attention was drawn to the kitchen window over the sink. I could see Rollie looking inside, holding up my Berretta for me to see. At the same time, I became aware of sirens getting closer and closer.

While the intruder was off balance, I raised my arm, pointed my index finger up and rotated it above my head. Rollie recognized the "play ball" sign and turned the Beretta toward the intruder as Darth Vader returned to face me. Gripping the Beretta with two hands, Rollie quickly took aim and pulled the trigger.

I don't know where he was aiming, but the bullet grazed Dmytri's head, knocked off his mask and taking off his right ear before whizzing by me and into the wall. Blood shot out the side of his head. Dmytri screamed and blew the mouthpiece off the costume.

Police raced through the door. Two cops tackled Vader and pinned him to the floor. Rollie walked in holding the Beretta and was tackled to the floor too. I was still sitting at the table as I tried to explain loudly that Rollie had saved my life.

Ida dialed 911 and asked for an ambulance to transport a man wounded by gunshot to the hospital.

The police chief showed up moments later and took control. Dmytri was read his rights, cuffed, and taken by police car to the hospital just down the street. The American Ambulance EMTs were dismissed. Rollie was cuffed, read his rights, and arrested on multiple charges of carrying a handgun without a license, discharging it within city limits, trespassing and disturbing the peace. Dmytri's weapon and my prized Beretta were seized as evidence, both confiscated as unlicensed.

With the police, the EMTs and the startled neighbors involved, the story couldn't be contained. Word spread like wildfire on every conceivable media and social network in the world. Truman, Rachel, and Eric called in quick succession. Sally called; Rollie's wife called; Mickey, Merle, and others from the Boat tried to get in; Otch and others came over with pizza, beer, and wings. Ida finally issued a statement on Google Baba-Twittazon, the largest retail and social networking site in the world. That pretty much halted all the anxiety from the public.

Homeland Security dispatched damage control people from Boston and New York who showed up before midnight. They set up headquarters in the police community room, though it was slightly smaller than they would have liked. Media people and picture crews massed into town. All the hotel rooms in the area were filled for a few days. Restaurants stayed open extra hours. Briefings were scheduled with the governor, the mayor, the police commissioner, the fire chief, and the officers who did the tackling, even though there was no new information to announce.

After four days, the story shut down as some new calamity happened elsewhere, and the media crews disappeared as quickly as they had arrived.

I thought it was not a very auspicious beginning to our new life as spies. The media was irrationally hyping my credentials as an engineer and a pioneer in technology at the Boat. I was worried that we had blown our new careers within a week of returning to Norwich. But Director Watson, Mattern, and Gwen were delighted with the publicity. They felt my new celebrity status would give me greater access to targets.

*** 

On the following Monday, with my two-week leave over, I went to my office at the Boat. I was chip scanned by everyone who'd ever given me a hard time. I hadn't been told that I'd been moved to the sixth floor with the other Level IIs, but I found out. The office was bigger, brighter, and more favorably equipped than my old one. I arranged my stuff and hung the photocopies of my degrees and certificates on the walls. There was more space now. I needed a few more pictures or art.

When I settled down to think, I messaged Gwen that I was at the Boat in my new office and ready for action. I didn't get an immediate response. I played some solitaire and Scrabble on the Cloud until Merle called and asked if I wanted to have lunch downstairs with the boys.

"Sure," I said. "Mickey hasn't given me my new assignments as yet."

That was a lie, but nobody else needed to know. Twenty minutes later in the cafeteria, I heard a ping from my communicator. I walked away from the lunch table to see what had come in.

It was a message from Gwen:

"It's summer in South Africa. What's your departure date?"

# Postscript

The Russian drone stayed on the court for nearly two weeks. The police had to put an officer outside to direct traffic. Sightseers were endless. I had temporary lights set up so it could be seen at night. Too many people drove by and honked. The honking was annoying, but I liked looking at it myself. It was like a piece of outdoor sculpture.

Bandaged and peppered with painkillers, Dmytri spent a single night in jail. When he showed up in court the next morning, a team of New York lawyers was there to represent him. The Russian UN mission claimed diplomatic immunity. He was released on bail. In a week, his lawyers had the charges reduced from felonies to misdemeanors, a small fine was assessed and paid, and he was quickly shuffled out of the country.

Rollie also spent the night in jail. When he was presented in the same court the next morning, I had the best defense lawyer in town there to represent him. Rollie's charges were more serious: he had discharged a gun and hit a person. He was charged with unlawful possession and transport of a firearm, discharging said firearm within the city limits and causing injury to a person, trespassing and disturbing the peace—and parking on Broadway more than twelve inches from the curb.

If convicted of a felony, he would be barred from ever having a pistol permit. His future was in danger. I worked with Ron, the bail bondsman and Rollie was released in my custody. The case dragged for months. Then, unexpectedly, the junior assistant prosecutor was offered a promotion and reassignment to Bridgeport. She was told she had to resolve *all* her outstanding cases before she could go. She quickly agreed to a few misdemeanor charges and I paid Rollie's fine. We walked and he was awarded the pistol permit.

A truck leasing company headquartered in Mexico claimed the tractor and flatbed trailer that Dmytri had rented in Quebec City and used to transport the drone to Norwich. The police found the truck the next day in Mohegan Park, in the isolated parking lot at the cul-de-sac by the swimming area. The vehicle was impounded. The Mexican company hired local counsel, and after the criminal cases were disposed, the city released the vehicle upon payment of removal and storage expenses.

The Russian Embassy in Washington claimed the drone and demanded its return. Instead, the Defense Industries Cabinet took possession of it and hired the CT National Guard 1109th TASMG at the Groton airport to document and dismantle it into all its component pieces. We didn't take it, so why should we return it? They had technicians here for four days. After my sculpture was gone, I had no idea when or how—or if—it was ever returned to Russia.

Because of the threatening remark Ambassador Katya Rocinkova made on my call to her from Sherbrooke—which was captured by both our surveillance and Russia's—she was recalled to Moscow even before the State Department could ask for her removal.

My Beretta M9A1 was mounted in the Norwich Police's public display case of interesting artifacts from their history, with an embarrassing but accurate account of how it had come into their possession. Ida and others told me about it. I never went to look.

The Russian Embassy demanded the return of the handgun and accessories taken from their citizen at the time of his arrest. After an extensive search, the Norwich Police admitted that the handgun was missing, maybe lost somewhere in their evidence room. The locals suspected that some insider had taken it as a souvenir. It was never returned.

Ida agreed to give Rollie another chance, provided *I* didn't apply to get a pistol permit. I agreed.

# Acknowledgments

Between 2011 and today,
- With the political gridlock in America, with no end in sight,
- the high rate of unemployment and underemployment,
- the growing number of Americans on public assistance,
- the millions of illegal aliens working here, and the political football it is causing,
- the wind-down, and maybe another wind-up—of the wars in Iraq and Afghanistan,
- the sequestration and proposed downsizing of the US Defense Department,
- the energy boom from fracking, followed by volatile fluctuations in energy prices,
- the continuing $CO_2$ pollution of the atmosphere,
- the fear of global warming,
- the Affordable Care Act implementation,
- the government deficits and rising, massive total debt,
- the quantitative easing by the Federal Reserve bond buying,
- Iran going nuclear, threating Israel with extinction,
- the unrest in one after another of the Arab nations,
- the declaration of a caliphate in portions of Syria, Iraq, Yemen, Libya, Somalia and others,
- the never-ending Israeli-Palestinian conflict,
- gold and silver prices rising to new highs, then falling into stagnation,
- marijuana and drones going mainstream,
- China ascending, and
- Russian resurging—

––I couldn't help wondering how these issues might look in twenty or more years. I began keeping files of news stories, Internet messages, and the like, relating to emerging technology, energy, terrorists, domestic and world issues that would have to play out in some fashion over the coming decades. They were not just going to disappear!

This story extrapolates these entangled conditions and events, in what I believe is a totally possible approach, to reach what I think the United States and the world *might* look like some years from now. Possible? Probable? Agree or disagree? Whose analysis is better?

Thank you to all my tireless friends, supporters, colleagues, and family––and most importantly, to my wife and partner, Millie, who have listened patiently and at times not so patiently as I have talked about these ideas and my theories of what could be possible, probable, in the future. I listened as you argued the absurdity of some of my thoughts and projections (though I've included them in the story anyway). I want to make special mention of my friends and former classmates here and around the world, in Canada, Germany, England, Norway, Egypt, Israel, Panama, for their patience and advice from a different view of the world.

In particular I need to thank Paul Duevel, my former colleague on the boards of our local bank, hospital, Rotary Club (my sponsor in 1998), and many other civic interests. He read an early partial manuscript, pointed out some huge incongruities, and made many valuable suggestions that significantly shaped the final text. He did so again, a second time, with a near final draft, for which I owe him a great debt of gratitude. To Ralph Bergman, attorney and friend, thank you for listening and arguing with me at so many lunches and for reviewing and commenting on the near final draft as well.

To you, my readers: this story is for your enjoyment and to spark your imagination about where we might go from here. I hope it provokes discussion among you, and I hope you realize that we, each and every one of us, can influence the future––by becoming an active part of the process and a voice for our freedoms.

Remember, there are only three kinds of people in this world:
    Those who make things happen,
    Those who watch things happen, and
    Those who wonder what's happening.

# About the Author
# Martin Shapiro

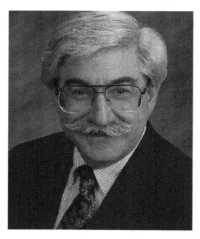

Martin Shapiro is a graduate of the Harvard Business School and the Rensselaer Polytechnic Institute. An industrialist turned author, he has an extensive history of civic and religious work and has served as a professional director of various enterprises.

As a writer, Shapiro explores the full expanse of mankind's journey, from our ancient past to our not-too-distant future. His Scroll of Naska series consists of four books that tell a tale of intrigue and adventure in biblical times, while this most recent entry, **2039**, heads in the opposite direction to follow a married couple's struggle in the not-too-distant future.

Shapiro is a member of the Poet and Writer's Circle at the Harvard Club of NYC, the Christian Writer's Guild, and the Connecticut Author's and Publisher's Association. He annually attends the Writer's Center at the Chautauqua Institution and Canyon Ranch in Tucson, where much of his writing takes shape.

A past president of the Norwich Rotary Club (2006–2007), he has contributed over a decade of service to Rotary Clubs International.

Contact the author at **mshapiro2039@aol.com**.

Made in the USA
Middletown, DE
21 May 2017